MW00379555

Pat Addams

© 2008 *It's the Little Things* Reg # 1878218150

This book is a work of fiction. Names, characters, places and
incidents are either the product of the author's imagination or are
used fictitiously. Any resemblance to actual events or locales or
persons, living or dead, is entirely coincidental.

2008 US Copyright 1-127907966

It's the Little Things

Pat Addams

It's the Little Things is dedicated to two very special people.

First, to Joel Cooper, if it wasn't for you I never would have existed.

Second, to Sharon Joy, your love and support allowed Joel to set me free.

– Pat Addams

Pat Addams

Chapter 1

Rebecca Willis, Becca to everyone except her parents, had always wanted to be a reporter from the moment she could speak. While other children preferred cartoons, Becca watched documentaries and news shows. While most children admired sports figures and action heroes, Becca was in awe of the TV news anchors. She admired their ability to separate themselves from the stories they relayed, no matter how tragic. Moreover, Becca loved the way words could paint a picture, especially if the picture was about something real.

When Becca's ex-lover, Roberto Sanchez called her for a meeting at his publishing company, she assumed it was another excuse for him to try, once again, to rekindle their relationship.

Roberto had received the 'Rush-Hour' manuscript, as it was self-titled, just one day prior to calling Becca. Typically Roberto didn't open unsolicited manuscripts, let alone read them, however this one arrived by private courier with his missing sister's name as the sender.

Roberto immediately opened the package and withdrew its contents. Taped to the top of an inner package was a single sheet of paper that read; **No police. Just print it. I'll give you two weeks to get copies on bookshelves across the country or I'll start mailing you pieces of your sister.**

With trembling hands, Roberto broke the seal on the inner package and slid out the hand-written manuscript. A blood-stained pendant fell out and clattered onto his mahogany desk. Roberto recognized it at once. He had given it to Melina last year on her birthday.

Melina Sanchez had been missing for ten days before the manuscript arrived at her brother's office on Third Avenue in Manhattan. Melina had recently been accepted into the New York University School of Law J.D. Program. This was a huge honor bestowed only on a handful of college graduates from the thousands that applied each year.

Melina had just graduated as valedictorian from UCLA with a master's degree in Criminal Justice. She had moved to Manhattan two months earlier and had been staying with Roberto while she waited for the fall classes to begin.

Fearing the worst immediately, Roberto notified the police when Melina didn't come home from her meeting with the NYU admissions office. Ever since they were little children, Roberto and Melina had shared an almost psychic connection.

Their parents had immigrated to southern California from a small town in Mexico called La Joya, about ten miles south of Tijuana. Roberto was two years old when his family crossed the border and Melina was pushing at the seams of her mother's womb.

Throughout their adolescence, Roberto and Melina only had each other; as their parents, Roberto Sr. and Carmen Sanchez, worked around the clock for less than minimum wage to ensure that their children would have a better life.

In the course of staying ahead of the increasing migration of Mexican immigrants who were willing to work for less and less than their predecessors, the Sanchez clan kept moving further north. It wasn't until they landed in a part of Los Angeles called Mission Junction, that Roberto and Melina finally had a place to call home. Not far from Dodger Stadium, Roberto Sr. and Carmen found work that allowed them enough free time to enjoy the previous fifteen years of sweat and saving.

Roberto Jr. had also graduated from UCLA, although not as a valedictorian. That same year, Melina skillfully completed her freshman term and decided to declare Criminal Justice as her major.

Roberto's bachelor degree in business administration and his minor in communication landed him a job with the New York based publishing firm John Wiley & Sons Inc. Though not a firm with a well known name like McGraw Hill or Random House, Wiley had been around since 1807 and primarily published textbooks and professional books.

Two months before Roberto was to say goodbye to the west coast and his family, Roberto Sr. and Carmen were murdered.

Passing through Chinatown on their way home from the stadium they were carjacked at gunpoint on West College Street just south of the Gold Line's stop at the Chinatown station. Two Asian teenagers looking for their next hit of crystal-meth mistook Carmen's actions when she reached into her handbag to give the hoodlums money. They were both shot repeatedly in the face and chest.

It was only after Melina's persistent encouragement that Roberto continued on with his plans and moved to New York City. Three years later, with nothing holding her back; she joined him on the East Coast.

The Friday evening Melina's dinner went uneaten; Roberto had initially tried to call his sister on her cell phone. After an hour of having his efforts sent to voice mail he decided to take the relatively short walk from his apartment on Seventeenth and Third Ave to the NYU Admissions Office on Broadway a few blocks east of Washington Square Park.

Keeping an eye on both sides of the street for his sister, he followed the route he had given to Melina just hours earlier. When he arrived at the 721 Building, twilight was beginning to descend on lower Manhattan. Rushing up the stairs to the second floor, Roberto found the Admissions Office closed for the evening; and still no sign of Melina.

During the week and half that followed; the police kept reassuring him that they were doing all they could. More than 2300 people go missing in United States every day; deciphering which ones are truly abducted and which ones have simply run away becomes more and more difficult for the police with each passing year. Unfortunately cities and states simply don't have the manpower to pursue every missing person without being given a solid lead to follow.

Then the manuscript; and the heart wrenching dilemma it brought with it; *No police*. But since the police were already involved; what did that mean. On an instinctual level, Roberto knew that the author of this insane proposal was well aware of the police's involvement to that point. **No police**; simply was referring to the manuscript.

Roberto screamed with helplessness. Concrete proof relating to his sister's disappearance lay literally in his lap. The same piece of evidence that confirmed that she might still be alive could also be her death sentence if shared with the very people who could help save her.

After a sleepless night pondering his alternatives, Roberto realized the only person he could possibly turn to in his dire need was someone he hadn't spoken to in close to a year.

Roberto had met Becca Willis during his second month on the island of Manhattan. Most of his first month was spent settling into the apartment on Seventeenth Street; a one room studio that had been renovated into a bizarre two bedroom loft by someone with a vast understanding of maximizing square footage. Roberto simultaneously mastered Manhattan's mass-transit system while establishing himself as the head of the new Hispanic Division within Wiley Publishing.

Once he had settled in to his new home; the evenings became long, and Roberto began to feel the loss of his parents and the absence of his sister more heavily than he had been. It was time to branch out and launch a social life amidst the concrete jungle that is New York City.

Roberto's administrative assistant, Marissa Colmenares, a voluptuous grad-student from Venezuela, told him about speed-dating. Marissa said her cousin met her fiancé at a speed-dating event down in the Wall Street area. She jokingly stated that she would rather go shopping for a man at Bloomingdales rather than K-Mart. Even though Roberto was looking for a woman, he understood Marissa's meaning.

Speed-dating, for those of you living in a cave this past decade is an event where equal numbers of men and women have a chance to meet each other one on one for six to ten minutes. The women get to sit at tables and the men move from table to table. After everyone has rotated to the different tables, you make your selections. When mutual selections match, typically, the woman is given the gentleman's phone number for additional contact.

The speed-dating event Marissa recommended was sponsored by a company called New York EasyDates, and focused on single professionals aged twenty-something to thirty-something. The event was held at a place was called Suspenders, a cozy bar located on Broadway just north of Wall Street.

The interior of Suspenders was laced with dark wood accents. The atmosphere was further enhanced with antique styled lamps that barely illuminated several recesses. In addition, each nook and cranny was filled with comfy furniture; the ideal setting for an intimate tryst.

Sitting at the bar anticipating anti-climatic results from the upcoming event, Roberto's attention was drawn to the bar's entrance; with long black hair and ice-blue eyes that could stop time, Becca Willis entered Suspenders.

Roberto found himself being drawn forward as if this radiant vision of beauty had cast a hook into his soul and was reeling him in. Becca's gaze locked with Roberto's across the room and she smiled as though they had known one another for years.

Before the event was even completed, Roberto and Becca had mutually selected each other and departed Suspenders to continue their ten minutes elsewhere.

Chapter 2

Reluctantly Becca went to Roberto's office at Wiley Publishing the same Friday afternoon that he had called. There was such an air of desperation in his voice that she couldn't refuse his request. As an experienced reporter, over the phone, Becca had asked all the proper probing questions seeking Roberto's motivation to no avail. The last thing Becca needed in her life just then was a replay of their on-again-off-again two year romance. Roberto really did seem to have something else in mind when he asked, almost begged, for her audience.

"How long would it take to print and distribute this RJ?" Becca asked using the nickname she had bestowed upon him immediately upon discovering that he was a junior.

"It would be cutting it very close, I ran the timeline model this morning, but it could be done in the fourteen day time-frame"

"Thirteen."

"Que?" he asked, falling easily back into the vernacular they had mostly shared.

"You received this yesterday; and I'm guessing we should probably consider one day already off the countdown." At this point Becca hadn't read the manuscript yet and was focusing solely on the safe return of Melina. "Have you talked to your associates here at the firm?"

"Not yet. Between the acquisition of Hungry Minds Inc., and the world-wide expansion of the 'For Dummies' series, all the Wiley's are scattered across the globe until the middle of next month."

"All the Wiley's have wandered away?" Becca couldn't help herself. No matter how grave a situation was, her downfall was an inability to pass up a play on words.

Roberto just starred at her in disbelief.

"I'm sorry RJ, I didn't mean…" she cut herself off knowing there was nothing to say to retract her verbal faux-pas. "What do we need to do to get the ball rolling, so to speak?"

"I'm ready to move forward and risk everything." Roberto began, "Meaning that I'm probably going to lose my job over this, but if it means getting my sister back, I'd risk even more." Reaching into his briefcase that lay open on the desk between them, Roberto withdrew the manuscript and within a shaky grip extended the document to Becca. "I need to have you to read this to fully understand what I am about to mass produce."

(Unedited excerpt from the manuscript)

I want to be called 'The Rush-Hour Madman'; so few of us in history have had the chance to label ourselves. No, I don't think of myself as a *madman* or that I'm *insane*; but I do like the title. It's fitting; as you'll see. Maybe you will decide that my actions in the past or 'nearly present' are a little questionable, possibly *mad* by your standards; but who the fuck are you to judge me. You are faceless.

I'm writing this all down so that you will understand that this is not an act of political or religious terrorism. I do have political and religious views and opinions; they just aren't strong enough to foster hate or action. What I do, what I've done, is sparked purely by a desire to experience intensity. To get my heart pounding in my chest as an athlete might during a championship, or as the bomb squad might during a countdown decision between the red and green wire.

This would be a good time to mention that I've left clues within this manuscript as to the date and time of my grandiose plan. Not that I expect you, of all people, to figure it out. However, it does add to the *thump-thump*. Good luck. Don't get too close. Remember, you are faceless.

It is a grandiose plan, a little extravagant maybe excessive, but how else am I to make my point. When the idea first entered my brain I thought there was no way I'd be able to pull it off. But, you'd be surprised how easy most of it was. The hardest part was hiding from *Big Brother* throughout the setup; I needed lots of money, a couple fictitious companies, and of course, the explosives.

I am not going to be very secretive about my targets either; simply because I don't think it would matter. Originally I was torn between two locations as my initial target. Not anymore, not for a long time. Tell Mr. Smith to start spreading the news.

Thump-thump.

Every story has a beginning, middle and end. Not this one. Most of this story is about the middle, the end is yet to be played out. Let me share with you some of the beginning; I remember everything as if it happened yesterday.

The first time I used an explosive on a person it was quite unplanned. I learned a lot from that experience; from then on, everything I did had a plan.

I grew up in a suburban town called Lynbrook, Long Island. On a good day I could be in Manhattan in about 30 minutes. My family was considered middle-class by 1970 standards and I really didn't want for much of anything. Separated by two and a half years each, I have two younger brothers.

Lynbrook was a very diverse town; people from all sides of the tracks brought together within a school district.

Go Owls.

As I was beginning my sophomore year at Lynbrook High a decision was made to acquire the elementary school across the street to expand the resources for the over-crowded high school. Construction, which included a connecting extension bridge over Union Avenue, would begin that coming summer.

Due to the depth of the planned 3-year project, class schedules needed to be adjusted. Junior and senior classes were set to be conducted from 7:30am to noon, while the freshmen and sophs would go from 12:30pm to five. What could possibly be any better than that? My parents disagreed.

Woodmere Academy here we come.

Wrong.

Not for me at least.

As a sixteen year-old the Academy decided that it was "too late" for me to be brought into their program. Thank God for that. My brothers both went; and, for all intents and purposes that was the last I'd be close with them. Not their fault, nor mine, just logistics.

I should also mention that this was also a pivotal moment in history regarding my relationship with my parents. I don't know if they took to heart the comment made by Woodmere Academy that it was "too late" for me, or if they just got too busy with their own shit and the lives of my brothers at their 'new' and 'better' school...

Fuck it, it doesn't matter anyway.

No regrets. Everything happens for a reason.

I've always preferred my own company anyway.

At least I got to see them at their funeral.

Timing is everything.

I loved the new split-schedule at school. Are you kidding me; twenty minute classes until noon, and then freedom. Basically, the whole day was mine to do with as I wanted.

I began making bombs around the age of thirteen. Originally I would just empty out a few bricks of firecrackers, carefully pack the gunpowder into the cardboard core of a toilet paper roll, seal off the ends with candle wax (or melted crayons), and then poke a hole in the side to insert a fuse. After which, I would tightly wrap the "shit-kicker" as I called them with duct tape. The whole process was very thump-thump.

I made several of these shit-kickers over the years; blowing up mail boxes or whatever I could find out in the trash. A delayed fuse made it easy to light and go. Unfortunately, most of the time, I didn't get the ka-boooom I was expecting. I figured it had something to do with the weakness of the waxed end-caps. So I modified the concept and began using those cute little 8-oz coke bottles. These worked much better and the glass shrapnel was an added bonus.

💣

Anyway, I was telling you about the first time I killed someone. Her name was Amanda Farber; she lived with her mom and step-dad down by the bay. That sounds like a glamorous location, but actually it was a very poor part of town. Amanda would take the regular city-bus back and forth to school as the regular school-buses didn't service her neighborhood.

Amanda was in a few of my classes. She always sat in the back and never participated. Everyone thought she was slightly retarded and therefore not even worthy of being picked on.

To me, there was something dirty and sexy about Amanda. I think it was part where she lived, her disproportionately large breasts, and the fact that I felt I could dominate her. Whatever the reason, I thought a lot about fucking her.

It was on a rainy Thursday afternoon in late April as I was pulling out of the school parking lot that I saw Amanda waiting for the public bus. She was hunkering down in the corner of the enclosed bus stop waiting area. The wind was blowing the rain in at her at an angle; you could see the misery on her face.

"Here I come to save the day!" As shoe-shine boy becomes Underdog becomes Predator-dog, I pulled up next to the bus stop. Amanda barely looked up at me as I rolled down the passenger window of my Dad's station wagon.

"Hey!" I shouted into the wind and rain, "get in; I'll give you a ride. The buses are running late today because of the weather."

Amanda looked up and down the street, and then shook her head 'no'.

"Come on." I said in my most inviting voice. "I'm going to be passing right by your house." She made eye contact and I knew my smile would solidify the invite.

It did.

Amanda somewhat reluctantly slid into the wagon and closed the door. "Welcome", said the spider to the fly.

I quickly checked the rear-view mirror. Between the bad weather and the split-schedule, there was no one around. Nobody to see me take off with the 'slow-girl'; not that I meant her any harm at that point. It just would have been bad for my rep. I wanted to fuck her, not date her.

I realized that she probably hadn't been with anyone yet; therefore, getting her naked was going to be difficult; unless of course her step-daddy tucked in more than just her into bed at night. I do love a challenge though.

I drove onto one of the back streets off the main road and pulled over. Amanda shifted closer to the passenger door, if that was even possible.

"Relax", I said "you just look so uncomfortable all wet." I reached over into the back seat and grabbed a towel. You never know when you may need a towel. I handed it to her and said: "Here, take your jacket off; I'll turn up the heat."

Amanda's jacket was soaked through and through; I tossed it into the very back of the station wagon. "It should dry out by the time we get you home."

As she was patting herself dry I asked her how her science project was going. Science was one of the classes we shared. Amanda just shrugged her shoulders which pushed her tits together forming a beautiful mound separated by a 'v' of cleavage.

You've got to love wet T-shirts.

I started driving again and asked, "Do you mind if we make a quick stop so I can check on my science project?"

"What is yours?" she replied.

'Got her', I thought to myself. "I'm doing an experiment on mold growth," I lied "and I need to record the progress on some of the items."

"OK," she said "but I need to be home soon so I can get dinner ready for my step-dad before he goes in for third shift."

"So, what's your project?" I asked again, still trying to find an opportunity into her pants.

"I'm tracking the growth of bean plants in different types of light." Amanda said, starting to open up a little.

"Hey look, we have something in common," I said "we both are watching stuff grow."

Amanda tilted her head and smiled. I thought to myself, 'she certainly is going to see something grow today and there isn't any mold on it!'

Back then Long Island still had a lot of rural areas mixed within suburbia. Small farms, that hadn't sold out to the developers yet.

I turned down another side street and then onto a dirt road partially hidden by the overgrown shrubbery. This led along a tree lined property divider up to an abandoned barn; a long forgotten vestige of the Hollingsworth Farm.

The Hollingsworths owned most of the surrounding area until that fateful night when Sarah Hollingsworth went nuts and killed her husband and four kids. Good story, but not mine.

I found this little hideaway back when I was a freshman. I actually came across it by mistake because I got lost riding my bike home and took off in the wrong direction. Once found though, I kept it as my own private sanctuary. I never even shared the find with my close friends. It was mine. I've always been a very private person; a loner who is never alone.

The barn was embraced by so much ivy it was barely noticeable against the adjacent woods and foliage. I parked the car near the side door and turned off the engine. I could see the look on Amanda's face and realized the next thing out of my mouth would make or break the rest of the afternoon.

"I could really use your help in there," I said in my most soothing voice, "but if you want to wait here... I guess I'll understand."

I can't imagine what was going through her head. Here I was, one of the most popular kids in school asking this nobody to basically 'hang out' with one of the cool kids. I don't know if it was a desire for acceptance, or what, but Amanda took the bait.

"No, no." she declared "I'll help you. Whatever, you need."

Perfect, first foot in the web.

I opened my door and moved around to the passenger side. When Amanda saw that I was actually going to open the door for her, she took her hand off the handle and let me maintain control.

The rain was still coming down so I lifted up my jacket and made a makeshift umbrella for us. Amanda slid out of the car and pressed her body next to mine.

Oh boy was it on now.

No turning back.

I was getting my stick wet today, or so I thought.

I had installed a deadbolt lock into the barn's side door. Years ago I had secured the rest of the entrances and I had the only key to this door. I had originally done this to test the security of my sanctuary. Days and months, then years had gone by, and only I appeared to know, and or care, about this place.

I left Amanda leaning against the wall by the inside of the door until I got the light turned on. The bare bulb hanging down from the ceiling swung back and forth on its cord. Shadows from beams and pillars crisscrossed and swelled in hypnotic patterns all around the inside of the barn.

I put my arm around Amanda's shoulder and escorted her towards the back corner where the horse stalls stood in the gloom. I could feel her hesitation and yet she let me lead her forward.

"Is there anymore light in here?" she asked in almost a whisper.

"Mold grows best in the dark." I said, surprising myself that I actually remembered something from class; because as I said earlier, there was no mold growth experiment going on here.

Now it was Amanda's turn to be surprised.

I spun her around and pinned her up against the stall door with my body. My hands went immediately for those melons of hers while I told her how badly I wanted her.

Needless to say my advances were not well received by Amanda. Actually it would be rather accurate to say that she freaked the fuck out.

I pressed my hand against her mouth to stifle the screaming; not that anyone could hear her, but it was driving me bananas.

"Calm down! Calm down!" I yelled at her; which by the way didn't help matters. So, in a much calmer voice I continued, "I was just joking. I wasn't going do nothing. I was just playing with you. I'm sorry."

Amanda quieted down and I asked her if it was okay for me to remove my hand from her mouth or was she going start up again.

She nodded her head so I took my hand away.

No sooner did I do that and *wham!*

Her knee connects with the boys like she's banging it out of Shea stadium. My balls ricochet up inside my body, hit my lungs and the breath goes right out of me. I double over and go down; meanwhile I got a sideways view of Amanda B-lining it for the still open door.

All I can think as I'm struggling to my feet is what a moron I am. How could I have left the door open?

I wonder what was on my mind.

There was no way I was going to beat her to the door; and I wasn't in the mood to play cat and mouse outside in the rain. But as fate had it, as it usually does for me, Amanda tripped over her own feet and lay sprawled on the dirt floor fifteen feet from the exit.

As I stepped over her trembling body, I asked her if she was okay while I continued to my target. I pulled the door shut. The deadbolt clicked into place with a loud *th-chunk!*

Amanda knew she had made a mistake.

Crying and whimpering, she shuffled backwards on her butt away from my advances until she could go no further. Her back was literally against the wall. She seemed pathetic and no longer an object of my desires and that made me even angrier. I was already angry that my advances were rejected and that she drove her knee into my boys, but now I wasn't even going to get laid.

In the back of my mind I must have known that Amanda was getting in on a one way trip as soon she got into the car. I was too focused on getting into her pants to realize that I didn't have a plan.

💣

I've been told I get a 'look' in my eyes; I'm not exactly sure what this means, but those who have seen it know I'm done fooling around.

Amanda must have seen or sensed something as I walked towards her; because she was too busy pulling up her shirt and telling me I can have whatever I wanted to notice the shovel in my hands. Otherwise, I'm guessing she would have ducked.

I caught her clean in the face. Her head spun around like she had heard a startling noise behind her. Amanda's hands dropped to her sides leaving her shirt pulled up propped over her huge chest, and much to my own surprise, I got aroused.

I know this is going to sound kind of sick; but, I thought to myself, while the body is still warm... I mean, I've had worse lays; girls that just lie there while you stick it to them. How could this be any different?

I dragged Amanda's body over to some hay bales I had set up as a makeshift living room and draped her over the couch.

This girl had one heck of a body. Once I had her naked it was easy to ignore the dent in the side of her face and the blood that was crusting around her ear.

As I'm driving myself in and out of Amanda, using my own spit as a lubricant, I realized that this was a perfect opportunity to use one of my shit-kickers on a person. Because let's face it; Amanda wasn't going home to prepare anyone's dinner that day.

The prospect of using one of my shit-kickers was overwhelming and the excitement that ran through me was incredible. I climaxed immediately.

It was the best orgasm I've ever had.

💣

In the act of moving Amanda back to the original location I had had in mind, the old horse stall, I recall thinking how soft and supple her body remained. I was always under the impression that rigor began to set in within about an hour.

Positioning the body face down with the knees drawn up underneath and her butt sticking straight up in the air, Amanda looked like she was praying to Mecca. I wonder if she was facing east.

Not bothering to redress myself I hurried out to the wagon and grabbed my backpack. My pants wouldn't have fit properly anyway, if you know what I mean.

I had one of my earlier versions of shit-kickers with me; the ones made from toilet paper cores and duct tape. It took some doing, and a lot more spit, but I managed to cram it into Amanda making use of the hole I had previously widened. I got it all the way in leaving only about a half inch of the fuse dangling out. I wanted to watch so badly but knew it could be risky; so, I lit the fuse and high-tailed it out of the stall.

I wasn't worried about the fuse not working; I had dropped enough of these babies into the bay to know that they were waterproof. What did concern me was when I heard Amanda start screaming again. I guess she wasn't dead.

Previous experience told me I had fifteen to twenty seconds on the delayed fuse and habit had started a mental countdown in my head. When Amanda came staggering around the corner of the stall heading straight towards me I was at eleven.

I'll admit I panicked. A feeling I never wanted to have again. My feet were frozen to the warm ground.

Twelve, Amanda stopped and looked around in utter confusion. Thirteen, her hands clawed furiously at her crotch as her face contorted.

Fourteen, Amanda's eyes wide with bewilderment settled upon my presence.

Fifteen, she took a step forward with an arm outstretched in hopeful assistance.

Sixteen, a sudden sharp pain stopped her advance and stretched her facial features in agony.

Seventeen, ka-boom!

What I saw appeared to happen in slow motion.

Amanda's head snapped back as her abdomen exploded open in a spray of blood and entrails. Everything came forward in a mist of red. I was assaulted with tepid hunks of intestine, bits of flesh and muscle. Something salty stung my eyes and I was momentarily blinded.

Rubbing my eyes until my tears washed away the burn I slowly regained focus at the carnage. I had pieces of Amanda stuck all over my naked body as she lay there ten feet from me with her lower half splayed open.

What a mess. Luckily the basin that held rain water for the horses was still operational. I used Amanda's clothes as washcloths to clean myself up and insure that all the blood on me was not my own. Then I began the time consuming process of cleaning up. I gathered all of Amanda scattered parts and dumped them into a trash barrel along with what was now definitely the dead carcass of her remains.

The following day I returned and filled the barrel with industrial strength lye. The caustic solution began eating away at the barrel's contents almost immediately. The fumes however were overpowering and I had to leave. I wanted to watch, but again I figured it was hazardous.

Two days later all that was left were shiny bones which I buried behind the barn.

Chapter 3

Becca jumped when Roberto stepped back into his office. She had been so immersed in the manuscript that she actually forgot where she was for a moment. Roberto had been gone for nearly two hours, leaving her alone in his office to read a copy of the original while he set in motion the process of printing the vile document.

Roberto sent Marissa his admin home early for the weekend. Marissa, being the hopeless romantic that she was, immediately thought she was being dismissed so that her boss and Ms. Willis could be alone. Marissa always felt she had a vested interest in their relationship since it was she who recommended Suspenders all those years ago.

Once alone, away from prying eyes that would wonder why the Head of the department was operating the scanning equipment, Roberto began the tedious process of feeding single sheets into the Epson GT-3000. One of the many short-cuts that developed out of the 'timeline model' Roberto had created was to print the manuscript exactly as it was written. This eliminated the time consuming process of reproducing the handwritten papers into typeset pages, and also eliminated the need to involve additional staff.

Becca rubbed her eyes and shook her head as Roberto sat down into one of the dark brown leather chairs in front of his desk. "This is the craziest stuff I've ever read RJ. You have to take this to the police. Too many lives are at stake; this madman is talking about a terrorist act that could make the 9-11 tragedy look like a walk in the park."

"I can't. If I don't follow his instructions it would be as if I killed Melina myself."

"You don't know that." Becca began to say more but Roberto sprung up out of the chair, veins sticking out on the sides of his neck, his face a violent shade of red.

"I DO KNOW THAT!" he screamed, spittle flying across the desk, "I WILL NOT RISK LOSING MY SISTER!"

Becca stood without saying another word, laid the open manuscript face-down on the desk to hold her place, circled around the desk and wrapped her arms around Roberto. She felt him release his fury and slump into her embrace. He began to weep as she rocked him; she told him it was going to be alright, that everything was going to work out. Becca reassured him that she was there to help in any way she could. She agreed that **No police** meant no police; but, they needed a plan.

She persuaded Roberto to get some sleep, convincing him that he was no good to anyone, especially himself in his present state of mind. Not wanting to leave the office, Roberto stretched out on the matching dark brown leather couch against the wall opposite the window overlooking Third Avenue. Roberto surprised himself by falling asleep almost as soon as his head connected with the armrest.

Becca covered him with a light blanket she found in the supply closet and thought back to another time. In what seemed like a lifetime ago, they had shared the intimate comfort of that very same blanket.

It had been their third date since meeting at Suspenders only eight days earlier. RJ had been such a gentleman; never pressuring her for more than an innocent kiss and virtuous hug at the end of each encounter, but Becca was ready for more.

They had eaten dinner at Domenico's on 40th Street, a three-and-a-half star Italian restaurant just around the corner and over one avenue from Roberto's office. The couple's plan to see a late movie at the AMC Loews on 2nd Ave was interrupted when a quick stop back at the office turned into a night of passion. First at the office and then rounds two and three back at RJ's apartment. It had been the beginning of what Becca thought to be, finally, her last boyfriend.

Settling back into the executive style chair behind the desk, Becca returned to the manuscript, simultaneously reading and devising her own ideas on how to proceed in this rapidly unfolding horror show she found herself in.

While napping on the couch, Roberto experienced a nightmare where he found himself transported back to a time of new beginnings...

Roberto Sr. brought the old Ford pickup to a squeaky stop. Dust from the dirt road circled the vehicle and made visibility impossible. Carmen awakened in the passenger seat and asked her husband why they were stopping.

Were they across the border yet?

Crammed in among their meager belongings in the tight compartment behind the bench seat, Roberto Jr. leaned forward at the sound of his mother's voice.

As he listened to his parents exchange words he did not fully comprehend he was still aware of the concern they expressed. Watching the dust settle as if a curtain was lowered, the young boy became conscious of the men approaching the truck.

As his father attempted to open the driver's door his mother frantically tried to hold him back. The boy could only stare helplessly when his mother's face grimaced and her hands went to her distended abdomen. He could hear his unborn sister scream a warning of impending doom.

Roberto Sr. stepped out of the dusty blue pickup closed the door behind him and headed towards the men standing twenty feet in front of the truck. The boy reached out to his mother and placed a small hand on her shoulder. Carmen laid a sweaty hand over his all the while keeping her eyes fixed on her husband.

The child and his mother were spectators as the most important man in their lives conversed with men that now appeared ten feet tall. They watched in horror as the man who was transporting them to a better life turned and gestured to the vehicle unaware of the weapon that was being aimed at his head. Carmen's hand instinctively drew up to cover her son's eyes from the act of violence that ensued.

Roberto Jr. heard his father's head explode as his mother and sister howled in unison.

The band of savage men approached the truck, moving on all fours as their clothes were stripped away, leaving them naked, covered with blood-red scales shimmering in the sun. Barking and growling like rabid dogs, the men surrounded the vehicle and began pounding on the metal. Snarling faces full of jagged teeth, left smears of foam and spit on the windows as portions of the trucks exterior were torn from its frame.

The boy sat in the dirt and watched as the pack dragged Carmen away from his outstretched arms. Unable to move and unable to scream, Roberto Jr. witnessed his mother's body being torn apart. Her death screams reverberated through his soul as her skin was peeled off her remains. The muscles over her abdomen were then pulled apart to reveal the soft white tissue of the womb that protected his sister.

Roberto Jr. leapt to his feet and ran forward, driven by a supernatural force to save his only sister. But the savages were gone. Only the headless body of his father and the ravaged hollow carcass of his mother remained.

A thin trail of blood gleamed in the dirt, and with a panicked sense of urgency, the young boy began to follow the path, praying that he wasn't too late to save his sister...

The panicked sense of urgency followed him into his waking state.

Roberto knew that time was running out and he had just slept away precious time Melina couldn't afford.

Chapter 4

"I got us some coffee and sandwiches from the Koreans downstairs." Becca told Roberto as he stood up and stretched.

"How long was I out?"

"About an hour, you needed it. Did you sleep at all last night?"

Roberto just shook his head. He could still see the trail of blood when he closed his eyes.

"Do you want turkey or ham?" Becca asked as she handed him a Styrofoam cup filled with black coffee.

"I can't eat; I've got to get downstairs and prep the equipment."

"Don't make me force-feed you RJ. You know as well as I do you need to eat."

She was right and she did know better than most; Roberto was Hypoglycemic. If he didn't eat at regular intervals and his blood sugar dropped he could blackout or worse have seizures.

They sat down together on the sofa and as Roberto moved the light blanket Becca had covered him with, their eyes met knowingly and they both smiled for the first time since she arrived at the office.

While they ate Becca shared some initial thoughts she'd been having about the manuscript. She was having very mixed emotions about printing and distributing the document. Anticipating another flare-up objection from Roberto she quickly stated that they must proceed and follow the lunatic's instructions without fail to protect Melina as best they could. Becca didn't feel the need to share with Roberto her bleak view that Melina was going to die anyway; that is, if she wasn't dead already.

Becca's read on the self-proclaimed Rush-Hour Madman was that he now needs the recognition that he had been missing out on his whole life. The part of the manuscript that she had read so far, read like a confession. The Madman had gotten away with so much in his lifetime that he was profoundly proud of, but no one knew about it. It had finally gotten to the point where he desperately wanted to be recognized for his "accomplishments".

Roberto could see her point but lacked the foresight to see where she was going with it; time was of the essence and he needed to get busy. The disk that held the scanned pages needed to be uploaded into the computer. Page placement needed to be mapped to correspond to the binding process. The printing presses needed to be calibrated. Paper stock needed to be transported from the warehouse and loaded into the feeder bins. A cover needed to be designed since the Madman didn't provide one; and then the phone calls to hundreds of dealers and distributors across the country, and at this point in the process Roberto didn't have a clue what to tell them to insure shelf-space.

While relaying all that he needed to do to Becca, Roberto spoke mainly in Spanish. Although she was born Rebecca Martina Valdez Willis; half Irish and half Puerto Rican, daughter of Felicia Catalina Valdez and Jonathan David Willis, she was red white and blue through and through. Becca rarely conversed in Spanish even though she was fluent in it as well as three other languages. However, English is the language of the United States of America and Becca will argue with most to that point.

However, when she and Roberto began dating they spoke predominately in Spanish to one another, at the time it felt like a special bond they shared and she let it carry on too long to ever comment on it then, or now.

Becca explained to Roberto that he was already ahead of her. She agreed that he needed to get busy producing the manuscript while she began trying to find the Madman. Roberto asked her to repeat herself, positive that he misunderstood what she said. Becca clarified by explaining that the breadcrumbs were all there in the lunatic's text. Not only was he providing supposed clues to a near-future terrorist attack; but he was so pompous about his past deeds that he appeared to be blind to the remote possibility that he didn't cover his tracks.

Roberto begged her not to go looking for trouble but didn't have a credible argument when she asked him why he had called her in the first place.

With the manuscript under her arm, Becca gave Roberto a hug and a kiss on the cheek, and told him she was going home to read some more, get some sleep, and drive to Long Island in the morning. Promising each other to stay in touch throughout the next day, Becca left and hailed a cab to her own apartment on the Upper East Side.

(Unedited excerpt from the manuscript)

I can't begin to tell you how exhilarating it was to relive that moment. Writing it all down was so much better than just thinking about it. Little details kept coming back to me. And you know... it's all in the details. I'll have to remember to put a flower on her headstone as a thank you next time I'm in town.

I go back to the old neighborhood every couple of years. I like to see what my brothers are up to. Neither of them lives in the town we grew up in, but they are close enough that I can take a stroll down memory lane when I visit.

❧

After I removed Amanda from attending the balance of the school year, I learned something about you faceless fucks. You don't care about anything or anyone other than yourselves and you happily lie to your friends and neighbors that you do. You may think that I'm no different, but you're wrong. You see, unlike you, I don't pretend to care about anything or anyone other than myself.

I am pure.

I watched the town pretend to care about the missing poor girl and then quickly forget. You ignored the family's suffering and anguish like it didn't exist. Personally, I think you all missed out. While you went about your daily rituals and mundane existences, I relished the extended pain and misery that had been created.

Taking a human life was a new and exuberant feeling for me. However, since so much went wrong with Amanda, I needed to know what it would feel like when I had a plan.

I knew enough to stay away from another of my schoolmates and create even the smallest of patterns. I definitely wanted to use the Hollingsworth barn again. I wanted to take my time with this next subject; you know, savor the moment.

❧

I decided that two types of people would be perfect for my selection; the homeless and the hookers. Either one would be someone not readily missed, if ever. I came up with a little game to make the final selection. As fate had it once again, in the long run the better of the two choices was made for me.

Living on Long Island wasn't a tropical paradise, but we had our fair share of beaches. Atlantic Beach, Long Beach and my personal favorite Rockaway Beach; they were all within 10 miles from my house in Lynbrook.

I spent a lot of time on the beaches in the afternoons, especially during the week. Don't forget I was done with school at noon and my part time job at The Back Barn, a wine and cheese bar and restaurant didn't start until 5. I'll tell you more about The Back Barn later, but for now you can know that it was my very first car bomb.

To add to the *thump-thump* of my shit-kickers I developed an extra-long delayed fuse. I'm very proud of this, the process took quite a while and there were many discarded attempts. I realize that by today's technology with remote detonation and the beauty of C4 plastique this seems trivial to you, but I was a 17 year old kid with a dream.

The fuse would burn without extinguishing for a period of twenty to thirty minutes. This allowed me plenty of time to set up the shit-kicker and be far away before the excitement began.

My game was called 'gender specific casualty'. The rules were quite simple actually; a wounding counted as one point while deaths counted as five. The only delay to the scoring occurred if a wounding became a death; so I decided to only count the initial results, hence if someone died later, I only calculated the one point from the original wounding. Casualties were separated into male and female categories, taking in no additional consideration based on age. I didn't want to over-complicate the game. Just like flipping a coin, male meant one thing and female meant the other.

During this particular round I was set up at Atlantic Beach, I found there was a lot more traffic on the sand there during the weekends than at the other two beaches. On that day, the men represented the homeless and the women represented the whores. No meaning behind my selection although fitting.

I arrived at the beach early and set up two blankets as if I expected more people to join me later. This also allowed me a degree of privacy. Digging between my two blankets, I planted a double-strength glass shit-kicker about three inches beneath the sand leaving the tip of an extra-long delayed fuse barely poking through the surface.

Once I had the game-bomb set up, I waited for other people to set up 'camp' around the area I had already staked a claim to. Even though the official start of summer was a week away, the beach quickly filled with a wide variety of families and groups of teens. I casually rolled up one of the unused blankets and brought it back to my car.

Upon my return the vacated space was occupied by five very well built seniors from the Lawrence High School cheerleading squad. I remember thinking to myself that this is going to be a terrible waste of talent as I passed them and continued on with the game as planned.

I learn my lessons well. I always say, have a plan and stick to the plan; at least I do since Amanda

At the car I changed into a hideous pair of plaid swim trunks and affixed a temporary tattoo of a black panther to my left shoulder and a barbed-wire band design around my right bicep. I glued a fake moustache to my upper lip with rubber cement to insure its hold as I took a quick dip in the cold Atlantic.

Pat Addams

Returning to my established ground-zero, I found two of the five cheerleaders remaining. Not bothering to disguise my voice I inquired about the missing ta-tas. With my eyes hidden by a pair of mirrored sunglasses nobody was the wiser that I wasn't looking at their faces as they told me that their friends were off trying to find the boys they had come with.

I explained how this was their lucky day because I was about to leave. I promised to wait so no one else would take the vacated spot. Double-D was so thankful that she gave me a hug that I can still feel today.

When the rest of the group arrived there was an even amount of boys and girls.

Does it get any better than that?

I couldn't wait to see who would win; the homeless or the whores?

Talk about *thump-thump*.

Last piece of business was lighting the fuse and heading to the boardwalk with my score sheet. As planned, I lit a cigarette, asked anybody if they wanted one and received eight out of ten yeses. Stupid jocks; didn't they know smoking can kill you?

I rolled up my other blanket as the boys set theirs down. I asked if I could hang while I finished my cig and was told 'of course'.

I sat cross-legged between the blankets with five boys to my left, five girls to my right and one fuse in front of me begging to play.

I said my goodbyes, wished them well and as I snuffed the burning ember of my cigarette out in the sand, I touched the fuse and watched it snake below the surface.

Game on.

Completely unobstructed, ten feet above the sand, my view from the boardwalk was perfect. Having changed once again at the car and keeping a close eye on my watch, I arrived at my front row balcony seat approximately fifteen minutes after igniting the shit-kicker. I couldn't be sure about the time because my waterproof watch stopped working when it got wet in the Atlantic.

The lack of time coordinates added immensely to the *thump-thump*. I couldn't look away even for a second. What a great game. The jocks and cheerleaders moved back and forth over the divide between the blankets.

I was amazed that they avoided stepping in the sand.

It was very *thump-thump*.

I was concerned about them carelessly unearthing the shit-kicker and ruining the game.

Finally the group appeared content with who was on each blanket and they all laid down to soak up some rays. I expected the ground to erupt at that very moment they had found their stillness; but still nothing.

A bright blue and yellow beach-ball came bounding into my peripheral vision tempting me to look away from the game board but I held fast in my vigil. The ball continued to be batted up and over by the throngs of beachgoers until it amazingly came to rest at ground-zero. I now had everyone's attention.

I leaned forward with my hands gripping the railing in front of me and almost cheered on the impending destruction as if I was a spectator at an Islanders game watching Bobby Nystrom on a power-play breakaway.

Double-D picked up the ball and gave it weak smack into the air and watched it travel backwards over her head. Still nothing; I settled back down onto my wooden perch and wondered if I had a fuse malfunction as Double-D leaned over the divide to plant a kiss on jock-boy laying to her right.

The blast took me by surprise; which is to say nothing for what it did to Double-D and her friends.

People were up and screaming; running away in a fanned out circle from the epicenter of the action. There were so many wounded it was hard to count let alone determine men versus women. Plus, too many wounded were running away.

The dead were much easier to count.

Just one: Double-D, she appeared to have taken most of the discharge in the chest and face; both of which were now mostly missing. I wish I had brought binoculars with me to get a better view. The top of the coke bottle was lodged into her throat and acted like a faucet. I either caught the tail end of her desire to survive or just the final beats of her heart; but the little fountain of blood that shot up out of her neck through the broken bottle was like poetry.

Jock-boy took a hefty direct assault of glass shards to the face and I'm pretty sure he won't be lettering anytime soon. I mean how can you without eyes? Everyone else got off rather light thanks to Double-D's double-D.

Needing to make a quick adjustment in tabulating the final score, I decided to call an audible and only count those that remained on the beach needing medical attention.

It was close, but the one death swayed the results; the hookers won.

Chapter 5

Melina regained consciousness.

Slowly she opened her eyes but still could not see. The darkness around her was so complete that she could have been blind in both eyes.

Fruitlessly stumbling around in the obscurity, Melina could find no escape. Her left ankle was shackled to a thick chain secured into a rough wood paneled wall allowing her only about ten feet of mobility. Despite her best efforts she could not free herself from the shackle nor free the chain from the wall.

(Unedited excerpt from the manuscript)

Back then finding a hooker was easy. 42nd Street in Manhattan was well known for dollar peep shows and backroom blowjobs. In addition, every street corner on the West Side surrounding the two tunnels to New Jersey was littered with whores'au jus.

Chloroform was also easy to come by as it was readily available at the school nurse's station and in the gym teacher's first aid kit. The seventies were fabulous in its ignorance.

I picked up an adorable little red-head at the corner of 10th Ave and West 30th. She couldn't have been any taller than 5'4" and that included the high-heels she was wearing. Just like McDonald's drive thru, I pulled up to the curb and Roxie leaned into the open passenger window asking what I wanted.

I ordered a foxy-Roxie blowjob for ten bucks. Once she determined I wasn't a cop, using her foolproof method of asking if I was a cop, the stupid whore got in. Now, if she had asked me if I was going to murder her; she could have saved herself a lot of pain and suffering.

Turning right and heading south down 9th Ave, Roxie directed me into a dark parking lot just off of 25th street near one of the Section 8 housing projects. Lovely neighborhood, but I wasn't planning on hanging around.

When I was originally planning the abduction part of the conquest, I considered letting the whore get me off first before I made my move. But I decided that it was too risky and would allow her a degree of control.

I had the chloroform soaked rag ready to go in a plastic bag next to the seat by the driver's door. As Roxie was slurping her mouth around the pole sticking up between my legs, I slipped my left hand into the bag and grabbed the rag. I already had my hand on the back of her head so when I asked her, "would you want to know when you were going to die?" it was easy to grab a fistful of hair when she stopped choking herself and looked up at me.

My left hand holding the rag, fully covered her mouth and nose as I held her head firmly in place over my lap. Roxie put up the briefest of resistance before she went completely limp. I pulled her off of me by her hair and shoved her to the floorboard in front of the passenger side.

I immediately drove off to find a safer neighborhood to finish wrapping the package for transport back to my barn on Long Island. It's funny; but in all the excitement, I hadn't even noticed that I had cum.

💣

I wasn't worried about anyone seeing my package bound and gagged in the backseat of the wagon as I drove out lower Manhattan via the Brooklyn Battery Tunnel. Toll booths were only occupied on the northbound side of the Gowanus Expressway; never a charge to leave the city, only to get in.

Of course you could use one of Brooklyn's three bridges to the city which were always toll-free both ways, in and out. But there were too many lights and too many bums wanting to wash your windshield for a buck on those routes. Besides I didn't know how long foxy-Roxie was going to be unconscious, and a moving package could draw even a bum's attention.

When Roxie came to I was about 20 minutes from the safety of the barn. Driving 60 miles per hour down the Belt Parkway just past the Howard Beach Exit, my package came alive with a vengeance. Grunting and snarling through the duct-tape covering her mouth while bucking and trashing like a trapped shark, I could feel the entire wagon shake as foxy-Roxie became aware of her situation.

The mania behind me went on for a non-stop 10 minutes and then all at once my package went silent. Strange, but for some reason, the silence had me more concerned than all the commotion did.

I took the next exit off the Belt onto Sunrise Highway and pulled up to a red light at Francis Lewis Blvd. I was finally able to put the car in park; and after unbuckling my seatbelt, I swiveled around and looked over into the backseats.

I have to confess I was impressed with what I observed.

Roxie no doubt was a resourceful little thing; somehow she had herself bent up under the seat and was utilizing the seat's under-spring to saw away at her duct-taped wrists behind her back. I think she almost would have had it too if she didn't stop when she saw me looking over at her.

Bug-eyed and savage, she stared angrily up at me and began her thrashing again. A car behind me blared on its horn because the light had changed to green. I spun around, threw the wagon back into drive and sped off looking for the nearest side street to pull off into and deal with the crazed foxy-Roxie.

Making a sharp right onto Market Rd, I heard a thud from the back and turned around. One way or another my package had up righted itself into the seat and was thrown into the door as the wagon screamed around the turn onto Market. I watched in the rearview mirror as Roxie slid back to the center. A quick hard left onto Sidney Place slammed her into the other door with another thud.

Sidney Place ran across the back end of the Green Acres Mall parking lot and then intersected with a small wooded park to the east of the Mall. The new plan was to get to the seclusion of the park without further incident and re-wrap my package.

As I doubled the posted speed limit of 20 miles per hour, Roxie's face appeared in the rearview mirror with her red hair standing straight out in chaotic spikes and her beautiful green eyes protruding from their sockets.

When Roxie lunged forward; I jammed on the brakes.

My adorable little red-head shot forward and face-planted into the windshield. Her neck snapped sideways and she crumpled into the seat next to me. I reached down feeling for a pulse to make sure she didn't spoil the rest of my weekend.

She didn't.

Chapter 6

Becca stayed awake reading the manuscript and making notes most of the night. Early Saturday morning, using her remote access, Becca logged onto the New York Post's database from her apartment on East Sixty-Ninth Street. Staring out her ground floor view, she watched as the city began to wake even before the sun. Once her encryption software confirmed that there was no spyware threat, she quickly entered in the six-digit randomized code from her New York Post issued RSA SecurID600 key chain before the numbers cycled to the next sequence thereby locking her out.

The Post's database was linked to some of the world's most extensive search engines as well as incorporating some high-tech internal software called SNIPH. SNIPH was an acronym for Spy Network Infiltrating Protected Hardware. Basically what SNIPH did was 'sniff' around the wireless information highway looking for virus protection software. Once located, SNIPH would copy the program in reversed code. This 'mirror image' would then be readily accepted and integrated within the original virus protection program almost like welcoming in a long lost cousin. Except the cousin snuck in a two way radio and opened up a line of communication back with the Mother Ship. The SNIPH program allowed certain individuals at the New York Post exclusive access to extended data within law enforcement bureaus, low-level government agencies and world-wide confidential news media.

Although Becca had security clearance to utilize SNIPH, she uncovered enough information in the Post's archives to set up her first day in search of the Madman. Becca had decided upon two starting points to test her theory that the Madman was being more truthful than he probably should be in his manuscript.

First was the death of Amanda Farber, which if proven true, would begin a trail back to the school she attended and then to her classmates. Once deductive reasoning was applied, it should be only a matter of hours before the identity of the Madman would be uncovered. Becca was relying heavily on the accuracy of the details the Madman provided himself, but she truly had nothing else to go on.

Exhaustion hit her hard as she sat stuck in traffic on the Long Island Expressway and she downed her second Red Bull energy drink. Becca thought she had left early enough to get out in front of the weekend travelers hurrying to points such as the Hamptons and Montauk to enjoy the last few weekends of the summer.

Becca had spent many weekends in South Hampton when she first got her job as a freelance reporter for the New York Post, one of the countries oldest publications. Her assignment was to simply dig up dirt on New York's rich and famous. Becca hated the assignments, but after being turned down time and time again by the local networks for an anchor position, she needed the work.

Growing up in East Flatbush, Brooklyn, Becca struggled through her first ten years of school. Her attention always seemed to be drawn elsewhere other than the subject matter at hand. Becca would drift off, daydreaming as they called it, developing her own tales far more interesting than what the lesson plans offered. She would be studying the mannerisms of her classmates and teachers, creating behind the scene stories in her head. The only exception was history and current events. In these classes, Becca at least maintained a B average.

Becca was destined to a life of mediocrity. Her mother and father never achieved more than a high school diploma and that was the extent of the expectation place upon her. Her parents were happy to sign off on a report card predominately littered with C's and D's as long as their only daughter was not strung out on drugs or pregnant.

Becca wanted so much more for herself. Then one evening, after overhearing her parents discussing a meeting they had just returned from with her guidance counselor, Becca decided to take control of her future. Mister 'call me Jeremy' Young; her supposed trusted advisor at Samuel J Tilden High School, recommended to her parents that Becca enroll into the DECA work program as part of her eleventh grade curriculum.

The worst part for Becca was the fact that her parents agreed, although she wasn't surprised. Her mother had spent the last thirteen years working in a factory sewing j-hooks and eye-clasps into the elastic strap of brassieres. Everyday her mother would pray that she wouldn't loose her job to either a machine or the Chinese. Meanwhile, Becca's father, after losing his bartending job at almost every Irish Pub this side of Dublin, had finally landed a steady job two years prior as night watchman for the Holy Cross Cemetery. Since the cemetery was walking distance from their home, the fact that her father was no longer allowed to drive wasn't an issue.

Becca had always thought she would be a famous television reporter, and not just any famous television reporter, but the first Puerto Rican-Irish-woman lead news-anchor New York City had ever seen. Becca learned something about herself that night; she realized that she had an unwavering determination once she firmly put her mind to something.

For the next two years, Becca studied and focused as she never had before. Mister 'call me Jeremy' was so impressed by her resolve and relentless improvement in her grades that he personally visited with Columbia University's admissions director to insure Becca's acceptance into the Ivy League's only School of Journalism.

Money wasn't plentiful for the Willis'. Their house on Fifty-Second Street was owned outright, willed to them when Jonathan Willis Sr. and his wife Kathleen were trapped and killed in a hotel fire while on vacation in Philadelphia. Even so, Becca's parents, Jonathan and Felicia could barely make ends meet. It seemed like every time they were able to get slightly ahead of themselves financially, something would breakdown and need repairing or replacing.

In addition, Jonathan had serious drinking and fighting problems, which not only cost him most of his jobs, but also took a toll on the family in court costs, lawyer's fees and the restitution that constantly needed to be paid to those with broken noses, fractured jaws and other assorted broken limbs.

It wasn't until Becca was heading into high school that her mother finally laid down the law. Felicia demanded that Jonathan clean up his act and get a decent job or she was leaving. She meant it too. Felicia was soft spoken as long as a situation wasn't a threat to her family or herself. At those times, standing a mere five-two, Becca's mom could instantly turn into a ten-foot tall fire-breathing dragon.

For as tough and rough around the edges as Jonathan was, Felicia was his whole life, and he would do anything to keep her happy. His wife had tolerated a lot of nonsense from him over the years and he made changes for her that a gambling man would have lost his shirt betting against.

When Becca told her parents she had been accepted to Columbia, it was the first time Jonathan openly wept. He was so proud of his little girl and so distraught with himself. He had been going to A.A. meetings for almost two years and in doing so he realized how much he had taken away from those he loved. Becca now had the ability to achieve something beyond his wildest dreams; and he recognized that he was to blame for putting her future at risk because he had crippled them all financially.

Mister 'call me Jeremy' almost fell off his seat he was laughing so hard when Becca came to his office the Monday preceding graduation. Becca had thanked him for all his support and everything he had done to help her get into

Journalism School; but, unfortunately her family just couldn't afford a school like Columbia. She had explained that she still would be pursuing a career as a news-anchorwoman, but she'd be applying to Brooklyn Community College instead.

For the first time in her life did the phrase, "You must have misunderstood…" get followed up with words so positive. Becca was going to Columbia on a partial academic minority scholarship. She often wondered which minority in her got the scholarship; the Hispanic or the Irish.

Working evenings as a cashier at Ramos Supermarket at the corner of Utica and Snyder Avenues just two blocks from her house, Becca lived at home and commuted to Morningside Heights on Manhattan's Upper West Side for school.

After four years Becca graduated with a Bachelors Degree in Journalism and an awareness that life doesn't always happen the way you think it should. Becca's grades were not adequate for a continued scholarship in the Master of Arts and Science Program and she was forced into the job market before her credentials could substantiate her desires.

Without the credentials, television stations required experience; and without experience, television stations required credentials. Frustration and rejection became close allies of Becca's until an old friend, Mister 'call me Jeremy' came to her rescue once again and used up another political favor by landing her a freelance position with the New York Post.

(Unedited excerpt from the manuscript)

My package remained docile for the rest of the trip to the barn. I did make a slight adjustment to the original plan based on the ferocity of my adorable little red-head. I wanted to exploit her power for my own indulgence; a small reward for having to deal with her escapades on the ride home from the city.

Why not take full advantage of the situation?

Most of you would have done the same thing.

💣

I had installed a track into one of the beams in the barn. I suspended a harness that hung down from a single chain and then split into two with leather straps at both ends. I had several different ideas on how to use this devise and it came in very handy when I decided to play with foxy-Roxie before killing her.

The barn was now also equipped with several shackles secured to the wall and as I displayed my package in spread-eagle fashion, a female version of da Vinci's 'Vitruvian Man' came to mind.

Finally I had a chance to relax; I pulled over an inflatable chair a few feet in front of my new wall art and sat back in anticipation of her awakening.

Roxie was an absolutely beautiful work of art. Perfectly proportioned, relatively still young enough to be full and firm and a well toned mid-section you could bounce a quarter off. Despite the golf ball sized knot in the middle of her forehead, I'd have to say she was just what the doctor ordered.

Truthfully, I liked her better unconscious, because as soon as she opened her eyes the innocent beauty went straight out the window. Her face contorted in a primal rage that was not very becoming of a young lady. Not to mention the vulgarities and threats that came spewing out of her mouth. I should have left the tape on.

Planning does have its benefits, I put on my headphones and cranked up the 8-track of Beethoven I had brought. It was either that or Pink Floyd and I felt Beethoven's 3rd, Eroica, was more fitting to what was about to go down.

Even though Roxie's mobility was seriously impaired; she still managed to do a lot of twitching and jumping while I was trying to caress her smooth and supple ivory skin; actually, she made it nearly impossible. It was unfortunate, because I've been told I have a very gentle touch.

Then, when she spit in my face I think I lost a little control. I found myself slapping her repeatedly with open hands. I got quite a workout and I believe foxy-Roxie got my point. Hanging her head down with blood trickling from her split lips she appeared to have run out of things to say and I was able to remove my headphones. I wasn't really listening anyway.

My little general was standing at full attention and I decided it was time to prepare for the evening's grand finale. I tried to re-tape her mouth but the blood made that impossible so I gave up. I thought about using more chloroform but I wanted my foxy lady awake.

Before I unchained her ankles I secured the leather straps from the harness around both her knees. A metal rod I devised kept the chains separated and also insured that my prey's legs would remain spread when I lifted them off the ground.

Everything worked out so much better than I had expected. Who would have thought that a whore would have such an issue with getting boned?

Roxie floated in the air. Her wrists were shackled to the wall and her legs were pulled up and suspended by the harness. I slid myself inside and let her do all the work. She bucked up and down on me so furiously I barely could contain myself. After I double checked to make sure I was still attached; I decided that I definitely had to play this rodeo game again.

Once I was finished, I dressed and left Roxie hanging there in the dark. I did however offer reassurance that I'd return in the morning to murder her.

I remember sleeping so soundly that night.

💣

Chapter 7

Becca's first instinct was that there was more truth than fiction to the Madman's recounting of his escapades; especially the earlier tales. His constant reference to John and Jane Q. Public as being "faceless" implies that he feels he is not only above the law, but also out of reach. Becca hoped to use his blatant lack of cover as a means to find out exactly who the Madman is; and therefore, be able to track him down quickly.

Becca had never met Roberto's sister, and she hoped to discover where Melina was being held captive and save her life. However, Becca's priority was to uncover and prevent the terrorist plot that the Madman so brazenly professes to be planning. Becca prayed that she wouldn't be put in a situation that would pit her against Roberto in their quests. She knows that Roberto's priority is the safe return of Melina, but there may come a time in the very near future when she has no choice but to involve the authorities.

Roberto wasn't exposed to the tragedy of September 11th the same way Becca was; or all New Yorkers for that matter. Roberto arrived in the city almost three and a half years after the catastrophe. Even though the terror, and the pain, and the anguish were experienced by the entire country; New York City experienced ground-zero, and despite the individual loss, the city came together a collective whole. A unity that forever changed millions of attitudes was born. There will not be an acceptance of selfishness again.

Nightmares of the events that changed our nation plague Becca to this day. Many of us recall the heartbreak of that fateful day and know exactly where we were; Becca watched the events unfold on the wall monitors of the New York Post's office on Sixth Ave. Gazing in horror as people chose to jump from the burning tower; Becca watched as her fiancé made that very decision.

(Unedited excerpt from the manuscript)

As I write and relive some of my earlier experiences, I realize that I might be coming off as a little sick, maybe twisted, slightly perverse; but, I don't know if you are truly getting the rush I feel that would help you understand that none of this is sick, or twisted and definitely not perverse. These were, and are, some the purest most creative experiences anyone could imagine. Especially when you are able to combine that raw adrenaline surge with sexual gratification; certainly, beyond any doubt in my mind, it is as close to God as anyone can be.

I'm sure what I just said means nothing to you; and I am not in the least surprised. You are after all, faceless. You are not even worthy to share in these triumphs; and therefore I smile as I see you writhing in the soil of your own self-loathing.

Chapter 8

As she finally broke free of the congestion on the L.I.E. and turned onto the Cross Island Parkway, Becca thought to herself that she must be the one who's crazy. Who did she think she was fooling? Did she really think that it would be that easy? Becca hated it when she had these moments of self-doubt. They never lasted long enough to have any form of significant impact on her, just enough to make her feel that she wasn't adequate, that she didn't deserve the praise and recognition that she had worked so hard to achieve.

Quickly putting those thoughts behind her, Becca refocused on the day ahead. After looking into the Amanda Farber story, the second item on her agenda was the Hollingsworth Farm and the Madman's beloved barn. Becca needed to verify their existence and ideally hoped to be able to explore them.

Exiting onto Francis Lewis Blvd, Becca continued south and turned left onto Rosedale Road which became Brookfield Road on the other side of Hungry Harbor until it intersected at Mill Road. A right on Mill, a left on Peninsula, another right onto Franklin and a left onto Broadway; Becca zigzagged her way to East Rockaway Road and Main Street where she finally turned down Rhame Ave to Lawrence Street. Last on the left, at the road's dead-end, the Farber's house sat in need of some serious repair.

The headline from the May 6, 1987 edition of the New York Post read:
LONG ISLAND PARENTS DECLARE THEIR OWN DAUGHTER DEAD
That article was the most recent reference that surfaced when Becca entered Amanda Farber's name into the Post's database. The headline was eye-catching and did its job which was to sell newspapers. The article on the other hand was merely informative and left nothing to warrant further interest from the reader.

The article swiftly went from its focus on a family suffering with the loss of a missing daughter and struggling to understand the circumstances surrounding her disappearance; to an expose on the proper protocol required to liquidate someone's estate if there is no body available to substantiate a claim of death.

The article did confirm for Becca that Amanda Farber never returned home from school one Thursday afternoon seven years earlier. Interestingly enough, Amanda's step-father, Bud Farber, was initially suspected of foul play but was later cleared due to lack of evidence.

Stepping through knee-high weeds, navigating onto broken slab remnants of a stone walkway that led to a weathered porch, Becca reached the bent screen door which whined on its hinges as she pulled it back. Green paint chips fell from the wooden door as she rapped loudly with bare knuckles.

After waiting a reasonable period with no response Becca knocked again, louder and longer this time. Still, with no response. Standing up on tiptoes, Becca peered through the small diamond shaped frosted window set into the top half of the door.

"GO AWAY!" Resounded from the other side of the door in a deep male's voice and Becca hastily took a step backwards, almost stumbling down the three porch steps into the weeds. Quickly regaining her composure, Becca began rapping incessantly against the wooden door making her determination known to those inside.

An unshaven, highly perturbed Bud Farber nearly tore the door off its hinges as he swung it open and stared inquisitively at the tiny woman who dared to ignore his demand to depart. "What could you possible want woman!?" he roared into Becca's face. Becca was accustomed to dealing with individuals who were less than willing to be cooperative in her line of work and had long ago found a little trick that seemed to work.

"I was hoping you could help me." Two quick bats of the eyes, a demure look down, eye contact with raised eyebrows and then wait. This trick only seemed to work on men, but Becca was okay with that.

Bud seemed to soften just a little around the edge. "Who are you; and what could I possible help you with?"

"My name is Becca Willis and I'm a reporter for…" Obviously the wrong thing to say because Bud instantly turned a shade of scarlet Becca had only seen in a box of crayons. With veins sticking out the side of his neck and forehead, Bud took a hostile step towards Becca and this time she did stumble backwards off the porch and landed on her backside gawking upward as the verbal onslaught came out of Bud Farber's mouth.

"How dare you!"

Spittle rained down upon Becca as he continued; "You have some nerve coming here asking for help after what you people did to me!"

Bud appeared to contemplate saying more and decided to simply turn away in a huff and head back inside. The porch reverberated under each thunderous step he took. Becca just watched and waited for the perfect moment.

With his hand high on the door's edge, Bud looked back at Becca to emphasize the symbolism that he was about to impose when he slammed the door shut. Becca then spoke just loud enough to be barely heard; "I know what happened to Amanda."

Chapter 9

Becca sat down without moving aside the newspapers and magazines that were strewn all over the couch and Bud made no attempt at apologizing for the clutter. The living room was dark and drab, littered with empty beer cans, fast food wrappers and discarded pizza boxes. The fragrance that assaulted you upon entering the premises was a combination of stale trash and loneliness.

The mention of his step-daughter's name froze Bud in mid-slam, which allowed Becca time to explain that although she was a reporter she wasn't there on newspaper business. Dancing around the true substance of the manuscript, Becca shared with Bud the disappearance of Melina and the time predicament she found herself in. His assistance not only could help save the life of her friend's sister, but it could also uncover definitive evidence about the disappearance of Amanda.

Becca waited for Bud to gain control over his emotions. The prospect that he could finally have answers after all these years was an overwhelming concept and brought the big man to tears.

As Becca flipped through the Class of 1980 Lynbrook High School yearbook that Bud had brought down from Amanda's room, she listened to Bud relive a Readers Digest version of the last forty-three years.

When Bud had met Amanda's mom, Emily Tebbe in 1965, Amanda had just turned three years old. Emily's husband had been called to active duty and deployed to serve in the Vietnam War just one month before Emily found out she was pregnant with their child. On Amanda's first birthday, notice arrived that her father would never be returning home.

The war had taken Bud's only family as well; his two older brothers had joined the ranks of the missing and were presumed dead back in 1964.

Sharing similar yet very different losses, Bud and Emily found each other at the local VFW in Westbury at one of the weekly support group meetings. It was a fluke that changed both of their lives. Because although Bud lived in Westbury his whole life, Emily was simply visiting her sister who suggested that she attend the meeting. Married one year later, they celebrated Amanda's fourth birthday as a family in their new home in Bay Park, Long Island.

The most maddening thing to Bud was the way the press, the vultures as he called them, swarmed down upon him as the evil step-father when Amanda first went missing. With absolutely no evidence to support their claims, the press painted him as everything from a child-molester to an overbearing, unreasonable parent who any child would want to run away from. Friends and neighbors stopped associating with the Farbers. Bud's third-shift position at the Waste Management Plant was eliminated after twenty-two loyal years of service, and Emily was asked to no longer volunteer at the local library.

Once the press was finished destroying Bud and Emily at the most devastating time of their lives, they seemed to get bored with the story, or lack of continued developments, and moved on. However, in the wake of their pandering, even the police found no justification in waging anything more than a meager investigation into Amanda's disappearance.

Bud got a job driving a taxi to barely pay the bills, while Emily sat in silence day after day, year after year. Bud and Emily deteriorated before each other's eyes as the years passed, but neither noticed. Both had given up hope of ever seeing their daughter again, yet they couldn't move on. There was nothing tangible, nothing concrete to latch on to, nothing to allow them the closure they so desperately needed.

Seven years after Amanda's disappearance, Bud had come home from the Nassau County Court of Clerks Office with the paperwork that finally declared Amanda legally dead. He had shown it to Emily in hopes of finally releasing her and allowing them to hopefully move on.

Emily stood up and slapped him across the face.

When Bud returned from work the following day he found Emily dead, hanging by her neck suspended from the second floor balcony.

(Unedited excerpt from the manuscript)

In retrospect, I should have given my captive audience a glimmer of hope at a possible future beyond the weekend. I'm not sure if it would have made a difference; maybe.

Somehow Roxie endured the pain and pulled her wrists out of the shackles in the wall. She completely filleted the skin off her hands in doing so. She must have also broken or dislocated a few knuckles in the process as well. It appeared she did her best to undo the leather straps that kept her suspended upside down at that point.

The bloody mess she created made total escape nearly impossible. Once the leather became wet with her blood, the weight of her body pulled and tightened the knots even more. I couldn't even undo them; I had to use a knife.

I give credit where credit is due, and I gave foxy-Roxie an E for effort. Not only did she try to escape, but she tried to kill herself so I wouldn't have the pleasure.

Using her teeth she gnawed at her own wrists, shredding the delicate veins within; almost successfully.

My biggest regret was that I wasn't in attendance to watch.

Her eyes were rolled up exposing the whites, and her arms dangled motionlessly, but I could see her taking shallow breaths. I grabbed hold of both her arms and lifted. The skin of her right hand had pulled off somewhat and hung attached like a partially removed glove.

It was pretty cool.

I tugged on her arms a little and let go allowing her to swing back and forth for a while.

Unfortunately I decided that she wasn't going to provide a lot more entertainment to me in her blood depleted state of laziness. I pulled over the trash barrel and lifted foxy-Roxie over *the rim. I cut off the knots that she had ruined on my harness and let her body crumble to the bottom of the barrel.*

Although I gave her credit for what she tried to do; I was still pissed that she took a degree of control away from me.

I had purchased a 3-ply facemask and a pair of goggles from the Ace Hardware on Main; so that when I splashed some of the industrial strength lye into the barrel, I could watch.

Roxie wasn't feeling as lethargic as I thought. Her body instantly began to twitch and spasm. Her head, arms and legs beat at the side of the barrel in the most unharmonious fashion. I was only able to watch for a brief moment as the caustic liquid ate away at her flesh. Her flailing around concerned me about the possibility of back-splash, so I quickly covered the barrel with its lid and waited for the bad drumming to stop.

The remains of foxy-Roxie is history as they say; like water under the bridge or water over the tunnel, I guess it depends on which side of the city you live on.

💣

Chapter 10

Becca just sat there staring at the silver haired man as he wiped fresh tears from his eyes. Her hand held a page of the yearbook frozen in mid-motion of being turned. Bud rose from his chair and headed into the kitchen where he opened the refrigerator and got himself another beer. Settling back down in his chair he said, "I'm sorry; it's been so long since I've had company I seem to have forgotten my manners. Would you like something to drink? I'm afraid all I have is beer. I could make us some coffee."

"No thank you, Mr. Farber. I'd just have a few questions for you and then I need to get back on the road."

"Please call me Bud, Ms…" Bud tapped his forehead with the fingers of his right hand. "Ugh… Ms…."

"Just call me Becca, Bud. That's what my friends call me."

Bud smiled warmly, "Thank you." He whispered and once again needed to wipe his eyes.

"To begin with Mr. Farber, I mean Bud; I want to express to you my outrage and disgust at what happened to you by members of my profession. I know nothing I can say or do could possible make up for the losses you suffered. I do hope however, that I can find answers for you about what happened to Amanda; and ideally be able to help you serve justice to the person responsible for taking her away from you and Emily."

At the mention of his wife's name, Bud instinctively looked up at the banister circling the landing above the living room in which they sat. Becca had to force herself to not follow his gaze. Instead she stood up, and with the yearbook in her hand she walked over to Bud stepping over a pile of trash.

Kneeling next to him, Becca set the yearbook on his thigh open to the page that held Amanda's senior picture. "She was a beautiful girl; you must have been very proud of her."

"She looked just like her mother, right down to the dimple in her left cheek." Bud spoke in a faraway voice and then paused. Anticipating that he wanted to say more, Becca waited before she interjected.

"She was a quiet girl, not many friends, if any. Amanda spent most of her time in her room with her books. That girl loved to read." Bud paused as if seeing in his mind a time long forgotten. A smile came to his face as he continued. "I remember how happy she was when her mother finally agreed to change her name."

"What do you mean? Her name wasn't always Amanda?" Becca asked.

"No. Not her first name; her last." Bud explained, "Amanda came home very upset one day from school. This was back in middle school, sixth grade I believe, the girls in her class were picking on her because her parents had a different last name than she did. They told her that it meant that she didn't really belong to the family, like she was more of a pet than a real daughter."

"That's horrible." Becca interjected.

"Well you know how kids can get." Bud said, "Anyways, Em had always wanted to maintain a bond for Amanda with her real father who passed away in 'Nam so she left her with her birth name; Amanda Tebbe." Bud took a long swig and finished off the beer in his hand. Becca grabbed the yearbook as he stood and headed back to the kitchen for another all the while still talking. "Poor child never knew her real dad, yet Em insisted that was her name to keep. I tried talking to her, Emily that is, but she wouldn't budge. Stubborn woman; God rest her soul."

Bud parked himself back into his chair as he had probably done millions of times before, pulled back the aluminum tab on the beer can and sucked at the ensuing foam that bubbled out the opening. "When Amanda came home in tears that day Emily finally broke down and agreed. We took her to the courthouse the next day and legally changed her name to Amanda Tebbe Farber." Bud's smile beamed. "I don't think I've ever seen her happier than she was that day."

Becca let Bud soak in the memory before she flipped to another page in the yearbook she had been marking with her thumb. "Who is this?" Becca asked pointing at a photo of the senior science class. There was one boy partially hidden by another, but he definitely had Amanda in a lecherous gaze. "I don't know." Bud said, "That was a long time ago."

Becca pressed, "Did Amanda ever talk about anybody from school; a particular boy maybe?"

It was apparent Bud was uncomfortable with this line of questioning or he was just feeling emotionally drained from the morning's conversation; either way, his tone changed and Becca decided it might be a good time to go. "I told you before missy; Amanda didn't have no friends, and she sure as hell didn't have no boyfriends if that's what you're driving at."

Becca apologized and explained she was just trying to help. She thanked him for his time and promised to let him know as soon as she found out anything. Bud was kind enough to let Becca borrow the Class of 1980 Lynbrook High School yearbook with a sworn promise of its safe return. Becca was sure he let her take it more for the promise of another visit, than for anything else.

Becca almost gave Bud one of her New York Post business cards and thought better of it; so she scribbled her name and cell-phone number on a magazine lying on the coffee table in front of Bud's easy-chair.

"Just one more question if you don't mind before I go." Becca asked as she approached the door. "Go ahead." Bud replied amiably enough from his perch in the chair. "The article I read about Amanda being declared…" Becca trailed off not being able to say the work 'dead'. "What about it?" Bud prompted and Becca continued, "It was issued after your wife…ugh…you know...but the article never mentioned it."

Bud once again looked up at the landing and this time Becca followed his gaze. When she looked back at Bud and their eyes met he said, "Because no one knows. You're the first person to find out that my Emily is gone."

(Unedited excerpt from the manuscript)

Well, I almost got what I wanted with Roxie. At least it satisfied that part of me that wondered what it would feel like to kill with a plan. It was definitely a more rewarding experience when planned.

Additional *thump-thump* appeal is always a good thing.

I got side-tracked for a while as the school year wound down and graduation parties ensued. I really wanted to use the harness thing again, but as it turned out, almost two full months passed by before I had an opportunity. I'm not saying I didn't kill anybody in those two months, just that I didn't get a chance to play on the swing.

Let's see if I remember their names; there was Sandy Berkley, Linda Copeland and Patty Thompson. I remember them more vividly as the Strangled Trio.

Sandy was some slut I picked up at The Garage, a local bar that had bands on the weekend. She blew me right there in the alley behind the bar by the dumpster. She actually thought I was being passionate when I wrapped my hands around her neck until I couldn't feel her pulse anymore. You should have seen her expression change when she realized she wasn't going to hear the band's second set.

Linda was fun, she didn't recognize me, but she was one of the lucky Lawrence High School cheerleaders from the beach. We met at the Green Acres Mall. I thought I smooth-talked Linda out to my car and into the backseat; but, it was actually her idea from the start. It turned out she was pretty kinky, she liked doing it out in public with strangers. Linda took her last breaths while I was still inside her. Who's kinky now?

Patty was an older, attractive waitress from the diner down the road from The Garage. I would sometimes stop in there before returning home. I watched Patty as she left the diner when her shift ended at 2. I followed her in my car for about 5 minutes until she pulled into an apartment complex and parked around back. Leaving my car parked on the street, I walked silently to the rear of the building. Patty was still gathering some groceries from the open trunk of her car when I came up behind her.

Startled at first, Patty recognized me and wondered what I was doing there. I told her I had just moved in and asked if she needed help. Without a second thought Patty just smiled and thanked me. People are stupid. As soon as she turned around I wrapped the fishing line I had in my pocket around her neck. Her hands instinctively came up to her throat and I pulled tighter until she stopped rubbing her ass against me.

I couldn't believe how hard I was.

💣

Killing became addictive, I really enjoyed it. Taking a life gave me the same high as using my shit-kickers. The only difference was that while a shit-kicker ended with a lot of noise, taking someone's life ended in silence; and when you combined the two, it was perfect harmony, yin and yang, black and white, life and death.

Good times.

Graduation was uneventful, an anticlimactic dog and pony show mainly focused around a select few faceless fucks. I considered rigging one of my glass shit-kickers up on the podium and playing a version of gender-specific to determine which college I accepted. Both Syracuse and Ohio University were willing to let me grace them with my presence. I couldn't risk becoming part of the game if my timing was off, so I chose to pick my college another way.

During graduation there was a moment of silence for Amanda when we got to the F's. One of the teachers said a few nice things about her and prayed that she was safe and happy wherever she may be. Her parents weren't there; I heard they were having a hard time with the press. I guess her step-father used to beat her while her mother watched. I'm delighted I was able to help her get away from all that.

💣

Chapter 11

A door opened and slammed in the dark. Melina was accustomed to the routine, and she shut her eyes tight before the bright light was beamed at her. Already sitting, Melina scooted backwards until she came in contact with the wall.

When she heard the metal bowls set into the dirt she began salivating as she awaited the sound of a small bell which let her know she was allowed to move from her spot against the wall. Early in her captivity she learned these rules well at the business end of a whip.

'Ting' went the bell and Melina scrambled forward, moving on her scrapped knees to her food bowl. Using only her face to avoid the crack of the whip, she maneuvered the unknown meat to the edge of the bowl and into her mouth. Lapping at rancid liquid in the other bowl, Melina could feel the eyes of her captor watching her from beyond the beam of blinding light and wondered what was coming next.

(Unedited excerpt from the manuscript)

With high school finally over, I was able to work more hours at The Back Barn. I became close with the owner, Scott Lee and very, very close with his girlfriend, Angela Henry.

You would think with a last name like Lee that Scott would be at least some part Chinese, but you'd be wong. He was nothing more than a wannabe thug. A spoiled rich-boy from the Cedarhurst area, his parents had money and were prominent members of the Seawane Country Club. However, Scotty Lee; and he hated being called that, preferred to make you think he had grown up on the tough streets of Brooklyn under the El with Vinnie and Tony and Rocco.

Scott and I got along real well and I quickly went from a dish-washer to a bus-boy to a bouncer in about a week and a half once I was able to put in the hours. I loved working at The Back Barn and it wasn't because I was totally infatuated with Scott's girlfriend either. I had power; as the bouncer, I had control as people came and went.

For those of you that are doing math, let me remind you that the drinking age was 18 back then; and in New York that was for full service, not that 3.2 crap most of the country was feeding the rest of you 18 year olds. You're right though, I was still under age, but I'm going to let you in on another little secret. Our drivers licenses were dot-matrix printed on a piece of un-laminated paper. You can't believe how easy it was to change 1962 to 1960 with just a pin and a sharp pencil.

The Back Barn was popular as an after-game meat-market. After every home Islanders game that place was wall to wall pussy, both downstairs in the restaurant and upstairs in the bar. I found out why too. Scotty was a high-level drug dealer; mainly trafficking in pure Pink-Peruvian flake. That's cocaine for you idiots. I watched the door to his office on several occasions as back-room parties and transactions took place. Many times, I simply provided a barrier for Scott as he got his stick wet with a random bimbo.

Angela managed the downstairs restaurant but sporadically she would come upstairs. Those times I prevented her from going into the office I'm sure she knew why. Maybe that's why she chose me for her displays of blatant disrespect to Scotty. I didn't care; she was 9 years my senior and unbelievable hot.

Scotty wasn't bothered by Angela flirting with me; I think he thought of me as just a kid. But I could tell by his rage that last night of my employment that he was truly angrier at me for breaching his trust than he was at Angela for fucking me.

💣

Chapter 12

As Becca drove from Bay Park to the school in Lynbrook she couldn't shake the jitters Bud had left her with. Emily was buried in the backyard.

When Becca first questioned Bud about what he meant by saying that she was the first to find out that Emily was gone; Bud stood and escorted Becca to the kitchen window that looked out over the jungle of overgrown weeds in the backyard. Terrified of what the press may do to him, Bud told Becca the tale of how he had kept quiet and taken care of business on his own. Emily's sister, her only other relative, had passed away from cervical cancer two winters prior. There was absolutely no one who would question Emily vanishing. Once her sister was gone,

Emily had no reason to leave the house on Lawrence Street, and therefore she didn't. Bud did all the shopping and errands for the household since his job had him driving all day anyhow.

Bud shared that he had left Emily hanging like a new chandelier for almost two full days while he contemplated what to do before he realized that his delay actually solidified his only course of action. Then as the years drifted by and Emily's Social Security check began to arrive, Bud knew he had made the right decision back then.

"You see that tree?" Bud asked without the need to point since there was only a solitary tree amongst the ruins of the lawn. "That's my Emily now."

Becca didn't want to hear any more, she already assumed what transpired twenty-one years ago and just wanted to leave. But, Bud placed a cold hand on her shoulder and continued to talk as he starred out the window.

"When I cut her down she didn't look like my Emily anymore. Her eyes had begun to dry up and sink into a face that reminded me of those Holocaust victims. Her hands and feet were black; I guess from all the fluids in her body being forced down by gravity." Bud continued in a faraway monotone as he relived that day in his mind. "I heard her legs snap when she landed, I didn't think to try to break her fall, I mean; what was the point?" Bud left his hand on Becca's shoulder even though he felt her shudder. "I put her in one of those large green trash bags and moved her into the kitchen. Right here where we're standing as a matter of fact; I just couldn't look at her broken body while I waited for it to get dark."

"It had rained earlier in the day, so the ground was heavy but soft. I dug down about five or six feet; exhausting work I tell you. It took most of the night before I was done filling the hole back up with my Emily finally resting at the bottom. I planted that tree sapling right in the middle. It's an American Black Cherry; I picked it up that morning at Rainbow Nursery and Landscaping over on Atlantic."

The next sentence that came out of his mouth convinced Becca that, for whatever the reason, no matter who was to blame, Bud Farber was insane. "I think it was the fertilizer that made all the difference. That little sapling sprang up like it was no body's business; and when those flower's first appeared in the spring, I'd swear they had Emily's eyes. Best tasting cherries I've ever put in my mouth."

Becca swiveled away from the window and marched towards the door as Bud continued to call after her. "You missed the season this year. Emily starts dropping them about mid-June. I'll call you and we can make a pie."

(Unedited excerpt from the manuscript)

Angela was incredible. I think I've said that before, but it warrants mentioning again. I remembering her telling me her heritage, German and Irish and something; but what I remember the most was the Cherokee Indian part. Her skin was an exquisite golden bronze and when she looked at me with those almond shaped blue eyes I would melt. No doubt about it, that girl had a rare hold on me.

After the doors closed for the evening, usually around 2 in the morning, Scotty would stay upstairs cleaning and prepping the bar area while I usually went down to help Angela in the restaurant. There was a small serving island where we would tally up the register receipts and count the cash.

This particular evening there had been a scene earlier when Angela came upstairs right as the new bartender, a busty brunette named Gloria, came strolling out of Scotty's office adjusting her skirt and wiping her nose. Scott basically laughed in Angela's face when she told him she had enough of his fooling around.

Downstairs in the island, Angela stood behind me and began rubbing my shoulders. "Can you believe how that asshole treats me?" she asked.

"You deserve better." Was all I could say before I was spun around in the swivel chair and sucked into Angela's mouth.

I had fantasized about that moment for as long as I had known her. I was willing to risk whatever else might happen if she continued following the script I had laid out in my head; which somehow, she did.

Unbuttoning my shirt and then stripping down my jeans to my ankles, Angela worked me with her mouth. Hiking up her skirt she revealed herself and straddled over me. With her feet on the shelf under the counter and her hands gripping the brass rod that ran along the underside of the islands top shelves, Angela rode me. Just as I hit maximum overdrive, all hell broke loose.

"What the fuck!" was all I heard repeatedly as Scotty came bounding down the stairs with a baseball bat in his hands. Luckily the chairs were not stacked on the tables yet, otherwise he would have had a straight line approach to the island. "How do you like it?" Angela asked him as she slid off me. "I'm gonna fuckin' kill you, you son-of-a-bitch!" Scotty screamed as he clobbered chairs out of his way.

I didn't wait to figure out whether or not he was referring to me or Angela. I pulled up my pants and rolled over the back end of the island's counter and headed towards the kitchen.

It then became apparent who he was after; me.

He altered his direction and began moving through the aisle way between tables to cut me off. "I'm gonna fuckin' pulverize you, you ungrateful piece of shit!" For emphasis, Scotty shattered one of the decorative table lamps. "Stop fuckin' running! You're only gonna make it worse!"

Considering that I had a pretty good point of reference on how getting killed could truly be made worse; I picked up a chair and threw it at him to slow him down. He did stop for a moment but only to make perfect contact with the bat at the approaching chair. I almost wanted to applaud, but thought it better to keep moving.

Neither one of us saw Angela running across the tables until she lunged out and tackled Scott. I watched the two of them crash into the wall and hit the floor and then I was in the kitchen and out the back door.

The engine in my car sputtered twice before it caught and I was able to speed away just as Scotty barreled out the rear door and tossed the bat end over end at my receding taillights.

Wight, wong or indiffwent; this wasn't over and I needed to strike first.

Chapter 13

Becca called Roberto and explained to him why she would probably never be able to eat cherries again and asked how he was doing. "I'm exhausted. I couldn't sleep until I got the pages loaded and mapped into the mainframe." Roberto replied, "I think I can pull this off as long as there are no surprises."

"I have faith in you." Becca said encouragingly.

"I hope so for Melina's sake." There was a pause and Becca could hear him trying to hold back the emotion he felt. When he continued his voice was strained, "I should be able to begin printing at least the cover by early this evening. I was just about to go down to the warehouse to bring up some card stock."

"Wow, that soon? I thought you originally said it would be all weekend before you even started up the presses."

"I did too until I reevaluated my timeline model and realized I didn't eliminate the timeline that is inherently incorporated for typesetting. I subtracted it in my head, but never transferred it onto paper."

"Have you spoken to your distributors yet?" Becca asked.

"No, I still have no idea how to present this; besides, the people I really need to talk to aren't in until Monday. As soon as I get the presses rolling I'll be able to get some sleep. I can't think straight right now anyway."

"I didn't sleep a lot last night either. Right now I'm functioning on caffeine, taurine and whatever else they put in Red Bull."

"You be careful Becca. I don't have time to visit you in the hospital."

"Don't worry about me. I have a sister to save and a Madman to stop before I can make any other plans. You stay focused and I'll talk to you later."

"Good luck at the school and thanks; I love you Becca." Roberto hung up before Becca could react to his last statement.

Becca couldn't believe how mad she got at Roberto for using the 'L' word. It did help her regain her edge though; she was no longer envisioning biting into a cherry and having blood run down her throat.

By the time she arrived at Lynbrook High she was fully focused on tracking down clues to the Madman's identity. She probably already had enough information to plug into the SNIPH program to do a cross-referenced data search, but any degree of shrinking the information would greatly reduce the result time in the search engines.

The front doors to the building were not only unlocked, but they boasted a sign announcing try-outs for the inaugural season of the girl's varsity football team.

Becca hoped the administrative offices were open as well despite the fact that it was Saturday. The squeak-slide sound of sneakers on the gym floor emanated from the double doors set in front of her down the long hallway. The office was to her right, and a buzzer sounded as she opened the glass door. A large brutish woman, with dark brown hair pulled tight into a ponytail, popped up from behind the four and a half foot high counter and startled Becca.

"What do you want?" The question implied that Becca was already a major inconvenience and that whatever this was about, it had better be quick.

"I was hoping you could help me." Two quick bats of the eyes, a demure look down, eye contact with raised eyebrows and then wait.

"Look sister, I ain't your type, besides I think you're looking for Mrs. Ferman the admin." Becca realized the woman speaking to her was probably the gym teacher because as she stepped around the counter her legs looked like she could crush beer cans between her thighs. "I've got to get back to my girls. Have a seat over there and Mrs. F will be right back."

Becca watched Thunder-thighs stomp out of the office and swagger down to the gym. Mrs. Ferman passed her about halfway down the hall where they stopped and exchanged words. Both women turned and looked in Becca's direction, had a few more words together and then parted. In contrast, Mrs. Ferman was small and thin with flowing grey-white shoulder length hair.

Upon entering the office, Mrs. Ferman went immediately around the counter before addressing Becca. This was obviously her establishing a position of authority for some reason.

"Hi, Mrs. F, I'm…" Becca was cut off by a sharp tongue. "Don't Mrs. F me. You don't know me, and I sure as hell don't want to know you." Becca was clearly confused at the venom that sprang forth out this sweet looking older lady. "You can look as baffled as you want missy; but we are done talking to the press about the district's decision. If you have a problem with history in the making…"

It was Becca's turn to interrupt. She came right up to the counter's edge and leaned into Mrs. F's space. "Listen you assumptive, crotchety, old coot; it's only 11:30 in the morning and I've already had enough insanity for one day. I don't know who you think I am or what I'm doing here; but I have no idea what you are babbling about." It was rare that Becca let her temper get the best of her, and considering her mixed Puerto Rican and Irish heritage, most took that as a blessing.

The color drained so completely out of Mrs. F's face that it was hard to tell the difference between her skin and hair. She backed away from her side of the counter and sat down at one of the cluttered desks. "I'm sorry, but Ms. Armstrong said you were probably another reporter trying to cause trouble for the girl's football team." Becca was definitely a little taken back at being pegged as a reporter and made a mental note to be more cautious in the future. Her boss at the Post had warned her about how some people have an almost sixth sense when it comes to reporters and salesmen.

"Look Mrs. Ferman, I'm not going to lie to you, I do work for the New York Post but I'm not here about football. I'm here about a girl that went missing over twenty-eight years ago." Becca held out the 1980 yearbook towards Mrs. F to corroborate her statement. Mrs. F stood up and joined Becca at the counter and took the book into her hands. "You mean Amanda Farber?"

(Unedited excerpt from the manuscript)

I went right back the following evening around midnight. I had a double-strength shit-kicker with me. I had modified the fuse by wrapping it within 3 wooden matches. The plan was to duct tape the bomb to the engine of shit-for-brains Scotty's car. I didn't have a lot of prep time, but the few tests I had conducted told me that the radiator should get hot enough to ignite the matches.

I knew that coke-dealing, get-pissed-at-me-for-fucking-his-girlfriend, asshole Scotty-boy lived out by Babylon about 35 minutes away; plenty of time to get the engine hot. As much as I wanted to be there when the car blew, it was more important to quickly remove that sorry-assed son-of-a-bitch from the earth's population.

Better him than me I thought.

I peered in through one of the side windows to get a fix on where Scotty was, since there was no Islanders game, the bar wasn't that busy. I saw Scotty and Angela sitting together at one of the pub tables all lovey-dovey.

Go figure? I guess adversity breeds understanding.

No matter; and it certainly didn't change things. Especially when I noticed the shiner around Angela's left eye. They deserved each other and I promised myself I'd have to come back another time and help her join him on the other side of living.

Scott's midnight blue vintage '65 Chevy Camaro RS was parked in back in its usual spot away from the main parking lot near the dumpster. As I slid my hand into the front grill to grab the hood release latch I heard the kitchen back door open. Another few seconds and I would have had the hood open and my hand in the cookie jar. I swiftly shuffled around to the far side of the car and hunkered down.

Julio, the new dishwasher, had stepped out for a smoke. From the smell that drifted over to me it was clear that it wasn't a Marlborough. Quickly enough, Julio got his groove on and headed back inside. I debated taking another look in the bar but decided against it and proceeded as planned.

I knew from talking with shit-for-brains that he didn't have an alarm system on the Camaro; just the stickers saying that he did. He always said, why pay for something when you don't have to?

Thanks for playing, you fucking moron.

This time I actually had my hand on the release latch and was about to pull when I heard footsteps coming around the building. Luckily the car blocked me from their approach and I was able to crab crawl backwards behind the dumpster this time. I knew one of the people coming towards the car was Mr. Lee himself even before I heard his grating voice. The sound of his cowboy boots was unmistakable, especially with the boot-straps he accessorized them with.

I couldn't see who else was with him; not that it mattered, as long as they couldn't see me. The raised trunk lid of the Camaro further obstructed the view; but I did see silhouetted shadow movements on the ground created by the street lamps from Sunrise Highway.

Large items passed from one to the other and hands were shaken. As the trunk lid was slammed down, I ducked further back into the gloom behind the dumpster and waited until I was finally alone with the car again.

Contemplating aborting the mission until another evening; I was concerned about who was coming out next and would my luck hold out for a third time. The thump-thump quickly won me over and I stuck my hand into the grill and released the hood's latch.

Hurriedly I secured the shit-kicker around the hose leading from the engine to the radiator while taping the modified fuse directly onto the radiator. Just as I brought down the hood gingerly so as not to make any noise, the fucking kitchen door opened again.

This time I waited as Julio made a trash drop into the dumpster and finished his hand-rolled cigarette. While I sat there lingering, I made the decision to pop open the Camaro's trunk and see what was inside.

Best decision of my life.

The cash that I uncovered was enough to enhance who I was and what I could do. If you ask me now; that was the pivotal moment of everything that's to come. If it wasn't for Julio and the trash; I would have simply left after setting the shit-kicker in place.

By the way, it worked; took about 15 minutes for the engine to get hot enough, but right at the corner of Merrick Road and Ocean Avenue, a beautiful car ceased to exist. The news said the explosion also blew out all the stained-glass windows in the church across the street.

Man that would have been something to see.

💣

Chapter 14

"You can call me Mrs. F dear, and I'm sorry about that little mix up. You would think the world was going to come to an end the way some people are reacting to us having a girl's football team."

"That's quite alright, Mrs. F; about Amanda, you remember her?"

"That was my first year here in the office. I was a substitute for two years before that. I remember it because I was able to relate to the parents. Well, sort of."

"What do you mean?" Becca pressed.

"Well…this is hard to talk about; it's been so many years…I can't believe how I've suppressed the memory…" Mrs. F sat back down, slumped forward and rubbed her forehead.

Becca listened as Mrs. F retold her tale of a pregnancy as the result of a rape; of a child born to a girl barely ready to be a mother; of a mother who despised her child for reasons unfounded; of a child who ran away at the age of thirteen; and of a runaway whose crumpled body was found near a railway station.

Mrs. F explained how she felt an affinity to the Farbers and the pain they felt at having driven their daughter away. She always hoped that Amanda would return; but as the months and years passed, she only hoped that Amanda was okay wherever she had run off to.

Without divulging any information about the manuscript, Becca lied and told Mrs. F that she was working on a story about teenage runaways. She was hoping that Mrs. F would be able to shed some light on Amanda's relationships with her classmates; or better yet, be able to provide information on a few of the students that were in some of Amanda's classes for direct interviews.

"You've got that yearbook there; what more do you need?" Mrs. F asked a little suspiciously.

"Don't misunderstand me, Mrs. F." Becca smiled warmly, "I'm not asking you for anything that isn't public record. I can't believe how lucky I am to have found someone that was actually on staff back then." Becca noticed a slight furrowing of Mrs. F's brows and aptly added, "Most people nowadays move from job to job; it's nice to know that there are still a few of those around that are able to commit to a position." Becca didn't know what the hell she was talking about but hoped that Mrs. F was buying it. She regretted calling her an 'old coot' earlier.

"Listen Ms….What did you say your name was?"

"Willis. Becca Willis."

"Listen Ms. Willis, I have been around a very long time, and I will probably die here. That is the choice I made. In a lot of ways I get to pretend to see my little girl grow up and move on; time and time again. We all have our crosses to bear and we age while we carry them. Now, I have a lot of work to do so let's cut to the chase; what is it exactly you want to ask me?"

"Fair enough," Becca turned the yearbook to the photo of the science class and laid it open on the counter between them. "There are no names captioned with this photo. I was hoping you could tell me what the names of the students in Mr. Brook's science class were."

(Unedited excerpt from the manuscript)

In spite of becoming sixty thousand dollars richer; killing Scotty Lee left me feeling very unsatisfied. If I hadn't been in such a rush; that was a life I would have enjoyed taking slowly. I apologize if I gave you the impression that I liked him; I liked the position of power he gave me, but he was a fake.

I was also pretty perturbed at Angela; she took advantage of me and put me in harm's way. There is a hefty price to pay for that type of disrespect.

The first thing that I wanted to do was remove that pretty face of hers. No point in being distracted; she already played me for a fool with that tune once already. It's time to become truly faceless my Cherokee princess.

A wise man once said, 'Revenge is a dish best served cold', and Angela would need to wait. I was running out of time before I was off to Ohio University; and don't worry, I'll tell you later how I chose between the 2 colleges.

But for time being, I have other things more pressing that warrant my attention.

Life is also about keeping things in their proper order.

Priorities my little faceless fucks; so just like Angela had to wait for hers; you'll wait for yours.

As I sit here and chronicle my past actions that have brought us here to this moment in time, we are both waiting for an event that has not happened yet. I am so pleased, and hope you can appreciate what I have done. I am sharing the anticipation and the thrill; the rush of the count-down and the excitement of choosing between red or green wires.

Can you feel it in your chest?

Maybe not; I haven't taken you up to the edge yet, I've become very caught up in myself as we've strolled down memory lane. You need to understand a little more about me to recognize the depth of my undertaking. This is a plan set in motion decades ago. I continued to have my 'fun' along the way, but without initial concepts and baby-blueprints set in place at times when the ultimate design was in its infancy; none of what is about to occur could ever have happened.

Compare me to the power of Mother Earth, because it is the closest you can get. Envision the tiny eruptions, see the minor quakes, and watch as the tides erode the land. Every movement orchestrated as each breath of the Cosmos aligns with the other, one event building upon another; until at last, total catastrophe, destruction and devastation of epic proportions.

Who do I think I am? That's easy; I am the manager of your favorite retail store. I am your local business owner. I am your faithful insurance agent. I am your personal banker and financial advisor. I am the one you blindly trusted with your private information. I am the one you shared your secrets with. I am the one sitting across from you right now; and you, you are faceless.

I enjoyed that little dissertation almost as much as I enjoy drawing those little bombs you see between several of my paragraphs.

Anyway, I am on a time schedule here, and need to make a quick trip into the city to pick up a package that will insure that this manuscript gets into your hands. If there is enough time, I will tell you more about it, and then you'll be totally up to date.

Right after I deliver and secure the package, I promise to finish telling you about Angela

Chapter 15

Leaving the school with no more information than she had arrived with; Becca sat in her car contemplating her next move. Mrs. F was willing to cooperate, but simply was unable to provide the information Becca had been looking for. Computerized school records that stored classroom details only went back as far as 1990. Budget, time and personnel restrictions made it impractical to transfer any written archives that existed prior to the school adapting a computerized system of record keeping. In addition, the school was under no obligation to even maintain written archives for information more than ten years old.

Feeling the effects of the Red Bull wearing off, Becca popped two Excedrin, more for the caffeine than the pain relief, although she did have a monster of a headache. Becca decided to make a quick trip to the infamous Hollingsworth Farm site before heading to the closest Panera Bread to make use of their Wi-Fi connection. Shuffling through papers she had printed earlier that morning, Becca compared historical data to a recent map showing the town of Lynbrook she had picked up at a local Mobile station.

Becca had uncovered a vast and colorful history of the Hollingsworth family who had settled on Long Island during the late eighteenth century from Ireland. Among a few other families, such as the Wicks, the Nostrands, the Riders and the Cornwells; the Hollingsworths took residence on what was once the tribal territory of the Rockaway Indians.

While the other families of the area prospered off the land with farming and other businesses including a wheelwright shop, a grist mill, several general stores, a greenhouse, a small hotel and a tavern; the Hollingsworths struggled in every endeavor they attempted. It was rumored that the family was cursed for building its primary residence upon the Rockaway Indian's sacred burial grounds. As crops failed and businesses bankrupted, the Hollingsworth homes were foreclosed by the bank. In efforts to survive, the Hollingsworths began to sell off huge acres of their land to neighboring families.

Subsequently in 1903, as the railroad made its way through Long Island, the Hollingsworths leveraged their few remaining assets and lobbied for rights to own and operate a railway station. The station, named Bridgeport, had its share of problems right from the start. Flatbed trains carrying manure for fertilizer stalled at the Hollingsworth's Bridgeport station which was aptly nicknamed, "Skunk's Misery". Then in 1911, an engine blew up and killed a man; not even a year later, flooding from spring rains caused an accident and killed an engineer and two others. The family never recovered from lawsuits following the accident and the deaths, and the station was virtually abandoned.

By 1926, all of the Hollingsworths had acquiesced to the truth of the ancient burial grounds and left Long Island. They moved further west and settled down as broken sects in Pennsylvania, Ohio and Indiana until the only Hollingsworth left on Long Island was Valentine Hollingsworth who married a local Rockaway Indian woman named Reanna. Together they farmed the land that remained as the Hollingsworth's Long Island legacy. After two years, the Hollingsworth Farm finally began to produce meager crops of corn, potato and pumpkin.

In 1944, Reanna died while giving birth to their son Thomas, who continued the farm's operations after Valentine died in 1962. Ironically, Thomas inherited the Hollingsworth Farm at the age of eighteen, the same age his father had assumed it from his father before him.

Finally, in the spring of 1964, Thomas married Sarah Davies, a young woman of Welsh-German descent. The couple had four children, two boys and two girls, each just about one year older than the next. The farm continued to be managed by the family until 1970 when Sarah slaughtered Thomas as well as her own children thus ending the Hollingsworth name on Long Island.

Becca knew there had to be more to the story of the Hollingsworths and thought to herself that once this nightmare was over, she would spend some time researching the family's lineage and maybe write a book. She was ready to take a sabbatical from journalism and possibly this was her opportunity to break into some serious writing. The sensationalistic form of writing she had found herself doing for the Post just wasn't giving her the same satisfaction that she got from the story-telling type of journalism she had first wanted to pursue. She remembered the little girl sitting in front of the television dreaming of becoming an anchor.

Then life happened, and eight years had gone by in a job that was supposed to be a stepping stone. Becca had become so sidetracked from her original plans that she had almost completely forgotten about them.

Becca drove to the corner of Hempstead Avenue and Merrick Road and continued east on Merrick Road for approximately one mile before turning right onto Whitehall Street. Becca noticed the crowded suburban housing developments on what used to be Hollingsworth property, one house looking just like its neighbor to its right and left. Absolutely no originality or individualism, every home painted the same color and shape, as if they had been stamped out of a factory's mold.

Whitehall ran northeast parallel to the railroad tracks; about one mile up, Whitehall then intersected back with Hempstead. Turning right and heading southeast, Becca ending up back where she started at Hempstead and Merrick. The old Hollingsworth property was a perfect equilateral triangle. Becca stopped and made a quick scribble in her notebook that was always at her side. The 'Hollingsworth Triangle' was a perfect title for her book.

Unfortunately, Becca found nothing out of the ordinary occupying a once historic landscape, just normal 'Stepford Wives' type of suburban neighborhoods. Becca wasn't sure what she expected to find or what she hoped to find, but nevertheless she felt somewhat cheated. She had anticipated more.

Staring at the local street map that she had picked up at the Mobile station, Becca could envision the Hollingsworth Farm sitting amongst the fields before mass civilization occupied its terrain. Becca's focus was drawn to a grayed out area in the center of what was, as she now thought of it, 'The Hollingsworth Triangle'.

Making a U-turn at the intersection of Merrick and Hempstead, Becca drove a half mile and turned left onto Hendrickson Avenue. Hendrickson ran straight through the triangle formed by Merrick, Whitehall and Hempstead; and also passed directly in front of the grayed out area on the map.

On the south side of the road, between President Street and Central Avenue was a series of two-story commercial buildings. Becca pulled up through the main gates, rolled down her window at the security hut and waited for the guard to notice her.

Chapter 16

Roberto sat down in the soft dark brown leather executive chair behind his mahogany desk to proof the draft of the manuscript. Since the Madman didn't number the pages, Roberto had the tedious task ahead of him of comparing the printing draft to the original.

The paper was printed double-sided and in an order that allowed the binding machinery to cut, stack and fold sections. Each section was comprised of about twenty pages. Individual sections were then married to their sequential counterparts. The complete set of sections then went through a process that compressed them all together, and then fed them along a conveyer belt where the folded margins were thinly sliced off. Roberto was using the same process of binding that was used on the soft-cover editions of the 'For Dummies' series; a double gluing method that first secured all the pages together, and then set the printed cardstock cover in place around the gathered book.

The printing and binding equipment that performs these automated tasks is a single-unit, monster of a machine. Three of these monsters occupy the entire seventh floor of the Wiley Publishing Building on Third Avenue. Running the full length of the block between East 39th and East 40th Streets; blank paper stock is fed into one end and then stacks of finished books come out the other end.

With the draft laid open on the desk in front of him, Roberto began to verify the sequence of pages to the original. Trying to simply view each page as a picture for the comparison process, Roberto, unfortunately, found himself re-reading sections of the depraved text.

As each of the brutal acts moved from the paper through his eyes to his mind, Roberto's heart sunk deeper in his chest. The realization that Melina was being held by this obviously insane individual was too much for him to deal with in his current state of exhaustion. Tears welled up in his eyes and soon overflowed the lids.

Pushing himself away from the desk and the tainted script, Roberto hung his face within his hands and wept uncontrollably. Shakes racked through his body and he howled at the overwhelming sense of helplessness he felt.

Eventually regaining his composure, Roberto stood and went to the washroom to splash cold water on his face. When he returned he noticed the draft copy of the manuscript had closed upon itself and he hadn't been marking the pages he already proofed.

The clock on the wall read 2:38 in the afternoon.

Roberto needed to close his eyes for a while and regroup, he felt as if he was coming apart at the seams. The last thing he wanted to do right then was touch the Madman's paper. Just the thought of holding something in his hands that connected him to the deranged psychopath was too much for him at that moment. It was almost as if in his weakened state of mind and body, the Madman's essence would seep off the document and penetrate his skin, infecting him with the same disease that crippled the Madman's own mind.

Realizing how irrational he was sounding to himself, Roberto pulled out the top right draw from his desk and withdrew a travel alarm-clock. Moving back to the couch and setting the alarm-clock for one hour later, he set it down on the magazine table next to him. Roberto draped the brown, black and cream colored blanket over his head to ward off the sun that bounced back into his office from the mirrored building across the street.

Closing his weary eyes attempting to replace the visions of blood and terror that danced across the inside of his eyelids, Roberto thought about Becca. He also recalled the fond memories related to the light blanket that now cradled his head. He felt his heart rate slow down. He had slipped up earlier when he told Becca that he loved her. But he did, he always had, even when they were breaking up, he never stopped loving her. Reflecting back on the troubles they had shared, Roberto always knew that he was to blame. He tried so many times to change but constantly fell back into the same old insecurities that had plagued him since his parents died.

Roberto had enlisted the support of a psychologist (at two-hundred-and-fifty dollars an hour) after he and Becca had split for what was then the final time. It wound up costing him a thousand bucks to tell a complete stranger stuff he already knew. He had, and has, complicated feelings surrounding abandonment issues. These feelings stem from not only the death of his parents, but from leaving his sister behind in California when he moved to New York.

As Roberto finally drifted to sleep he thought that he could have been a psychologist. How hard is it to ask someone, "So how does that make you feel?" or "What do you think that means?" He could make that scrunchy 'I'm concerned and understand' face while he bobbed his head up and down. "Well, that's all the time we have this week…same time next Tuesday? Will that be a check or charge today Mr. Sanchez?"…

The sun was shining, birds were singing and children were laughing. Roberto and Becca walked hand in hand through the park. They had been together for three months and Roberto never felt happier. As they passed by a fountain, Becca pulled him into the onslaught of manufactured raindrops. Cowering as if the water burned, Roberto playfully complained and spun Becca around in his arms. They stood beneath the water in each other's embrace as onlookers smiled at young love.

Laughing and running, still hand in hand, the young lovers approached the water's edge and sat down in the soft grass to dry under the sun's beaming warmth. Watching paddle boats drift lazily back and forth on the calm surface of the water, time seemed suspended.

All of the universe's focus was shining on the two souls pressed against one another.

Nothing else mattered.

Roberto turned to look into Becca's eyes and felt at peace. Her smile was the world to him. He would do whatever was necessary to forever see that expression on her face.

Now seated on a bench behind three painted Stallions that galloped in rhythm but at different heights, Roberto and Becca watched as a young Melina of eight or nine road on the blue and red Stallion closest to the edge. Laughing and full of life, the young girl reached out for the brass ring as the revolving Carousel made its pass by the ticket booth. Just barely reaching the rings, Melina stretched farther and farther with every pass. Turning and smiling, Melina asked her older brother for help.

Unable to withdraw his hand from hers, Becca kept him seated at her side.

As the Carousel made its way back around towards the suspended rings by the ticket booth, Roberto watched as Melina leaned out so far she seemed to float off the blue and red Stallion.

The Brass ring wrapped itself around the young girl's wrist and stole her away from the safety of her steed. Roberto lunged forward but the Carousel had already moved him away from her position. The Stallions raised their heads snorting and whinnying in front of him. Lions and Tigers began growling behind him. The Carousel moved faster and faster as the sky darkened. Becca was gone and Roberto held tight to a brass pole at the speeding Carousel's edge.

Whipping by too fast to get off without breaking his neck, Roberto saw glimpses of Melina pinned to what was the ticket booth. Slats of multi-colored wood jutted from the earth like jagged broken teeth. Melina was displayed in the center on a blood-red pinwheel that spun clockwise, toppling the girl end over end as Becca stood by her side with arms outstretched like she was introducing the latest model of a new car. Melina screamed and Becca laughed as Roberto frantically looked for a way off the accelerating Carousel.

Grabbing the reins of the nearest Stallion, Roberto swung his leg up and over into the saddle of the green and black beast. Pulling the steed's head around and kicking with all his strength, Roberto rode the massive steed in the opposite direction of the spinning Carousel. Swerving between galloping lions and tigers, jumping over approaching benches, ducking as crossbeams flew overhead. Roberto managed to arrive at the position where his sister was held captive.

Moving now at the same speed but in the opposite direction from the Carousel, he was able to maintain a stationary position across from Melina.

When Roberto sprang off the green and black Stallion everything disappeared and he fell silently through a black abyss. With no point of reference, Roberto didn't know if he was falling or floating…

The alarm-clock snapped Roberto back to the present. Still shrouded in darkness, he yanked the blanket from his head and fumbled with the clock until it stopped its incessant beeping. Not fully remembering the details of the dream, and thankful for the same, Roberto washed down three Advil with the leftover cold coffee he had picked up with his lunch.

Returning to his desk with a different method in mind to proof the manuscript for sequence accuracy, Roberto picked up the phone and dialed Becca's number.

Chapter 17

Clearing her throat with a loud "Ahem", Becca finally got the attention of the security guard away from whatever had held his interest on the small television in the guardhouse.

"Mr. John hasn't arrived yet, he said your meeting wasn't scheduled until three." Becca watched as the young man with blue eyes and a bright yellow shirt strained his neck to get a better look down her shirt.

Quickly deciding not to pretend she was there for the meeting and risk getting caught in a lie, Becca told the guard that she was in the area doing research for a book and was hoping that he could help her.

Two quick bats of the eyes, a demure look down, eye contact with raised eyebrows and then wait.

Todd Hemsoth, as his badge proudly proclaimed, was more than happy to help. Becca stepped out of her car to let Todd enjoy the entire panoramic view and asked him a few questions about the facility that stood before her.

Todd was only nineteen and therefore wasn't able to answer any of Becca's inquiries regarding anything that happened outside of his little bubble of existence. Unaware of a world that existed prior to the Reebok Pump, Napster, Rollerblades, Beanie Babies and Tickle Me Elmo; Todd was only able to offer information related to current events.

Born and raised around the corner on Hillside Avenue right behind the West End Elementary School, Todd had graduated Lynbrook High the previous summer. After talking to Todd for a few minutes, Becca realized why he was working in a guard house on a Saturday afternoon on the last weekend in August.

Todd wasn't that outgoing, or all that bright; and this was probably the job he would still have forty years from now. College was not in the plans for Mr. Todd Hemsoth.

As Todd spoke he continued to be infatuated with Becca's breasts; she ignored this by looking out at the huge facility that stood before her only one hundred yards away.

PANDA BEAR FARM was painted in large lettering across the sandy colored two-story building above the top floor windows; the 'P' was formed by an actual Panda Bear facing to its right so it slightly resembled the letter. Todd explained that the business had been there for as long as he remembered.

Todd exuberantly shared that every year at Halloween time, Mr. John, who Becca assumed was the owner, converted the parking lot into a haunted hay ride. There were carnival games, contests with prizes, and Mr. John paid you double to dress up and help out. Other than that, the only thing Todd knew about the company was that they sold 'stuff' to the supermarkets. Todd was all about the details and Becca surmised she would get more information out of the stump she passed on the street corner.

Thanking Todd for his time and giving him one more good stare at her chest, Becca got back into her car and pulled into the lot to turn around instead of backing out. Making an extra wide circle in the lot Becca caught a glimpse behind the main building and saw another structure off in the rear of the property.

Stopping briefly at the security hut to inquire about the other building, Becca asked; "What is that building in the back?"

Todd came running around to the driver's side eager for another peek, and Becca felt visually violated once again as she received her answer. "Oh, that is for Mr. John's toy company; he makes all those great gag gifts you see. Like whoopee-cushions, fake gum, bugs in ice, joy-buzzers, fake vomit and fake dog-dodo..." Becca cut him off before he could recite the entire catalogue he obviously had memorized.

Becca was wrong; some details did matter to Todd other than cup sizes.

Putting the car back into gear, ready to leave, Becca came to an abrupt halt as a black Mercedes-Benz convertible blocked her path.

(Unedited excerpt from the manuscript)

Okay, so back to the beautiful Ms. Angela Henry or the temporarily beautiful Ms. Angela Henry we should say. I snatched Angela up right from her own house, just one week after they had a memorial burial for Scotty Lee.

There wasn't enough left of him for a regular funeral. I heard they cremated his remains which seemed redundant to me, but what do I know.

Anyway, Angela stopped working at the Back Barn after Scotty left her. Primarily because the cops had shut it down. When they were investigating his alleged murder, they came across a whole bunch of illegal drugs and weapons in addition to numerous documents that led them to further arrests. Scotty's associates were not happy with his record keeping. Fortunately Angela kept her nose clean, no pun intended, and the cops weren't able to pin anything on her.

💣

I parked my car out of sight in the alley that ran behind her house and made sure she was alone before I rang her bell.

She was so happy to see me.

Sitting on her living room couch, we reminisced about the good ole times and how crazy it got that night she jumped on my heat-seeking moisture missile. However, Angela acted like I wasn't disrespected that night, and that wiped away any possible second thoughts I was having. Because, when she opened the door and I looked into those almond shaped baby blues, I almost decided not to go through with my plan.

When Angela didn't apologize for that night at the bar something happened and I snapped. I literally saw red. I grabbed the lamp that was next to me on the couch and smashed it into her face.

I don't know if I heard the lamp crack or her nose, but something shattered, maybe both.

Angela's hands went right up to her face as blood ran freely between her fingers. Standing up, getting ready to run I guess, Angela began violently choking on her own blood and doubled over. I jumped up behind her and grabbed two fistfuls of hair and began smashing her head into the thick glass coffee table until she stopped choking.

It worked just like CPR.

Splayed out face down over the glass table, blood began to pool around her head and gather in the engraved floral design at the table's edge. Her shirt had gotten pulled up in the struggle and the small of her back was exposed. Exotic golden skin, the sensual curves of her waist and hips got my motor going and I had to have it.

I stripped off her jeans and lowered mine. I was so hard it hurt. I drove myself into her from behind while her head squeaked against the glass table as it moved back and forth through the clotting blood. When I was finished I dragged her unconscious body up the stairs and threw her into the bathtub. There was no way I was fucking up the interior of my car.

After I cleaned her off in the tub and dragged her into her bedroom for a clean set of clothes I realized I wasn't done with her. I gagged her and tied her to her own bed with stockings I found in her dresser. This time I wanted her awake, and I wanted it to hurt.

💣

Always prepared, I had both smelling salts and chloroform with me in my backpack.

Angela never even questioned the bag when I arrived; it amazes me how much you stupid faceless fucks take for granted, never questioning something that seems out of place or unusual. Never looking over your shoulder; forever trusting that life is just la-de-da- fucking beautiful.

That's okay though, I've decided that you can't help yourselves. You are beyond your own help; and, despite your ineptness, the Mexicans will still hold a moment of silence for you next November. They will respect the memory of your losses.

Nothing like ruining someone else's holiday.

I apologize for that unexpected commercial break sponsored by Mexico's sugar skulls and chocolate molds.

Now back our show, already in progress...

I woke Angela with the smelling salt and proceeded to tear up her southern exposure. All the while I was explaining to her how she disrespected me. I didn't want to think I did this kind of thing all the time. She needed to know that she earned it, that she deserved it.

When I climaxed, and it took a while the second time, I think Angela thought it was finally over. I showered off again and got dressed. When I bent over to kiss Angela on the forehead and thank her for a wonderful evening she began thrashing her head from side to side. It made it very difficult to not hurt her when I placed the chloroform rag over her mouth and nose. I think I accidentally pressed too hard against her shattered nose because her eyes rolled up to the whites and she passed out.

Maybe it was just the chloroform, doesn't really matter.

I dressed Angela's limp body trying not to get aroused again. It was difficult because she had the most beautiful golden skin. Even to this day, I can think of her soft yet firm body, her almond shaped baby blues, her glowing smile and that infectious giggle; and I get turned on something fierce.

She definitely had a hold on me, too bad she fucked it up. She could have been 'the one'.

I quickly spot checked the house, wiped down anything I thought I may have touched, and carried Angela over my shoulder out through the back door and to my car.

Angela lived local so it only took about 10 minutes to get her to the barn.

I was looking forward to what was coming next.

Chapter 18

Becca stayed in her car as the man in a perfectly matched Armani Techno Track jacket and shorts set stepped out of the black Mercedes and removed his sunglasses. Standing next to the immaculately clean convertible the debonair gentleman just starred at Becca behind the wheel of her six years old, blue Nissan Maxima. He stroked his slightly scruffy face with thumb and forefinger just along his jaw line as he continued to soak in Becca's presence.

Finally approaching her vehicle, never taking his eyes from hers, the gentleman crouched next to open window of the driver's side door. Extending his hand out to the very edge of the open window as if conscious of not breaching her personal space, the man introduced himself. "Good afternoon." He said with a slight nod, "I am Christopher John." Becca reached across and placed her hand in his and thought to herself how strong and smooth it felt.

Feeling uncharacteristically flushed, Becca slightly stammered when she replied. "I…I'm…I'm afraid you may think I'm someone else."

Smooth as silk, with Becca's hand still in his own, Christopher John replied, "Who else could I possibly want you to be other than the vision of beauty that sits before me now?"

Now, unquestionably blushing, Becca said, "I simply meant that I understand you have a three o'clock appointment and unfortunately it isn't with me." Becca couldn't believe she just flirted and withdrew her hand from the warmth of his.

"Ah, I see my trusted security guard has yet again performed his duties beyond any employer's wildest dreams." Christopher John spoke with a smile, but a quick glance at the security hut caused Todd to retreat like a frightened mouse back into its hole.

"No harm done." He continued, returning his gaze into Becca's eyes. "So, what brings you to my humble abode and how can I be of service? I seem to have caught you trying to escape."

Becca was torn between telling everything to this charming man and maintaining the fabricated story she had told Todd. There was a moment when she thought she had seen a flicker in his eyes, as if he had been reading her thoughts and knew she was about to lie.

"I'm writing a book on the Hollingsworth family, they were one of the original…"

Christopher John held up his hand and she immediately stopped talking as he interrupted. "Then my dear you have come to the right place. I would be honored to share with you my vast knowledge on the subject. I'm a bit of a local history buff myself."

Becca was truly taken off guard. This was the last thing she expected when she took the left off Hempstead onto Hendrickson not even an hour ago.

"My schedule has the better of me for the remainder of the weekend Mrs…."

"It's Miss. Miss Rebecca Willis" Becca interjected, stressing the Miss part. Flirting again; Becca had also used her given name for some reason. It had been decades since she heard herself say it out loud. In her mind she just thought is sounded better; I'd like to introduce Miss Rebecca Willis and Mr. Christopher John. Becca flushed again and hoped he wouldn't notice. But, he seemed to notice everything.

"As I was saying Miss Willis, would it be to forward of me to ask for the pleasure of your company for dinner this Monday evening? We could discuss the subject of your book among other interesting topics, I hope."

Becca felt swept up off her feet, she hadn't felt that way since… Becca blocked the thought from her mind. "I'd be honored to have dinner with you Mr. John. Where and when shall I meet you?"

"If you felt comfortable enough giving me your address, I'd be happy to pick you up around seven if that isn't too late?"

"That would be wonderful except I live in Manhattan."

"Not a problem, Miss Willis. I'll plan to spend the evening at my apartment on the Upper West Side. I can schedule meetings in the city for Tuesday. It will actually help me take care of some pressing matters that need my attention with one of my Manhattan based businesses."

Becca was overwhelmed. This guy had jackpot written all over him. Armani clothes, Mercedes-Benz convertible, at least three companies and probably a home or two. Becca produced one of her business cards from her purse and wrote her home address on East 69th on the back.

Christopher John took the card, glanced at it and filed it into his jacket pocket. "Does the Post know you are doing freelance work on the side?" he asked with eyebrows raised in a comical gesture.

"They will when I sell a million copies of my book." Becca was quick to reply.

Just then another car pulled in behind the Mercedes, and an older Asian woman looked out the open window with an expression of confusion. Christopher John stood and said something in Cantonese to the woman. She replied back smiling and nodding and then put her car in reverse withdrawing to the street where she sat and waited.

Reaching in slightly past the window's invisible barrier this time, Christopher accepted Becca's hand and gently squeezed as he said, "I await our encounter this Monday with great anticipation Miss Willis. Until then I bid you a splendid afternoon and wish you success in your perusal of what was."

Not knowing how to respond, Becca just smiled and waited for him to break eye contact and return to his car. Becca waved at Todd who pretended not to see as she drove back out onto Hendrickson and turned left.

Giddy as a schoolgirl, Becca turned on the radio for the first time that day. Singing and bopping along to the original, Martha and the Vandellas version of *Dancing in the Streets*; Becca relished in the excitement of her upcoming date with Mr. Christopher John.

Placing her hand on the copy of the 1980 Lynbrook High School yearbook that sat on the passenger seat, Becca followed Whitehall back to Merrick Road and headed east to the Panera in Rockville Center.

(Unedited excerpt from the manuscript)

When Angela awoke, she found herself in a rather precarious predicament. She was standing atop an open wooden crate filled with dirt; her wrists were shackled and her arms were raised, held high by chains trailing down from the crossbeam overhead.

Here's the best part; while she was still unconscious, I sliced a thin line, about a half inch, into her flesh. The cut followed the contours of her face; beginning from one temple and moving down and around under the jaw line in front of her ears all the way around to the other temple. It was a little difficult to keep the depth of the cut consistent up along the sides of her face; the skull kept getting in the way, so I had to slightly angle the razor there. No big deal, just not as clean as I would have liked it.

Using 5 of those office-type metal binder clips, I grabbed a hold of the flap of flesh I had made under her chin and attached the clips.

She looked like an Amish dude with a beard.

Oh yeah, I ran fishing line with a needle around the clips through her face. I wanted to make sure they didn't slip off.

Then I wrapped and secured the 5 lines up over the crossbeam just loose enough so her face didn't peel up to soon.

I tried to be so careful not to mess up the performance before it started, and in retrospect I should have prepared the face before I hung her up. I had dressed Angela in a white T-shirt and boxer set and although I draped a towel over her, some blood snuck through and stained the top of the T-shirts collar.

Oh well, what are you gonna do?

Sitting in my front row chair, I grew impatient waiting for her to wake up and I considered using the smelling salts again.

I needed to remember that: the chloroform lasts differently on different people.

Finally the show was about to begin. Angela's eyes fluttered open and she began to struggle but quickly stopped. A thin trail of blood seeped down her slender neck and decorated the left shoulder of the T-shirt.

"What are you doing to me?"

I was amazed she spoke. I didn't expect conversation.

"We are playing a new game I made up. It is called 'Are You Faceless', and you're tonight's first contestant. Congratulations."

I got up and brought my chair over by Angela and stood up on the seat. Looking right into her almond-shaped baby blues, I wanted to make sure she understood the game; since she asked.

"Here's how you play. In round one, I'm simply going to release your arms and give you a chance to escape. Sounds simple doesn't it. I'll think I'll give you about 5 minutes; it depends on how entertaining you are. I have to think about the ratings. You know how that goes."

The horrified expression that captivated Angela's face was priceless. I wished I was able to take pictures.

I would have one hell of a scrap book.

You know something to show the grandkids one day.

"Round 2" as I continued to explain the rules, "gets a little more difficult. If you look down; and I don't advise doing that right now, you will notice a watering hose set into the dirt which you are standing on."

Angela began to whimper at this part. I think she might have figured out what happens in round 2 before I even finished explaining the game. So without further ado; I jumped right to the most important part, the scoring.

"Now Princess don't forget that this is all about the show, so don't be selfish. I'll be judging on originality as well as technique; and I'll let you in on a secret since this is your first time, I want to see some creativity, and remember less is more, so please not a lot of screaming. Are you ready to begin?"

Even though Angela responded, "No, no, please no."; I'm pretty sure she meant "Yes! Let's get this show on the road!"

Lights, camera, action!

💣

Chapter 19

Sipping on a double low-fat Chai latte and finishing her sugar-free chocolate-chip cookie, Becca stared at the laptop as if it would speed up the search process. Utilizing Panera Bread's Wi-Fi network, Becca was able to log in to the Post's SNIPH database.

Without the information she had hoped to obtain at the school, Becca imputed the names of every senior male student into SNIPH, all two-hundred and fifty-seven of them. It was no wonder the school was looking to expand back then to the elementary school's building. Becca set the parameters for the SNIPH search engine by utilizing three pieces of information she highlighted in the copy of the manuscript Roberto had given her. Looking for commonality from the names she entered of the male seniors, Becca instructed SNIPH to cross-reference those names against database archives from Ohio University in Athens, Ohio for the years 1980, 81 and 82. Filtering the process by similar names found in the registry from Woodmere Academy on Long Island, for the years 1978, 79 and 80.

While Becca waited for the search results she found herself daydreaming about Christopher John. Thinking about his jet black hair and his grey-blue eyes, and the way he seemed to peer into her soul when he looked at her; Becca found herself getting slightly aroused.

Feeling like everyone in Panera was looking at her and able to read her thoughts Becca glanced around.

Just in her mind.

Suddenly feeling warmer than a minute ago, she fanned herself with the small colorful cardboard menu that sat propped on her table.

When her phone rang she realized that she had been so engrossed in fantasy, that although her eyes were open, she wasn't even aware that she was still in the restaurant. In her mind she was back at her apartment Monday night after dinner having a glass of wine with Christopher John. Knees touching as they sat and laughed together on her living room couch.

The caller ID said 'NEVER AGAIN', which meant that it was Roberto calling from his office. She made a mental note to change that ID. Not that she ever planned to get back with him, but she knew she wouldn't want to hurt his feelings if he ever saw how she had him listed. She realized she would need to change the ID attached to his cell number as well; that one said 'RJ aka SAD SACK'.

Snapping open her phone on the fifth ring, Becca noticed the digital time readout flashing 3:37pm.

It felt much later.

"This is Becca, how can I help you?" answering as if she didn't already know who was on the other end.

Becca felt guilty for harboring some bitterness towards Roberto, especially considering all that he was going through. But Becca was never one to hold back any punches, regardless of the situation, and she was still ticked-off about the 'I love you' comment he made four hours earlier.

"It's me, Roberto." He paused as if he expected her to just start talking now that he announced himself.

"Are you busy?" he asked obviously sensing something in her silence.

"I was just working on the computer, trying to gather some more information about our friend." She replied blandly.

"Where are you?" he asked and Becca almost went through the roof. Taking a few deep breaths before she responded in the wrong manner, she simply said, "I'm using a Wi-Fi connection out here on the Island. I may want to check out one more thing before I head back to the city. It all depends on what I can sniff out here in the next few minutes."

Becca was proud of herself, and in all fairness to Roberto, she did tell him she would keep in touch throughout the day. But it amazed her how easy it was to fall back into those personal issues with someone you shared a past with. Especially if it was a past riddled with ups and downs, and one that ended poorly. Every little thing that seemed to come out of Roberto's mouth had her saying to herself, 'Oh yeah. That's why we broke up.'

"How are things going on your end?" Becca inquired, already feeling better towards Roberto and ready to just move forward.

"Took a quick nap; I was starting to see double."

"I know what you mean. I just downed a double dose of caffeine and I don't feel a thing. Did you start printing yet?"

"Probably be able to start the cover in the next few hours. I need to have those done before I can even start printing the text."

"Any thought to what you're going to say the distributors?" Becca asked as she watched the SNIPH program's 'working' bar continue to endlessly cycle.

"I was hoping we could brain-storm on that together." Roberto said, and then with a lilt in his voice, "Maybe dinner later?" Becca exhaled loudly enough for him to hear. "I don't know, I'm exhausted, I was thinking about just grabbing something on the road later."

Roberto took the hint and realized that once he got the presses rolling and he had done all he could, he could use a good night's sleep as well. "How about Sunday brunch then and you can fill me in on the rest of your day?" he asked.

"Sounds like a plan. I'll call you in the morning." Becca disconnected before something stupid came out of Roberto's mouth again.

Becca also recognized that the sooner she told him about Christopher John, the better. She didn't know why she was even concerned; she and Roberto had been apart for almost eighteen months.

He must have assumed she had moved on at this point. Even though the reality of the situation was that she hadn't dated anyone since they had split for that final time; but, Roberto didn't know that.

The laptop beeped to get her attention. With a smile on her face, Becca looked at the screen which read:

SNIPH SEARCH SUCESSFULLY COMPLETED
COMPILING DATA PLEASE BE PATIENT

(Unedited excerpt from the manuscript)

Round 1 was intense.

I had a lot of fun; Angela, not so much.

Very thump-thump, I'm sure the ratings soared.

I was on the edge of my seat the whole time. I let it go on for a lot more than just 5 minutes; it was that entertaining.

I immediately got an added bonus I wasn't expecting. When I unchained Angela's wrists and let her arms down, the skin on her neck extended just enough to open the wound around her face.

I was right there too.

The agony that flashed in Angela's eyes was pure and exquisite. Blood ran in tiny rivers that were immediately devoured by the white T-shirt. As the shirt sucked up the blood, it molded itself around Angela's perfect tits, it was all I could do to not grab hold and squeeze. But, this was her game to play, not mine.

Angela proved to have very good balance, at least in round 1, not as much in round 2. At first, Angela tried to pull the fishing line down from the rafters.

Excellent move and I awarded her points for creativity. When that didn't work she began fumbling at her clips attached to her face. Working gingerly at first, Angela realized that she needed to be a little more aggressive if she wanted to remove them. Accepting the pain that was to come, Angela pulled down with both hands on the clip attached under her chin.

Lots of points for technique with that bold move. I was impressed.

Angela successfully removed the center clip from her face in a spray of blood that left a ragged flap of skin flopping down below her lower lip.

Unfortunately Angela did let out a whopper of a howl and I had to remove some of those hard earned points she had accumulated.

It also appeared the chin-tear move took a lot of the fight out of Angela. Her head bobbed forward and part of her face peeled up as the remaining clips tore the flesh away from the muscle.

Fresh, wet, blood covered the entire T-shirt and soaked the boxers as well.

It reminded me of Carrie at the prom.

Angela feebly raised her hands and grabbed the fishing lines above her face and used them for support. She swayed back and forth a little, but with her hands on the lines, there was no tension pulling at the clips. Another good move, but I couldn't reward her with any points; there just wasn't enough entertainment value.

I let her rest that way for a little while and then headed over to the water basin.

It was time for round 2.

*

Chapter 20

Melina sat in the dark and continued to pick at the wood that surrounded the metal plate that housed the end of the chain.

She had made some headway over the last ten or twelve days. She couldn't be exactly sure how much time has elapsed since she had become aware. She had no point of reference how long she was unconscious at the onset of her abduction.

She remembered the elevators not working at the NYU Admin building and deciding to take the stairs. She recalled that the main staircase was cordoned off and she was forced to take the rear stairwell that led down to the parking garage. A good looking gentleman gave her directions back to the Broadway side of the building... and then nothing, until she woke up chained and naked on a dirt floor in the dark.

Melina had begun counting days based on how often she received food and water. Guessing by the weight she lost, how weak she felt and how infrequently she needed to relieve herself; Melina figured she was only being fed once a day.

As she dug splinters and the occasional larger shard from the wall, Melina took great care to form a neat pile. She would then systematically gather the shavings in her hand and take them to the farthest reach her tethered ankle would allow and bury them in random locations. Feeling around the metal plate at the progress she had made gave Melina a glimmer of hope. At least she felt that she was doing something towards facilitating an escape.

Melina had learned a lot about her will to live and about her own body's ability to adapt. Being immersed in absolute darkness Melina found her sense of hearing had become finer tuned as did her sense of touch and visualization.

In her mind she had a clear picture of her perimeter. Every facet, every bump in the ground, every pebble in the dirt, every knot in the wood paneled wall and every link in the chain was mapped perfectly clear in her mind's eye.

Melina grew accustomed to her captor's routine as well. She had a relatively good idea where the chair and whip were in relation to her position and the door.

She learned quickly not to speak unless spoken to; and most of all, to follow instructions without hesitation. It only took one mistake per rule to learn that being hit with the whip was no fun.

Melina was driven by an intense desire to one day return the favor.

Ignoring the pain as a sliver of wood slid under her nail into the tender flesh, Melina pried out a long shard that gave her some purchase behind the metal plate. The sound of keys jingling in the distance signaled feeding time or worse; but left her no time to hide the splinters she had gathered in the last several hours.

(Unedited excerpt from the manuscript)

I turned the knob ever so slightly on the valve; I wanted the water to just dribble into the crate.

So far Angela was putting on a fantastic show.

I was looking forward to Angela's face peeling off; but, I loved the slow anticipation round one offered, and I was hoping for the same in round two.

Live and learn; I should have packed the dirt tighter, because as soon as the water mixed into the crate everything happened very fast. I barely had a chance to get situated back into my front row chair.

The dirt mound Angela had been supporting herself on began to crumble. The water rapidly created mud.

At first Angela raised up on her tiptoes, but she couldn't maintain any balance that way. Her feet slipped out from beneath her and her hands naturally flayed out to the sides looking for support.

Angela fell forward out of the crate.

Her face tore off from the meat of her head and was accompanied by a ripping sound that reminded me of wet Velcro. As the remnants of her skinned face swung back and forth from the rafter; her body flopped around on the ground in front of me like a fish out of water.

I sat watching for a while, leaning forward from the edge of the chair. It was obvious Angela was writhing in agony, but with out her face, expressions weren't very distinguishable. She had no eyelids, no eyebrows and her lips were missing.

There was such a sinuous mess of tissue and muscle that it took me a moment to realize that her eyes were somewhat pulled out of their sockets as well.

Pop goes the weasel.

I stood and rolled Angela onto her back. She was getting way too much dirt in her face. I went over and turned up the flow of water and pulled the hose out of the crate and sprayed Angela's bloody form. Her arms began to thrash around as she tried to ward off the spray.

It became apparent that the water on her exposed face must have felt like acid so I steadied my aim and thus began the bonus round.

The crowd went crazy and our ratings soared through the roof.

At some point while I was chucking and jiving around Angela's raised hands, warding off the stream of water, I must have hit the mark. Like the clown's mouth on the Midway I popped the balloon. Angela started choking and gagging violently. Either it was on water or blood, or maybe a combination.

Bottom line is, Angela drowned.

Weird way to die considering everything else that had happened to her that night. Don't you think?

I unhooked her face and scalp from the fishing line and almost put it on like a Halloween mask. I didn't have any mirrors in the barn though so I just slipped it back on where it had come from.

I couldn't put my finger on it; but, Angela just wasn't as pretty as I had remembered her.

A barrel, some industrial strength lye, a few shiny bones and a shovel; you should know the routine by now.

Sorry no parting gifts for today's contestant.

💣

Chapter 21

Becca wrote down the seven names that matched the search criteria she had fed into the SNIPH program.

Seven matches was more than double what she expected to find given the narrow triangulated corridor she had established. She was hoping to pinpoint the Madman's identity based on the immediate results but realized more background searches would be required.

Packing up her laptop and ordering another double low-fat Chai latte for the road, Becca aimed her car back towards Manhattan.

For nearly six years Becca had avoided approaching Manhattan from the south end. The absence of the Towers was too apparent from that route. Even though, the forever changed New York Skyline was unavoidable from any angle, Becca preferred to use the Triborough Bridge and skirt down the FDR Drive to her apartment on the Upper East Side.

All these years later, Becca could still see Jeremy jumping to his death when she closed her eyes.

They were planning to be married the following May after an intense two year long courtship. Becca had maintained contact with her high school guidance counselor, Mr. 'call me Jeremy' Young, throughout her years at Columbia. In the beginning she felt she owed him the courtesy of updates on her grades and progress; but, rapidly they became close friends and soon Becca found herself picking up the phone just to talk.

Twelve years her senior, Becca had an enormous crush on Jeremy; and Jeremy had grown quite fond of Becca. It wasn't until the evening of Becca's graduation that the two of them realized something else was at work between them. A congratulatory hug became a lover's embrace, which then became a weekend in the Catskills.

The two of them were joined at the hip for the rest of that summer.

The only time the couple had a disagreement was when Becca was struggling to break into the field of television journalism. Jeremy suggested that she contact the local Hispanic stations and Becca went ballistic.

The disagreement was more like World War III. Becca argued that it was bad enough she got into school based on her ethnicity; but, she would be damned if she was going to be labeled for the rest of her life. Jeremy tried to explain that it would be nothing more than a stepping stone; a place she could get the experience she needed to land a career with one of the bigger networks.

As Becca's Irish and Puerto Rican blood began to boil, and she screamed at him that she would rather work for the Enquirer than sell out her American heritage and play the race card; Jeremy realized he had no chance of making sense to Becca.

The day Jeremy met Becca for dinner at Tony's Italian Garden on Remsen Avenue; it had been three days since the argument. Neither of them had brought it up since, but it hung there in the air between them like an invisible force field.

Jeremy pulled the chair out and seated Becca at their favorite table on the back outdoor patio. When Jeremy began the conversation by saying, "We need to talk." Becca broke down and started crying. "I'm sorry." She said, "I was just so frustrated; please don't break up with me."

Immediately getting up and coming to her side, Jeremy knelt beside Becca and took her hand and started laughing. Through waterlogged eyes, Becca asked what he found so funny.

That evening Jeremy explained how much he had fallen in love with her and wanted to know if she felt ready to move in with him. He told her that he couldn't imagine his life without her and would do anything to make her happy, even if it meant getting her a job at the Enquirer. Becca asked if he was serious and he replied by explaining that his townhouse in Bergen Beach was a two bedroom and that he wouldn't mind parking his car on the street, so she could use the driveway.

Becca let him know that she would love to move in, and wondered what took him so long to ask; but she was more interested in what he said about being able to get her a job.

As fate turned out, Jeremy's contact at the Enquirer had recently taken a position with the New York Post as editor of the entertainment section and was looking for a full-time field reporter. Unfortunately, as the monkey's paw turns, the very same phone call that set Becca's career in motion also placed Jeremy in the World Trade Center on the morning of September 11th, 2001.

Jeremy told Becca as he kissed her goodbye that Tuesday morning that he felt guilty about taking a day off from school so early in the school year, but he needed to meet her boss's nephew at the American Express office downtown to help him with his admissions essay to Princeton and he also needed to interview him for a letter of recommendation that he was to write on his behalf. Jeremy made Becca promise to not let her boss know; but, Jeremy made it clear that, the spoiled brat of a nephew, didn't stand a chance of being accepted. Not even, if the President of the United States wrote a letter of recommendation; but, a favor received equaled a favor owed.

Four months after Becca accepted Jeremy's proposal of marriage, they shared the commute on the B-train as far as the DeKalb Avenue stop in Brooklyn. There Jeremy transferred to the R-train which branched off into lower Manhattan.

Becca smiled and wished they could leave the house together every morning. Holding on to the overhead railing and trying not to be groped by other commuters, Becca continued on the B to the Rockefeller Center station, and walked to the editorial offices of the New York Post.

Not quite in the office for fifteen minutes and without her routine morning cup of tea; at 8:46am, Becca's world darkened as the first plane struck the North Tower. Praying along with the rest of humanity, Becca hoped for the best.

Forty minutes later, all hope was lost when she saw her future jump to its death.

Finally, back at home, after a long, crazy day on the Island, Becca put her feet up on her white scalloped couch and closed her eyes.

It was only 6:20 in the evening but it felt like midnight. Setting her internal clock for 8:30, Becca let her mind drift through random images left by the day's events. Bloody cherries, spouses hanging from the rafters, mean little old ladies and steroid enhanced gym teachers. A town and a generation oblivious to the history of the land on which they lived; acting as if they were the first people to set foot on the moon.

Floating faces of Jeremy, Roberto and Christopher; faded in and out of her mind's eye, overlapping, blending and morphing into one another; and then, nothing, Becca fell into a dreamless slumber.

Chapter 22

Roberto had finished proofing the printing draft of the Madman's manuscript and was ready to set the cover into motion. Once he spot checked a random sampling of pages to insure the scanning process had functioned properly; Roberto devised a method to check the sequence of the pages, in order not to find himself reading again. By placing a paperweight diagonally across the proof and one across the original, he was able to simply turn up the lower right corner and compare just a few words. This method allowed him to verify accurately that the order of each page was in sync.

The cover was a simple enough design, black bold lettering on a yellow background that read THE RUSH-HOUR MADMAN. As an afterthought, Roberto scanned the letter that was enclosed with the manuscript and included it on the cover below the title.

Roberto wanted the public to know that he had no choice.

Without knowing exactly what he was going to say to the distributors, other than that they are free, Roberto still was unsure how he was going to market the manuscript to insure shelf space.

One decision Roberto did make was that he would deal solely with his two main chains, Barnes and Noble and Waldenbooks. This way he only had to worry about making a couple of phone calls on Monday verses a couple dozen.

Even by streamlining the distribution process, Roberto still felt confident that he was satisfying the Madman's request. Roberto had himself convinced that he would see the safe return of Melina as long as he delivered as requested.

Barnes and Noble had almost 800 stores throughout the 50 states while Waldenbooks had another 560 plus. If he sent out only a dozen for each store, he could get by with a production run of only 16,500 copies, thereby limiting the expense to the Wiley Company.

Despite everything else that was running through his head, he was still concerned about possibly keeping his job.

With the covers running through the press, Roberto headed back down to the warehouse on the ground floor to gather the paper stock required for printing the book. As he headed down the open freight elevator, wondering why the printing presses were not conveniently located near the warehouse and shipping docks, the lights flicked overhead and the elevator came to an abrupt halt.

Immersed in the red glow of the emergency lights that lined the elevator shaft, Roberto surprised himself by swallowing the panic that surfaced like an angry shark and began calculating his options.

Within five minutes Roberto realized that the emergency generator was up to its old tricks and he needed to get back to one of the main floors. From there he would use the stairs to get down to the electrical room located in the sub-basement where he would activate the emergency generator manually.

The freight elevator predominately ran behind a solid wall on the back end of the building. The only floors that opened up to the elevator were the two basement levels, the ground floor and the seventh and eighth floors where the printing presses were housed. Gauging from the twilight that crept in the windows on the seventh and eighth floors above, Roberto figured the elevator stopped somewhere between the second and third floors.

Climbing up the chain-link cage that comprised the upper third of the freight elevators walls, Roberto was able to grab hold of the ladder that was recessed into the wall behind the back of the elevator.

Planning to use the slight ridge that ran around the inside perimeter of the elevator shaft at the floors where the elevator had access to the building; Roberto headed up instead of down.

Roberto was positive he had secured the gate doors that led into the warehouse on his last trip down when he retrieved the cardstock for the cover. Without the elevator being in place outside the doors to trigger the release latch, Roberto would not be able to open the gate doors into the warehouse. In contrast, there were no gate doors on the printing press floors, just secured platforms surrounded by a low chain-link fence kept the unaware worker from plummeting down the shaft.

So, Roberto began the slow upward climb; carefully placing his feet and hands on the rungs that were covered in a thin film of mechanical grease that must have spit out from the freight elevator's gears over the years.

Halfway up, the long day began to play a major factor in Roberto's concentration. Twice he lost his footing and twice he almost fell backwards down the three flights he had climbed. No doubt, a fall like that would have certainly broken his neck.

With his arms and legs straining, threatening to give out at any moment, Roberto dared to look up and saw he had only one more floor to go. At that very moment, the building's slow-to-react emergency generator sparked to life.

Lights flickered and illuminated the elevator shaft from the seventh floor; Roberto was momentarily blinded as the freight elevator below roared back to life and began ascending up the shaft. Roberto just hung there frozen in disbelief. Staring at the rising elevator, envisioning the top metal frame of the cage slicing into his flesh as it passed him by.

Roberto's mind finally grabbed hold of the wheel and sent messages to his arms and legs. Hand over hand, foot over foot, Roberto scrambled up to the ridge that lined the shaft outside the seventh floor. With his back pressed flat against the greasy wall, arms out to the sides for balance, Roberto began side-stepping around the edge.

Working his way into the first corner as the elevator passed the fourth floor, he realized that he wasn't going to make it.

The elevator was rising too quickly.

'Don't think! Go!' his mind yelled at him and he began his side-step shuffle at double-time pace.

Just as he cleared the last corner and was two feet from the opening to the seventh floor, he lost his balance and fell forward.

Fortunately the elevator was only ten feet below him and all he suffered was a twisted ankle and bruised forearm as he hit the floor and fell into the freight elevator's wall. From his position on the ground, he watched as the monster printing press came into view and then disappeared as the elevator continued its climb.

At first alarmed, Roberto quickly remembered that the elevator needed to rise all the way to the top of the thirty-six story building to reset itself after a power failure. Once stationary at the summit of the shaft, Roberto rose to his feet and tried to put weight on his ankle and found that although it was tender he would be able to manage walking on it. Pressing the button for the seventh floor, Roberto sidetracked his trip to the warehouse to make a quick stop and confirm that the interrupted power didn't affect the printing press.

(Unedited excerpt from the manuscript)

I know you'll never forgive me if I don't tell you how I chose Ohio University over Syracuse. First, I want you to appreciate that regardless of the method, the outcome would have been the same. I was destined to be at OU at that moment in time as you will soon realize.

Apart from that, I did play another game of 'gender specific casualty'. This time I played it at night at one of my favorite clubs in the city, The Limelight.

The Limelight was a dance club that proudly supported the lifestyle of sex, drugs and rock 'n roll.

No fucking Disco.

I think it was Disco that first drove me to making shit-kickers. Just kidding; but, I would have loved to shove a few of them up the Bee-Gee's asses if they wouldn't have enjoyed it so much.

This all went down at the beginning of the summer, about a week after my birthday; I was still working at the Back Barn but had a rare Thursday and Friday off.

Anyway, The Limelight was a multi-level club built inside a deconsecrated church. It really doesn't get any better than that; and yes, I feel bad they had to shut down for two months during repairs. If they had kept a better house cleaning policy, I might have picked another location.

There were always beer bottles strewn all over the dance floor getting kicked around; you never knew where one was going to end up. I thought what a great place to play hot-potato with a live shit-kicker.

That Thursday night, head banging on the dance floor to heavy metal with some hot brunette, I almost tripped on one of those discarded bottles. The brunette thought it was the funniest thing she had ever seen; but, instead of getting mad, I got even.

I invited 'Miss. I think it's funny you almost fell' to meet me back at the club the following night. I told her it was going to be a blast and she didn't want to miss it.

Friday, I arrived late; I wanted to be sure the club was full. I snuck in a one of my double-strength glass Coke-bottle shit-kickers with an extended delayed fuse inside my pants.

'Is that a bomb in your pants or are you just happy to see me?'

I needed to stall a little. I figured it would look suspicious if I walked in, lit a fuse and walked out. The bouncer may not have been able to recognize me, or even been able to put two and two together, but I always say, it's better to err on the side of extreme caution.

Something else I say is, 'there's no better way to kill time than getting your dick sucked'. I looked around and found the brunette comedian from the other night and with absolutely no convincing required, I escorted her up the back stairs to one of the private rooms on the third floor where she swallowed samples of my DNA.

We moved down to the dance floor and forced our way to the center. I slipped the shit-kicker out of my pocket and lit the fuse and dropped it to the floor.

Nobody fucking noticed, not even the stupid cock-sucker I was dancing with.

It amazes me how blind you are, absolutely unbelievable.

I gave the shit-kicker an initial shove with my boot and then watched for a few minutes as it went this way and that way, then it was time to go. I told the cock-sucker to hold our place on the dance floor while I went to the bar to get us drinks.

I headed straight out the front door and got in my car around the corner.

I would have loved to stay and watch, but my personal safety was a concern. There was no way to tell where the shit-kicker was going to be when it finally went off.

As I drove past the front of The Limelight heading home I heard the explosion and the subsequent screams. The quality of the acoustics was deafening and gratifying.

According to the news Saturday morning, I had set a new personal record with 12 dead: 9 men and 3 women, thanks to a group of Asian men that were dancing together. The 27 others who were merely wounded or hospitalized comprised of 18 men and 9 women.

So, the ladies lost, and I made a phone call to Ohio University Monday morning.

💣

Chapter 23

The clock on the wall above the kitchen door read 8:39pm when Becca's internal alarm clock rang. Getting up off the couch and giving her body a dramatic stretch, Becca pulled over a small step stool and took the clock off the wall. Without a need to confirm that her internal clock was accurate, Becca adjusted the wall clock eight minutes to read 8:31. Later, she smiled to herself as she noticed the time display in the lower right corner of her laptop in perfect sync with the clock above the kitchen door.

With a Stouffer's Meat Lasagna in her belly and a glass of Merlot within reach, Becca typed the seven names SNIPH had provided to her earlier.

Becca awoke from her nap with the knowledge of how to narrow down the search results. This was a common occurrence for her; many times when Becca struggled with a dilemma, she awoke with the answer. It was as if her mind continued to work on the problem long after she stopped consciously thinking about it. An old phrase came to her, something her mother would say to her when she was younger and struggling in school; "Let go and let God."

Becca let her mind drift to thoughts of her mother; it had been quite a few weeks since she had seen Felicia. Although they spoke on the phone every couple of days, her visits out to Brooklyn seemed to get further and further apart.

Living in an assisted resident facility; Felicia was suffering in the later stages of dementia at the rare, but not uncommon, age of fifty-five. On Becca's last several visits, Felicia needed to be shown photos confirming Becca's identity; and, when they spoke on the phone Becca felt as if she had dialed the wrong number.

God does work in mysterious ways; because, if it wasn't for the dementia, Becca doesn't think her mother would have been able to cope with the loss of her husband.   Becca's father, Jonathan Willis, having finally found the inner strength to control his drinking and maintain a steady job to support his family, was beaten to death in the summer of 2003.

As the night watchman for the Holy Cross Cemetery, Jonathan mainly got little but exercise each night as he patrolled the 95 acre facility. Then, one rainy July night in 2003, Becca's father stumbled upon a group of teenage thugs who were desecrating the grave of Louis Capone. Although no relation to the Chicago crime boss, Al Capone; Louis was a renowned hitman for the notorious Jewish and Italian-

American organization, Murder Inc. Louis died of natural causes in 1944, but there were still people holding a grudge some sixty years later.

Surprising the hoodlums in the midst of their vendetta against the dead gangster, Jonathan tried to scare them off the property with only a flashlight and a nightstick. One of the teenagers snuck around Jonathan's back and struck him in the head with a shovel. Once they had him on the ground, the gang circled around and kicked him to death.

It was later that summer, when Becca's mom began setting the dinner table for two again, that Becca first took her to the doctor.

Initially being misdiagnosed with a form of grief induced depression; Felicia's symptoms went untreated at a stage where the disease could have been controlled. Even Becca herself didn't realize the severity of her mom's condition simply due her age; and by the time reality of the disease became apparent, it was too late to do anything but accommodate her mom's failing mind.

Selling the house on 52nd Street, Becca helped Felicia move to the Park Manor Assisted Living Community on Coney Island Ave in Kensington. Now, four years later, Becca's visits have dwindled from every weekend to about once a month; and, the saddest part about that to Becca, is the fact that her mother doesn't even know.

The laptop beeped bringing Becca's attention back into her apartment on East 69th. SNIPH had completed its most recent task and Becca stared at the two names flashing on the screen; Kenny Thomas and Brendon Thomas.

Kenny and Brendon Thomas were the only two names from the Woodmere Academy database that shared a last name with one of the Lynbrook High School seniors and with the freshman list of Ohio University for 1980. Becca had relied on the Madman's accounting about his two brothers that got shipped off to the Academy and it paid off in a big way.

In her earlier search formula she was only looking for common last names, she didn't factor in possible repeated names from the Academy. The new search hit the proverbial nail on the head. Becca was now positive she had the identity of the Madman.

Turning to the senior photos in the yearbook she had borrowed from Bud Farber, Becca followed her finger through the T's; Craig Talbot, Harvey Terrell, Beverly Thatcher, Michael Thelman and finally, Jack Thomas.

Preparing SNIPH for a global search, Becca raised her glass of Merlot and toasted the Madman's arrogance as she pressed the enter key and watched as the hourglass began its end over end dance.

Chapter 24

After resetting the cover in the printing press following the power outage, Roberto decided to call it a night. There was no point for him to head back down into the warehouse, and it wasn't because he was scared. His ankle hurt, and he was tired, and he wouldn't be printing the book before Sunday morning anyway.

Before leaving the Wiley Building, Roberto flipped the circuit breaker on the ground floor which circumvented the emergency generator and restored normal power. Around the same time Becca was waking up from her nap, Roberto was telling a taxi driver his address.

Walking with a noticeable limp, Roberto hobbled up the one flight of stairs into his apartment at the corner of 17th and Third. Turning the faucet in the tub and allowing the hot water to run a while, he searched below the bathroom sink for a bag of Epson salt. His ankle had swelled considerably; and despite how strongly he needed to go to bed, Roberto was concerned about walking without assistance the following day if he didn't soak in a hot tub.

Settling into the salted water, Roberto wondered what sadist determined the average size of a bathtub. With knees bent and arms uncomfortably propped up to their sides, Roberto leaned his head back into the wall and placed a damp washcloth over his face. Trying to forget his panicked climb up the greasy elevator shaft, Roberto searched for a moment of stillness. The past fifty-four hours were something out of a horror movie and Roberto felt as if the movie were just beginning.

(Unedited excerpt from the manuscript)

Ohio University was a great experience. Not only did I perfect the fine art of being incognito; but, I had the opportunity to meet Reverend Wayne West, leader of the Satanic Church of Brotherhood.

It is amazing how modern day society misleads when it doesn't understand.

I'm not going to go into a lot of detail here for two main reasons; first, I don't think, actually I know, you would never, could never, appreciate the truth. Secondly, I don't want you to make this all about Satanism. I can already see you faceless fucks trying to label all of this. Not everything fits into a pattern, not everything can be explained with an answer that makes you comfortable. Truth be told, if you even had an inkling about what's what, you'd never close your eyes again. Besides I've already told you what's what as far as this dissertation goes; you're just too fucking stupid to remember.

Being at OU gave me absolute freedom. No more sneaking back into the house through the backdoor. No more pretending to be someone my parents wanted to meet.

Unfortunately, it also meant no more barn, no more swing, no more lye, no more sanctuary and no more innocence.

It was a time to grow up and plan for tomorrow.

It was a time to begin realizing the bigger picture and deciding how I was going to redecorate.

When I first arrived at OU, I had a roommate, but since I'm a very private person, I concluded that one of us needed to go. Funny how things work out, even though I slit his throat in the woods at Old Man's Cave in Hocking Hills, he got to keep the room and I left school early.

Before I forget, I want to share with you my last weekend at the Hollingsworth's barn.

Sad as it was, I made the best of it.

Growing up there was a group of 4 guys; I guess you would call them my friends. We had known each other since Waverly Park Elementary, stuck together through South Middle, and predominately hung around the same places during the Lynbrook High years. By the time graduation rolled around we were simply acquaintances.

Maybe it was just me.

Anyway, I'm going to tell you a story here that I've never shared with anyone; because, frankly it is a little embarrassing. However, I think it is necessary that you have some background as to how I selected the barn's final unwilling participant.

Revenge after all, is a dish best served cold; or, in this case, on a swing and a little charbroiled.

As much as those guys would love to see their names in print, I'm only going to mention one of them, Adam Blackman. The only reason he gets an honorable mention here was because he had two very hot older sisters, Andrea and Alexandria. We spent a lot of time at Adam's house, especially in the summertime around the pool.

After graduation, Adam's parents organized a Sunday barbeque-pool party to get the 'old' gang together one last time. I almost didn't go; I was still working crazy hours at the Back Barn, getting off at 3am and then returning by 5 that same afternoon.

When I called Adam to let him know there was no way I could make it, Alexandria answered the phone. Alex was 4 years older than us and built like a Super-model.

I had been fantasizing about Adam's sisters ever since I knew what my dick was for.

Alex took the lead in the conversation before I even had a chance to ask for her brother. She told me how excited she was that I was coming over and how she couldn't wait to see what kind of a man I had grown up to be. I had no fucking idea what she meant by that, but my dick told her I'd be there around one.

💣

Chapter 25

Roberto had fallen asleep and was lucky he didn't drown. He awoke in a tub filled with cold water and a fire in his heart. Normally being a man of proactive action, Roberto was furious with the way he had been manipulated these past two days into being a man of reactive action.

Stepping out of the tub to wrap himself in a towel, Roberto felt the sharp pain of his twisted ankle shoot up his calf as he stepped upon it.

Cursing in Spanish, Roberto put his fist through the drywall. Loose tiles fell to the floor and the medicine cabinet swung open as expired medicine bottles toppled into the sink.

Roberto slammed the mirrored cabinet door shut, half expecting the glass to shatter. With arms braced on the edges of the sink, Roberto stared at himself in the mirror. There was a piercing intensity in the expression that stared back at him.

He had no idea what had happened to him in the bath, but he liked it.

Enough was enough he screamed at himself. Tomorrow he was going to print the psychopath's manuscript. He was going to help Becca find Melina, and then he was going to tear the mother-fucker limb from limb.

Climbing up to the bedrooms by means of a small round rung ladder in the living room that traveled up through a cutout in the loft's floor; Roberto lay down in his bed with no intention of being able to sleep. Putting a pillow over his mouth, to spare the neighbors, Roberto let out a primal roar. Pounding his arms and fists into the mattress and kicking his legs with no regard for his tender ankle, Roberto looked like a child in the throws of a temper tantrum; and like a child, Roberto was fast asleep before he knew it.

Chapter 26

Refilling her wineglass in the kitchen, Becca heard her laptop beeping in the living room. The sound indicating the completion of the SNIPH search on Jack Thomas had Becca almost running from the kitchen. Nearly spilling the wineglass as she carelessly placed it down on the glass coffee table; Becca sat down and leaned forward as she read the first and only line of the program's results:

OLD MAN'S CAVE CLAIMS LONG ISLAND YOUTH

Becca clicked on the link and read the story about Jack Thomas. A sad tale of a boy from Lynbrook, Long Island who perished in a fifty-foot fall down a crevice into the lower caverns at Old Man's Cave in Hocking Hills, Ohio. Jack, the oldest son of Robert and Shannon Thomas, was in his first trimester at Ohio University in Athens, Ohio. While exploring the famous caves with his roommate; who preferred to remain anonymous, Jack crossed over the protective railing to peer down into the multi-layered lattice of the underground caverns. These subterranean marvels were formed when the glaciers melted some twelve thousand years earlier and were known to crisscross the entire state of Ohio. Jack Thomas's body was returned to his family after an almost impossible fourteen hour recovery mission. Damage sustained during the initial fall and the subsequent recovery process made identification impossible. If it weren't for the assistance of Jack's college roommate, the body would have remained a John Doe.

Becca didn't believe a word of it. Swilling back her Merlot and feeling the heartburn set in before the Merlot got to her stomach, Becca ate four extra-strength TUMS and went to bed.

(Unedited excerpt from the manuscript)

While everyone else was stuffing their faces or playing Marco-Polo, I watched as Alex broke away from the party and headed into the house. She hadn't said anything to me the entire afternoon and I wondered if I had misunderstood her on the phone. Then she stopped just inside the backdoor that led into the family room and turned back as if looking for me. Playfully flipping her long black hair from side to side, Alex disappeared with a hop-step into the darkness of the house.

I took that as a signal, so I waited a few moments and then followed her into the house.

Alex's slender body was just vanishing around the corner that connected the family room to the kitchen. I caught just the faintest glimpse of her red bikini bottom and followed it like a beacon in the night.

As I entered the kitchen, Alex was still on the move. Taking the back stairs that led up to the bedrooms on the second and third floors, I continued my pursuit.

When I opened the door and stepped into Alex's room on the third floor, her bathroom door was just latching.

I was really enjoying this game even though I had no control. I was feeling a different kind of *thump-thump* and it was giving me one hell of a stiffy.

I closed the door and lay down on her bed waiting for her to reemerge. I slipped off my swim trunks and tried a few provocative positions before I settled on the one that best showed off the hardware.

Alex opened the bathroom door to a view of me propped up against the oversized pillows on her bed with my arms bent up behind my head and my hard-on locked and loaded ready for take off.

Alex emerged from the bathroom completely naked. At first I thought she had changed into another bathing suit before I realized it was just the contrast between tanned and un-tanned skin.

The brief moment I got to enjoy the view left a lasting memory I carry to this day. ...and the award for Most Voluptuous goes to...

Years later when I looked her up to repay her for that day, I found her 150 pounds heavier and decided to let bygones be bygones.

💣

Chapter 27

It was still dark outside when Roberto woke up Sunday morning. The feeling of empowerment had solidified into a clear focus replacing the rage that he had felt the night before.

Quickly dressing, Roberto left the apartment without shaving and hailed an uptown cab on Third Avenue.

At the Wiley Building, Roberto went directly to the warehouse to gather the paper stock to finish printing the book. He was running out of time. Not time according to the Madman's schedule; on that note, he was actually way ahead of the deadline.

He was running out of the alone-time he had with the presses, away from his employee's inquisitive eyes. Roberto was feeling very confident about being able to complete the limited book run prior to Marissa and the staff returning on Monday. It would be a lot easier to explain packed up cartons in his office, rather than a psychotic manuscript running through the press.

The freight elevator groaned and complained, but made the trip to and from the basement without incident. Leaving the paper stock at the loading platform, Roberto walked the hundred feet to the opposite end of the seventh floor to inspect the printing press.

Mentally running down a list of intentions for the day, Roberto walked around the perimeter of the giant machine. Calibrating ink wells and folding spindles, aligning cutting blades and glue wheels, Roberto's mind wandered to thoughts of Becca as it often does. However, this time there was less remorse and more constructive thinking involved.

If a silver lining could be found amongst the massive grey cloud that had descended upon his life, it was Becca's return. Roberto felt very confident about being able to secure Melina's safe homecoming once he had satisfied the Madman's request; and as a sideline bonus, Roberto wanted nothing more than to have another chance with Becca.

Pulling the skids of paper stock over the press's frontload feeder with an ancient hand-jack, Roberto checked his watch to see if it was late enough to call Becca and schedule their brunch meeting. It was only 7:45 and although he couldn't wait to see Becca, he decided to wait another hour before he called.

He wasn't going to make the same mistakes he had in the past.

Pat Addams

Becca always told him he was too needy and smothering when she was giving him reasons why the relationship wasn't working for her.

Loading enough paper to print the first five thousand copies, Roberto walked the full length of the press to retrieve the printed covers and move them to the side-loader where they would be automatically attached to the printed book. Sliding the hand-jack into the skid beneath the covers and cranking the hydraulic arm, Roberto was so distracted by his thoughts about how to win Becca back, that he missed the handwritten note taped to the stack of printed covers.

(Unedited excerpt from the manuscript)

Still pulling her hair back into a ponytail, Alex stopped cold in her tracks trying to comprehend my naked presence in her bed. I just assumed she was impressed with 'what kind of man I had grown up to be'.

I scooted over to the edge of the bed and invited her on for a ride. Instead of happily approaching the bed, Alex lunged at me with hands furled and teeth barred.

My brain took over; thinking it was being attacked by a mountain lion, I rolled backwards across the bed and landed on my feet. My happy-stick; not so happy now, pointed accusingly at her as she scampered over the sheets still on the attack.

"What the fuck is wrong with you? Are you fucking mental?" Alex screamed at me as I backed into the wall. I grabbed a field hockey stick that was propped up next to the dresser on my left and swung it to keep Alex at bay.

Alex stopped momentarily swiveling her head from side to side.

I actually think she was looking for a weapon of her own.

If the rest of her family wasn't downstairs, I might have taken things in a different direction; but, right then all I wanted to do was get the hell out of the room with my dick still attached.

"You invited me... on the phone the other day. Don't you remember?"

Alex smirked as if now understanding what was happening.

She settled down and kicked over my swim trunks that lay on the carpet next to her feet. "I wouldn't spit on you if you were on fire. You're a nothing more than a snot-nosed little punk, who is very lucky I'm not calling my father up here to kick the living shit out of you."

Accepting that as a dismissal, I slipped my bathing suit back on and left the room.

I was just about to close the door when Alex said, "If you tell anybody about seeing me naked..." She let the threat trail off as if it was understood.

I was too confused at that moment to tell anybody anything anyway. I had no idea what had just transpired until I walked back outside and saw Alex's sister Andrea, laughing.

I went around and said my thank yous and goodbyes to my friends and the Blackmans, including Andrea; I didn't want her to know that I knew what she had done. I had just recently played with foxy-Roxie and had a pretty good idea about how I was going to get back at Andrea; but, I wanted it to be a total surprise.

I didn't mind letting her think she had gotten away with it for the time being. The main thing was that I felt better knowing what had happened.

I have to hand it to Andrea, it was a good prank.

Not worth dying for; but we all make mistakes.

Chapter 28

Becca tossed and turned all night. She couldn't turn her brain off. Frustration tore at her seams as thoughts and ideas scratched at the surface but never solidified. She had been so sure about the Madman's ignorance.

Becca had been so busy staring at the woods that she missed the trees. She needed to regroup, reassemble her thoughts from the beginning and formulate a new starting point.

Opening the side door into her small gated garden area, Becca ignored the early morning pedestrians eager for a glimpse down her nightgown as she bent over to pick up the Sunday paper.

Closing the door while raising her middle finger, Becca thought about moving out of the city.

Becca was approaching her thirtieth birthday and was no where near accomplishing the goals she had set down for herself when she celebrated her twenty-first. She wasn't married, she didn't have children, she wasn't a news anchor, she didn't own any property, and she hadn't been to Europe or Asia.

Quickly taking control of her mind before the 'poor me syndrome' could settle in for the day or possibly an extended stay, Becca put a pot of water on the stove and opened the paper to her favorite section; The Daily Word Jumble.

Becca found these puzzles to be grounding. Whenever she felt overworked, overstressed, or over-Roberto-ed, she would immerse herself within a Word Jumble and let her mind reset.

Something about the mixed up letters gave her a mind massage. The incorrectly arranged letters would enter her brain on individual flashcards and magically shift their positions into comprehendible words.

Becca would sit back almost like a spectator and watch the inner show. Many times while her brain was playing with the flashcards, Becca's mind would simultaneously solve other problems she had been worrying about.

This was her waking form of 'Let go and let God'.

Becca stepped out of her nightgown and into the shower as the water heated. She took with her the four words from the paper; TONI, VILED, CANSEE and CHERISA, each set up on individual sets of mind flashcards. Closing her eyes, she let the hot water beat down upon her neck and shoulders.

The movement lifted the note up at the edge as Roberto jerked the hand-jack forward to get the heavy stack of covers rolling. Seen only in his peripheral vision, it was still enough to freeze both his momentum and his heart. Taped on top of the stack of printed copies of the cover, was a note written in the all-to-familiar print Roberto had come to loath.

> I like the letter on the cover.
> Nice touch. Makes it look like a real book.
> Just wanted to stop by and see how you were doing.
> Have a great day.

Roberto snatched the letter off the stack and crumbled it into a ball and threw it at the windows that faced out onto 40th Street.

He stood there trembling.

Roberto no longer felt alone.

He was sure the Madman was watching from somewhere. He surveyed the windows and rooftops of the buildings across the street, then moved and performed the same ritual across Third Avenue and again across 39th; nothing.

Roberto was convinced the power outage the night before was no accident either. He needed a gun; but, first he needed to print a book.

After toweling off, Becca used her finger to scribe in the fog on the mirror. INTO, DEVIL, SEANCE, CASHIER. Becca stared at the words, not sure at first where they came from or what they meant.

She had been thinking about Jack Thomas. Becca was sure she had missed something so obvious that once it was found, it would be as plain as the nose on her face. A giant redwood.

The whistling of the boiling water brought her out of her reverie and into the kitchen where she made herself a cup of Oolong tea. Becca sat down at the small kitchen table, moved the Sunday paper onto the chair next to her and set the Madman's manuscript onto the round wood table. It was 8:30 Sunday morning and Becca needed to come up with a new game plan. Instinct told her that the answers she was looking for were still hidden within the text.

Booting up the computer and logging into the SNIPH database; Becca wanted to be able to cross-reference and research some more of the landmarks the Madman referenced in the manuscript.

The Madman liked playing games and the distribution of the manuscript was just another game for him. Becca wanted to win; and she was bound and determined to do it with his own bat and ball.

(Unedited excerpt from the manuscript)

Once again I was given a sign that the universe was on my side. Fate delivered Andrea right to my doorstep; well, to my doorstep at The Back Barn.

I had just been thinking about her that very afternoon. Being a faithful planner, I was wondering where I would be able to grab her when the time was right. I really didn't know much about her other than the fact that I was looking forward to our upcoming play date.

She came in on a Thursday with a few of her girlfriends. They had been to the Islanders game and they were shit-faced. Andrea didn't recognize me as her brother's friend, or as the recipient of her nasty prank. She did sort of recognize me though, but couldn't put her finger on where or how. It couldn't have been any more perfect.

It's amazing; remove something familiar out of its familiar context and you faceless fucks have no fucking clue what it is anymore.

Your consistent ignorance, complacency and general lack of being touch with your surroundings, have not only made my life easier but have given me the motivation to do what I do.

Thank you.

I was working the front door that night and had an ideal vantage point as I watched Andrea and her friends parade themselves around the bar hustling for drinks. They ended up scoring more than the Islanders had that night and they left unescorted.

I grabbed Andrea's arm as she was passing by my post at the door. She swung around and pressed her body up against mine, leaning on me for support and slurred, "Oh, it's you again." I asked her if she was alright and if she needed a ride home. It would have been a shame if something happened to her before we had a chance for our little get together.

Andrea explained that her friend had driven and they just lived up the street in the apartments across from the Green Acres Mall. I told her to wait and I'd take her home later but she needed to go because she had to be at work early for inventory.

She worked at Victoria's Secret; and, speaking about secrets, Andrea didn't have any now. In less than thirty seconds she told me where she lives, where she works, and that she has at least one roommate.

About five weeks later, I know it was after the Back Barn had been closed down; I grabbed Andrea as she left work and brought her to my barn.

She never even looked around as she opened her car door.

💣

Chapter 29

Hot tea splashed onto Becca's face. She had been slowly raising the cup to her mouth; eyes transfixed on the manuscript, when the telephone's ringing made her jump. Using the sleeve of her bathrobe to wipe off her cheeks and under her chin, Becca let the call go to voice mail.

Ten seconds later the phone rang again.

For a second time, Becca ignored the call. Soon her cell phone began to ring.

Becca couldn't remember ever hearing Roberto swear before and he seemed to be making up for lost time.

All she heard initially was 'mother-fucker' this and 'mother-fucker' that. Roberto was mixing English and Spanish together and none of it was making any sense to Becca. Originally, Becca thought Roberto was angry because she didn't answer the phone right away, and she was about to tell him off.

When she realized that he was saying that the Madman was there, she went cold from the inside out.

Becca dressed, grabbed her car keys and then realized she had a great parking spot and didn't want to lose it, so she double-checked her billfold for her Metro-card and headed for the 6 train. As she walked west on 69th to Lex and over to the station on 68th at Hunter College; Becca mused to herself how even at a moment like this, the fact that her car was in a spot that was good until Tuesday, was equally important as the fact that Roberto was totally freaking out.

No sooner than she had stepped through the turnstile, a 6 train pulled into the station.

Becca wore jeans and a loose fitting T-shirt featuring a worn out photo of John Lennon and the caption 'IMAGINE'.

Choosing to stand for the three quick stops to 42nd Street and Grand Central Station, Becca could see the dismay on the faces of the men that shifted over to make room for her in the seats.

No matter what Becca wore she always seemed to attract the attention of the opposite sex. That was the basis of the first real fight she had with Roberto; and, in her mind, the beginning of the end.

Six months into the relationship, when Becca was finally feeling totally comfortable with Roberto, he snapped at her about an outfit she was wearing. They had just come from an afternoon showing of *The Phantom of the Opera* and were having an early dinner at Jekyll and Hyde, a haunted-theme restaurant and bar near Central Park South.

The waiter, an actor wannabe, made it very obvious he was infatuated with Becca and her low cut blouse.

Conducting himself with blatant disrespect to Roberto, the waiter continuously kept hitting on Becca; who, in Roberto's opinion led him on by not telling him to back off.

Becca, and all woman for that matter, who are constantly being leered at, who are constantly having crude comments thrown their way, who are constantly made to feel like sponge toys on the subway; become oblivious to that type of attention. It is meaningless to them, just a normal part of the day. If the attention should ever stop, *that* would be noticeable. It's like getting used to the sound of traffic or crickets outside your window at night. You don't notice it because it is always there. But, if it should stop; that's when you know something is wrong.

Roberto didn't see things that way; simply because he wasn't one of 'those' guys. He didn't ogle other women.

He wouldn't make crude comments just because a woman was wearing a short skirt or a low cut blouse. He truly respected a woman as an equal and not a sex object.

It probably had a lot to do with his childhood. He and Melina were everything to each other. Equal partners in survival.

The entire cab ride home to Becca's apartment after dinner was consumed with Roberto's jealousy over the waiter's advancements.

Roberto's issues with Becca's alluring attire and her playful banter became the center point of their relationship from that moment forward. Roberto proved himself to be insecure, insanely jealous and possessive. Becca began to feel smothered and after enduring the new Roberto for six incessant weeks after dinner at Jekyll and Hyde, she broke things off for the first time.

After another six weeks of phone calls, letters and singing telegrams; Roberto won her over enough to get a second chance.

(Unedited excerpt from the manuscript)

Finally my dish of revenge was ready to be eaten. I came up from behind Andrea and took hold of her head. Covering her mouth and nose with a chloroform laden rag, I crammed her into her car and shoved her unconscious body across the bucket seat of her forest-green Cutlass Supreme.

Settling in behind the wheel, I stole my friend's sister's car.

My car was waiting for me at the Valley Stream train station where I would make the switch after we played on the swing at the barn.

This was my last weekend at home and so far everything was going according to plan.

Earlier that week I had removed what I felt could be incriminating evidence from the Hollingsworth's barn. I left the wall shackles and overhead harness intact for my time with Andrea

They were easy enough to remove before I set the fire anyway, and I was determined to have another go on the swing.

I was a little concerned that I was expecting too much and would be disappointed by Andrea. I figured that it was going to be hard to top the amazing time I had with foxy-Roxie.

But, my little prankster Andrea didn't let me down. I attribute most of that to a well thought out plan and the lighter fluid. Plus, I had never fucked anyone on the rag before and it added some great visuals.

I think of her every time I'm with someone who is having their period. They always ask, "Do you mind"; and I honestly tell them no.

I feel like I'm stabbing them to death with my dick.

💣

Andrea awoke with wrists shackled to the wall and her knees strapped into the harness. I laid her out on a table so as not to put any undo pressure on her arms and legs while she finished her chloroform nap.

I figured she might as well be comfortable before she died. I was planning on taking my time with the barn's final victim.

As an added touch, I personalized the moment; something I carry on to this day whenever I'm given the opportunity. I remembered that Adam's family was never able to go see the Greatest Show on Earth. His sisters were afraid of the clowns.

What a pity; I love the circus.

💣

I was wearing a clown mask I picked up at Woolworths, and when Andrea saw me, I swear her eyes actually popped out of her head. It was one of the coolest things I've seen. They moved about a half inch forward and then recessed back in. No matter how hard I've tried, I haven't been able to duplicate that reaction.

Terror tears streamed out of Andrea's eyes and she begged me to stop.

The funny thing is I wasn't doing anything.

For the longest time I just stood there and watched her mind crumble. I was having a great time.

I finally understood that old saying, 'Less is more'.

The first time I fucked her I kept the clown mask on and remained silent. Even though she just hung there like a dead fish, the effect of ramming my cock into her bloody hole got me off quickly, and Andrea actually thought we were done.

She kept saying "okay...okay" and asked if she could go home now. I explained to her that she was home and I removed the mask with a musical TA-DA.

Now, she not only recognized me, she actually got an attitude; like I was going to be in big trouble.

I found it interesting that despite everything she had just been through, she was posturing herself like she was in a position of authority. I believe the bottle of lighter fluid and matches in my hand changed that position.

Andrea decided that it would be a good time to apologize for the little joke she had played on me with her sister.

I told her not to worry about it. I felt that we were even.

I sprayed a thin line of lighter fluid across Andrea's chest and she started jerking side to side while I held out the book of matches and lit one.

Great bodies ran in the Blackman family and Andrea's full, firm breasts giggling from side to side were rather stimulating. I was too busy getting aroused to notice that the match flame burned itself out just above my finger tips. I was ready for more and positioned myself back between her legs.

I sprayed a little more fluid onto Andrea's chest and flicked a lit match at her. I missed the lighter fluid but Andrea's body began jack hammering up and down on my shaft all the same. I rode with it until she stopped and then sprayed some more fluid on her and flicked another match.

Direct hit.

Blue flame danced across her chest in a zigzag pattern and she began jerking up and down hard on me. The flame went out quickly but left a red welt on her skin.

Crying and praying and pleading for her release, Andrea promised not to tell anyone if I let her go.

I told her okay and then sprayed a thin line of lighter fluid up her stomach, between her tits and onto her face. The fluid landed in her open mouth, went up her nose and into her eyes.

Screams and body gyrations provided the perfect symphony as I ignited the pool of fluid on her abdomen. Fire ran up the length of her body and wrapped over her face like a mask.

It was hard to keep her on me she was bucking so violently. I had to grab onto the harnesses chain just to stay onboard.

The flames extinguished fast again as the lighter fluid evaporated on her body. But her face ignited her hair which must have been doused in hair products and soon there was a little fire ball setting there between her shoulders.

As soon as I came I became aware of the stench and I had to get off. I dipped a bucket into the water basin and splashed it onto Andrea's charred head. The skin had bubbled and peeled away in most places and she looked like a bald-headed freak.

Her eyelids were gone revealing a cloudy white sightless orb glistening in each socket. Her lips had swelled and split and were still oozing puss and blood.

Smoke trails floated off her black and red skull like strands of hair defying gravity.

Not a very pretty sight and she still stunk. I unchained her as quickly as I could and dumped the barn's final playmate into the famous lye barrel.

Well Adam, at least you know what happened to your sister now; no need to thank me.

The following day I used what was left in the bottle of lighter fluid to start the blaze in the barn. I've never felt such a sense of loss before.

So many good times... so many fond memories... all going up in flames.

I stayed and watched until I heard the fire engines off in the distance.

'We don't need no water, let the motherfucker burn. Burn motherfucker; burn'.

Chapter 30

Becca stood in the archway of the Wiley Building's seventh floor and watched Roberto as he moved around the giant machine. Shirtless and sweating, he moved in harmony with the machine's hum. Gliding from station to station, turning a knob here, pushing a button there, Roberto had a grace and determination Becca hadn't noticed before.

Moving out of her view, Roberto disappeared behind the end of the press and did not emerge around the other side.

Becca shouted a hello that was consumed by the machine's constant droning.   Roberto had sounded pretty high strung when she had spoken to him on the phone, and who could blame him considering the note he had just found. Becca didn't want to take any chances of mistake in identity so she made a wide birth around the press to meet up with Roberto at the other end.

Roberto was standing with legs spread and hands on his hips in a stance that made Becca think of Superman, all he was missing was the cape billowing out from behind him. Roberto's gaze was transfixed on the rear end of the press. He turned his head as Becca approached and smiled.

"First one should be coming through any moment."

Becca moved next to him and stood in silence. Roberto reached his arm over across her back and gave her a slight tug into his side and thanked her for coming down.

Becca could sense a change in Roberto but elected to not comment on it yet.

A compression lever activated at Becca's feet making her jump.

The receiving tray came alive and rose off the ground to accept the finished product from the press. Yellow books with bold black lettering began churning out of the machine.

Roberto grabbed a copy, still warm in his hands, turned to Becca and stated with absolutely no expression; "I hope you have a plan, because I'm going to kill this motherfucker."

With the press running smoothly, Roberto loaded enough paper to print the next five thousand copies while he and Becca went downstairs to get something to eat and talk about their next moves to save Melina.

Sitting in the Starlight Diner on Third Ave between 38th and 39th Streets, Roberto ordered a stuffed southwest omelet in contrast to Becca's fruit cup and yogurt. Becca quickly rehashed the previous day's events, intentionally leaving out the part where she had met and agreed to a date with Mr. Christopher John.

Becca shared with Roberto that although she had uncovered the Madman's identity, he seemed to have staged his own death while at school in Ohio; leaving her right back to where she started.

Surprisingly, Roberto was not as devastated at the news as Becca had anticipated. Becca assumed that Roberto would have been distressed when he found out that Melina's whereabouts were still a mystery. However, once Roberto began sharing his progress in the production and distribution of the manuscript, Becca understood that he was still living in the fantasy assumption that Melina would be returned safely.

Becca leaned back into the red vinyl covered booth and sighed deeply. A large debate was going on in her head centered around two main topics. First, having arrived at a dead end in her attempts to find the Madman, Becca was seriously contemplating going to the authorities with the Madman's threat. Secondly, she wanted to tell Roberto about Christopher John; it was going to come up sooner or later, and she wanted it out in the open sooner, rather than later. Part of that debate though, was asking herself why she even cared what Roberto thought and what that might mean on a deeper level.

As if reading her mind, Roberto took the lead in the conversation about their next steps. Reaching across the table, brushing aside the empty plates that lingered, Roberto grabbed hold of Becca's hand and said, "First, I want to thank you for all you've done." He looked directly into her eyes and Becca thought for the second time that day, that there seemed to be something different about Roberto.

"I've done a lot of thinking lately, and I'll admit most of what I'm about to say solidified only in the past couple of hours…" Roberto paused as the waitress cleared away the empty plates and refilled his coffee cup. Becca indicated that she was fine when asked if she wanted more tea, and Roberto continued. "I still have faith that Melina will be set free once I get the manuscript on the shelves. At this rate, that should happen by Thursday, Friday at the latest."

Becca's facial expressions relayed her opinion on that matter but Roberto chose to ignore it, but added, "What choice do I really have?"

"You can go to the police." Becca dared saying preparing herself for Roberto's aggressive response that didn't come. Instead he said, "I know you think that is best, and I'm concerned about the terror attack that the Madman is mentioning as well. The last thing I want on my conscience is the blood of innocent people. Especially if there was something I could have done to prevent it from happening. But follow my thinking and tell me if you don't agree."

Becca was dumbfounded. Who was this person sitting across from her? In all the years she had known Roberto she had never seen him exude such a take charge attitude. Maybe this situation was the catalyst he needed in his life to start riding on top of the waves instead of being thrown around by them.

Continuing with his line of thought, Roberto raised the fingers on his right hand as he explained his points to Becca.

"The Madman wants the manuscript in the public's hands before anything is going to happen. He is taunting them with the challenge of uncovering his plot prior to actually committing the atrocity. Since the police will have access to the manuscript at the exact moment it hits the bookshelves, it is safe to assume he doesn't care if they have it then. He is only holding my sister to insure that the manuscript gets published and distributed. Once I do that, he doesn't need Melina anymore; and she is safe."

Roberto paused giving Becca an opportunity to disagree; when she didn't he continued. "Now let's look at the timing. The madman gave me two weeks to get the manuscript out. I'm doing it in one. I think it is a safe guess that part of the Madman's game is the panic and fear he will be instilling in the public, and he is going to want to savor and enjoy that. I don't think a planned attack will occur anytime sooner than the beginning of October and possibly later."

Roberto emptied his coffee cup just as the waitress was making her rounds and it was instantly refilled. Becca just sat and watched as Roberto added a small dollop of cream and stirred the brew with a stained spoon.

Becca was impressed with his logic and so far had nothing to add.

"If you…" Roberto started and then changed to, "If we, go to the police now, all that we are going to accomplish is signing my sister's death warrant; and possibly worse. We are being watched by this maniac. He proved that point last night at my office building. If we don't do what he has asked, we both could end up in his next book."

That was a startling revelation to Becca and she uncomfortably looked around the diner. A man was staring at her over his shoulder from the counter chairs, upon being seen he quickly turned back to his meal. Shivers ran down Becca's spine. She turned and noticed another man standing on the sidewalk, hands cupped over his eyes as he pressed against the diner's window looking in. His eyes swept over her before he turned and walked away.

Becca didn't need this shit; that thought had never crossed her mind when she was out looking for the Madman yesterday. She was the cat not the mouse. Now she felt like the mouse and there was a big angry cat walking around her hole.

Roberto could see the change in Becca's attitude and had a pretty good idea of what had happened. Becca, for as long as he had known her, was always someone to jump in with both feet, very focused with a pinpoint view of a situation.

Life was straight up, black or white to Becca. No shades of grey in that girl's world. It was one of the things that attracted him to her. Roberto also knew that Becca could be prone to moments of self-doubt and he wanted to keep her focused.

Earlier when he was listening to Becca tell him about coming to a dead end while tracking the Madman, Roberto thought about something he had read in the manuscript and wanted Becca to check it out.

Roberto's voice dropped to a whisper and he leaned into the table, his stare burrowing into Becca eyes when he stated; "I want my sister back; and then I want to kill this man. I want to wrap my hands around his throat and choke the miserable life from his body." Becca's gaze slowly regained their focus as Roberto further explained his theory about the Madman and why he wanted her to make another trip to Long Island that day.

(Unedited excerpt from the manuscript)

Okay, you faceless fucks, where were we?

Ohio University was an absolute playground. I got to meet and kill people from all over the world.

My favorite part of Ohio was the vast landscape. OU is located in Athens, which is at the south eastern end of the state. Not very far from West Virginia, the terrain is heavily wooded and sits within the Allegheny Mountain's plateau.

If you listen closely you can hear the beginning of *Dueling Banjos.*

During my stay at OU, which only lasted 2 years; I became very familiar with an area of woods to be found off the South Green of OU's campus. A dense forest situated between Township Highway 402 and State Routes 104 and 83. The area was cordoned off with "Danger! No Trespassing!" signs all around and was therefore virtually uninhabited.

I used the land for a new thrill game I devised. My own style of fishing, a game of catch and release where I would lure my prey into the woods, have my initial fun with them and then let them escape; sort of.

My initial fun usually entailed bondage, rape, torture and drugging. Not necessarily in that order, and not everyone was lucky enough to experience the total package.

The game began in what I referred to as Home-base. Not as comfortable as my barn; but it was quite adequate.

The area was designated a high-risk hazard zone due to the unmapped remnants of the old Snow Fork Coal Mine labyrinth. The old coal mine stretched down from Nelsonville, an area about 7 miles northwest of Athens. In contrast, the Nelsonville area of the mine was well mapped and secured.

I stumbled upon Snow Fork when I was on a reconnaissance mission of OU and the surrounding area; I needed a new way to dispose of the bodies when I was finished playing with them and Old Man's Cave in Hocking Hills was too popular of a location to use comfortably. Although, I believe my roommate would have enjoyed the company. Even the dead get lonely.

I'll have to write that song one day. It can be the opening track for the 'You're dead but still a loser' album by Stabby McStaberson.

💣

After I left home and the sanctity of the Hollingsworth's party barn, I didn't have the same resources available to me.

That is definitely the most difficult thing about relocating. You have to figure out where your new favorite shops are going to be, which gas station is going to get your business, where are you going to stop for your morning cup of coffee, how you are going to dispose of the corpses... little things like that.

But life is all about adjusting.

Making due with what you've got.

Learning to adapt.

Being able to chuck and jive.

I am very fortunate: I can become one with nature, I get in tune with my higher self, I trust in the process... I have faith.

Unlike you faceless fucks; my faith isn't blind.

I've been shown the truth.

I have always known that I am being guided on my journey by my Creator.

I am blessed.

The forces of the universe will not allow me to go astray until my task on this plane of existence is complete. I will be led to the answers of my asked questions. I will be given the assistance and support and protection I deserve and require.

💣

Home-base was an abandoned mineshaft entryway set dead center in the woods. No pun intended.

Snow Fork coal mine traversed southeast from Nelsonville; running underground below the town of Athens and the campus of Ohio University. Several minor tributaries of the mine ended within the wooded area behind the South Green.

This little stretch of paradise was completely unmapped by the ODNR (Ohio Department of Natural Resources) and was therefore designated as "indefinitely quarantined".

A perfect outdoor playground protected from prying eyes.

The entryway was rather large and fully enclosed. From the outside it looked like a rundown shack leaning against a small hill. Once inside though, the area opened up nicely, about 200 square feet; plenty of room to play.

The rear wall was actually the hillside, and it was also the home of a poorly covered mineshaft. I remember an eerie howl crept up on a constant breeze that rose out of the ground between the rotting boards.

The sound made me feel like I was performing for an audience of tortured souls trapped within the earth.

With every thrust, with every stab, with every torment I inflicted on the participants in my 'Catch and Release' game; I could hear the howling growing in intensity, savoring the pain and the agony and the fear.

I would feed it as I emptied the life force from my victims. Depleting their energy and sharing it with the forces of Nature and the Universe.

There was so much about it that reminded me of the Hollingsworth's Barn that I truly felt at home.

I was able to secure the game's participants into various positions depending on my mood. I had a variety of shackles and harnesses secured to the walls in addition to several tent spikes I had bored into the ground.

I skillfully utilized ropes and pulleys, broken glass and sandpaper, a variety of blunt objects and of course the crowd's favorite; my very own cock of redemption.

There was nothing better than forcing myself down the throat of someone convulsing and gasping for air as their trachea constricted around me.

So many memories and so little time to share them with you...

💣

I would get such a charge from the terror I was able to instill.

In all my travels and other experiences, I've never found anything that got me so turned on, or gave me such a feeling of empowerment. In retrospect, the liquid acid I dosed them with probably had a lot to do with the extreme terror they exuded; and people say that drugs are bad.

There were so many people that would come down to Athens to experience the party atmosphere that Ohio University had a reputation for that I had no trouble at all finding a constant stream of participants eager to play my game. By not limiting myself to the students and teachers I never ran into the problem of creating suspicion and was able to play almost every weekend. I quickly realized that the majority of the young co-eds that came to party at OU from the outlying towns didn't exactly tell their parents where they were going for the weekend.

It was almost too easy to get a girl to come with me so I created a minor selection process just to make it slightly challenging. I realized that several of my earlier experiences were with individuals that shared a common first letter in their names. Amanda, my first; Angela, my beautiful Cherokee princess; and Andrea, that stupid fucking bitch and the barn's last.

Anyway, I decided that I was going to pull girls into the woods based on their first names. After I had established a few trial runs with randomly named participants, and honestly, I don't remember their names. Not that they weren't important to me; because they all were, they each still have a very special place in my heart. I can see all of their faces, the unique curves of their breasts, the slender curves of their waists and hips, the smalls of their backs, and the terror in their eyes.

When I close my eyes, I can still taste them on my lips and smell their fear.

I've loved them all for what they have given me.

None of them will ever be forgotten.

Just because you are all faceless does not mean I am heartless.

I do remember the other names, the ones I picked because of their names. I skipped the letter A out of respect. Starting with B, I took 25 ladies into the woods and had my way with them. They either came willingly, at the promise of a free high, or they arrived unconscious thanks to Captain Chloroform. No matter how they ended up in the woods, it was always a good time.

One of the aspects of 'Catch and Release' I enjoyed most was the unknown element. Although I had a primary plan, a basic outline of the game, I never knew which way my mind would take me. On a few occasions I became so engrossed in the rape and torture element of the game that I didn't realize I had killed my participant before I could release them.

Not that it was a big deal, there was always next weekend, but I think I missed out.

At those times I seemed to be operating outside of myself; doing things that I couldn't remember doing while in the moment.

For example, when I took Frieda with me into the woods, I found myself with both hands grasping the sides of her head. I had cut a small hole in her throat and was literally fucking her brains out. My thumbs were using her eye sockets for leverage as I thrust her head back and forth over my cock. Don't misunderstand me, a warm hole is a warm hole, and I was there in the moment when I came inside her head; my point is that I don't remember what actually transpired prior to me sticking my dick in her neck.

Reflecting back on those times, I think I might have attained a higher spiritual plane and been at one with my Creator.

There really is no other explanation.

For the most part, during a game of 'Catch and Release' I would set them free after some initial getting-to-know-you time.

Disoriented from either loss of blood, liquid acid drops in the eyes, a few broken bones and foreign objects inserted in places that are usually for exiting only; who knows, it could have been any number of things and probably a combination of several. I still enjoyed playing with lighter fluid and matches and most of all I loved having my dick inside these faceless participants while we enjoyed some of the game's other elements. You just can't duplicate the type of thrusting on your cock that you can get from a good torture session.

At any rate, after 'Catch' came 'Release'. I would allow the participant an opportunity to experience a false sense of escape. These episodes worked best when I would tell them I'd be back in an hour and warn them not to go anywhere. Like clockwork, I could rely on them to wait about five minutes and then start working on their restraints.

So predictable.

Obviously they were able to free themselves and once they realized their clothes were nowhere to be found they took off naked. Running aimlessly in desperate hopes of freedom and survival, my ladies would never cease to entertain me with their different reactions to escape. Some would be crying, some would be laughing, some would move with quiet stealth; and yet all would break down into a panicked run when they heard my approach.

I enjoyed the same varied liberties with the 'release' part of the show as I did with the 'catch' process. A few of the participants were corralled into preset entanglements of barbed wire. This was fun; they would get themselves so tangled and cut up, they literally could not move without fucking themselves up real bad. 9 out of 10 times they would ask for my help as I stood there watching.

Interesting how still and trusting someone can become when they have no choice.

I would track down others and beat them senseless.

Maybe fuck them again, not always. After that, I'd hide off in the dark and wait for them to regain consciousness. As soon as they were up on their feet, I'd let them go a little way and then jump them again. I'd have them so unsettled and confused they were easy to steer around back to Home-base.

In those instances I could actually see their inner strength crumble with defeat as the realization of their futile escape became their final reality.

All in all I learned more about human psychology in the woods than I did in the 12 credit hours I took in Porter Hall.

💣

I know you're curious and actually I want to see if I can still do it too... Brooke, Colleen, Dolores, Eve, Frieda, Gloria, Helen, Iris, Jacqueline, Kayla, Lucy, Megan, Naomi, Olivia, Pam, Queenie, Robin, Stephanie, Tara, Ursula, Valerie, Wendy, Xui Mei, Yvette and Zoe.

💣

In maintaining the truthful manner in which I have been sharing my accomplishments with you faceless fucks; which is so much more than you deserve.

I need to tell you that Queenie was taken out of rotation.

I had been wondering how certain letters were going to play out and Q was one of those I thought I might have to skip. But, as fate had it, yet once again, I met a beautiful dark-skinned goddess from Atlanta, Georgia right after I checked off the letter K and couldn't risk waiting for her proper turn since she was just visiting some friends.

Ursula was another one I took some liberties with. After searching all Thursday and Friday night for someone with a name that began with U, I finally settled on a middle name.

I think she said it was her grandmother's.

Yvette and Zoe were students; I had met both of them early on in the game and got their phone numbers to call on when their turns came due.

Everyone else was just fortunate enough to be at the right place on the right day at the right time.

You would think that X was going to be difficult as well until you stumble upon the roster for the Chinese-American Cultural Society Annual Dance.

Just between you and me, I loved fucking Xui Mei. Just sticking my cock into her seemed like I was torturing her. She screamed and bled so much I thought she was having her period.

I grabbed a few of her friends over the next several months after I finished off the alphabet and it was always the same thing. Screaming and blood; I was in heaven, so to speak. It seemed that I had uncovered a clan of Asian virgins delivered to Ohio just for me.

What are the odds?

Chapter 31

Melina had made tremendous progress prying out large shards of wood from behind the metal plate that was bolted into the wall. After almost getting caught in the act, she now carefully regulated the times in which she continued her excavating.

Her captor seemed to be in exceptionally good moods the last two days when he came to check on her and deliver her food. He would sit in his chair and whistle a variety of tunes that reminded Melina of Disney movies or maybe cartoons, she couldn't exactly place the songs but enjoyed the change in atmosphere.

"Stand up; I want to look at you."

Melina almost choked on the meat she was chewing. Her captor had never spoken to her before. All of the rules she had learned came from doing things the wrong way and being corrected by the whip. She had learned fast, and more than a week had passed since the last unexpected crack of the whip tore open her tender flesh.

Melina stood quickly.

"Turn around." The command came from the darkness in front of her.

Melina slowly turned completely around. Feeling vulnerable, captured in the beam of the high-powered light, Melina's arms unconsciously covered her exposed breasts.

"Don't."

Melina instantly dropped her hands to her sides and prepared her body for the onslaught of the whip.

It never came.

Standing naked before her captor Melina could hear rustling sounds as something was being removed from what sounded like a paper bag.

Feeling her heart pounding in her chest and reverberating in her eardrums, Melina waited, frozen, not breathing, anticipating the worst.

A shape came lofting out of the darkness and into the light. Instinctively, Melina gasped and cowered backwards as the brown paper bag landed and upended her empty metal food bowl.

Dark laughter emanated out of the darkness.

Melina cautiously crept forward to inspect the bag's contents.

Her skin crawled awaiting to be flayed open at any moment. Half-expecting the searing pain and crack of the whip she had become accustomed to receive when a new element of behavior was being taught.

Again, it never came.

The bag contained a sixteen-ounce bottle of water, a bar of Ivory soap, a small washrag, an array of travel-size items, a toothbrush, toothpaste, shampoo, and lastly a package of Wash n' Wipe towelettes.

"Clean yourself up."

Melina hesitated as she was overwhelmed with the possibilities of what this gesture might mean. First she thought that this ordeal was finally over and she was going to be set free.

She was no longer concerned about taking revenge and only envisioned herself outside in the sun.

Finally free from her chains and torture.

Then her mind took that notion and flipped it upside down and inside out.

Melina's heart was encased within a new darkness. A black shrouded fear, denser than anything she had adapted to in the past two weeks.

Melina was positive she was being prepared for death.

Fear wrapped her in its cold embrace and she stood motionless with one arm extended inside the paper bag.

"I said clean up." The words came at her through clenched teeth.

A shiver scurried down Melina's spine.

She heard the chair jut backwards on the dirt floor and knew the whip was being taken down from its perch on the wall.

After a quick stop back at her apartment on 69th Street where she changed her clothes and packed up her laptop; Becca was back on the road by 11:30.

Regretfully she pulled out of her prime parking spot leaving it vacant for the next lucky New Yorker to hunker down in until Tuesday.

Wondering to herself where she was going to find a parking spot later, especially on a Sunday, Becca cursed and gave the finger to a cab driver who intentionally made it difficult for her to merge into traffic.

So far Becca was having a wonderful day.

Hot tea in her face, a psychopathic killer possibly stalking her, the loss of a prime parking space; and now, Sunday traffic out of the city.

Becca fought her way to the FDR and headed south to the 59th Street Bridge into Queens. She planned on taking the city streets most of the way to avoid the congestion on the freeways.

Taking Queens Blvd all the way to the Van Wyck Expressway; Becca opened up her laptop on the passenger's seat and booted up.

Using her wireless connection, Becca logged into SNIPH and located the cemetery where Jack Thomas was supposedly buried. Not being very surprised to find that the Madman was buried on grounds that were originally owned by the Hollingsworths, Becca set a course for the Rockville Cemetery on Merrick Road. She could have saved herself a trip if she had known about this yesterday. The cemetery was situated less than two miles from where she had met Mr. Wonderful at the Panda Bear Farm facility.

The thought of Christopher John put a smile on Becca's face. His chiseled features, his jet-black hair and his grey-blue eyes had a power that illuminated the bleak day she was experiencing.

Becca soon found herself fantasizing. Seeing him thrusting between her legs, sweat glistening on his chest, muscles rippling as he drove himself deep into her wetness. Imagining that she was arching her back and clawing at the sheets of her bed as they climaxed in unison.

"Holy shit", Becca said aloud as she came out of her reverie. She wasn't even seeing the road ahead of her, yet she appeared to have exited where she was supposed to.

Repositioning herself on the seat, feeling the stickiness between her legs where she had ruined her underwear, Becca headed down Peninsula Blvd to Lynbrook Ave until she turned left onto Merrick and parked in front of the Rockville Cemetery.

Roberto's idea was to interview Brendon and Kenny Thomas, the Madman's brothers. Becca's first reaction was that it was a ludicrous notion and that there was no pretense to conduct an interview. What was she supposed to do? Just walk up to these strangers and say, "Hi, I'd like to ask you a few questions about your brother who died twenty-eight years ago."

Roberto explained that he had a gut feeling about this and that she of all people would find a way to get them to open up. She knew he was right and after listening to him, agreed that some information might be obtained from the brothers.

Becca had learned that Roberto reread the manuscript while the first print run was laboring through the press. He had shared with Becca that he needed to read it through a 'different set of eyes' as he had called them. Roberto said that he read the manuscript like a detective would; like she would.

At the time the compliment made her blush although Roberto didn't notice.

The Madman did mention early on in his manuscript two points that had Roberto thinking that some degree of contact might have been maintained throughout the years. Roberto felt the Madman expressed a quality of loss when he talked about being separated from his brothers due to the split-schedule in high school.

Secondly, the Madman pointed out that he paid respects, in his own way, to Amanda Farber's memorial when he made visits to his brothers. This was the key in Roberto's mind that the brother's knew something, even if they weren't completely aware of the information they possessed.

If nothing else, it was a lead that kept them moving forward.

Becca searched for a while before she stumbled upon the gravesite. Cemeteries don't have directories posted at the entrance like your local shopping mall. Becca mused to herself that maybe it wouldn't be such a bad idea.

People could be buried by category.

Loving Parents on the first floor, Juniors and Misses up the escalator past the Music and Book Lovers Section, Grandparents close to the entrances and bathrooms, and of course Psychopathic Madman in the corner next to Victoria's Secret.

Becca was pleased with the change of attitude her thoughts of Christopher John had bestowed upon her. She was truly looking forward to their date Monday evening. She caught herself daydreaming again and almost missed the tombstone that marked her destination.

Hidden in the far northwest corner of the Rockville Cemetery, separated from the natural flow of the surrounding headstones and set into the ground in what appeared to be a deliberate non-perpendicular angle. The tombstone of Jack Thomas was shrouded by the overhanging branches of a Weeping Willow tree.

Cautiously moving closer, Becca read the epitaph.

JACK MARTIN THOMAS
It's the Little Things
Born, June 2, 1962
Died, September 13, 1980

A chill wrapped its hand around her soul and she began to shiver in the shadows.

Despite the blazing August sun, nothing was able to chase away the shivers that wracked her entire frame.

Becca hurried back to her car and turned on the heater.

Similar to what she experienced at the diner, an irrational panic embedded itself in her mind. With eyes wide, Becca surveyed the landscape of the Rockville Cemetery and then the sidewalks up and down Merrick Road.

Although no one was in sight, Becca was sure she was being watched.

(Unedited excerpt from the manuscript)

One of the greatest lessons I've learned in life is that: You are not who you think you are; rather, you are who you are perceived to be.

If you have the ability to wrap your mind around what that truly means, you will discover that anything is possible. There can be no limitations imposed upon you.

Using that concept as a basic premise, I was able to graduate from Ohio University without having to waste my time actually graduating from Ohio University.

After 2 years and 37 murders, I moved back to the east coast where I interviewed with a Brooklyn based toy company.

I presented myself as the greatest commodity since sliced bread and easily established myself as the company's new Director of Far-East Operations.

While in Ohio, I had acquired quite the appetite for Chinese food and was determined to get a job that delivered me directly to Asia's doorstep.

For one and a half years, all on the company's dime, I was blessed with the opportunity to savor the local delicacies and experience the subtle nuances between them.

My business dealings took me through Taiwan, Hong Kong, China, Korea, the Philippines and Thailand; so many women, so many screams, so much blood.

I was having such a good time.

The added thump-thump of being in a foreign land was exhilarating.

I felt untouchable.

That was until I was approached by a local who sat down next to me at the bar in the basement of the Sheraton Hotel and said, "I've been watching you. I know what you've been doing."

Chapter 32

As the miles between Becca and the gravesite of Jack Thomas increased, the ridiculous notion that she was being observed decreased.

Becca dismissed the irrational fear by convincing herself that it was nothing more than the eerie design of the Madman's grave. The slight off-centered tilt of the headstone and the Willow Tree's tendrilous shadows were two aspects; however, the fact that Jack Thomas wasn't actually buried there, was the main contributor to her unease.

Who really was buried there beneath the shadows?

Someone was laid to rest in the corner of the Rockville Cemetery under the name of Jack Thomas; but it definitely wasn't Jack.

Becca was positive of that.

Becca knew, in concept, who was buried there. It was Jack's unfortunate roommate from Ohio University. But in all her searches with SNIPH and other sources, Becca wasn't able to uncover a name. Whoever Jack Thomas had murdered in his place was not missed and raised no eyebrows of suspicion.

It was time to put an end to the vicious existence of Jack Thomas and Becca was looking forward to having a hand in doing just that.

After the previous day's escapades that yielded one dead-end after another, Becca had been deflated in her efforts to uncover the Madman's identity. Roberto's drive and focus during breakfast had reenergized her at a point where she was almost ready to turn the manuscript over to the authorities.

Feeling invigorated, Becca could now see the real possibility of accomplishing one of three things. Maybe even, score a hat trick in the process.

Save Melina. Save the World. Save her career.

Jack's brothers lived relatively close to one another. Kenny and his wife Kyra lived in the town of Roslyn with their two children, Ryan and Erin. Meanwhile, Brendon and his wife Ruby along their three children, the twins Brad and Alex plus their youngest daughter Catherine, lived only two and half miles away in Old Westbury.

It's amazing how much information could be obtained in SNIPH even though it wasn't pertinent to your quest. Becca probably would be able to find out when Ruby had her last Pap smear if she was interested.

Driving due north from the Rockville Cemetery up Peninsula Blvd. Merging onto Clinton Street in Hempstead and following the road as it became Glen Cove Road north of Old Country Road in Westbury; Becca proceeded to Brendon's house first.

Twenty-five minutes after she was shivering in the August sun, Becca's blue Nissan Maxima was turning onto Winsor Drive in Old Westbury.

Loaded with the age old premise that, '*It is always best to hide behind the truth*'; a saying that her father had instilled in her when she was young, Becca stepped out of the car to the sounds of children playing.

(Unedited excerpt from the manuscript)

I was in mid-swallow and almost choked to death as the Heineken diverted down the wrong pipe.

The elderly Chinese man to my left waited patiently for me to get my breathing back under control before he continued; "I think we should take a walk. Don't you?"

My initial reaction to run was quickly diffused when I looked into the old man's eyes.

There was something there that said not to worry.

I don't expect you faceless fucks to understand what passed unspoken between us in that instant.

How could you?

You and your culture are not developed enough to even scratch at the surface.

For the next six years I had all of my 'clean up' work taken care of for me.

I resigned as the Director of Far-East Operations and moved to Hong Kong on a permanent basis. I established my own company called The Paper Airplane; however, I maintained contact and continued to do business with the Brooklyn toy company that gave me my start in the Orient.

Nobody can ever say that I don't appreciate those that have taken care of me during my career development.

I hired a staff of 22 individuals and expanded my client base to several US based manufacturers. My company dealt in a wide variety of products from electronics to Halloween goods.

I wouldn't be surprised if some of you reading this have bought something from me in the past.

I was nicknamed 'The Farmer'; at least that was the closest English translation from the Cantonese.

In Thailand they called me something else that translated to 'Harvester of Souls'.

That was my favorite.

The affiliation I formed with a few Asian associates was quite simple. There was always a high demand for fresh organs on the Asian Black Market; especially white meat, and I had the ability to deliver the products in demand.

In return for providing top quality goods; I was well compensated and no longer had to concern myself with the clean-up and disposal end of the business.

I had several apartments established under alias names in many parts of town. So that, no matter where I was conducting business, I always had a place to hang my hat. Among other things.

It was a perfect working relationship. Everyone was getting what they wanted until I butchered the wrong girl.

💣

Chapter 33

There were sounds of laughter and children coming from the backyard of Brendon Thomas's house.

Becca hoped this interaction went well. The last thing she wanted to do was ruin a family's Sunday.

The driveway was on the side of the house and Becca hoped that someone would have seen her arrive. When nobody came to inspect the strange car that had arrived, Becca decided that it would be inappropriate to use the gate that led to the backyard; so, she followed the inlaid stone walkway through the front yard towards the front door instead.

The door opened almost immediately and Becca was warmly greeted by a dark skinned woman who instructed Becca that the Mister and Misses were in the backyard.

Explaining that she wasn't expected and wished to just have a brief word with Mr. Thomas, Becca was left standing in the archway of the open door while the Thomas's house-assistant disappeared from the front foyer.

The house was gorgeous. From where Becca stood she could see that someone, probably Ruby, had impeccable taste for the finer things in life.

Dark, rich woods accented by stunning chandeliers peaked out of the dining room to her left. Soft, luxurious leather sofas, nestled in dense plush carpeting, beckoned a warm invitation into the living room situated to her right. Straight ahead, Italian granite countertops set beneath white maple cabinetry could be seen accenting the kitchen where the Thomas's house-assistant reappeared and indicated that Becca should follow her.

Walking through a kitchen that had more square footage than her Manhattan apartment, Becca was led out sliding glass doors onto a raised deck that overlooked the Thomas's backyard.

Brendon Thomas stood manning the enormous stainless steel Grand Turbo 52" grill. He was operating with the fluid motions of a professional short order cook. Flipping steaks, turning hotdogs and chicken wings, searing hamburgers and rotating corn, Brendon appeared to have enough food cooking for ten times the amount of people Becca saw in the backyard.

"I'll be right with you." Brendon spoke into the grill and Becca wasn't sure if he was talking to her or his meat.

Closing the lid on the massive grill, Brendon wiped the sweat from his brow with his forearm and then used a towel that was lying on the table to dry his hands and extended the right towards Becca.

"Hi, I'm Brendon Thomas. Clara said you wanted to talk to me about a family matter. What's this all about?"

Although Becca had decided that she was going for the direct approach she found herself using her standard opening; particularly when talking to men.

"I was hoping you could help me." Two quick bats of the eyes, a demure look down, eye contact with raised eyebrows and then wait.

Becca was always pleasantly surprised when she could actually see the change in a man's demeanor with this approach. Nine out of ten times, the man's chest would puff out a little, his voice would deepen slightly and he would wear a half-cocked smile on his face as he responded.

"I'll do my best." Brendon's reply came out in a somewhat deeper register than before.

As if in response to her husband's increase in testosterone levels without her being present; Ruby gracefully ascended the deck and stood by Brendon's side.

Ruby was stunning and in incredible shape for a mother of three. Long dark brown hair flowing just past her shoulders bounced as she wrapped her arm around her husband's waist and addressed Becca.

First speaking to Brendon, Ruby said, "I didn't know we were having company, honey." Ruby's eyes then turned and surveyed Becca from head to toe before she commented without any pleasantries; "I'm not sure if my swim suits will fit you if you planned on taking a swim."

'Holy shit; what a bitch.' Becca thought to herself. She had encountered many women like Ruby in her lifetime. Something about that silver spoon must leave a bad taste in your mouth as it forces you to look down your nose at people.

"Actually sweetheart," Brendon began, sliding himself away from Ruby's grasp; "Clara said Ms…"

"Willis; Becca Willis, I'm with the New York Post."

As Becca fished in her satchel for her notepad and a business card, Brendon pulled out one of the deck chairs from beneath the table and motioned for Becca to have a seat.

"Hang on. Let me turn down the grill." Brendon said as he accepted Becca's card.

Ruby just stood with arms crossed as she watched Brendon adjust six of the eight dials on the Grand Turbo and then join Becca at the table.

"Have a sweet Seatheart." Brendon misspoke to Ruby as he indicated the chair to his right.

Ruby elected to stand between Becca and Brendon instead and said, "No. I'm fine. I need to keep an eye on the children thank you.

Becca glanced over the deck's railing and saw another couple out on the lawn surrounded by five kids all playing a game of duck-duck-goose. They definitely appeared in need of Ruby's supervision.

Duck-duck-goose was claiming lives allover the country. It was becoming a raging epidemic.

"Where are my manners? Would you care for something to drink?" Brendon's exaggerated gesture, like he just remembered he could have had a V-8, did not bode well with Ruby as she sneered openly at him.

Not giving Becca a chance to respond to Brendon's inquiry; Ruby demanded, "I'm sorry; I may have missed it; but, why are we being honored with your presence today?"

This was it.

The moment of truth.

Time to lay the cards on the table.

Diving right in without testing the water, Becca turned to Brendon and said; "Brendon, I have reason to believe that your brother Jack is still alive."

Becca held her breath as Brendon and Ruby exchanged looks. Brendon's hands went to his face as Ruby's hands went to her hips.

Ruby rolled her eyes and what came out of her mouth was not even on Becca's remote possibility list of responses.

"Not this again."

Chapter 34

Melina began washing herself and prayed that she would not feel the sting of the bullwhip.

Moistening the washcloth with the bottled water and lathering up the bar of Ivory soap, she began scrubbing away at two weeks worth of dried dirt, sweat and fear from her body.

Although she could not see him because of the 1000-watt floodlights that stood atop tripods; Melina could envision her captor settling back down into a director's style chair. Her enhanced sense of hearing actually 'felt' the canvas cloth stretch beneath his weight.

Melina heard the whip drop out of his hand and land in a cloud of dust on the floor to his right. Relaxing slightly as the threat of her skin being flayed open diminished, Melina continued to ponder where this change of events was going to lead.   Pouring the water sparingly over her head, dampening her long black hair, Melina twisted off the cap on the travel sized bottle of Johnson's Baby Shampoo.

A small dollop in her hand worked into a full froth of suds in her dirty hair.

Melina had always been a lather and rinse shampooer. But, given the amount of grime that had accumulated in her hair since her last shower; she definitely required the full use of the instructions. This was absolutely a lather, rinse and repeat day.

Melina closed her eyes and tuned in to her heightened senses. Her sense of touch and hearing were like fine tuned instruments.

Sounds entered her ears in high definition on distinct audio tracks; her nails scratching back and forth on her scalp, the shampoo bubbles crackling and popping in her hair, the overhead hum from the commercial lighting and the subtle creaks of the canvas chair in front of her.

Textures in subtleties she never imagined stimulated her skin as she felt the slightest change in the air around her. Her bare feet on the cold earth felt even the smallest pebble as she shifted her weight from left to right.

With her eyes closed she could see beyond the blinding light.

Vibrations emanated off every wall and out of every corner illuminating all they touched. A picture painted within Melina's mind as vivid and as real as if it were taken with a camera.

Melina had a clear image of her captor sitting in his director's chair. Positioned slightly off center and angled with one arm slung across the back. His gaze fixated on her while she bathed herself.

He slid a hand into his waistband.

Turning to face him, Melina brought her soapy hands down from her hair and lathered her breasts. Moving her hands in slow circular motions over her nipples she felt herself becoming aroused.

Despite her initial revulsion at what she was doing she couldn't stop.

She was enjoying turning him on.

Melina watched as he unbuckled his jeans and unzipped his fly. Grabbing hold of his enormous penis he stroked it up and down. All the while, he never took his eyes off of her. Sliding her soapy hands down her stomach, Melina slid two of her own fingers inside herself and gently rubbed as she watched him stroke himself faster.

One hand inside of herself, one pinching at her nipple, Melina's body quivered as she climaxed.

Her body lurched forward and she almost lost her balance.

Melina's heightened sensitivity released endorphins into her body and she felt like she was floating.

With eyes still closed and hands still gently caressing her body, she watched as her captor brought himself to fulfillment. White semen spouted in high arcs from the end of his penis and Melina found herself wanting to rub the warm spew all over her body.

"Finish up. I have something to show you."

The deep voice brought Melina out of her trance and she questioned if any of it had actually happened.

The bright lights bore down on her and she could see nothing beyond their glare.

Looking down at herself she was covered in spotty patches of soap suds. Using the remainder of the water in the bottle Melina quickly rinsed out her hair and toweled off with the small washrag.

Standing naked and feeling exposed and defenseless, Melina involuntarily crossed her arms across her breasts before she realized she put herself in peril of being whipped.

She had been told not to do that.

(Unedited excerpt from the manuscript)

They were coming to kill me.

Fortunately I had an extra special relationship with the wife of one of my associates; a young and beautiful girl from the Shenzhen province of Guangdong, named Mei Ling.

It seems I had grabbed the wrong piece of white meat from a disco in Wanchai on Lockhart Rd. called Neptune's. Usually you didn't find many tourists there. Neptune's was primarily a local hangout for Amahs and the girls that worked the hooker bars.

Anyway, after literally fucking this girl to death, I put in my standard call for room service. I envision everything on their end went along just fine. Like always, I left the body parts undisturbed as requested, although I recall I got a little creative with a box cutter on this one.

Which was fine; as long as I left the vital organs intact for harvesting, I was given free range to do whatever I desired.

It wasn't until the next day that all hell broke loose.

💣

Mei Ling gave me a heads up regarding the problem I had created.

Apparently the blond from Neptune's who I had turned into human confetti after coercing back to my apartment that previous evening; was the daughter of my associate's client.

Can you imagine the embarrassment my associate faced when he went to deliver the kidneys?

It's almost funny when you think about it. Picture yourself standing there with pieces of the guy's daughter in a cooler as he is showing you a picture of her and asking for your help in locating her.

According to Mei Ling, her husband didn't find it very humorous and ordered that I be eliminated.

Another valuable lesson I've learned in life is that a good offense is a strong defense; so I turned myself in to the Royal Hong Kong Police. It was a risky move on my part but it insured my safety. It is difficult to make someone disappear when they have brought themselves to the attention of the authorities.

💣

I spent the next 15 hours in the RHKP station in Tsim Sha Tsui. I never spent a second behind bars although I was fingerprinted and photographed.

My associates visited me under the pretense of being my legal council and offered me a deal I couldn't refuse. I was given the option of leaving Hong Kong immediately or getting killed.

I chose to leave.

For my silence regarding any activities I may have been involved in while I resided in Hong Kong, my associates arranged for my timely release from police custody.

To satisfy the press and any other onlookers; I was charged and fined with the minor crimes of wounding, as well as possession of illegal ninja weaponry.

Could have been worse.

💣

Chapter 35

Still trying to wrap her head around the response she had received to the statement that Jack Thomas might still be alive after twenty-eight years, Becca leaned back in her chair.

Ruby wanted nothing to do with the conversation and apparently that outweighed any catty jealousy she had felt earlier. Ruby marched herself down the wooden deck steps, all the while muttering to herself. Becca overheard a few choice words but could not make out the exact content. It was obvious though that this was a touchy subject in the Thomas household.

Becca was eager to find out why.

Turning to Brendon, Becca said "I'm guessing this has been discussed before. Do you mind if I…"

Leaning back in his chair, arms cradling the back of his head as he looked skyward, Brendon interrupted Becca. "Let's wait for my brother Kenny. He should be up here any moment."

Confused, Becca peered over the deck's railing down into the lush yard below. Ruby was slightly bent at the waist, hands still on her hips as she spoke to the other couple seated amongst the playing children.

As if choreographed, all three heads turned in unison and stared up at Becca.

The gentleman rose from his position on the blanket and began walking towards the house as the two women put their heads together and continued talking. Becca could feel their cold stare as their heads shook back and forth.

"Kenny, this is Becca Willis; a reporter from the Post."

Becca stood as Brendon introduced her to Kenny as he came up the steps to the deck with a Corona in his hand.

Becca couldn't believe her luck at having both brothers together.

"I told you he was alive." Kenny stated to Brendon in that, as a matter of fact tone.

"We'll see." Brendon responded; "Nobody has proven anything. Even Ms. Willis used the term 'reason to believe'; not 'I have evidence'."

Kenny sat down as Brendon moved to his right into the seat he had originally offered to Ruby. An awkward moment of silence engulfed the table as the two brothers stared at Becca waiting for her to talk.

Other than a slight difference in hair color, Brendon and Kenny could have been identical twins. Becca wondered if 'grown up' Jack shared the same attributes as his two younger brothers.

Becca decided that she needed to revise her strategy considering that she wasn't thrown out with she suggested that a twenty-eight year dead brother might still be around. Rather on the contrary she just appeared to be rehashing an old topic.

Knowing that Brendon and Kenny have entertained this subject before, Becca wanted to gather as much information as possible while revealing the least amount of information as possible.

Experience had taught her that when you can get someone talking for at least eighty percent of a conversation; they seem to walk away quite satisfied that it was an even two-way communication.

Becca opened up her notepad setting the pretense that she would be more asking the questions than answering them.

Glancing down into the yard Becca saw that Ruby and Kyra had gathered the children and were walking further away from the deck towards the pool area.

Lunch was going to be delayed.

Fanning herself with her notepad, Becca commented on how the day sure was heating up. Unbuttoning one more button on her blouse, nothing risqué, but in line with her comment of being hot, Becca began one more time; "I was hoping you could help me." Two quick bats of the eyes, a demure look down, eye contact with raised eyebrows and then wait.

(Unedited excerpt from the manuscript)

It was January when I repatriated to the land of the free and the home of the brave. New York was way too fucking cold for me after basically living in the tropics for six years, so I headed south.

I spent the next two and half years in Florida. I'll give you a time frame for those of you who are paying attention. Remember the Sun-Sentinel headline: Dead German Tourists?

You're welcome.

💣

Living overseas was a very eye-opening experience for me. I always disliked you faceless fucks and my time spent observing you from a new perspective gave me an opportunity to fester that dislike into a full-blown disgust.

When you realize, as I have, that your existence is an abomination: a disease, writhing against the harmonious flow of the Universe: you too will beckon for its ruin.

Look at yourself for what you are. Remember, you are not who you think you are: you are who you are perceived to be.

You are the Seven Sins seven times over.

💣

Returning to the States, I needed to find something to sink my teeth into: and I wanted to make my presence known to you faceless, deplorable, nauseating fucks.

This was the moment in time when pen was brought to paper and the birth of my grandiose plan poked its smegma encrusted head from the labia of my desire.

My disgust for you faceless sacs of flesh runs deep. I've enjoyed walking among you pathetic drones counting the years and the days and soon the hours. All the while laughing as I compiled everything I needed to orchestrate the beginning of *The Rush Hour Madman*'s reign of terror.

💣

I told you early on that I've left clues within this manuscript. Have you noticed any? Or, do you sit there as oblivious as ever?

You don't even think I'm referring to you when I call you a faceless fuck. Do you?

You are un-fucking-believable.

And then you're going to wonder why you drove directly into the center of your own apocalypse.

I'm going to walk you right up to the cliff's edge. I'm going to tell you exactly how I accumulated the money, the explosives and created the companies that will be held responsible.

Why?

Simple; first, it won't make a damn bit of difference. I can tell you today and still go out and do again tomorrow.

That's right, you are that fucking ignorant.

Second; as I've said all along, I'm doing it for the *thump-thump*. It would be nice to think that maybe, just maybe, a few of you faceless buffoons might make this exciting.

You can thank me another time for the *thump-thump* I've given you. I realize that we hardly know each other, but trust me when I tell you that you should be feeling it.

Because, while you're reading this...

The clock is ticking.

The date has been set.

The targets have been selected.

Picture me on the rooftop; kicking back, ready to enjoy the panoramic show. Thanks for playing.

💣

Chapter 36

Brendon and Kenny exchanged a quick glance after they both watched a bead of sweat run down Becca's neck, take a right turn over the rise of her breast and then disappear into the valley of her cleavage.

The brothers turned identical shades of red as they realized Becca was monitoring their fixation on her chest. Ninety-nine percent of all men fail the ADHD test when administered by a female nurse.

Look at the bird.

Brendon spoke first while Kenny stole another glance down Becca's shirt.

"How can we help you?"

"Well," Becca began "you can tell me why your wife reacted the way she did."

"Oh, I'm sorry about that. Ever since she had Cat; that's what we call our daughter, she gets a little jealous when I talk to sexy women." Brendon realized that calling Becca 'sexy' was probably inappropriate and he tried to back-peddle with his mouth.

"I don't mean sexy... I mean you are sexy... I'm sorry, I mean beautiful... I mean..."

Kenny stared at Brendon thoroughly enjoying his brother's social blunder and said; "Hey Bro, would you like some fries with your foot?"

Brendon's face was now a shade of red that Becca had honestly never seen on a human before. Brendon looked over railing to insure Ruby was nowhere within earshot; probably something he should have done earlier, but he was still safe.

Becca spoke up saving the drowning brother from potentially swallowing his other foot.

"First of all, thank you for the compliment. Second of all, that's not what I meant. I want to know why your wife said, "not this again" when I mentioned your brother Jack."

Kenny was the one who answered.

"Both our wives, Ruby and Kyra, have decided that we are wrong and they are right when it comes to the matter of our brother Jack."

"Spoken like a true Stepford." Brendon interjected.

Kenny chose to ignore the comment.

"We have all sat around discussing this for years and years. We would polish off one bottle of wine with dinner and sit around in the living room drinking a second."

Kenny paused as if remembering a happier time, then shook his head.

Turning to Brendon, Kenny said, "Man, do you remember some of those crazy scenarios we came up with?"

Brendon just smiled and deferred providing an answer; allowing Kenny to continue.

"In the beginning, we used to joke that Jack killed himself just so he wouldn't have to finish college. He never really wanted to go. I can still hear some of the arguments he had with our parents." Kenny paused and took a long swallow from his Corona. "Jack was always of the opinion that he didn't need a college degree to succeed." Turning to Brendon, Kenny said, "If you ask me, I think Jack got screwed when we went to that split schedule."

Kenny took a little time and explained to Becca all about the Lynbrook High School construction plans, the split class schedules and how he and Brendon were transferred to Woodmere Academy.

Becca listened as if she was hearing all of it for the first time. Becca had decided that, if she could avoid talking about the manuscript, she would. There was no reason to alert the brothers about Jack's psychotic nature.

Becca's past experience involving sharing negative news about someone's family member, whether they were dead or alive, was usually faced with denial and an abrupt end to a conversation.

Although hearing Kenny share insights about how Jack conducted and presented himself to his brothers and parents was fascinating; it was not pertinent or relevant to what Becca was trying to uncover.

Needing to steer the conversation back to Jack's death not his life, Becca waited for Kenny to pause and asked, "So, it sounds like you both thought Jack really did die out there at OU… What changed your minds?"

Chapter 37

Melina readied her mind and body for the worst. She heard him stand up abruptly; heard the canvas director's chair fall over and collapse. She assumed he was picking up the whip.

How could she have been so stupid?

She had already been warned previously when she covered her nakedness. It was a small blessing that she didn't feel the sting of the whip earlier. It was rare that her captor didn't use the whip to teach her right from wrong according to his standards and rules.

But this whole interaction was out of character.

He had spoken to her.

He had allowed her to bath.

He had allowed her to make a mistake.

Thinking that she had more than enough scars to remind her of this ordeal, Melina smiled. In its own way, that thought, was a positive reflection on her eventual release from this situation.

She couldn't be reminded of this ordeal unless it was in the past.

The whip slicing through the air and splitting open her flesh with a crack never happened.

Instead another paper bag landed at Melina's feet.

"Get dressed; we're going for a little walk."

Chapter 38

"Jack was always an enigma to us growing up."

It was Brendon who continued the dialogue. "Right around the same time we went to the Academy, Jack became even more distant from the family than he normally was."

Becca began writing in her notepad hoping to catch something that would offer a clue to what became of Jack Thomas.

"Jack and I used to share a room together when we were younger. Kenny was in the room next to us and our parent's room was across the hall. Jack separated himself from the family by relocating into the room that was originally used for a live-in housekeeper. It was located off the kitchen in the rear of the house and it was always *off limits* to Kenny and me."

Brendon looked over at Kenny who just stared at the empty Corona in his hand and nodded.

"Jack spent less and less time at home. We all used to be very close. Playing ball games in the front yard after school everyday; or just, messing around in the basement together." Brendon let out a deep sigh and finished off his own Corona. Standing up he removed the empty bottle from his brother's hand and walked over to the cooler next to the stainless steel grill.

"Are you sure you don't want one?" Brendon asked Becca who simply shook her head and asked; "What do you think Jack was doing after school?"

Brendon popped off the caps from the Coronas with an opener that was built into the side of the cooler. He fished out two lime wedges from a Tupperware container and crammed them into each bottle's neck as if he had done it a million times before. Handing Kenny a beer, Brendon repositioned himself into his chair and took in a long swallow of the golden liquid before he began talking again.

"Nobody really knew what Jack was doing after Ken and I got sent to the Academy. That split schedule at Lynbrook gave him a lot of freedom. By the time we got home from our full day at school, Jack was already gone. After a while we stopped asking our Mom where he was. The answer was always the same. I don't know; maybe at work, maybe at the beach, maybe at his friends house."

"Don't misunderstand me, its not that our parents didn't care; I believe they cared a lot. It's just that... what could they do? Jack was very popular at school. He always got passing grades. He was never in trouble with the law. He wasn't messed up with drugs. He just preferred to be somewhere else all the time and our parents let him."

"It all happened so quickly. I don't think my parents even realized what was happening until it was too late. Soon Jack was graduating and packing up for college before they were aware they hadn't seen him for the past two years."

"When Jack took off for Ohio, it didn't mean anything to me. I was already used to him being gone. It wasn't like anything changed. What do you think Kenny?"

"Kenny?" Brendon repeated and still got no response from his brother.

Kenny was so deeply lost in thought that Brendon had to reach out and snap his fingers in front of his brother's face before Kenny even realized that he was being spoken to.

"I'm sorry," Kenny began, "I was just remembering Mom's reaction when I told her I saw Jack at his funeral."

Chapter 39

Melina reached in the plastic Target shopping bag and removed the Hanes' 3-pack of white v-neck undershirts. Opening the bag, Melina withdrew one of the three v-necks and hesitated for a second before slipping it over her head.

She couldn't believe this was happening.

The undershirt fit snugly around Melina's torso. The material was soft against her skin. It had been too long since she had clothes on and the security they offered was overwhelming. Melina fought to hold back the emotion that was sure to bring tears. A chill ran through her body and her nipples protruded through the flimsy material.

The Target bag also contained a colorful pair of men's boxer shorts wadded up at the bottom. Melina reached in and pulled them out by the waistband and inspected the design on the shorts.

Staring at the graphics of four cartoon boys, Melina couldn't recall their names although she had seen them before. The tag said South Park.

"My favorite episode was when Satan beat the shit out of Jesus."

Melina couldn't respond. Firstly, she had no idea what to say. Her mind was still reeling around the bizarre change of events that had transpired in the last hour. Secondly, she had no idea what he was talking about and didn't want to risk pretending that she did. So, she did the next best thing and kept her mouth shut.

The chain around her left ankle rattled as she lifted her leg to place it into the opening of the boxers. Melina froze unsure on how to proceed. She had become so used to the shackle that she had actually forgotten that it was there.

"Lay down." His voice commanded her from the darkness beyond the flood lights. "On your back. Legs spread. Arms above your head."

Melina complied immediately.

"If you even breathe funny while I'm unchaining you…"

He didn't finish the sentence.

He didn't need to.

Melina understood what would happen.

Stretched out on the floor, Melina looked down over the length of her body and watched as her captor emerged from between the towering flood lights.

Chapter 40

"You saw Jack at his funeral?" Becca leaned forward in her chair as she probed Kenny for more of the story.

"Well not exactly. According to our mother; I saw a trauma induced hallucination; or how else did she put it…?" Kenny looked towards his brother for the answer, but then it came to him and he swiveled back around in his chair and faced Becca.

In a repetitive tone, Kenny recited the agreed upon explanation as concluded by those who would accept nothing less; "My grief stricken mind must have latched onto a stranger who had features similar to my brother's to help ease the loss of the most important person in my life."

Kenny inhaled and exhaled deeply to emphasize the monotony of what he had just proclaimed.

"Wow." Brendon interjected and applauded in mock fashion; "I can't believe you still remember that verbatim.

"Well you know what they say;" Kenny retorted, "Photographic minds are a sign of genius. At least someone in the family is destined for greatness."

"Not in your wildest dreams…" Brendon began but was interrupted by Becca.

"Excuse me boys. Can we decide who is greater than whom later?"

Both Brendon and Kenny blushed and faced forward.

To Kenny's right and out of his peripheral vision, Brendon mouthed the words 'I am'. Becca smiled, she was enjoying the playfulness the brothers shared and lamented on the fact that she was an only child. Turning her attention to the younger of the two, Becca asked Kenny to continue his accounting of Jack's funeral.

"It was a horribly strange week anyway; I should have kept my mouth shut, there was no reason to further upset Mom." Kenny turned to Brendon as he finished the sentence. Brendon just sat in silence staring at the lime that stuck to the inside of his now empty Corona bottle. Brendon's head bobbed up and down ever so slightly. Lost in thought and listening to Kenny retell the details of the week that followed the phone call to Shannon Thomas with the news that her eldest son was dead.

"September 13th, 1980 was a Saturday. I'll remember that for the rest of my life. We all had just come home from a cookout over at our Grandmother's house, our Grandfather had just passed away a few months earlier and we were still spending a lot of time over there."

"I can see the calendar hanging next to the phone on the kitchen wall. It was an MC Escher calendar and September featured that one with the crazy stairs and the roly-poly lizard-things. We all stood in silence as mom played back the message that sat around all day in the machine waiting for someone to listen to it. We missed the call by moments as we left the house earlier that day. We had had such a nice day too. Our cousins had come over that day as well; we played ball in the backyard, explored the old house, walked up to Smitty's on Broadway and got some ice-cream…"

Kenny paused, looked up at the sky and then out across the yard to where the women and children were playing by the pool together. He let out another deep sigh and continued; "It was a day Jack would have enjoyed."

"We could tell right away, even before my mom called the school back that it wasn't good news. You could just tell by the tone. We all watched as my mother's heart broke and she collapsed into the wall beneath the phone and the MC Escher calendar."

A single tear escaped Kenny's eye and he excused himself from the table under the pretense of getting him and Brendon another beer.

This time, no one asked Becca if she wanted one.

Kenny explained to Becca how Jack's remains were brought back in a sealed pine box stained black.

Brad and Shannon Thomas drove the ten hours to Ohio University the following day after the phone call to retrieve their son and his belongings. Upon arrival, they were informed that a Last Will and Testament was found in their son's room outlining what was to be done with his body. Although strange, and terribly uncommon for such a document to be found in a college student's dorm room, it was to be considered a legally binding document outlining the wishes of a sound minded adult.

The most disturbing facet of the Will was that it was constructed by a law firm located in Lynbrook and was dated on the exact day of Jack's eighteenth birthday. According to Kenny, the discovery of the Will was the beginning of the end for his mother. Just the few bizarre requests that were contained within the Will and the depth of Jack's involvement in preparing such details tore at Shannon Thomas's inner soul. She was left pondering the question; to what extent did she not know her own son? The more she thought about it, the more withdrawn she became and the more she realized her son was nothing more than a stranger to her.

The most devastating blow to the Thomas family was Jack's written refusal to be buried at the Saint John Cemetery in Queens with the rest of the family's descendants.

Without any explanation to the family, Jack had purchased the corner plot at the Rockville Cemetery and had prearranged his funeral. Not only was the plot paid for, but so were all the funeral arrangements right down to the hiring of an organist and the music to be played.

In an effort to provide some answers to their distraught mother, Brendon and Kenny met with the funeral director prior to the actual burial. They were informed that a young man had negotiated the rights to the plot earlier that summer. It was a rather expensive dealing since that area of the grounds was not designated to be used for a gravesite, but the funeral director said that the young man was quite persuasive.

The brothers discovered that Jack had personally set the headstone into the ground and provided a number for a local stonemason to be called when his body arrived for burial, so the epitaph could be completed.

Yes, the funeral director found the entire transaction extremely unorthodox; however, he was of the opinion that he was just dealing with some wealthy kid who had a morbid fixation on his own mortality. Besides, the amount of money that was paid for the plot and the subsequent confidentiality far exceeded any concern he may have had regarding any issues of morality.

As Kenny spoke, Becca drew a large dollar sign with a question mark next to it and circled it several times. Becca had been taking diligent notes as the brothers talked. Roberto had pointed out earlier in the day; that the brothers may know something even if they don't know they know it.

Having seen the gravesite earlier, Becca had a clear mental image of the family crammed into the corner of the Rockville Cemetery. The giant willow tree, causing crisscrossed shadows to slash through the sunlight as the family buried their first born. A mother, a father, brothers, friends and schoolmates all gathered around a crooked tombstone already bearing the name of the departed.

A familiar chill ran up and down Becca's spine; and as much as she didn't want to hear more, she asked the probing question.

"Kenny, tell me what makes you think you saw Jack at his funeral?"

(Unedited excerpt from the manuscript)

While living in Florida I began creating an intricate web of deception; an ever outward spiraling mass of people, places and things. The fundamental nouns of your destruction.

Now playing at the Fillmore Auditorium... The Fundamental Nouns. Opening band hits the stage at 2:30. Don't be late.

💣

I bought a small house just north of the Ft. Lauderdale border in Pompano Beach; it was far enough away from the cops, the crack and the beaches; but near enough to grab prey when I wanted.

Florida reminded me a lot of my days at OU. Between the naturally loose locals and the tourists on vacation; it was unbelievably easy to get women to come home with me.

I had a rental property on one of the side streets off A1A in Lauderdale. It was difficult, there weren't a lot available given the prime location, but I found one that even had a side entrance into the kitchen from the carport.

It was actually one of the best setups I've had so far; offering total privacy during the delivery and disposal stages of the slaughter process.

I began experimenting with butchering my quarry after I was done playing with them; it's amazing the wealth of knowledge you could teach yourself on the internet. I created a small company and began selling cuts of meat to a few local establishments along the Boardwalk.

If you've traveled to Ft. Lauderdale in the early 90's it's possible that maybe you've eaten some of my company's product.

I realized the risk I was taking greatly outweighed the *thump-thump* I was receiving; and although it was exhilarating, I needed to find a different outlet for my merchandise. Besides, I was missing out on personally witnessing the product being consumed.

I joined a company called Colorado Prime Foods. They were a shop-at-home food service company based right there in Pompano Beach.

Once again fate had delivered me to the doorstep of my next great adventure.

I could have moved anywhere in Florida.

But I didn't.

That's fate.

That's powerful.

The company was very fortunate to get me as their Director of Human Resources; and since I was a seasoned salesperson, I was also able to facilitate sales calls to the homes of potential clients in the Ft. Lauderdale and Miami areas when we became overbooked.

The General Manager couldn't believe his luck when my resume fit so perfectly with what the company was looking for.

Absolutely amazing... Don't you agree?

My Colorado Prime endeavor was perfect for so many reasons. I'll give you my top three; first, as HR Director I was privy to all of the company's personnel files. I had access to social security numbers, mother's maiden names, birth places, high school graduation information and copies of driver's licenses.

I commenced stockpiling hundreds of identities and placing them in my web for a variety of uses.

Second, the telemarketers I hired were predominately young females; a never ending supply of blonds, brunettes and redheads. A plethora of legal teenagers, out on their own for the very first time; ready to take on the world and typically from out of state. They were vulnerable, trusting and easily manipulated back to my apartment by the beach.

Even under normal circumstances, a high percentage of telemarketers don't show up for work on the second day anyway. It's just the nature of the industry.

That percentage rose slightly at Colorado Prime; but for different reasons, it wasn't that the job sucked, it was more that they were having too much fun entertaining me and my cock of torture.

Remember our earlier lesson?

A warm hole is a warm hole.

And number three...

My telemarketers called on several locations throughout the southern states and scheduled no cost, no obligation appointments for the Colorado Prime sales force.

It was a simple, non-threatening process; the prospective clients would be met in the comfort of their own homes by a Colorado Prime representative. They would be presented with a custom tailored program designed to bring savings, quality and convenience into their lives. Since they were already shopping for these items anyway... it was a no-brainer sales pitch.

When we were overbooked with in-home presentations in the Ft. Lauderdale and Miami areas; I was more than willing to help out. It was a great opportunity to expand the delivery range of my privately prepared meat. I would watch the prospects gobble down free samples of what they thought was Colorado Prime Filets while I ran through the pitch book with them.

Honestly, I didn't care if they bought the program or not.

Most of the time the company thought that the prospective household had canceled their appointment; it happened all the time anyway. So in those situations, when nobody knew I was there; usually I was the only one left breathing by the end of my presentation.

Colorado Prime offered many add on products to help lower the overall cost of their program. My favorite was the German Solingen Cutlery set; my demonstration typically left them speechless.

I would get such a fucking hard on watching them eat Fillets of Phoebe, or Short Loin of Lucy, or Shank of Charlotte.

Most of the time, I couldn't contain myself.

I found myself stabbing the husband to death and getting freaky with the wife before I was able to review the payment options with them.

Damn, those were some good ole times.

It was nice not having to worry about cleaning up after dinner.

Chapter 41

"I've always had what most people call a photographic mind." Kenny paused to give Becca a chance to interject at this point.

When she didn't, he continued.

"It's not like you might expect it to be. I mean, I can't do it on purpose, it just kind of happens." Kenny paused again, so Becca obliged him with a response this time. "Wow, that sounds interesting; what do you mean by, 'it just kind of happens'?"

"Well I'm not really sure how it works, but it seems that the harder I try to create a photo memory, the less chance I have that that memory is even retained. But, if I wasn't trying at all to create a memory, I seem to be able to vividly recall it when something triggers that specific recollection's hidden imagery."

Not really understanding the point, Becca asked Kenny to be more specific with an example.

"Okay, let's say that I'm just flipping through a magazine and pass over an ad for washers and dryers on sale at Sears. Even though I barely acknowledged the ad as I was turning the pages, and had no conscious memory of seeing an ad for washers and dryers; if Kyra, my wife, mentioned needing a new washer and dryer, the full page color ad would appear in my mind as if I was looking at in my hand. I would even be able to read you the small print."

Kenny waited to see if Becca had a question before continuing.

"Now on the other hand; if I sat down and diligently pored over that same ad with the intent of remembering it, I wouldn't be even able to recall any of the details if more than a few days had passed by." Kenny smiled and added, "But mark my words; if I didn't try to memorize it, that stupid ad is going to stick with me the rest of my life."

Kenny leaned back in his chair, folded his arms across his chest and nodded his head as if he had finally nailed the explanation. Kenny looked to Brendon to concur with the clarity of his explanation but Brendon just shrugged and said, "I've never understood it so don't look at me."

"So how does this all fit into you seeing Jack at his funeral?" Becca asked for the third time hoping to make some headway before the wives decided it was time for lunch.

"Oh right." Kenny said as if he had forgotten what he was originally talking about. He finished the last swallow of his beer and set the empty bottle on the table next to Brendon's.

From Becca's angle, the two bottles on the table with the sun off in the distance between them, reminded her of the Corona television commercials; *Miles away from ordinary* was the slogan. Becca couldn't agree more.

Kenny picked up the pace of his story, talking while he stood up and stretched.

"I can't be one hundred percent positive; but, I am damn sure I saw Jack that day. I guess that is what all the discussion has been about all these years.

Having nothing concrete, it is purely speculation. Almost like debating the existence of God."

Becca's heart skipped a beat at that last comment; and not a good skip like when she had met Mr. Christopher John. This was a bad skip accompanied by a familiar chill based on Jack's self-claimed alliance with a higher power. Becca was nauseated thinking about how pleased Jack would be at the thought of having *his* existence compared to a debate on the existence of God.

Kenny could see the trouble in Becca's eyes and asked her if she was okay before he continued.

"I'm fine; but, do you have any water in that cooler?"

Brendon sprang up out of his chair seemingly thrilled at being able to provide Becca with something to drink finally. Brendon grabbed the empty Coronas from the table and bounded over to the cooler to retrieve the drink order.

In a lame attempt at humor Brendon asked Becca is she would prefer a Diet Water or just a regular. Even Kenny rolled his eyes and groaned. Becca complied with a forced giggle and a smile and requested the Diet so she could keep her figure. Becca's comment won her body another mutual stare from the brothers which she didn't mind in the least.   The playful banter chased away what Becca now labeled as, *The Jack Thomas Chills.*

Kenny held onto the new beer in his hand without taking a swallow as he resumed the story of seeing his supposedly dead brother.

"Let me finally get right to it."   Becca's smile didn't go unnoticed and received a warm nod from Kenny.

"We were all lined up, crammed inside that corner, facing out into the expanse of the cemetery. I was standing there on the far side of Brendon and my parents.   That crazy tombstone was in front of us, then the hole in the earth and then all those people were arched around as if we were on stage.   I've never felt claustrophobic before; but I had an attack right then and there at that moment. It felt like we were being backed into the corner of the cemetery, and that fucking tree didn't help."

"I'm sorry," Kenny interjected, "I usually don't curse."

"Don't worry about it," Becca offered "I do it all the fucking time. Please continue."

The brothers exchanged another one of those quick 'looks' that spoke volumes between them and once again warmed Becca's heart. She truly did like these two and wondered how someone like Jack could have been born of the same genes.

Kenny picked up where he left off by saying, "I felt like I was going to faint. I couldn't breath. I looked around for a break in the mass of people suffocating us. Looking for a break in the bodies, somewhere where fresh air was seeping in; that's when I saw him. He was in the back. Smiling."

"Jesus." Becca spoke without even realizing she had said it aloud.

"No, not Jesus; Jack. But, it's funny you say that because he sort of did look like Jesus."

"I'm sorry? What?" It was Becca's turn to be confused.

"He was in disguise." Kenny explained. "Jack used to make movies when we were younger. He used to call them his Super Eight Super Features. Our parents got him one of those eight millimeter cameras for his thirteenth birthday and he would spend hours at a time making short films. I recall Jack making dozens of movies over the next three or four years."

Brendon came out of his reverie and added, "I remember those!"

Both Becca and Kenny looked over at him waiting for him to say more and then realized that anything else Brendon was remembering was staying in his head.

So Kenny continued; "I always thought Jack was going to be the next great movie director. He was so creative. He made some fantastic spoof films; Shazam - Capt Marvel, SWAT, Spiderman, The Bionic Man, Old Frankenstein..."

Kenny trailed off in thought and Becca sat looking at two space cadets now. Maybe she should have cut them off from the Coronas. Who knew how many they had before she got there.

"Ahem!" Becca cleared her throat and Kenny refocused; first on her chest and then back on his story.

"Jack would play most of the characters himself. He was really good at movie quality prosthetics. He would drive our mother crazy with fake wounds and injuries. She used to warn him about how one day..." Kenny's eyes welled up with tears and he needed a moment. "Well you know how mothers are."

Brendon reached out and put a hand on Kenny's shoulder. Becca knew there were some deep feelings and unresolved issues regarding Shannon Thomas that the brothers needed to explore; but she wasn't qualified and this wasn't the time.

Kenny regained his composure and proceeded without any additional prompting from Becca this time. "Most of the time you wouldn't recognize Jack in his films; he was that good. His hair and makeup techniques just kept getting better and better. The only reason I knew Jesus was him at the funeral was because I explored his room when I wasn't supposed to."

Even after all these years, Kenny sheepishly looked down while admitting he had snooped in his big brother Jack's room.

"It was right before he left for Ohio University and even though he was hardly around the house I was so nervous he would come home and catch me. Jack used the back door a lot, and if he had arrived while I was in his room I would have had no place to hide. I remember my heart was racing; I was thirteen at the time and certainly didn't feel like the baby of the house anymore, but Jack scared the heck out of me. Jack could get this look in his eyes..."

Kenny and Brendon shared another moment of total, unspoken agreement.

"I actually peed in my pants once when Jack looked at me with that death-stare of his simply because I came down into the basement when he was busy doing something. I still don't know what he was doing, but I didn't go into the basement ever again while he was home unless I knew where he was."

Becca couldn't imagine what it would be like growing up with someone as disturbed as Jack appeared to be. A small saving grace was that Brendon and Kenny didn't appear to know how twisted their brother really was; or more appropriately, is.

"When I rummaged through his room, I did it so quickly that I wasn't really looking for anything in particular. I did it more because I wasn't allowed to. It was actually exciting; my heart racing like that gave me sort of an adrenaline rush. I get that same feeling now when I do my rock climbing or mountain biking."

Becca saw the words *thump-thump* in her head and experienced another rush of *The Jack Thomas Chills*. At least Kenny didn't need to get his rush by killing. Becca wondered what gave Brendon his thrill.

"I must have come across Jack's theatrical costumes and prosthetic makeup when I was looking through his stuff; because, when I saw Jesus amongst the throng of mourners at Jack's funeral, I had a photo memory flash of the entire outfit."

Chapter 42

At first all Melina could see was his silhouette framed by the lights behind him. The unmistakable long-tail suit jacket he wore flowed seductively with every step he took.

Finally when the horrifying image of her captor came into view, Melina screamed and recoiled into a fetal ball trembling.

Moving at a melodramatic pace, his true features distorted by face paint; the clown swaggered towards Melina.

Savoring the terror he was instilling in her, the clown demanded that she lay still while he unchained her ankle. Melina always had an uncontrollable fear of clowns and had trouble keeping her leg from twitching when he touched her.

"I have a key in my hand and an axe hanging on the wall; which would you rather me to use to free your foot?"

Melina tried to speak but found that the words she tried to produce had no muscle to escape her chest. The fear that gripped her was extreme and paralyzing. She had never felt so close to the brink of a mental breakdown. Melina could actually see in her mind's eye a signpost up ahead offering rest and relaxation from reality. All that was required was a simple thought. A heartfelt acceptance of her inability to cope with life; it was truly an effortless price to pay for peace and serenity.

Melina was mere seconds from paying the price to free her mind from its physical and emotional terror when her captor spoke again.

"A pity; your silence has selected the latter."

Regaining the inner strength that had sustained her through her ordeal so far, Melina was able to barely force the words from her throat.

"K...k...key."

Melina faced her fear and stared at the clown as he unchained her ankle. His grey-blue eyes held her gaze as he worked the key into the lock. Face painted half white and half black with alternating colors for eyebrows. His hair was slicked back and Melina didn't know if it was black or just appeared that way from the gel. A thin red line slashed down through each eyebrow and over his eyes to the crest of each cheek bone. Lips painted in the same blood red as his eye makeup; white side turned up in a smile, black side turned down in a frown.

The raw power that emanated from her captor was tangible in the air between them. Melina instinctively knew not to try to escape or she would end up dead or worse.   Telling herself to bide her time.

Telling herself that her chance would come.

Telling herself that for now she needed to be patient and docile.

Melina lay prone on the floor and waited to be told what to do next.

Chapter 43

Kenny closed his eyes visualizing the experience all over again and narrated to Becca what he saw.

"There was no mistaking what I was seeing. My mind flashed item by item. The wig, the beard and moustache, the shirt, the glasses, even the necklace; each item the Jesus looking stranger wore matched up perfectly to the exact same items I stumbled across in Jack's room.

There was no doubt in my mind.

It was Jack.

I began calling his name and trying to break free from the grip my mother had around my arm. Trying to side step around the cramped family huddle jammed in the corner of the cemetery, I was quickly becoming the center of attention.

Fighting to get over to the gathering of mourners and confront the disguised apparition; I was being jostled and grabbed by everyone every step of the way. People though I was having a breakdown; and, in a way, I guess I was.

Attempting to get the situation under control my logical mind tried to rationalize what I was seeing. Here I am standing at my brother's graveside, casket still hovering above the six foot hole, and I'm calling out his name like he's standing across the street and I'm trying to get his attention.

It didn't make sense; and I knew that.

But it didn't eliminate the fact that I had just seen someone wearing the exact theatrical prosthetics I had come across in Jack's room not three months earlier.

I needed to break free of the family and confront Jesus-Jack to find out what was going on. It was the only way to prove or disprove what I thought I was seeing. I could explain what had happened to the family later.

But when I looked up Jesus-Jack had disappeared."

Becca was at a loss.

How do you respond to something like that?

Becca had no doubt in her mind that Kenny did see Jack at his own funeral. Did she let Kenny and Brendon know what she knew? In the short time she had spent with Jack's brothers she had come to truly like them.

Was it fair to leave them wondering if it was true or not.

Becca decided to hear more of what the brothers had to say before she determined how much of her story she would share.

Looking up from her notebook, Becca found Kenny with his head hung down and a single tear staining his face. Brendon was leaning back in his chair; his head nestled in a makeshift hammock of his interlaced fingers looking up into the sky.

"Kenny." Becca said softly and he looked up.

Becca laid the notebook on the table to her left and leaned forward to gather Kenny into her embrace.

Kenny let out a sob as he settled his face into Becca's neck. "I never told my mom how sorry I was that I hurt her that day. She was already dealing with so much pain..."

Becca squeezed Kenny tighter and whispered into his ear; "She knows. She knows."

Brendon cleared his throat to alert the two that the wives and kids were on their way back from the pool. Becca and Kenny unhooked themselves from each other and leaned back into their respective chairs wiping away the tears from their eyes.

Ruby and Kyra stopped at the blankets in the yard below the deck with the children at their sides. Ruby took a few steps forward and called up to Brendon. "Can I see you for a second?"

(Unedited excerpt from the manuscript)

A lot had changed in the States while I was away. Major US retailers went belly up while others thrived and consumed the old Mom and Pop shops. Everyone was going out of business. The middle class ceased to exist. The rich got richer and the poor got poorer. The welfare system was out of control, rewarding those who figured out a way to cheat the systems while it punished those honorable enough to try to make ends meet in a biased economy. We saw banks go bankrupt, the internet became a household appliance, and we watched the beginning of World War III but refused to call it that.

The funny part of that is that we are still in the midst of WWIII and you faceless fucks still sit around like nothing is happening. You people are so stupid I'm amazed it is considered a felony to kill you.

It's like squishing a bug.

Nothing more, nothing less.

Nobody cares.

You actually deserve to die and I'm happy to help.

🎇

It also got a lot harder to acquire certain items that made my life easier back in my youth. Chloroform wasn't as readily available and background checks and forms in triplicate were required to attain large quantities of industrial strength lye and ordering 500 Dermestid Beetle larvae put you on some sort of watch list.

Not a problem, I was able to create several companies that had legitimate reasons to obtain such goods.

I'd like to thank all of you that have provided your good names to my cause over the years. I do appreciate it; because without you, none of this could have happened. I'd especially like to thank those of you that have died and designated me as your benefactor; your constant influx of cash has been a great source of comfort to me and my organization.

Did you know that you could take out a life insurance policy on almost anyone?

Great country... armed, dangerous and wealthy.

To thee I sing...

🎇

Holy shit! I didn't tell you about the beetles!

Great band.

They totally changed the face of rock and roll.

But I'm talking about the beetles that totally changed the face of my victims in Ohio.

To be very specific, they ate their faces off.

They are up there high in the rankings on my top 10 list of the Coolest Fucking Things I've Ever Seen.

🎇

I need to backtrack for a moment and tell you about the Dermestid Beetles.

When I was at Ohio University playing my 'Catch and Release' game, the participants were left in a less than acceptable way for them to ever go back home.

Clean bones are easy to bury. It's the flesh that rots and begins to stink up the place; and it's that particular stench that starts attracting wild animals, curious pets and of course, local law enforcement.

I didn't need to deal with any of that.

I had enough going on; thank you.

Who needs those kinds of distractions anyway?

Like you faceless fucks deserve an explanation... Fuck you.

Anyway, I needed something to serve the same function as the industrial strength lye did for me back in the good ole' barn days; and lo and behold, the answer came to me in a dream.

In the dream I sat lazily in an old fashioned tree-swing, rocking gently back and forth as I watched my parents interacting in the yard in front of me.

My father had my mother stripped down and tied between 2 trees. She was spread out like a star. Legs and arms extended and pulled to limits threatening to dislodge the limbs from their respective sockets. My father held his cock in his hands, which ran 9 feet from his body and acted like a bullwhip. He repeatedly cracked the cock-whip across my mother's bleeding body; tearing hunks of flesh off her already filleted skin.

The dream was vivid in color, but utterly void of sound. My mother's mouth would contort in hideous silent screams as my father's face roared in silent laughter.

The backlash of my father's cock-whip began to slice into his own body. First snapping against my mother's flesh; cutting deep gashes, exposing torn muscle and some bone; then rebounding back into his own flesh. My father's relentless rhythm increased as his own skin fell away from his body. His cock-whip first split in 2 and then split again and again until he way flailing away at his own and my mother's body with ribbons of bloody skin as sharp as razors.

My mother's silent screams subsided as a final blow severed her head from her body. Long blond hair, darkened with blood, snaked out in tendrils as her head rotated end over end through the air and landed at my feet. Gashes in her face had popped one of her eyes and a milky substance oozed down her cheek. Her one remaining eye would follow me as I continued my slow arc in the tree-swing, back and forth, back and forth over her head.

Mounting my mother from behind, my father tried to fuck her with his ruined cock. Using the hole in her neck for leverage, my father thrust his bloody stump against my mother's ass as the red ants swarmed out of the ground and began to consume my parents.

I woke from that dream with knowledge I did not have when I went to bed the night before. All I took with me to bed was a question, and I was blessed with an answer through the power of dream guided by my Creator.

Less than 10 miles down the road I met Mark Rosser and his wife Pauli over at P & M Taxidermy in New Marshfield. I wonder if they remember the young college student they helped with his biology project.

Well P & M; that handful of Dermestid Beetle larvae became quite the colony. They ate extremely well those 2 years I spent in Athens. They had a rather extensive subterranean habitat as well.

I wonder what they've been feeding on these past 26 years.

Chapter 44

"Your brother has been working very hard to save your life."

The clown's words took Melina off guard and she stumbled as she finished slipping into the South Park boxer shorts.

Unsure of what she had just heard, Melina said, "Roberto?"

"You have another brother?"

"No… I just… I don't understand." Melina spoke softly and stared at the ground. Although she was feeling better with some clothes on, even if it was simply an undershirt and boxers; Melina was still very freaked out by her captor's face paint.

"Put this around your neck."

A vicious looking choke chain and collar landed at Melina's feet. The type of device one would use on a wild animal while either trying to train it or subdue it. Melina's heart began pounding in her chest as she thought about the possible scenarios her near future might hold. Every time her situation began to appear as if it could be brightening, a dark cloud of despair and fear crept back in.

Melina held the collar in her hands and inspected the tines that would be resting against her throat. The tines appeared to have been sharpened beyond what the original manufacturer had provided. Melina assumed it was an added touch courtesy of the Nightmare Clown.

Melina slid the collar gingerly over her head and around her neck. Very aware that the slightest pressure applied to the chain would cause the collar to pierce her throat; Melina stretched out her arm offering the leather strap to the clown in hopes of gaining his favor.

Pleased with her subservience, the clown smiled and accepted the proffered leather handle.

"As I mentioned; your brother has been working very hard to save your life and I've decided to reward him by letting you live."

Melina's knees involuntarily buckled beneath her and she fell to the ground. The sharpened tines of the choke chain penetrated her throat in several areas as tears of joy streamed from her eyes.

Chapter 45

Brendon and Ruby ascended the deck stairs hand in hand. Brendon's expression however spoke the truth, they weren't walking hand in hand; rather, Ruby was leading Brendon *by the hand*.

Ruby piloted Brendon with simple and subtle turnings of the wrist until Brendon was standing a half step in front of the couple with Ruby just slightly behind and off shoulder. The smirk on Ruby's face was unmistakable as she held Becca's gaze while Brendon spoke.

"It's getting late in the day…" Brendon began, and knowing that his wife was behind him he chanced rolling his eyes as he continued; "and the children need to maintain a schedule even though it is the weekend…" Pausing briefly as if he had forgotten his lines, Brendon added; "Plus, I really should capitalize on the free time I have to spend with the family since I am so busy during the week…"

Kenny raised his eyebrows, staring at his robotic brother, afraid of what was inevitably coming next. He had formed a strong bond with Becca in such a short time. Nothing lustful, although he did find himself focusing on the soft fullness of her breasts while they consoled each other just moments ago.

It had been a long time since he had talked about Jack's funeral and the pain that it always dredged up. Kenny needed the cleansing that came with sharing the experience every now and then. Kyra was done hearing about it and it didn't make Kenny love her any less; but he needed to unload that unresolved burden that he has carried for close to three decades.

The timing couldn't have been any better as well. Kenny had stayed behind at his house in Roslyn finishing up paperwork while his family drove over to Brendon and Ruby's house in Old Westbury. He was hoping to catch up on some work. That alone was a hysterical concept. There was no catching up on work; as a corporate lawyer for a financial firm the likes of American Express, you don't catch up on work. You don't get ahead of work. You just barely keep your head above the never ending flow of paperwork that comes your way.

Just before Kenny left his house to join his family the doorbell rang.

The driver from Fed Ex held out his electronic clipboard and asked Kenny for his name as if it might have changed since the last package he had delivered the day before. Kenny's company made sure he didn't get behind on the weekends by keeping him supplied with the most current pile of urgent paperwork.

The driver didn't hand over the customary thick document sized package with the tamper resistant tear-strip that insured nobody but Kenny would do the work; instead, he reached into the truck and withdrew a small rectangular box addressed to Erin, his daughter.

Her birthday would be on Tuesday.

He had almost forgotten.

Saved by the mystery box.

One mystery box arrived for the kids around their birthdays every year. Brendon and Ruby received one for each of their kids every year as well. Nobody ever knew exactly where the boxes came from or who the sender was; there was never a return address, or a card, or a letter indicating its originator. A box would just arrive addressed to the kids on their birthdays. Each box would contain an age appropriate toy; two if it was the twin's birthday, usually a red one and a blue one if it was feasible.

Brendon, Ruby, Kenny and Kyra had stopped discussing the origin of these mystery boxes a long time ago. It was finally determined that someone had signed the children up for a program like the book of the month club and that was the end of the discussion. Kenny could still hear Ruby's voice from that night when they were all sitting around after dinner having a glass of wine enjoying one of their 'Is Jack still alive?' conversations.

Ruby had slammed her glass down on the table, stood up and spoke with venom running down both sides of her mouth; "Your brother is dead. He is not showing up at family functions in disguise. He is not sending the children birthday presents. He is dead. Get over it. I am sick and tired of hearing 'Jack this' and 'Jack that'. It's a tough thing to face in life; but people die. Brothers die. I don't want the children hearing about any of this; they are getting older, this isn't healthy for anyone. Am I clear on this? Can we finally all agree and bury this ridiculous notion that Jack is alive? I am sorry; but your brother is dead and I don't want to hear about it being anything but that ever again."

The four sat in the living room in silence for the next ten or fifteen minutes. Quietly finishing their glasses of wine, no longer in the mood to discuss much of anything; Kenny and Kyra thanked Brendon and Ruby for dinner and headed home.

The subject of Jack Thomas hadn't been mentioned since.

Not until Becca Willis reopened the can of worms and spread it out all over the Thomas's family barbeque.

"Kenny...Kenny..."

Totally lost in thought, Kenny didn't hear anything that had come out of Brendon's mouth once he began reminiscing.

Ruby was staring at him over Brendon's shoulder and Kenny realized that his gaze was transfixed on Becca's chest while he was daydreaming. Too bad he thought; it would have been a nice view if he was focused. But he was too busy reliving Ruby's harsh words from a couple of years ago.

"I got another one of those boxes today... It was addressed to Erin, but I'm sure it is one of them."

Ruby sucked in air and let it out in a huff and pulled on Brendon's arm.

"Ken; not now please." Brendon pleaded.

Becca looked back and forth at the brothers realizing that there was more and prayed that she wasn't about to be dismissed. Time was running out and Becca was recognizing the opportunity that Roberto had foreseen.

Brendon continued and Ruby smiled sensing her victory at obtaining what she desired; which was, to get this Latino off her deck, away from her man and squelch any further discussions of Jack Thomas.

But Brendon threw a curve and forced a swing and a miss.

"Listen you guys; I need to get this grill cranked back up and feed the fam'... Ken, could you run into the house and grab the dogs... Becca..."

The pause brought Kenny to the edge of his seat.

Becca held her breath.

Ruby glowered.

"Becca, how would you like to join us for lunch?"

Becca exhaled and smiled.

Kenny leaned back and smiled.

Ruby snatched her hand away from Brendon's and stormed down the stairs.

Brendon called out to her as she strode across the lawn; "Lunch will be ready in about ten minutes, sweetheart; have the kids ready, thanks."

Brendon, Becca and Kenny all shared a warm moment of silence and then got busy preparing to eat. Brendon turned up the dials on the Grand Turbo with an audible whoosh; Kenny slid back the kitchen door and stepped through the threshold in pursuit of the hotdogs; and Becca gathered the empty beer bottles off the table and began setting out the picnic ware for lunch.

Chapter 46

Melina didn't feel the pinch as the tines of the choke collar pierced her neck.

Hearing the news that she was going to live outweighed everything else. For the first time since her capture, she finally had a true semblance of hope. As much as she had tried to maintain optimism and faith, it was a forced belief that she would live to see an end to her ordeal. No matter how hard she tried, Melina couldn't fully relinquish the notion that death and despair were hiding in the shadows, waiting for their chance to pounce on her for a final time.

In what appeared to be an uncommon act of compassion, the Madman released his grip on the leather strap of the choke chain as Melina's knees buckled. The razor sharp tines still found purchase in the tender skin around Melina's throat as the collar tightened. Small puncture wounds dotted the surface in parallel lines and leaked thin rivulets of blood down her neck, over the raise of her collar bone and disappeared into the ribbed neckline of the V-neck.

Melina's captor was thankful that his prey wasn't stupid enough to penetrate her jugular and thus ruining his plans to free her. He planned on using her to solidify the game he was playing.

She was the concrete evidence.

No sense in playing if everyone thought it was a joke.

She was the volume knob, and he wanted it turned up to full blast.

But as he watched the tears roll down her face and the blood roll down her neck he became aroused. She appeared weak and frail and he wanted to hurt her. She wasn't acting in a manner fitting of someone who was bestowed with the honor of being his first victim to live.

He began to question his intent of letting her go.

The blood had seeped deep into the T-shirt's collar and was working its way through the thin material adhering to the curve of her breasts.

He felt himself getting a hard on and envisioned himself strapping her into the swing and torturing her with the lighter fluid. In his mind he could easily see her bucking up and down on his cock as she was writhing in pain while he rode her hard in the harness.

It was a tough concept to ignore.

Chapter 47

Lunch was rather uncomfortable.

Ruby refused to even look at Becca, let alone talk to her.

There was a painful general silence that loomed over the adult's table; interrupted only by an occasional, 'could you pass me this?' or 'could you hand me that?'

In contrast, the chatter coming from the children's table was incessant. It was obvious to Becca that these first cousins had spent a lot of time together throughout the years.

Becca found herself reflecting on her own solo upbringing for the second time that day with a heavy regret. It would have been nice to share her joys and sorrows with a sibling, or a cousin, or even a close friend for that matter. That thought process eventually led her, as it always did, to mourning the loss of Jeremy once again. Along with that came the empty pain deep in her chest, the one that felt like a rock crushing her soul.

Then, as if following a script; her mind took her back to the time when she had first met Roberto; that scene highlighting the realization that she could love someone again. But, on the very next page, unable to stop the natural flow of the script; came the scene where Roberto turns into a needy, emotionally draining, jealous half-wit. That scene turns tragic as Roberto's own self-destructive qualities begin to amplify and he becomes a nightmare for Becca to disengage from her life.

Then, just as the scene where Becca meets the debonair Mr. Christopher John is queuing up in her mind; the scene where she is swept off her feet and falls in love with the entrepreneur, Kenny's wife, Kyra, placed her hand on Becca's arm.

"Do you have any children of your own?" Kyra asked.

Snapped out of her trance and realizing that everyone was staring at her, Becca could only offer a reply of "Huh?"

Becca had no idea what Kyra had just asked her.

How long had she been staring at the kids?

"You seem to be really enjoying the children and I was just wondering if you had any?" Kyra repeated her question without any hint of annoyance at having to reiterate the question.

"Oh no;" Becca said and instantly regretted the tone in which she said it. It came across like she didn't like children and nothing could be further from the truth, so she quickly added; "I wish I did… I thought I would by now…" Becca's mind shifted and recognized an opportunity to win over the women of the Thomas households.

It was another trick of the trade she had picked up along the way interviewing less than cooperative individuals. Depending on the situation; sharing a story that made you appear vulnerable had a tendency of opening people up to you that normally wouldn't tell you their proper name.

Becca shared with the table her tragic ordeal of love found and lost with Mister 'call me Jeremy' Young.

Ruby and Kyra Thomas were Becca's new best friends.

Brendon and Kenny took a turn watching the kids run around the yard while the women talked, cleared off the tables on the deck and enjoyed their own round of drinks.

Ruby opened a delicate white Zinfandel verses the Coronas the men were swilling.

Becca joined in with a half glass of her own to seal the deal of companionship. They shared stories of where they grew up, where they went to college, what their favorite books and movies were, what actor they thought was 'hot', and of course the weather.

There is an unwritten law that states: All conversations can't be fully complete until there is a discussion of the day's weather.

This basic principle allows everyone, everywhere, regardless of your social status, regardless of your familiarity with the other person; the pure, unadulterated ability, to share a common subject. No matter who you are, no matter what your occupation, no matter what level of school you've completed; you have an opinion on the weather and are always able to discuss said opinion.

Weather; the great equalizer. Bringing people together for centuries.

The three women sat on the deck and talked for a good half hour enjoying the afternoon sun before the conversation turned to the reason for Becca's visit in the first place.

Jack.

Ruby was the one who abruptly sliced into the conversation and changed the tone from light and airy to dark and serious.

As if following Ruby's command, a lone thick cloud cut across the sky and blocked the sun. A giant shadow covered the backyard and somehow muffled the children's voices that emanated from the swing set where Brendon and Kenny were supervising the five cousins.

"What gives you the right to walk into my house and disrupt my family time with all this nonsense about my husband's deceased brother?"

Becca was still hoping to get more information from Brendon and Kenny before she called it a day. She at least needed to hear more about the 'box' Kenny had mentioned right before lunch that had caused such a stir from Ruby and a "not now" from Brendon. Her answer to Ruby's question needed to be quick, specific and most of all, submissive; Ruby appeared to have a superiority complex, and Becca needed to play into that.

"You are right; I am so sorry to disturb your personal time." Becca began and diverted her eyes away from Ruby's stare as if she were not worthy to address her on the same level. "I should have called and received your permission first."

The smile that creased Ruby's face and the shift in her posture told Becca that she was moving on the right track. Now she just needed to provide a reasonable explanation why she was claiming that Jack Thomas might still be alive.

Becca took a deep breath and crossed her fingers hoping that she wasn't about to be thrown out on her ear.

Chapter 48

Melina didn't notice as the clown raised his fist high above his head.

She was still on her knees, head hung down, trying to gain control of her emotions. Hearing that she was going to live was overwhelming; even the warm blood that soaked her T-shirt was of no concern to her. She had barely even felt the tines when they punctured her skin; the news of her continued existence prevailed over all else.

With his hand clenched tight in a ball, the Madman in the black and white face paint began to envision smashing his fist into the back of Melina's head. His goal was to pummel her off her knees and shatter her face into the dirt floor. He wanted to kick her in the ribs and chest until blood came out her nose and ears. He wanted to hang her from the rafters and fuck her senseless.

How dare she ruin his plans?

With his fist frozen in its downward swing, the Madman realized that changing his plan wasn't an option. He had learned a long time ago how important it was to have a plan.

Even more important, was sticking to the plan.

Especially when things were going so well.

Unclenching his fist, the Madman used his hand instead to pick up the leather handle of the choke chain off the dirt floor; and when Melina was told to stop her crying, the tone of his voice insured that there was no hesitation.

Pulling on the chain enough to slightly jab the sharpened tines into the open wounds that Melina had caused herself, the clown escorted Melina on her hands and knees across the floor. They stopped in front of the door that her captor had used on so many occasions as he entered and tortured Melina with silence, bright lights and a vicious crack of the whip.

Melina had an acute sense of her surroundings from her weeks of captivity in the dark. Behind her now and slightly to the right was the set up of lights and the chair he would perch himself in while she ate like an animal. The very same chair where he had just pleasured himself as he watched her bathe; and right behind that, a short wall that normally held the bullwhip.

Melina had a strong feeling that other items were probably displayed there as well but didn't want to risk a glance over her shoulder to see. Despite her recent assurance that she was going to survive this nightmare, she wasn't taking any chances at provoking her captor.

The Madman bent down and leaned his face up against the side of Melina's head and whispered hot breath into her ear.

"Be good or be dead."

Then a black canvas bag slipped over her head and out went the lights once again.

Chapter 49

Becca knew to be direct with Ruby. Any beating around the bush regarding Jack Thomas would only be met with a swift kick in the ass and directions to the door. Although Becca hated to divulge any thing about the manuscript to the family she felt cornered by Ruby and therefore out of options.

Becca's mouth opened, ready to divulge information about the manuscript to Ruby. Instead, Becca's brain took a shortcut and intercepted the truth and began the story about doing research on the original founding families of Long Island. Becca had no idea where she was going with this line of thought; it had all started without a conscious effort and she assumed it would continue that way. Besides it would be perfect practice since she would have to use it tomorrow night on her date with Christopher John.

But it didn't matter.

Because as it turned out, Ruby didn't care about the specifics.

"I don't mean to be rude…" Ruby paused as if giving the comment thought and then continued, "Actually, yes I do."

Becca raised her eyebrows and felt her face flush.

It took a lot, but Ruby finally did it.

Becca wanted to smack that condescending bitch across the face so hard that she would think she was in a remake of the *Exorcist*.

Ruby could tell that she had finally gotten under Becca's skin and that maybe she had pushed over that line a little too far; so, she consciously tapered her tone down a notch.

"What I mean is, honey…" One more jab, Ruby couldn't help herself.

Honey was just like Ma'am to most women. Especially, when used with the right subtle tone and false smile.

Okay she was done; Ruby felt satisfied.

Ruby continued to explain her position to Becca as Kyra sat and listened. "I don't give a rat's ass if Jack Thomas is alive or dead. Honestly, I'd be a fool to think that he wasn't alive. I don't think my husband and his brother are feeble. Nor do I think that they would make up such tales."

"So, whatever your excuse, or whatever your motivation is; it is completely and utterly irrelevant. I don't care what you think you know; and I certainly don't want to hear anything that might get our husbands contemplating the existence of an older brother again."

Becca was dumbfounded at what Ruby was saying and looked to Kyra for some support in understanding. Kyra however, eyebrows raised and scrunched together just kept nodding in one hundred percent agreement with Ruby's dogma.

At the risk of being told it was none of her god-damned business, Becca asked; "I don't understand; if you think Jack might still be alive…"

Ruby was quick to the draw and obviously losing her thin margin of hospitality for the uninvited Latino guest.

"I'm going to say this slowly for you since you seem to have missed it the first time. I believe Jack is alive. There have been too many instances or sightings if you will, by our husbands to not believe them."

Ruby stopped talking, crossed her arms in front of her chest and stared at Becca as if simply repeating herself, even if she said it slightly differently, would clarify matters.

Just as Becca was about to use the 'what have I got to lose' tone with Ruby in a vain attempt at receiving an answer to her question; Kyra stood up and stepped between Becca and Ruby who had moved uncomfortably close to one another.

"Let me explain;" Kyra said as she took Becca's arm and walked her over to the deck's railing. Standing side by side overlooking the backyard, watching Brendon and Kenny play with the children on the swing set, Kyra spoke softly while still looking out across the yard. Becca followed her gaze and listened.

"Ruby and I are very bitter about the whole Jack Thomas issue. Ruby hides it much better than I do though." The two women shared a quick glance and smiled at the obvious misstatement before returning their eyes to the backyard revelry.

"You see Becca, if Jack was alive, Ruby and I would be the first ones to kill him." This time only Becca turned her head and Kyra continued talking facing forward. "Do you realize the torment those two brothers have put themselves through? First of all by losing their older brother at a time when all they could only reflect on was how much they never got to know him. Then, to be tortured with the notion that they thought they kept seeing him; at his own funeral no less. Think of the anguish, I don't know about Brendon; but, Kenny still talks to a therapist once a month."

"That's awful." Becca interjected, truly visualizing the circumstances from this angle for the first time. Her stomach turned and her heart ached for the two brothers she had just met only hours earlier.

Kyra sighed and took a deep breath before continuing. "For a while there, Kenny would think his brother was everywhere; in a passing car, across the street in a restaurant, in the stadium at a ballgame… Kenny thought he was sincerely losing his mind and I believe his therapist agreed. Can you imagine? According to Kenny, Jack not only made an appearance at both of our weddings; but, he was there at Brad and Shannon's funeral as well. What a tragedy… as if that wasn't hard enough on all of us anyway."

"Who?" Becca asked, forgetting for the moment the names of Jack's parents.

"Brendon's and Kenny's mother and father; they were murdered while on vacation in Florida about twelve years ago."

(Unedited excerpt from the manuscript)

Okay, sorry about the backtracking; if I had more time I'd do a rewrite so you'd have continuity.

Fuck you.

Honestly, I didn't know I was going to write so much. The original plan was to just introduce myself so you faceless fucks would have a name for your fear; but one thing led to another, and here we are.

I have had an absolutely wonderful time reliving the past and I can't believe this notebook is almost completely full.

Don't worry, I'm not cutting you off quite yet; I do still want to share some of this past decade with you and bring us closer to current events.

But, first...back to the Sunshine State.

◆

Any good butcher will tell you; no matter how frugal you are, there are always parts of the animal that just are not edible. And in my case, I had to be extra selective with what cuts of meat I was utilizing.

Only the best for my clientele.

Besides I didn't serve everyone; sometimes I couldn't, the meat was too bruised or torn apart.

I found myself with a similar dilemma to the one I had in Ohio; what to do with the remains of my playmates.

My beetle friends were definitely an option again, however I wasn't about to turn my house or apartment into a taxidermy prep-lab. Besides that would have burdened me with leftover bones to contend with and I preferred a one step solution.

I'm making this sound like I didn't have a plan and I hope you know me well enough by now to realize that that would be a mistake.

You're right.

Congratulations you faceless fuck.

I'm guessing that you've gotten at least one answer correct today.

Interstate 75, the Everglades Parkway, or better known as Alligator Alley; do I need to say more? I think not; but I will. 40

miles of remote access to nature's greatest garbage disposal...The Florida Everglades.

You'd be amazed at what an alligator the size of your car can eat.

💣

I feel like I reached a plateau while living in Florida; it all happened one night when I was torturing the twins.

Maggie and Carlie Mullen; they had just moved to the US with their parents from Boostertown, an area just outside Dublin, Ireland.

I'm surprised I remember that, but I guess you remember your last as much as you remember your first. It's either that or the fact that they were pure and exquisite specimens. Red hair that made sunsets jealous and green eyes that had lush fields weeping tears of dew with envy.

I'm such the romantic.

After a long day at Colorado Prime; believe it or not, I actually had real work to do in between all the fun I was having. It unfortunately was a necessary trade-off to maintain my position with the company that was providing me with a never ending supply of playmates.

What are you gonna do?

You've got to play the game.

Am I right?

Anyway, I was sitting by the pool at The Tap Room Beach Bar right off A1A. Conveniently located a few blocks from my Lauderdale apartment, the place was a great tourist trap where a land shark like myself was able to just lay and wait for his next victim to come along. The Tap, as us locals called it, had 3 bars, 2 of them outside by the pool, live bands and was spitting distance from the boardwalk.

I lost count exactly how many women came home with me from The Tap over the few years I lived in Florida ...it was like picking apples off a tree.

Good times.

Maggie and Carlie showed up at the perfect time. I was sitting in my chaise lounge early that evening brooding about my job at Colorado Prime and contemplating a career change.

I was reflecting on all of the individuals and families I had crossed paths with since Amanda Farber.

Literally spanning the globe in a wake of blood.

I had accomplished so much; however, I was feeling a sense of boredom. Or, more aptly put, a sense of redundancy.

Been there; done that... Next.

It just goes to show you that no matter what you do; no matter what you achieve; no matter how high you've climbed... If you're still breathing; you should want more.

If you don't; and I'm sure most of you faceless fucks don't, and I'm not in the least bit surprised; however, if you don't want more, if you have reached a point where you can honestly say "I'm done"... Do yourself a favor and fucking kill yourself. I don't care who you are or what you do; there is more and you should want it.

My point is that I reached that point where I wanted to do more. My problem was what do I do to kick it up a notch?

How do I increase the ~~thump-thump~~?

From the moment I returned to the States and moved to Florida I had begun to devise ideas and plans for this next level of mayhem.

It was time to put pen to paper.

It was time to mature from my slaying, my butchering, my torturing and my raping.

Enough was enough; wouldn't you agree?

I mean, how much pizza can one person eat?

❧

Steadfast in my new direction and pleased with my resolve to make changes in my life; I opened my eyes that day by the pool at The Tap and was blessed with Maggie and Carlie Mullen.

A gift from my Creator.

Confirmation of my recent epiphany.

I looked up at the twin Irish beauties and knew at that very moment that they were going to be lucky enough to be my last hands-on playmates.

I also knew exactly what game I wanted to play with them.

Question One; for $100... Can you feel your sister's pain?

10 seconds... You'd better hurry.

❧

Chapter 50

Utterly flabbergasted at the bizarre misfortune this family had suffered over the years; Becca asked Kyra what had happened to Brad and Shannon Thomas.

Kyra gave a quick glance over her shoulder apparently looking to see where Ruby was before answering that particular question.

Ruby was nowhere to be seen. She had disappeared off the deck while they had been talking.

Initially Becca thought that Ruby was just a bitch; but now she could see that she was a true matriarch. Her motivation seemed to stem from protecting the family's best interests; both emotionally and physically. Despite all the comments and looks Ruby had thrown her way; Becca felt a great deal of respect and admiration for Ruby. She was simply defending her territory.

The sliding glass door opened and Ruby reemerged from the kitchen with a platter of cut up fruit for the children. The colorful array of green, yellow and red apple wedges, purple and green grapes, plump red strawberries and white banana slices surrounding a bowl of dipping chocolate looked like it was torn from the pages of a *Good Housekeeping* magazine. Becca wondered if Ruby actually made it or was just presenting the labor of their house-helper, Clara. Then Becca realized that either way it didn't matter; because probably nobody in the household gave it a second thought.

Becca wondered how long it would take her to start taking the finer things in life for granted once she had become accustomed to them. Then she realized that she was assuming that just because nobody was making a big deal about some of the finer thing the Thomas's were able to enjoy, that they were being taken for granted.

Becca's head began to sway as her mind wrapped itself around the concept that maybe *she* was being the bitch. Like reverse prejudice.

Then Ruby spoke and clarified matters. "I'd offer you some dessert... But I'd prefer it if you would just leave."

Becca's mouth worked as fast as her brain sent the words. First filtering out the initial sentence which suggested where Ruby could put the fruit platter; Becca made a request of the two wives, but primarily focused her attention on Ruby.

"I *am* sorry that I not only disrupted your lovely afternoon with the family; but, had I realized how deep the scars were, regarding Jack Thomas, I never would have come here in the first place."

Becca paused to allow the words an opportunity to work their way through Ruby's thick hide and find a soft spot before she delivered the ultimatum.

"Three things are very clear to me; first, it is clear that you don't want me talking to your husbands for a variety of reasons." Becca took a deep breath expanding her chest and shot a small smirk at Ruby as she continued. "Second, it is also clear that you don't care what information I have that suggests that Jack is still alive; and third, you would love for me to leave and never have any further contact with anyone in this family."

"You have an acute awareness of the obvious Miss Willis." Becca was impressed that Ruby remembered her full name and was glad to see that she had gotten under her skin. That level of discomfort was exactly what Becca needed to seal the deal so she went for the final challenge.

"I'm glad you agree, Ms. Thomas, because this is what I propose."

Ruby's eyebrows raised and her head cocked to the side as she set down the fruit platter on the table. Standing just a couple of feet from Becca, Ruby's hands went to her hips and she squared off in a stance that was suggestive of Wonder Woman. Kyra stepped up closer to the two women and positioned herself on the ready to react to what appeared to be an escalating situation.

Becca was thrilled to have everyone's full attention; but definitely did not want to get into a physical altercation. As much as she would have loved to have just one good swing at Ruby; Becca couldn't risk any scratches or bruises to her face, she did have a hot date tomorrow night after all.

However, Becca was too far into her proposition to alter her approach and would just have to accept whatever reaction was about to come.

"I will never initiate communication with you or your husbands ever again. I will leave here today without saying another word to them. You can make up whatever reasons you want for my departure. You can tell them that I made a terrible mistake and was too embarrassed to admit it. Tell them I was misguided in my research... it doesn't matter. Bottom line is that you can do damage control however you see fit."

Becca paused to read the expressions on the wives' faces. Kyra was nodding as if relieved and in total agreement. Ruby on the other hand knew that it wasn't going to be that simple and was waiting to hear the rest; so Becca complied and finished outlining the bargain.

"All I want…" Becca glanced back and forth at the two women. "All I want…" Becca repeated herself enjoying the suspense. "All I want is to have a look at the box that came this afternoon." Becca smiled with raised eyebrows and continued to look back and forth between Ruby and Kyra awaiting an answer.

Chapter 51

As soon as the black canvas bag slipped over her head, Melina's finely tuned senses took control.

The past couple of weeks being surrounded in absolute darkness changed Melina on a deep and instinctual level. Her heightened awareness evolved quickly due to the added threat of survival.

The human body is amazing in its ability to adjust to circumstances. In particular, when those circumstances are so far beyond our control or influence; we seem to be able to tap into an aspect of our psyche that is connected to mankind's global evolution. We are able to gather strength, courage and wisdom from eras past, present and future. We are able to accomplish feats and perform acts typically impossible under normal conditions; and we do this instinctively, we dig deep inside and call upon this hidden reservoir of miracles in our most dire times of need.

Within the cloak of darkness, very much like a bat, Melina's senses of hearing and touch, and even her sense of smell, vibrated in harmony to form a vivid picture in her mind.

Melina had a keen understanding of her surroundings. With the absence of sight, Melina was able to see much better than she had ever been able to before.

The Madman reached around and opened the door that blocked their way.

He stood slightly behind her and to her left. He held the handle of the choke chain in his left hand and had his right hand positioned on the small of her back just over her left hip. He placed mild pressure on her body indicating his desire for her to move forward.

Melina complied without hesitation.

Stepping through the threshold, Melina instantly felt her surroundings alter. The change was overwhelming in its stark contrast. One moment Melina's bare feet felt the soft inconsistencies of a dirt floor and then the cool smoothness of tile. One moment her nostrils were filled with the distinct sweet aroma of old wood and then the dusty fragrance of plaster and paint. One moment she felt as if she was outdoors in a rustic setting and then in the next moment, her ears were filled with the subtle buzzing of overhead florescent lighting of an indoor setting.

The vast contrast between the two sides of the threshold she had just passed through felt disconnected. Melina's mind wanted to fill a gap between the two sensations with a passageway that didn't exist.

Without the benefit of true sight to explain the extremely different mental images she was getting; Melina's mind wanted to create something, a logical transition from one room to the next; the two rooms felt as if they were worlds apart. It wasn't like walking from one room with carpet into one without within the same house. These two rooms felt like they were on opposite ends of the world; as if day had become night without the transition of a sunset.

Melina decided that she must have been drugged in the one room; the room she had come to know as 'her cell', and then had regained consciousness in this 'other room'. It was the only way she could have her mind accept the vast differences. Melina assumed that the canvas bag must been laced with something like chloroform.

For all she knew they might have taken a car ride in between.

As they walked down a long corridor Melina could sense rooms they were passing on both the right and left. Her mind's eye created a detailed picture of her new surroundings. She saw herself in a hallway reminiscent of a hospital wing or an office building. She was also able to visualize her captor a half step behind her; his face painted black and white with red slashes and his long-tailed jacket adding to the psychotic Ring Master look.

His fingers slid into the waistband of her boxer shorts and he held her still. Melina could feel the chain hanging down between the choke collar around her throat and the handle in his hand swing back and forth as he reached out and opened a door to their left. The door must have swung inward as they were able to stand their ground and not step out of its way.

Gently pressing against her lower back once again he nudged her forward into the room. His sneakers were making small squeaks on the tile flooring as he stopped and started moving. Each tiny squeak sent tiny chills up Melina's spine. The sound was deafening in her heightened state and her captor seemed to notice because he appeared to do it on purpose.

Melina hated this asshole like she had never hated anyone in her life. If she wasn't holding onto the hope that he was truly going to let her live; she would take this opportunity to attempt a break.

She could envision herself having a small, but realistic opening at turning on her captor. Relying on her mental picture, she was sure that he had no weapons. True there was a lethal choke collar around her neck that would tear her throat to shreds in a matter of seconds; but she still played out a viable scenario in her mind that gave her a moderate margin of success.

Melina always kept her fingernails long and well groomed. She had been nurturing them with nail strengthening products for as long as she had a credit card to buy them. These past weeks while digging at the wood surrounding the metal plate in the wall of 'her cell' had also sharpened them considerably.

Sporting ten razor sharp knives on the end of her fingers, Melina played out the attack in her mind.

Her heart began beating hard in her chest and her breathing intensified.

Afraid that her captor noticed a change in her behavior, Melina supposed that she has passed a point of no return.

Subconsciously she feared that she had already made a decision; committed herself to a course of action, and now there was no turning back.

Melina felt that she had left herself with no choice but to go on the offensive.

Chapter 52

"What box?" Kyra asked, first looking to Becca then turning her attention to Ruby.

Ruby ignored the question and spoke through clenched teeth at Becca. "You barge in on my family uninvited; you disrupt our peaceful Sunday barbeque; you bring up personal family business that is of no concern to you; and then, you have the nerve, the audacity, to make an ultimatum."

Ruby must have just watched a Godfather movie; because for a split second there, Becca actually became concerned she was being confronted by Victoria Gotti, sister of the famed John Gotti and the Gambino crime family.

If Ruby wanted to play mobster, Becca was more than willing to comply.

"My dear friend;" Becca began, utilizing the Mafia's version of 'Honey', and enjoyed the twitch it prompted in Ruby's left eye. "I make no ultimatum here; and certainly imply nothing that can be misconstrued as a threat. I simply offer an amicable solution to what appears to be an impasse between us."

Not really following the strange turn in the conversation, Kyra asked once again; "What box?"

Both Becca and Ruby turned to Kyra with an expression that said 'Are you for real?' before continuing with their dialogue.

Ruby's left eye now twitched repeatedly as she spoke. "You have just frayed my last nerve Miss Willis. Your unwelcome presence can no longer be tolerated and I am peaceably asking you to vacate these premises immediately."

Since Ruby broke character, Becca felt there was no need for her to continue so she just laid it back on the line the best way she knew how; straight up, no bullshit.

"Ruby, I don't see why you are making this simple solution so fucking difficult." Ruby acted like she had never heard the f-word before; and as she muttered, 'Well... I've never...' Becca just continued on as if Ruby said nothing.

"I can leave now if you'd like; but I promise you, I will call your husbands at work. I will meet with them again. I will and can cultivate their belief that Jack is alive."

Becca saw that her point was hitting home and she probably could have stopped there, except she wanted to insure that she received no more resistance from Ruby.

"Lastly, Ms. Thomas;" Becca turned her head to Kyra to include her in the conversation as well; "when I do meet with your husbands alone in the city... I will be quite attentive to their needs... I will be very hands on in all my interactions with them... You will question every late lunch they have; every business meeting they have out of town; if they get stuck in traffic and are simply fifteen minutes late... You will wonder..."

Becca was bluffing of course, she would never, could never, do that to this family. She had grown to genuinely care about the Thomas's that afternoon; Brendon and Kenny were adorable, and she couldn't imagine creating any problems for them at home, let alone pouring salt into the open wounds they carried for their older brother.

Becca even felt a lot of respect and admiration for both Ruby and Kyra as well; they seemed to be strong, loving women that have dealt with more than most in keeping their family units healthy.

Even though her words were merely a bluff; Becca still felt horrible suggesting that type of behavior. But, Ruby had put her back up against the wall and left her with no other alternative.

So, now with all her cards on the table, and no more Aces up her sleeve, Becca made her final plea. "As I said before… I only want one thing and then I will go away forever… I want to see the box that arrived this afternoon."

"Damn it you two!" Kyra exclaimed, "What box!"

(Unedited excerpt from the manuscript)

The sisters stood before me like Manna from Heaven.

Barely 2 weeks in the country, speaking English with heavy Irish drawls, Maggie and Carlie asked me if I knew of any parties going on.

Timing is everything.

I've been very fortunate my whole life to be in the right place at the right time.

That isn't by coincidence.

It is by design.

It is also by that very basic principle that I will be delivering countless thousands of you faceless fucks to your judgment day. City by city, state by state, you will learn my name and feel my influence. I have been guided by the Creator to prepare catastrophic moments in time that are awaiting your arrival.

We are all driven by the Hands of Fate.

💣

It turned out the girls were looking to score some weed. Wacky-tobaccy.

I never got into drugs or excessive alcohol myself. Didn't much understand the appeal? Saw too much in my earlier days working at The Back Barn to see a glamorous side. Why would you want to dull your senses or alter your consciousness? I can't imagine not being able to savor every experience I've had over the years.

I would miss all the pain and fear I've inflicted.

Wouldn't you?

💣

Okay, I keep drifting off topic...

Maggie and Carlie Mullen. 19 year old twin test subjects.

Participants arrived at my apartment in Fort Lauderdale at approximately 7:30 pm under the pretense of testing out some primo Burmese-Indica hydroponic crypto bud. (Just 'cause I didn't walk the walk, didn't mean I couldn't talk the talk. Yo feelin me dog?)

More than willing to try a new high, and a first for myself in the category of bold moves; my new roommates watched me pour the Chloroform onto a pair of handkerchiefs and allowed me to hold them to their faces as they relaxed upon my living room couch.

Unconscious, the test subjects were stripped down and bound in separate rooms. Upon initial investigation, both specimens appeared flawless and truly identical.

At the time of regaining consciousness and communicating through simple yes and no blinks of the eyes; it was determined that Maggie was bound to the bed, and Carlie was chained to the wall. To avoid future confusion a small 'M' and a small 'C' were carved into the bottom of the test subject's feet.

It was noted that neither participant was ticklish.

Experiments involving point of contact pain ranging from blunt force to heated hatpins proved to be inconclusive regarding any shared feelings between the twin test subjects.

Back and forth I gave them equal opportunities to pinpoint (no pun intended) where their twin counterpart experienced the pain I inflicted. A correct answer would allow them a rest period where no repercussions would be imposed upon them. However, incorrect answers were dealt with swift and violent blows to the head in equal proportions. Meaning that if I sliced into Maggie's left nipple 4 times with a razor and Carlie couldn't guess the correct side and the correct number of cuts, jabs, slices, burns or whatever; then Carlie would get punched 4 times in the head.

Very simple instructions: all they had to do was lift the corresponding hand with the right number of fingers showing.

Not difficult; should have been an easy game to play.

But, they were wrong more than they were right.

More unsuccessful research was conducted by playing several games of 'What hole did I just fuck your sister in?'... And it was finally determined that there is no psychic connection between twins.

However, despite the negative results, I had a wonderful time; Carlie and Maggie were like having a Twix candy bar. When I was done with one; there was another waiting for me in the other room. I stayed up for days playing with the twins.

Finally I grew tired of my own debauchery. A symptom of the times, as I had mentioned earlier right before the twins arrived; I was done.

I had reached a pinnacle in my endeavors and was ready to move on to bigger and better things.

I did lament the end of another era I approached the obliteration of the twin's existence with the knowledge that the Irish duo was going to be the last of my hands-on brutal escapades.

Don't misunderstand me: I had no regrets, because after all, that is what life is all about: living without regret. How many of you faceless fucks can look back over your pathetic existence and say that you've lived without regret?

And, make no mistake, I had no intention of not killing more of you faceless fucks: I was just limiting the extent of my personal, hands-on, involvement.

I wanted to get back to making a lot of noise. I hadn't played a game of 'Gender Specific Casualty' since the Limelight.

Chapter 53

Melina turned and brought both hands up to his throat with cat-like speed and agility. Even with the black canvas bag covering her head her accuracy was impeccable. The nails on her thumbs cut into his flesh like they were slicing through soft butter. Warm fluid oozed over her hands and a whoosh of air escaped his punctured trachea. Racking her fingernails along the side of his neck as her thumbs hooked inside his throat she shook his head back and forth. Blood spewed from tattered jugulars on each side of his neck as his head snapped backwards and forwards with her increased ferocity.

When the canvas bag was torn off her head, Melina was blinded by the brightness of the overhead fluorescent lighting. White light blazed off the walls and white tile floors and burned her retinas. Melina didn't even realize her eyes were open; she was so immersed in her escape fantasy, she actually thought it was happening.

Blinking her eyes against the sting of the light, Melina looked down at her hands which felt sticky with blood that wasn't there. Her heart was pounding and her breathing was labored. Melina felt the weight of the choke collar around her throat and resisted the spiraling obscurity that swept through her mind. Blackness was approaching from all angles and Melina feared she was about to faint.

A familiar voice resounded at her side, echoing off the walls of the sterile room and fear helped her maintain consciousness.

"Welcome to the War Room."

(Unedited excerpt from the manuscript)

I left Maggie and Carlie alive; at least it looked like they were still breathing as I doused my apartment in gasoline.

I was in no mood to clean up and I really made a mess of the twins.

It was a very fitting end to my time in Florida. I was reminded of the final weekend at the Hollingsworth's Barn.

Fire is cleansing.

Ashes to ashes, dust to dust... all that crap.

The fire not only destroyed my apartment complex, but took out the entire block, killing 4 and leaving 3 dozen homeless. The Sun-Sentinel proclaimed the fire as the worst disaster to hit Ft. Lauderdale since hurricane Andrew ravaged the coast in '92.

Personally I found the comparison to be a little extreme; however, I did enjoy being associated with the raw power of Nature.

Although the paper did state that the police were investigating the fire, the paper failed to mention that one of the 4 found dead was chained to a wall.

I can't say I was surprised when Darren Applegate, an old co-worker of mine from Colorado Prime, was arrested and charged with arson and murder.

Darren seemed like such a nice guy when I hired him...

🖤

Chapter 54

While Ruby was telling Kyra about the 'birthday' box that had arrived while Kenny was still at their house; Becca realized how to seal the deal and end what was becoming a long afternoon.

Earlier Ruby and Kyra had both alluded to the perfect scenario. If Becca could have used this rational sooner, she would have avoided playing out a scene from *The Godfather* with Ruby and the afternoon could have ended on a slightly friendlier note. Meanwhile, no matter what happens now, Becca's ultimatum will be the only thing Ruby and Kyra will remember.

Becca felt like an ass, but there was more at stake than a popularity contest.

"Why do you want to see the box? What's it to you anyway?" Kyra asked with her brow furrowed and her head bopping side to side. All that was missing was some hand gestures to complete Martin Lawrence's Sha-Na-Na look.

Becca couldn't tell if Kyra was annoyed with her, or the fact that another one of those 'birthday' boxes arrived which would mean dealing with the whole '*It's from Jack*' thing again.

Becca was pretty sure it was a combination of everything; as even keeled as Kyra had seemed to be, there had to be a breaking point. Kyra had watched her husband share intimate details with some stranger for a good part of the day with no questions asked. Then, she rehashed some of her own personal heartaches with that same stranger, dredging up issues that had finally been buried; and to top it all off, that very same stranger threatened the sanctity of their marriage with an ultimatum of intentionally seducing her husband.

Looking at it that way, Becca was amazed these two women were still talking to her at all.

With Kyra's question still looming in the air and with the knowledge that she had the absolute deal maker on the tip of her tongue, Becca said; "I was hoping you could help me." Two quick bats of the eyes, a demure look down, eye contact with raised eyebrows and then wait.

Becca received identical looks from the women that said 'Are you fucking kidding?' but it was Kyra who continued to speak. "How is seeing the box going to help you?"

Becca smiled, the question was the perfect set up.

"Not help me...Help us."

Chapter 55

The room was stark white with three rows of fluorescent lighting fixtures overhead, each housing six four-foot bulbs. The illumination of the twenty by twenty-five foot room was absolute. Bright, even light bathed the room from floor to ceiling and wall to wall. Free of any clutter, the white maple conference table with matching chairs in the center of the room almost disappeared in the absence of shadows.

As Melina's eyes adjusted to the harsh lighting she became aware of the artwork that surrounded the room.

With her captor a half step behind her and to the left, Melina took a step forward to gain a better view of the art that lined the walls. Pleased with her initiative, the Madman kept pace so as not to inflict any undo pressure on her throat with the choke collar and thereby opening fresh wounds.

This was a room that was kept free of bloodshed.

Instead this was a room where bloodshed was planned.

Approaching the wall, Melina realized that she was not looking at artwork, but rather maps. The walls were covered with maps of varying cities. Each map was elaborately drawn on with what first appeared to be a spider's web. Upon closer inspection however, Melina realized that they were in fact routes planned out from a central point that varied from map to map and from city to city.

Tendrils in assorted colors stemmed forth and had time coordinates listed along their sides as they wove through city streets and ended at sporadic locations with small illustrations of bombs.

Leaning in closer, Melina saw that each small bomb illustration had more numbers notated along their sides. Yet still, the most frightening discovery Melina viewed on the maps was the specific sites of the illustrated bomb's locations. Mainly tunnels, bridges and airports, but Melina also noticed a few ferry docks, subway terminals and bus stations as well.

Melina gasped as she absorbed the magnitude of what each map exemplified.

In a voice that was unmistakably proud, the Madman boasted; "Beautiful, aren't they?"

Moving around the room, trying to make a mental list of the cities represented on the wall, Melina risked keeping silent and defied providing a response.

Not every map was easy to identify the city from whence it came; but the Madman sensing Melina's angst was more than happy to provide the information as they walked the five hundred square feet.

"New York, Los Angeles, Chicago, Houston, Philadelphia, Phoenix, San Antonio, San Diego, Dallas, San Jose, Detroit, Indianapolis, Jacksonville, San Francisco, Columbus, the one in Ohio not Georgia; but don't worry Georgia is represented on the other wall."

The Madman leaned his painted face inches from Melina's own and asked if she had noticed the pattern yet. Not waiting for a reply he snapped his head back away from Melina's face and continued around the room reciting cities names in an almost sing-song fashion.

Melina was revolted at his good cheer as he played show-and-tell; and the thought of using her nails as a weapon crossed her mind once again.

"Austin, Memphis, Baltimore, Fort Worth, Charlotte, El Paso, Milwaukee, Seattle, Boston, Denver, Washington D.C.; I wanted to visit D.C. and the Capitol first, but it's important to have a plan and stick to it. Don't you agree?"

This time he stopped and waited for her to answer; but as soon as she opened her mouth he spoke over her response. "Of course you agree. You'd agree to anything I asked. You're nothing more than a pet monkey at this point; a pet monkey who is smart enough to know that she might live to see tomorrow. If I asked you if you thought it was a good idea to suck my cock you'd agree wouldn't you."

Disgusted, Melina went to voice her affirmative answer but it got stuck in her throat and nothing came out.

Infuriated at her lack of response the Madman grabbed her face with his free hand and squeezed. The inside of Melina's cheeks scrapped across her teeth as he pinched her face together. Screaming at her, his voice bouncing off the walls in the small room, spittle spraying into her eyes and open mouth.

"Wouldn't you!"

With tears forming in her eyes and terrible pain mounting in her jaw, Melina managed a meager "Yes."

Pushing her face out of his clenched hand he reinforced his authority by stating; "Of course you would; you'd love to have my dick in your mouth." He smiled and used his thumb to wipe away the tears that trickled from the corner of her eyes. "I am like a God to you. I alone have the power over your life and death."

Fighting against her natural instinct to cringe away; Melina maintained control over her revulsion and allowed him to cradle his hand just under her chin.

She swore to herself though that if his dick ever did end up anywhere near her mouth, she would sever it with her bare teeth and rip his ball sack from his body in the process.

Having regained control of his emotions, the Madman placed his hand back against the small of Melina's back, slightly on her hip as well, and escorted her around the final turn of the room.

"Nashville, Vegas, Portland, Tucson, Albuquerque, Long Beach, Atlanta, Fresno, Sacramento, New Orleans, Cleveland, Kansas City…"

Chapter 56

Once Becca explained that her search for Jack Thomas was motivated by a desire to see him dead or behind bars for the rest of his life, Ruby and Kyra were tripping over themselves to cooperate.

"Why didn't you say so in the first place?" Ruby's entire demeanor changed to such an extent that she actually looked like a different person. "Oh, I am so sorry for the way I've been acting." Looking around, Ruby remembered the fruit platter on the table and motioned towards it; "Would you like some desert? Can I get you any thing to drink?"

Becca had had enough for one day; by her count that was two back-to-back crazy days on Long Island and she was ready to get back to the city. She found herself eager to communicate with Roberto and share the news of the day with him. He was more than correct in his assessment that the brother's would have valuable information to assist them in their quest to save Melina and stop the Madman.

The three women decided that Ruby would stay behind and cover with the family, while Becca would follow Kyra the short two and a half miles to her house to inspect the 'birthday' box. Ruby would explain that Becca received an urgent phone call and had to leave suddenly and Kyra made a mad dash home for feminine reasons.

A perfect plan that would raise no questions and allow Ruby and Kyra the freedom to minimize Becca's visit and regain a semblance of normality with their respective husbands.

Pat Addams

Ruby insisted that Becca take her cell phone number and keep her abreast of any developments that had to do with the demise of Jack Thomas; and further offered any assistance that she may be able to provide.

Ruby and Becca embraced each other in the driveway and parted like they had been friends since elementary school. It is amazing what a common enemy can do; throughout the centuries it has been bringing people of such different and diverse backgrounds together.

The commonality of hatred; a beautiful thing.

Backing out first, Becca watched as Ruby continued to wave goodbye while Kyra pulled her car out of the driveway and proceeded to lead the way to her home in Roslyn.

(Unedited excerpt from the manuscript)

It had been a long time since I made a bomb.

Holy shit a lot had changed.

I couldn't even buy descent fireworks anymore. Back in the day you could at least pick up an M-80 and it truly was a 1/4 stick of dynamite. We used to be able to light them and toss them into the bay where they would sink with the fuse still going.

That always amazed me... fire burning in water! I mean... what the fuck?

The M-80's would sink down a couple of feet and attract the attention of some of the Bluegills and Sunfish; and then ka-blam! The underwater blast would create a concussion bubble that not only knocked the shit out the fish, but also rose up and broke the surface with a plume of smoke.

I'm telling you... good fucking times.

The old M-80's were also great for jamming up the school's plumbing system. Light, flush and leave. You'd be back out in the hallway standing next to a teacher by the time you heard the pipe rupture.

Can't imagine why they stopped making those.

- 182 -

Nowadays, what they sell as M-80's are barely what the old Black Cat firecrackers used to be. They don't even sink! What the hell happened to a little thing called quality?

Nothing is like it was and you faceless fucks have just accepted that as the new norm. Planned obsolescence is a component of everything you buy and you don't care.

I'm guessing you don't even know what that means.

There is such a thing as being too adaptable. It is called complacency; it is a disease and you have a terminal case of it.

You have the attention span of a gnat and you wonder why I'm not worried about telling you so boldly about your impending fate. You are too stupid and too complacent to do anything about it anyway. Like I said earlier; it's like squishing bugs.

Speaking of squishing... The Chinese had the right approach at Tiananmen Square.

I was there. Talk about power and a fuck you attitude.

Do you even remember Tiananmen Square?

See my point.

At that particular moment in time I knew that I was going to target the countries major cities. I knew that I was about to invest a lot of time in the planning stages and I knew I wanted to have all my proverbial ducks in a row.

Meaning that after the first city would fall captive to my mayhem; the next in line would be ready without the delays of starting over in the planning stages. I figured it would be just as easy to plan the full scale attack verses one attack at a time.

I was right; it took a while, but I've had a great time along the way. I enjoy instant gratification as much as the next guy; but there is something to be said about the journey. It's not always just about the destination.

It's how you got there that really counts.

Part of this particular journey began with the realization that I needed to be on the inside of a global financial institution. With the details of the companies I needed to formulate and the amount of additional funding that was about to be required; working on the inside with the systems only made sense.

I narrowed it down to 2 choices; Bank of America and Citibank Bank.

There was only one logical solution in determining which institution was going to be fortunate enough to have me as an employee...

Cue the announcer...

"That's right folks; it's time to play another game of Gender Specific Casualty... Today we are on location in sunny Florida where we will be introducing our new friend... Captain C4. The Captain will be visiting the lovely St. Regis Fort Lauderdale Resort... A unique hotel that provides views of both the Atlantic Ocean and the Intra-coastal Waterway... The St. Regis Resort is a seaside property that offers an array of upscale amenities to satisfy even the most discerning of guests."

💣

Chapter 57

"Wine passes right through me, always has; I'll be right back, please make yourself at home." Kyra excused herself to the bathroom as soon as they stepped into the foyer.

Becca watched as Kyra ran up the stairs past an open door to a small bathroom and guessed that Kyra's trip to the toilet might be more than a quick splash.

Looking around from her vantage point just inside the doorway, Becca felt a very warm and inviting atmosphere to the décor. The lower level of the split-level house was rich with earth tones and uninhibited by harsh dividing walls. To Becca's left, a sunken living room flowed comfortably off a dining area that was separated from the kitchen by a short wall and bar. To her right, an elongated sitting room bathed in the afternoon sun wrapped around behind the stairs and followed a hallway that separated it from the main entrance to the kitchen.

The only doors Becca could see on this floor were the front door she had just come through, the door ajar to the guest bathroom and the glass doors that rested between the sitting room and the kitchen at the end of the hallway.

Becca was drawn down the hall to the inviting panorama view that lay just outside and off the back patio. Kenny and Kyra's house was atop a picturesque vista overlooking one of the oldest villages on Long Island.

Stepping out on the enclosed patio lush with potted plants and herbs, Becca inhaled deeply, savoring the sweet air sweeping in off the Long Island Sound as she admired the quaint layout of Roslyn.

Becca exhaled with a sigh of mourning for a lifestyle she may never have. Envy wasn't a common emotion for Becca, yet she found herself deep within its green fields. The afternoon had taken its toll on her; she wanted this house, she wanted the husband and she wanted the kids. Not necessarily the exact house, husband and kids; but the exact conditions. The extended family, the closeness they seemed to have, both logistically and emotionally. But most of all, Becca wanted the camaraderie; it was like nothing she had ever experienced or imagined experiencing in her near or distant future.

As always, thoughts like this provoked a weakness within Becca; her disappointment with the direction her life had taken her brought a heavy sorrow to her heart. She knew she was being overly critical but also knew that it didn't matter. She could tell herself that by comparison to most people in the world she should be grateful and doing cartwheels; and it wasn't that Becca was ignorant to that fact, it just didn't matter. The only other person Becca was comparing herself to was her own idealistic version of herself; and she had a God-given right to do so.

Thoughts of Jeremy and what could have been played through Becca's mind. Then, as always, those images were interrupted by visions of him plummeting from the World Trade Center over and over and over again. Had he not been so prematurely and tragically taken away from her, she might have everything she wanted. The house, the kids, the husband…

Staring off the patio, high above the Village of Roslyn, Becca knew what reel was going to be played next in her mind; she had watched this double-feature a hundred times, if not more. The film was entitled *Everything Changes* and portrayed a young Roberto arriving on a white Stallion wearing shining armor and singing songs of hope and everlasting love. Conversely, as Becca is swept off her feet and raised up to ride behind her savior; the horse changes color, as do the songs.

Traditionally the film plays until the oppressed and miserable Becca jumps from the galloping steed into an abyss of thorns and darkness; however, in today's showing the director seems to have altered the story.

Straddled behind Roberto on the white Stallion, they face off against the Black Knight. The Black Knight is also Roberto, ugly with insecurity and self-doubt. Becca watches from her perch on the white Stallion as her Roberto gracefully wields his sword with a swift and decisive movement severing off the head of the Black Knight.

Watching as fantasy-Becca, with her arms wrapped around the muscular waist of the now bare-chested Roberto, ride off into the sunset together; she is well aware that real-Becca has some serious issues that need to be dealt with.

First and foremost, she realized that it has been way too long since she had been laid; and, despite the fact that Roberto seemed a lot more confident this morning at breakfast, that certainly did not give him the right to make her horny.

Becca immediately recognized that thought process as a sham. Roberto wasn't making her horny; it was the cool breeze blowing in off the Long Island Sound. Gently caressing her thighs as it reached up the pants leg of her Chinos and simultaneously slipped down the inside her blouse, swirling around her breasts and teasing at her nipples.

Becca's thoughts steered to images of Christopher John standing before her. Both naked underneath the glow of a full moon on this very patio; wrapped within each other's sweaty embrace, her hand sliding up and down his stiff member while his hands slid down over the fullness of her rump lifting her up and guiding her down onto his throbbing erection.

Becca's nipples stood erect and pressed against the silky fabric of her bra as she slid a hand beneath the waistband of her Chinos. Becca's middle finger slid between the moist mounds of her labia and began vibrating against the hard button of her clit. As if in response to her needs the wind swept hard against Becca and carried with it a gentle chill that brought a soft moan to Becca's lips as she climaxed.

Quickly returning from her fantasy with CJ; already giving Christopher John a nickname before their first date, Becca straightened herself up and turned around, hoping to still be alone on the patio.

(Unedited excerpt from the manuscript)

I was introduced to Captain C4 while I was living overseas in Hong Kong. This was early on, before I had formed the alliance with my local acquaintances that eventually had me leaving HK in a hurry.

I had met Captain C4 purely by accident while on a business/debauchery excursion in Thailand.

Bangkok to be more specific.

The back alleys of Patpong to be exact.

This is where a man who has everything goes to get what he didn't even know existed.

The main street of Patpong is lined with clubs where you can see anything from live sex acts to feats of pussy never before imagined. Exhibitions like shooting a blow-dart through a straw across the room to pop a balloon, pulling out a dozen double-edge razor blades strung together, smoking cigars, drawing caricatures, bouncing ping-pong balls into cups with eagle-eye accuracy and of course, the disappearing arm up to the shoulder. You just haven't lived until you see a man parading around the center stage, shoulder deep in two beautiful Thai girls displayed over his head.

I learned quickly that the main street of Patpong was for the tourists. If you want to survive in Asia, you disassociate yourself from the tourists as rapidly as possible. You learn the language; and more importantly, you learn the culture and the customs. You conduct yourself respectfully and with reverence towards the locals.

You behave like an ignorant American tourist; you disappear like an ignorant American tourist.

The back alleys of Patpong are indescribable. How do you properly describe a sunset to a blind man who is also deaf?

Chew on that for a while you faceless fuck while I tell you about Captain C4.

First, let's clear up that I'm not talking about a person; Captain C4 is just my way of referring to C4 plastique; a stable explosive that has the look and feel of Hasbro's Play-Doh. As a matter of fact, that is exactly how I brought large quantities of it into the country. My product however was called Clay-Dough and was manufactured under my Hong Kong company's Paper Airplane logo.

It was so easy; I established a Taiwanese based demolition company and was able to legally import the C4 from Italy. The C4 was stored at a factory in Taichung, an area about 40 miles south of Taipei, there it was mixed with food coloring and packed in pre-labeled 2oz cans. The Clay-Dough was then shipped in bulk to my domestic warehouse in the United States for further distribution.

Way to protect our borders.

Keep up the good work.

🔸

It's too bad that we are running out of time; thinking about the back streets of Patpong and Bangkok, I am reminded of so many great tales of extended pain, slow deaths, violent raping and torture that it's a shame not to go into greater detail.

Maybe next time.

The back alleys of Patpong were a hidden in plain sight Black Market of sorts. You name it; you could get it. Even if you didn't know what you were looking for; it usually found you anyway and let you know that's what you were looking for. That's exactly what happened to me.

The place was pure unadulterated magic.

Walking around like I had been there a hundred times before, I blended into the shadows until I was summoned deeper into the darkness. Like a phantom's icy hand wrapping itself around my heart I was led forward under a makeshift canopy protruding over a hidden doorway.

No words were exchanged that night; just cash from my wallet in trade for a metal box labeled 'RDX-Composition4'. I grabbed the briefcase sized, military green container by its handle and walked back through the dark alleys.

A Tuk-Tuk cab was waiting for me at the end of Phat Phong 1 and Thanon Silom where the driver delivered me back to the Regent Hotel without asking my destination.

Pure unadulterated magic.

Guided by the hands of my Creator; protected by Fate; brought to you by Bounty, the quicker picker upper.

Once back in my room at the Regent, I broke the seal on the metal container and stared in awe at the 13.6 kg of C4 plastique wrapped in 10 individual packages.

I knew right away what I had just acquired and began remolding the clay for transport back to Hong Kong. Being in the toy business, I was regularly bringing back components, prototypes and molds in large metal sample cases. My permanent resident status card allowed me to walk right through customs in Hong Kong 9 out of 10 times without ever being asked a single question.

Even if I was stopped, the only thing they would have found were six clay molds for a new line of Halloween masks.

Last time I checked, Halloween wasn't outlawed.

Back in Hong Kong, I was extremely nervous about playing with The Captain; you know that whole foreign country thing. However, it was like giving a kid a new toy at Christmas and telling him he could only look at it.

Not happening.

I had seen enough movies to know that you detonate C4 with an electric charge; but how strong of an electric charge was the $64,000 question.

Hong Kong was a never ending source of suppliers eager to do business with you and were therefore always happy to provide you with whatever forms of samples you requested with no questions asked.

I had components to remote control race cars, beepers, cell phones, garage-door openers and even The Clapper at my disposal.

Obviously The Clapper got ruled out immediately.
Too much *thump-thump* even for me.

Using what I assumed were small quantities of the C4, I prepared a small number of 'test' bombs with varying detonation devices. I kept careful notes and buried them along the hiking trail of an area called Dragonback, a ridge above the relatively wild east coast of Hong Kong Island.

The beepers became my preferred method of detonation for several reasons: reliability was number one, unless an entire grid went down the command signal always got sent; distance was number two, thanks to satellite based networks a local command can be sent halfway around the world; and finally, multiplicity, meaning that numerous beepers can be programmed to receive a single command simultaneously.

Outstanding.

Now back to our show already in progress...

💣

Chapter 58

The flicker of a light in an upstairs window caught Becca's attention. She could see Kyra moving around in what appeared to be the master bedroom. Becca could only imagine the view Kyra would have had if she had been looking out the window a few moments earlier.

Oh well, Becca thought to herself, nothing she could do about it now. In fact, Becca realized that she didn't mind if Kyra *was* watching. The notion of Kyra standing up there and watching as Becca knocked one off, gave her a strange, yet pleasant feeling and she found herself getting wet again.

Shaking her head and telling herself aloud to get a grip on herself all the while thinking about how she just did; Becca headed through the glass doors off the patio and returned into the house.

Becca knew that if she didn't get laid soon, she'd end up doing something stupid with Roberto; especially after his show of confidence and bravado this morning. Checking her watch, she counted the hours until her date with Christopher John.

Twenty-seven.

She was pretty sure she could keep her own hands out of her pants until then; and fairly positive she could keep Roberto's out as well.

Feeling a little sticky, Becca entered the guest bathroom at the bottom of the stairs just as Kyra came bounding down from above.

Chapter 59

Having circled around the entire War-Room, Melina began to accept the depth of the Madman's plans. Each map represented a meticulously detailed, well thought out, coordinated attack on major cities around the country. It was unclear to Melina if all of these events would occur simultaneously or successively. It was however hauntingly clear to Melina that these events, would occur.

The feeling that she was in the midst of a giant tidal wave out in the middle of the ocean was unmistakable. Set on a course of mass destruction; the War Room illustrated that the wave was already formed and moving too fast to be ignored.

Leaving the War Room; still guiding Melina with his hand on the small of her back, they made a left turn in the hallway and continued further from the direction they had originally came.

Shoes squeaking once again on the tile floor as he hurried Melina in front of him, they passed several other closed doors on both the right and left sides of the hallway until they made the only turn available at the hallway's end; another left.

Now proceeding down a corridor that wasn't as brightly lit as the main hallway they had just exited, Melina felt the Madman's hand lift from her back.

"Keep walking." He told her and she complied by not slowing down at all although she now felt the weight of the chain attached to the choke collar as he slightly lagged behind.

Melina could sense him moving around behind her as they walked, but didn't dare a glance over her shoulder to see what he was doing. It was as if he was looking for something in his pockets; at least that was the picture that Melina had formed.

A few steps before the dimly lit corridor ended he seemed to locate what he wanted with a hearty "Ah…got it! They make these things so damn small now."

Melina risked stopping at the corridor's juncture with another hallway that jutted off to the left. Melina's mental imaging of her surroundings told her that this hallway ran down along the back end of what was the War Room. They had walked around in almost a complete square from where she had first regained consciousness and found herself on the tile flooring.

Melina felt the Madman's hand return to her lower back as he said, "Second door on the right." Only this time his hand wasn't open and flat against her body; it was as if his hand held onto another object. Melina could only guess that it was what he had just pulled out of his pocket.

Curiosity about the object began to gnaw at her even though she knew better.

Barefoot on the cold tiles, Melina noticed that there were no doors on the left and that the ones on the right were much more widely spaced out than in the hallway that ran parallel to this one up at the other end of the corridor.

Stopping as ordered at the second door, the Madman reached around Melina's waist with the handle to the choke chain still in his hand and turned the knob on the door before them.

The door swung inward into darkness.

"How well can you count?"

The Madman's question was so bizarre that it caught Melina off guard and she just stood there unresponsive. Panic struck deep within her as she prepared herself for the pain that was sure to follow disobedience.

The last time she didn't answer a question she had the insides of her cheeks ground off by her own teeth.

Instead the Madman chuckled and said in a manner befitting of talking to a small child or an idiot; "You know…like on Sesame Street…One, Two, Three…" He chuckled some more and then stopped abruptly.

Leaning in; just inches away from her face and speaking in a slow, deliberate, monotone through barred teeth he repeated; "How well can you count?"

Shaking uncontrollably with fear, staring directly into the eyes of the Madman in black and white clown face paint; Melina managed to say "F-f-fine; I can count just fine."

"Perfect!" The Madman exclaimed and nudged Melina into the darkened room as he tossed the handle of the choke chain at her feet.

Startled with the sudden change of what was happening to her; not that she had any preconceived notion of what she expected next; but it certainly *wasn't* what had just happened. Melina looked up at the Madman as he raised his other hand and jiggled it like he was slightly shaking something. Held within his grip he revealed the blue glow of an open cell phone.

Just before the door closed, immersing Melina into absolute darkness, the Madman shouted in his counting instructions; "Three minutes, no more, no less. I highly recommend that you cover yourself with the mattress in the corner of the room before you reach zero. Have fun. Ready, GO!"

Chapter 60

Kyra was in the kitchen pouring small amounts of water into Styrofoam cups filled with dirt that lined the window above the sink.   Sensing   Becca behind her, Kyra began talking without turning around.

"They grow up so fast. You blink and they're walking and talking; you turn around and they're out of diapers; you fall asleep and when you wake up you're putting them on a bus to school…"

Not quite able to relate, Becca offered, "You're talking about Ryan and Erin; not those plants you're watering…Right?"

Smiling Kyra turned around and leaned back against the counter and faced Becca. "Of course; but, at least with my plants I am always there to keep them safe. They live their lives on my patio garden. I am here to feed them when they are hungry; water them when they thirst; cover them if a storm blows in off the Sound…"

Kyra stopped and stared at the floor for a long time before continuing; finally looking up into Becca's eyes she said; "Today was a reminder of what we go through in our lives; the hardships we face along the way, the baggage we pick up and have to carry with us to our graves."

Kyra let out a heavy breath through her mouth and nose.

"Watching the children playing on the swing set today, reliving the whole Jack thing, the funerals; I remembered how precious life is... how we forget to appreciate every moment... how fast everything changes."

Becca seized the opportunity to readdress the subject of Brad and Shannon Thomas with Kyra. Becca needed to find out more about what had happened to the parents; but even as a reporter, how often do you get to tactfully bring up the subject of dead parents?

So with the opening that Kyra gave her, Becca asked; "Kyra, if you don't mind, I was wondering if you could tell me more about Brendon and Kenny's parents."

"There really isn't much I can tell you. They were both warm, generous people who accepted me into their family like I was their own daughter right from the start." Kyra paused and looked at Becca inquisitively and then added; "I'm not really sure what it is that you're after here?"

Sensing an abrupt change in Kyra's demeanor that had walls going up in all directions, Becca feared she was about to get closed out and changed her approach.

"I'm sorry; I didn't mean to pry... It's just that..." Becca threw in a dramatic pause for an added effect and diverted her eyes from Kyra's for some '*I'm so embarrassed*' seasoning before continuing. "It's just that; I feel so close to you guys for some reason." Becca shot a quick glance up at Kyra, then right back to the floor. "I know we all just met this afternoon; but... we talked about so much... and, I don't know..." Becca now finished by looking deep into Kyra's eyes as she went for the close. "I feel like I've know you forever. I don't have any sisters or close girlfriends; and I know this sounds crazy... but, I was kind of feeling like you guys were...like family... I'm sorry; I don't have any right... I'll just leave..."

Becca had legitimate tears beginning to form in her eyes. Even though she started her little speech as a ploy to get more information and insure that she would get to see the box; but, Becca found a lot of truth in what had just come out of her mouth.

Becca was reminded again of what her father used to say; '*It's always best to hide behind the truth.*'

Kyra took two giant steps across the kitchen and wrapped her arms around Becca and pulled her into a tight embrace and said; "No, no, no; I'm the one who is sorry. I didn't see it from your standpoint. I was being selfish and defensive."

Kyra stopped talking and just held onto Becca.

Becca's arms snaked around Kyra's waist and her head nestled into the crook of Kyra's neck. Becca was feeling more and more contemptible for manipulating the situation as a real tear slipped out of her eye, rolled off her cheek and landed on Kyra's shoulder.

The two women just stood there in the waning afternoon light, holding each other and rocking slightly back and forth in the middle of the kitchen.

Becca was no longer even sure what she was upset about.

Was it the true sense of isolation she felt at really having no family or close friends worth mentioning?

Was it the fact that she is so easily able to callously lie at the drop of a hat to get what she wanted; regardless of those she may hurt or deceive?

Was the fact that she was getting a little aroused at being held by Kyra?

That last thought took Becca by surprise. She knew she was focusing a little too much on the sensation of Kyra's breasts pressing against her own. She was well aware that she was enjoying the feel of Kyra's skin against her face; and, she was acutely aware of how supple and tiny Kyra's waist felt beneath her arms.

Becca's mind was about to further explore the sensations she was having when Kyra began speaking again. "I didn't mean to get so snippy before. It's just that Brad and Shannon's death was so sudden and so tragic that none of us ever really had a chance to properly deal with it."

Breaking the embrace, Kyra leaned back and slid her hands down Becca's arms until she had both of Becca's hands in her own. Becca's arms broke out in goose bumps, her nipples rose to attention and she felt a stirring in the pit of her stomach.

Becca couldn't believe she was getting horny again. Especially since she had never even considered being with another woman; she had always thought of herself as a 'good stiff penis' kind of gal.

Nevertheless, Becca had clear visions of her and Kyra getting sweaty together; slipping and sliding around on top of each other on the leather couch in the living room.

Unaware of Becca's thoughts, Kyra continued speaking as she held Becca's hands and looked directly into her eyes. "I guess some natural defenses of mine still pop up when the subject of Brad and Shannon is mentioned... Kenny still can't handle it emotionally. He is a basket-case for weeks and the therapist bills skyrocket anytime anything to do with his parents' takes place."

Kyra paused and Becca felt obligated to say something.

"I was wondering what you taste like?" Was the question on the forefront of Becca's mind; but instead she said, "Oh gosh, that's awful... What a terrible thing to have to live with... I am so sorry I brought it up."

Kyra smiled and nodded her head in appreciation.

"That's sweet of you to say; and honestly, as I said before, I really don't know what to tell you about them. It almost sounds unfair and incomplete to just say, that they were wonderful people who unfortunately ended up in the wrong place at the wrong time. But, that's really the gist of it."

Kyra paused, sighed and then added as an afterthought; "They weren't even staying there; they just stopped by because they had coupons to the spa."

A familiar chill ran up Becca's spine as the recesses of her brain began piecing together all of the information she had gathered on the parents throughout the day. It was a very similar process akin to when her mind would independently figure out the Daily Word Jumble.

Murdered, vacation in Florida, twelve years ago, wrong place wrong time, sudden and tragic...

Becca wasn't horny anymore.

She was now hauntingly afraid.

Needing to hear it aloud, Becca asked; "W-what spa...Where?" Becca had to ask the question although she already knew what the answer was going to be.

"At that hotel in Florida, the one that was blown up by that terrorist group back in '96… I think it was the HAMAS or the Palestine Islamic Jihad; it was something Palestinian… anyway; Brad and Shannon were there."

Backing away from the grasp Kyra had on her hands and sitting down at the kitchen table; Becca was feeling light headed when she asked Final Jeopardy; "You mean the St. Regis in Ft. Lauderdale?"

"Yeah; I think that was it."

Chapter 61

Hello darkness my old friend…

Melina quickly dismissed the song from her head and replaced it with a slow, rhythmic countdown starting from one-hundred and eighty. She wasn't sure what she was counting for; but, was positive that it had to be done.

Melina took a brief moment and mused with extreme admiration at how many different tasks the human brain can handle at a single time. Overlapping and complex issues seemed to be managed with the grace and calm of a well trained soldier.

One part of her mind was still singing the Simon and Garfunkel song although she had tried to dismiss it. It was, after all, an oldie but goody. Another part of her mind was counting; and it was counting backwards to boot. An additional part was pondering the nuances of the Madman's newest game; and on top of all of that, another part of her mind was sketching out the layout of a room she had never seen before.

Melina felt like she was having an out of body experience. Her heightened senses were working independently of any real thought process; it had become like breathing. Melina was picking up on the slightest vibrations emanating from the room on levels she could only imagine were similar to what a bat does with its returned radar screech.

But, Melina wasn't initiating a radar wave… Or was she?

Thinking that her body was somehow producing an initial radar-type signal wasn't that farfetched to her; especially considering the depth of detail that was forming in her mind about her new surroundings.

One-seventy…

One-sixty-nine…

One-sixty-eight…

In her mind, Melina 'saw' the room she had never been in before. However, it was a room that didn't make sense to her; yet, she accepted it as accurate because she trusted the vision. The room was a perfect square, a little larger than the War Room. The walls appeared to be padded and Melina was reminded of a recording studio. Even the floor was soft below her feet. The springy material beneath her bare feet reminded her of those colorful interlocking squares you see in children's playrooms.

The mattress the Madman had mentioned was leaning against the wall near the far right-hand corner; basically cattycorner to where she envisioned herself standing just inside the doorway.

Other than the mattress; there was no other furniture in the room with the exception of a man who was strapped to a chair. Positioned halfway between Melina and the mattress in the corner, the man just sat there, motionless in the dead center of the room.

Chapter 62

Earlier in the day, while Becca was SNIPHing around her apartment researching and cross-referencing information in the manuscript against the Post's database; Becca had typed in the St. Regis Resort Hotel in Ft. Lauderdale.

There were several articles that appeared regarding the 1996 bombing and despite the fact there was never an official claim of responsibility, the general consensus was that it was a terrorist act.

Two suitcase bombs filled with C-4 explosives were simultaneously detonated in the world renowned day-spa as well as the state-of-the-art fitness center. Several hundred people were killed and twice as many were wounded in the initial blast and subsequent collapse of the complex.

Due to the fact that the St. Regis Resort was hosting the sixth annual United Jewish Communities Philanthropic and Humanitarian Awards benefit that same weekend; all hands pointed to a Palestinian based attack. It was easy for the media to blame the Palestinians for attacking the Jews at the St. Regis. It coincided perfectly with all of the bombings that were taking place in Europe and Israel that *were* being claimed by HAMAS and the Palestinian Islamic Jihad.

Not only did the media not have to worry about instilling panic in the public eye that there was yet *another* threat out there; but it made for great headlines:

PLO attacks UJC in FLA
237 Die in St. Regis Hotel Bombing

When Becca heard Kyra mention the word 'spa' all the individual bits and pieces of information fell into place and Becca knew that Brad and Shannon were murdered at the hands of their own son.

Talk about information overload on top of an already overwhelming day. Becca's mind went into a tailspin and she felt like she was going to faint. Too many questions ran through her mind too quickly to assimilate them all into a cohesive thought process.

Kyra noticed the color drain out of Becca's face and quickly knelt before her as her eyes rolled back and she fell forward out of the kitchen chair. Slumping forward in almost slow motion, Becca ended up in Kyra's embrace for a second time.

Chapter 63

One-fifty-two…
One-fifty-one…
One-fifty…
Thirty seconds gone already.
Two and half minutes left until…Until what?

Melina didn't know exactly; but, knew it wasn't going to be a good thing and time was running out. What Melina did know; was that following the Madman's instructions was important. Therefore, she needed to work her way around the room to the mattress.

But, first things first; Melina carefully expanded the collar with the razor sharp tines and lifted it carefully up over her head. Making sure the hated collar was well out of her path, Melina tossed the choke chain on an angle behind her. She both heard it with her ears and 'saw' it in her mind as it landed with a soft thud on the floor in the corner by the door.

Relying on her mental vision of the room, Melina backed up until her outstretched arms came in contact with the wall. It was soft and padded just like the image in her mind. Still very new to having this heightened imaging sense, Melina was somewhat startled at having a feature of her mental image confirmed by the tactile sense of her hands. It was almost like she still didn't fully trust what she was 'seeing' without her eyes.

Although it was unnecessary, Melina turned her head to verify that there were no obstacles in her way as she set out to follow a path around the perimeter of the room to get to the mattress.

Melina decided that she was going to ignore the man bound in the middle of the room. Figuring the less she knew, the better off she was; at least in this circumstance. However, simply by focusing her attention on the man, even in an attempt to ignore him, Melina's new heightened senses zeroed in on him to give her a clearer image.

Melina was amazed at the detail and could only surmise that her mind filled in some of the nuances based on her imagination. She wasn't 'seeing' in full color either; it was very much like using night goggles, the type you typically see in the movies. Except those are always shown in greens; everything Melina was imaging, was based in blues.

The man appeared to be bound to the chair with common duct tape. Sitting prone in the wooden chair, his arms were strapped down to the armrests at the wrists while more tape wound around his chest and across the back of the chair. His legs were secured both at the ankles and below the knees to the thick wooden legs of the chair. The bands of tape that wrapped over his mouth and around his head had crusted trails of blood on them from dried up rivers that had previously flowed out of his nose and from his left ear.

The man was beaten very badly; both his eyes were swollen shut and his head hung forward so his chin rested on his chest. In an effort to see if he was even alive, Melina's imaging sense actually zoomed in on the pathetic vision of the man.

Not only did the image enlarge in Melina's mind, but her sense of hearing also seemed to fine tune in on the subject. Melina was able to distinctly hear the man's heart beating and shallow raspy breaths being sucked in through the torn cartilage of his busted nose.

Melina tried to close her eyes and block out the image of the beaten man; she could almost sense his pain and suffering as well as 'see' him.

It was an utterly fruitless effort. Melina wasn't seeing with her eyes; but she was learning how the simple power of thought could assist in diverting her mental imaging to focus on something else.

Just as she brought the mattress back to the center of her attention and began walking the perimeter once again, the overhead lights came alive and momentarily blinded her.

The sensory image in her head was wiped out in a giant flash of blue-white light and then Melina saw nothing.

In a total absurdity, the light coming on in the room blinded Melina completely.

One-twenty...

One-nineteen...

One-eighteen...

One-seventeen...

(Unedited excerpt from the manuscript)

The employees of the St. Regis wore white Polo shirts donning the resort's crest logo which they conveniently sold at the gift shop. Sporting a simple pair of blue slacks or shorts depending on the time of day; and presto, I'm incognito.

That's right you faceless fucks; it was that easy.

Did you ever wonder where the term 'As plain as the nose on your face', came from? You have an unbelievable knack for missing the obvious and accepting the routine.

You should be on your knees thanking me for shaking things up a bit for you. Finally giving you something to live for...

Get it? That was funny.

Fuck you, so anyway...

I walked into the St. Regis with 2 gym bags full of Captain C4. I left one with the concierge and told him to keep an eye on it for a minute while I took the other one up to the Health Spa on the 4th floor.

A gorgeous blond looked up from the receptionist station as I entered the facility; but once she realized I wasn't a guest, I guess I didn't rate for a proper greeting. As Blondie was ignoring me, I set the bag to the side of the counter she was standing at and told her to enjoy the rest of her day.

I retrieved the other bag from the concierge; who left my bag unattended thank you very much, and took the rear elevators all the way up to the Exercise Room on the rooftop.

If I worked out, this would be the place to do it; spectacular panoramic views up and down the coast as well as out over the ocean. I imagined what it would look like against the night sky; the entire rooftop exploding in a cascade of color and sound and glass. I almost waited until dark to blow the place; but, I figured there would probably be less people in the spa and gym later in the day and the bottom line was all about the headcount.

I'll be honest with you; I had my doubts that the Captain was going to cooperate that day. It had been a long time since I had played with the Captain.

Dragonback had been the first and last time.

I had been toting around the rest of what I got in Thailand for almost 8 years.

There is a time and a place for everything.

Patience is a virtue.

I had divided what was left of the almost 30lbs of C4 equally into the 2 gym bags and wired them for remote detonation from my cell phone.

Knowing that this was my last night in Florida for quite a while, I headed down to The Tap where I had made some good friends over the years. I didn't tell anybody that I was leaving. Not that it would have mattered one way or the other, it's just not my style.

I grabbed a spot on the north end of the pool and stretched out. Leaning back in the lounge chair I had a great view of the girls in their skimpy bikinis and since The Tap was only about a half mile up the road from the St. Regis; I also had a great view of the festivities to come.

Speaking of coming...

The most difficult part of the entire process was not letting my hard-on show too much. The thump-thump of anticipation was agonizing.

I was so excited I could barely contain myself; I needed release, and I needed it fast.

Unfortunately, my apartment around the corner wasn't available anymore, so I had to make due by grabbing some beach floozy and sticking it to her in bathroom at The Tap.

I rammed it into her so hard from behind that she was still walking funny a half hour later. She came wobbling over to me on my lounge chair like she had just gotten off a horse and asked me to buy her a drink.

I told her to wait a minute; I needed to make a phone call first.

💣

<h2>Chapter 64</h2>

"What happened?" Becca asked Kyra; unsure as to how she went from the kitchen chair to the living room couch.

"Welcome back." Kyra said, a huge smile blossoming onto her face reflecting the obvious relief she felt. "You fainted. You were only out for about a minute; you're lucky I recognized the signs or we would have the emergency squad on the way." Kyra draped a cool damp towel across Becca's forehead. "You still scared me though. I haven't seen someone faint since I used to take care of my aunt; she was hypoglycemic on top of having low blood pressure."

Kyra was still talking as Becca watched as she stood and walked back into the kitchen. "I think you over did it today; a combination of the sun, the wine, the emotions; you did go at it pretty good with Ruby earlier, I think we all had our fair share of an emotional rollercoaster ride today."

Becca silently agreed and added a few of her own items to that list. She had started the day with an, I'm-turning-thirty-soon poor me attack; followed by a Roberto phone attack; which wasn't to be outdone by an anxiety attack over breakfast, where every stranger was the Madman; and, we can't leave out the graveside attack of *The Jack Thomas Chills*.

Becca also included the intense emotions she felt just a short while ago when she was fingering herself on the patio and then imagining herself hot and sweaty on top of Kyra. Nevertheless, she had no intention of mentioning that, nor did she intend on sharing the startling revelation that Jack Thomas killed his own parents.

Becca did however tell Kyra that she was glad she was there to catch her and save her from a nasty head contusion. Sitting up and taking hold of Kyra's hand as she reentered the sunken living room, Becca swiveled her legs off the couch and pulled Kyra down next to her.

A quick flash of them dirty dancing together ran across Becca's mind, but she simply put her arm around Kyra and gave her a chaste hug and thanked her for taking such good prompt care of her.

The coffee table in front of the couch was cluttered with folders and files and Becca surmised that this is where Kenny sat doing work before joining his family at Brendon and Ruby's house earlier. Leaning forward Becca saw the Fed Ex box on the floor amidst a spread of scattered newspaper sections.

Kyra noticed the box at the same time Becca did and said; "That's what we're here for... Go ahead."

Becca hesitated for a split second then reached down and grabbed the box.

Chapter 65

One-twelve...
One-eleven...
One-ten...
Less than two minutes left.
Bright light radiated from the ceiling and bounced off the white walls. Tears streamed down Melina's face as she tried to regain her sight in the fluorescent glare.

Blindly inching her way around the perimeter of the room, using her hand as a guide against the soft padded wall, Melina reached the first corner. There was only about twenty feet to go before she would reach the mattress.

As her eyes slowly adjusted to the light, Melina looked into the center of the room at the beaten man bound to the chair. The spectacle was more horrifying in full color than it was in the blue tones of her radar-vision imagery.

Drawn forward as if they shared a common magnetism, Melina approached the unconscious man. Surely this is what the Madman wanted. He wanted Melina to be shocked, he wanted Melina to be horrified, and he wanted Melina to fear him and revere his capabilities.

Ninety-two…

Ninety-One…

Ninety…

Melina was intensely aware that she only had a minute-thirty to get behind the mattress; that panicky sense of time quickly running out brought sweat-beads to her forehead and the shakes to her knees.

Stepping up close to the man strapped to the chair, Melina became aware of a few shocking details that went unnoticed earlier. First, the man was not unconscious; Melina could clearly see the man's blue eyes shifting back and forth following her movements through the slits of his swollen eyelids and busted cheek bones. His head hung limply against his chest and he remained motionless because he was paralyzed from what appeared to be a broken neck.

Secondly, the man had a name; Todd Hem-something, he wore a name badge pinned to a bright yellow shirt. Most of the name tag was covered over. It was caught up in the duct tape that was wound around his chest securing him into the chair.

The last discovery was the oddest; Melina observed that the duct tape also secured what looked like a pack of playing cards or a cassette tape into the breast pocket of the man's blood stained yellow shirt.

When Todd saw Melina noticing the rectangular object his eyes frantically and erratically moved within their sockets as if trying to communicate a message to her. Melina felt, not so much as actually heard, the struggled murmurs emanating from Todd's chest and taped mouth. At that moment, on an instinctual level that seemed to evolve tenfold since her captivity in the Madman's Funhouse; Melina knew she was looking at a bomb.

Seventy-three…

Seventy-two…

Seventy-one…

Melina's mind shifted into overdrive; with about one minute to spare, Melina began the complex reasoning and factoring involving her options.

Save the man.

Save herself.

Save both the man and herself.

Why save the man?

He probably wished himself dead ten times over already.

Was there time anyway?

What if she could free the bomb and hide that behind the mattress?

What would the Madman do to her if she saved Todd?

How could she just leave him here to die if there was something she could do about it?

Would she be able to live with herself, knowing that she might have been able to help?

Fifty-One…

Fifty…

Forty-nine…

Melina began working at the tape covering the rectangular shape in Todd's pocket. The tape was thick and matted together from Todd's blood and sweat which made it difficult for Melina to gain a solid grasp on an edge to start pulling.

Trying to use her sharp nails to tear at the duct tape proved fruitless as the elasticity of the tape stretched against her efforts.

Thirty-eight…

Thirty-seven…

Thirty-six…

Melina grabbed hold of Todd's shirt just above the upper edge of the tape and punctured her nails through the bright yellow material. She felt Todd's skin peel from his body up under her nails as she raked them over his flesh. Slipping her fingers down inside his shirt and clutching her fists around the tape, Melina jerked her arms back and forth in a vain attempt at tearing the bond.

Todd's head whipped up and down on his already broken neck until Melina heard the final snap and realized what she had done.

Only the whites of his eyes were now visible through the slits of his swollen lids and bright red blood decorated the outside of his ear. Todd's head rested straight back between his shoulders, distended on a stretched out neck.

Backing away from the fresh corpse, Melina stared in disbelief at what she had just done. Unable to comprehend the fact that Todd was already as good as dead; Melina was mortified that she as had just killed another human being.

With her head still working in overdrive, Melina pictured herself as a changed woman, never again could she look at herself in the mirror without seeing a murderer. She didn't see how she could possibly ever have a normal life.

No relationships.

No family.

No children.

No future.

Everything she ever wanted, everything she ever aspired to be; was just taken from her, forever.

The Madman had won; Melina had nothing left to live for.

Then the lights went out again and Melina realized that having nothing left to live for also meant that she had nothing left to lose.

Eighteen…

Seventeen…

Sixteen…

In a terror filled moment of clarity, Melina became aware that she briefly lost track of the countdown sounding off in her head.

Unaware that her radar-vision had taken over at the exact moment she was immersed in the darkness again; Melina ran to mattress in the corner in a panic stricken rush. She didn't think she was going to make it.

Thirteen...

Twelve...

Eleven...

Reaching the mattress in the corner and grabbing it by its sides, Melina tried to lift up the mattress. The original plan was to cower in the corner and angle the mattress over her as a makeshift barrier.

The mattress was too heavy and it slipped out of her hands.

Nine...

Eight...

Seven...

Melina tried to wedge herself under the mattress, but since she couldn't lift it, it just slid forward and moved closer to the center of the room and the bomb.

Six...

Five...

Four...

Cramming herself into the corner, Melina squatted down, leaned forward and tightly secured her hands over the piping around the edge of the mattress. Lifting and leaning back with all her strength and determination, Melina was able to pull the mattress over herself like a blanket.

Three...

Two...

One...

The top of Melina's head was still out in the open when the bomb attached to Todd's chest exploded.

Chapter 66

The box was smaller than Becca had been imagining. No reason for it; she had just expected the box to be bigger. Maybe it was because it had turned into such a big deal that she was anticipating an enormous package clearly labeled:

HANDLE WITH CARE
SPECIAL DELIVERY FROM DEAD UNCLE

The box was partially covered by a pile of scattered newspaper sections; Kyra explained that she had just swiped them off the couch a few moments earlier to make room for their passed-out house guest.

Becca was so focused on *the box* sitting right there on the floor, mere inches from her feet, that it took her a second to realize that Kyra was jokingly making reference to *her* as the passed-out house guest.

Sections of Newsday and The New York Times were spread around the floor and Becca made a mental note to activate one of her courtesy subscriptions to The Post for Kenny and Kyra.

Lifting the box out of the scattered newsprint, Becca noticed that the box was lying atop of Newsday's Puzzle Section; both the Sunday Super Sleuth Crossword and the smaller, regular Daily Crossword puzzles had been partially completed. Filled in, she assumed, by Kenny as he was trying to take his mind off of the piles of work before him.

Becca's eyes were drawn however to the Daily Word Jumble that sat untouched at the bottom of the page. Delighted to see a different puzzle than the one that she had solved earlier that day in The New York Post's Sunday Edition. Becca's mind gobbled up the jumbled words for later digestion; SKAM, DYNAC, GRANDO and FLINTIO.

There was actually nothing out of the ordinary about the Fed Ex package. Nothing about it even suggested that it was one of the surprise birthday boxes, until Kyra pointed out the return address on the label. It was postmarked from Norway.

Kyra could see Becca's bewilderment and offered to open the outer Fed Ex shipping carton and show Becca the wrapped box that would no doubt be inside. It was the inner box that had begun all the talk that these mystery birthday packages came from Jack Thomas.

Tearing away the patented rip-cord from the shipping carton, Becca slid out a smaller package that was wrapped in hot-pink paper with yellow and white balloons printed in an all over design. The balloons were decorated with the 'Have-A-Nice-Day' smiley face, except that the words 'Happy Birthday' formed the smile.

In the upper left corner of the present was a manufacturer's label. Printed in fancy cursive gold lettering on a glossy black background, framed on either side by a one by one inch gold toy jack; the label read:

WINSTON HORGHBRALL
Importer of Norwegian Novelties Since 1980

Becca tipped the present back and forth letting the light dance across the lettering and the jacks. The jacks could have been satellites or stars for all Becca could tell; but they were obviously toy jacks to Brendon and Kenny Thomas, and proof that their brother Jack was alive and well and sending their children presents.

Becca's initial reaction was to laugh and ask Kyra if she was fucking serious. Becca couldn't believe she spent the better part of her day fighting and manipulating Kyra and Ruby for an opportunity to see a box that in all probability was anything other than the proof she was hoping it to be.

Kyra couldn't tell that Becca was disappointed with the outcome the mystery box had provided and asked her if she would like to write down the name and address of the manufacturer.

Becca hesitated for just a moment; long enough to dismiss all the sarcastic comments that ran through her mind and said, "Yes, I would. Thank you."

Searching for her bag that held her notepad and pen, Becca turned to her left and then looked to the floor. Thinking that she maybe left it in the kitchen or out on the patio, Becca began to get up, and then realized she had left it in the car when they had arrived at the house.

Leaning forward, Becca picked up the Newsday Puzzle Section off the floor and tore off a piece just below the partially completed crosswords. Becca noticed with a slight smile that the section she tore away contained the Daily Word Jumble. At least now she wouldn't need to rely on her memory; SKAM, DYNAC, GRANDO and FLINTIO appeared to be coming home with her. Becca returned the rest of the paper back to the floor.

"Do you mind?" Becca asked of Kyra, indicating the pen that lay on the coffee table closer to Kyra's knees than Becca's. It wasn't that she didn't trust herself to lean over Kyra and chance rubbing her breasts against Kyra's thighs; or maybe it was... either way, Kyra picked up the pen and handed it to Becca.

Resting the torn paper fragment against the wrapped present Becca wrote WINSTON HORGHBRALL and then copied the Norwegian address off the Fed Ex mailing label.

Thanking Kyra for her time, nursing skills and companionship; Becca excused herself for the long drive back to the city and allowed Kyra to get back to her family at Ruby's house.

They shared a warm hug in the driveway where Becca once again was concerned with her uncommon focus on how good Kyra's body felt against her own; and then proceeded to wind her way through the streets of Roslyn to the Long Island Expressway.

Chapter 67

By the time Melina realized that her head was still uncovered above the mattress it was too late.

The explosion was deafening.

Fortunately, Todd's body acted somewhat like a shield since the front of his body was facing away from Melina's position. Unfortunately, Todd's upper body was blown apart and showered down upon Melina's face.

Todd's head was blown clean off his body and shot backwards into the wall just a few feet above Melina's own exposed head. Todd's head hit the wall with such force that the skull spilt open like a cracked egg and dropped his brain on top of Melina's head like a hot yolk; while grey hunks of lung and red tatters of muscle splattered onto her face and into her open mouth.

Although the thunderous roar of the blast was absorbed by the soundproofed walls and floor, Melina's ears wouldn't stop ringing. Gagging and spitting out pieces of Todd from her mouth, Melina shimmied herself out from under the mattress scraping her skin against fractured bone remnants that had sprayed all over the room.

As Melina was using her hands to wipe off her face and pick chunks of brain out of her hair, the overhead fluorescents came on again. Only this time, Melina's eyes were closed and she wasn't blinded as she had been before.

Surveying the carnage, Melina navigated her bare feet through the shrapnel of bone and guts strewn around the room. Large broken shards of bone, primarily from Todd's ribcage, were penetrated deep into the mattress and were randomly sticking out of the padded walls at varying heights.

Although, the last thing Melina was feeling was lucky; she realized that she wouldn't have stood a chance in Hell of surviving if she hadn't gotten under the mattress in time. Looking around the room, she was surprised that she didn't end up with a piece of Todd's ribcage right between the eyes.

Rational thinking hadn't entered her mind yet and she still felt responsible for Todd. The fact that he was alive and that she possibly could have saved him; no matter how remote that possibility was, didn't alter her awareness that *she* had killed him. Because technically, in her mind, and in her heart, and in her soul; *she did.*

It was a simple black and white concept.

He was alive. She shook him. He is dead. End of story.

The only thing Melina wanted to do now was kill the Madman. The man who robbed her of any innocence she might still have had as a human being. Melina was determined that the man responsible for ruining her life would pay with his own.

Chapter 68

Roberto had just finished putting the last label on the last box and stood back to soak in the magnitude of what he had just accomplished.

The entire wall by the freight elevator was lined with pallets of the Madman's manuscript packed and ready for delivery to the over thirteen-hundred stores Roberto had pre-selected. The only thing left to do was to actually make the handful of calls to the regional buyers for Barnes and Noble and Waldenbooks.

Roberto had already perfected his story for the buyers to make it a 'no-brainer' for the buyers to make the appropriate decision to approve the delivery. Roberto didn't even want to entertain the possibility that there would be a problem on that front; there was no room for error in that regard.

He would congratulate them at being selected to receive an immediate promotional 'no-cost' delivery of the hottest new psychological thriller by an up and coming new writer. The early release shipment was designed to increase the public's demand since they were intentionally short shipping stock. He would further tell the buyers that once word got out about their stores being selected for the initial limited production run; customers would be flocking to the stores and lining up outside before the doors even opened.

Roberto didn't expect to run into any resistance, even if the buyers were too stupid to appreciate the promotional aspect of the offer, they certainly wouldn't miss the fact that it was a pure profit deal; one-hundred percent to the bottom line.

A true 'no-brainer' of a deal for any commissioned salesperson.

Despite having single handedly completed both the pre and post production elements of publishing a book in a time frame that would have most publicists heads spinning; Roberto stood before the sea of finished product with mixed emotions.

The incredible sensation of pride at completing what seemed like an impossible task was overshadowed by the daunting truths of reality.

He was nauseatingly aware that no matter what he had just accomplished he still may never see his sister alive again. Consciously sensitive to the fact that there was nothing more he could do about that; Roberto held on to the hope that his compliance with the Madman's request would equal her freedom.

Another reality was that this was probably his last weekend with the company that had taken such good care of him over the past three plus years. No other person within the Wiley Publishing Company had the same responsibilities or entitlements that Roberto enjoyed; other than those with the Wiley last name.

They had truly treated him like family; or at least like a Mexican step-son.

Regardless of whether or not he would have ever grown within the ranks of the organization, he had always been treated with respect and treated fairly. Roberto felt terrible; he felt like he had taken advantage of the Wileys and their generosity. But he couldn't afford to let them in on what was happening; he couldn't risk Melina's life on their potential decision to not comply with the Madman's request.

Roberto realized that he would have to make good to the Wileys for the cost he incurred to them by using their equipment for his own means. He was also cognoscente of the company's reputation and did not include their name anywhere on the final product. There was absolutely no formal link between *The Rush Hour Madman* and Wiley Publishing.

Roberto was very impressed with himself; in the past seventy-two hours he had undergone a major metamorphosis that years of therapy had never been able to accomplish. He felt self-confident, in charge, level headed and with a clarity of thought he never dreamed was possible.

On one level, he hoped that he would have the opportunity to share his newfound persona with Becca. She had put up with so much of his crap over the years that she deserved to experience a positive, nurturing Roberto; versus, the self-destructive, negative Roberto she had dated.

Part of Roberto's fresh thinking also gave him the comfort of accepting the possible truth that maybe it was too late for that. Maybe too much had happened over too long of a period of time. Although that would be unfortunate, Roberto was ready to face that as a reality and he knew not to push.

Life doesn't always happen the way you want it to.

So be it.

That was going to be Roberto's new mantra; 'So be it'.

Much better than his old one; 'Life sucks, then you die'.

So be it.

Roberto took a slow look around the printing room making a mental list of things to do before he could go home. The staff would be arriving in about twelve hours and he wanted to avoid any questions about what had transpired over the weekend.

He needed to move the skids by the freight elevator down to the shipping platform. He could wait until Monday morning to do the paperwork and manifests to ship out the orders. Besides, Marissa had a program to mass produce orders for all of the Barnes and Noble and Waldenbooks stores. He would worry later about what to tell her to keep her curiosity at bay.

Roberto wasn't worried about the boxes sitting down on the shipping floor. He knew the department well enough to know that no one would question how the orders magically appeared ready for pick-pack. Everyone down there would just assume that someone else brought them down and they'd just be thankful that they weren't asked to do it themselves.

The open mouth of the freight elevator stood ominously behind its gate like the opening to the pits of Hell. Roberto decided he was going to avoid stepping back in there until there were no other tasks to keep him from doing so. Despite his newfound confidence, he was still gun shy about getting back into that elevator after yesterday's fiasco. Just the thought of being in the elevator had Roberto unconsciously rolling his ankle and rubbing his forearm.

Looking at his watch he was surprised it was six o'clock already and he found himself thinking about Becca and wondering how things went out on Long Island. He thought that maybe he would have heard from her by then and wondered if he had missed a call.

As Roberto was walking towards his office to check his cell phone; he heard it ringing in the distance and broke into a run.

Chapter 69

Becca didn't realize she was only doing 45mph on the L.I.E. until the blare of the Semi's horn behind her almost sent her into the guardrail.

Startled and shaken from her reverie, Becca looked up into the rearview mirror and saw nothing but teeth; and as strange as it was, for a fleeting moment she truly thought that her and her Nissan were about to be eaten.

Stepping hard on the gas and swerving back into the center of the lane, narrowly missing getting a new paint job courtesy of the L.I.E. silver guardrail program, Becca watched as the decorated grill of the tractor-trailer shrank in the reflection of the rearview mirror.

Becca was so lost in thought she didn't even see the road ahead of her and she wondered how long she had been driving that way. She didn't even remember getting on the Long Island Expressway, let alone following the exit ramps onto the Grand Central Parkway. Becca was astonished to think that she had been driving on autopilot for almost forty-five minutes; but the proof was right there in front of her. Her mind spoke to her in a terrible impersonation of Rod Sterling; 'There's a sign post up ahead... your next stop, the Triborough Bridge Zone'.

Lost in thought would be an understatement of the level of distraction Becca had been immersed in; for close to an hour, Becca's mind had danced back and forth between a couple of interrelated topics.

Although out of the ordinary, Becca had come to terms with why she had been entertaining sexual thoughts involving Kyra; figuring that it had nothing specifically to do with wanting to fuck Kyra, as much as it had to do with just wanting to be fucked.

In her self-diagnosis, Becca surmised that Kyra was the focal point of some pent up sexual tension that peaked when arguments with Ruby went unfulfilled. Meaning that when Becca wanted to give Ruby the bitch-slap she deserved; Kyra, by extension, became the desire of the opposite emotion caused by her soothing rationales at a critical moment.

Becca was well aware that she was feeding herself a line of bullshit, but didn't really care. The bottom line was that there was a simple solution to her brief moment of lesbian tendencies; tomorrow, she was going to fuck Christopher John like it was the last night on the planet.

Problem solved.

Becca's mind was also preoccupied with a mental debriefing of the day's results as they pertained to locating Jack Thomas and saving Roberto's sister, Melina. Plus they were no closer to adverting the proclaimed terrorist attack on the city and that had her concerned on another level altogether.

Time was running out in so many different directions.

For Becca, the day's results seemed to be less than proof positive of anything that she didn't already know. The brothers may or may not have seen Jack since his perpetrated death; although some of their stories did add to the mystery, nothing about their stories helped in locating him.

If Jack Thomas really did make an appearance at family events, such as funerals and weddings, then that meant that he somehow had a bead on what was going on within the family circle. How that would even be possible, was worth further exploring. Becca didn't remember anyone talking about a Thomas family newsletter that Jack could have subscribed to; so how could he know about such things.

It also came to mind that a trap could be set. Promoting some type of fake family event that would lure Jack out of hiding. Becca paused as her mind wrapped around the elaborate concept of faking a family event; she felt like she was involved in a blockbuster movie script, not real life; and certainly not her life.

Becca's mind bounced back to the Kyra sex scandal and added another tidbit of justification for her earlier behavior. The added excitement that these past two days had brought into her life was making her feel alive in away she hadn't felt in a long time. She felt vibrant and motivated. She felt reborn. A new and improved Becca, who did things the old Becca never even dreamed about.

Images and thoughts of being back on the couch next to Kyra led to images of the mystery birthday box sitting on the floor right next to her feet the whole time.

As far as she was concerned, the box from Norway was a dead end. The images of jacks in the company's logo was more than likely a coincidence that helped foster the notion that Jack Thomas had anything to do with the gifts. It was unfortunate that both, Brendon and Kenny were so ready to latch onto anything that might suggest the survival of a brother they never knew. Becca's heart sincerely went out to them and she hoped that one day, she might be able to provide them answers to give them some peace of mind.

As soon as she thought it, she doubted that it would ever happen. Even if she was ever able to let the brothers know about Jack and what he had been up to the past three decades; it certainly wouldn't provide any peace of mind to anyone. If anything it may make matters worse.

Becca mind drifted down another tangent and envisioned how that conversation might go with the brothers... 'You were right guys; your brother Jack is alive. He faked his own death at college so he could continue incognito raping and torturing women. He had started murdering women while he was still in high school; maybe you knew some of them. Oh and by the way, more than likely there is something fundamentally wrong with your brother; it could be a hereditary imbalance. I'd keep an eye on your own kids if I were you. Hey, you never know. By the way, what do you do for fun?'

Becca realized as soon as the thoughts came into her head that she was way off base. Whatever was and is wrong with Jack Thomas has nothing to do with Brendon or Kenny and especially has nothing to do with their children.

Becca's mind continuing to jump from topic to topic and she began contemplating the idea about writing a book on Jack Thomas's motivation.

The Madness behind the Madman.

Becca liked the sound of the title; now, all she had to do was find the Madman and sit him down for an interview. Maybe they could chat over a spot of tea and biscuits.

The thought of writing one book led to another, and Becca's mind moved onto the book she was going to write referencing the Hollingsworth Clan as one of the founding families of Long Island.

That thought reminded her that she needed to become a little more knowledgeable on the Hollingsworth subject before her date with Christopher John. She had completely forgotten that she had lied to him about writing a book on the Hollingsworths when she had first met him.

Eventually Becca's thought process took her back to the thought of sex; only this time instead of Kyra, it was Christopher John thrusting his hips between her legs. It was at that very moment, that Becca was finally snapped out of her trance by the 40 tons barreling down on her with its open-mouthed decorated grill and its horn blaring.

Chapter 70

The only thing left of Todd was his pants; complete with legs, just sitting in the chair like he was waiting for the rest of his body to return.

Melina navigated through the scattered remains, being careful not to poke her bare feet on the sharp splinters of bone that lay strewn all over the floor. The experience had left her teary eyed and exhausted. She had gone from one mental and physical rollercoaster to another; and there were no lines in between the rides.

She was the only one at the Madman's theme park.

Step right up, you're next; and don't worry, we never close.

Melina came upon the lower half of Todd's right arm still duct taped to the wooden arm of the chair. A long split of wood and a spike of fractured bone jutted from the broken chair arm and stuck straight up from the floor like a lawn dart.

The spectacle looked like someone was reaching up for assistance, except there was no hole to be pulled up out of; yet, Melina reached down and offered a helping hand. Grabbing tight around Todd's wrist, Melina leaned back and pulled. The severed forearm dislocated from the foam flooring with ease and Melina found herself plopping onto her behind just as the door opened and in came the face painted Madman.

Picturing herself from his view, Melina saw herself sitting on the floor amongst the carnage with her legs spread apart, blood and guts crusted to her face, hunks of grey matter still stuck in her hair and her arm extended in a bizarre handshake with a bodiless forearm.

The Madman just stood in the doorway speechless as he surveyed the room with his mouth agape. His focus moved around from corner to corner, taking in everything as if he was able to see exactly how events had played out in his absence. Slowly his mouth opened wide into a broad smile and his eyes sparkled as he began laughing.

Attempting to speak and laugh at the same time, the words initially came out in choppy fragments. "Wow! Looks like... I missed... one hell... of a party! Say goodnight to your friend and get up."

The last sentence came out with no laughter or smile on his face.

Melina hesitated for just a split second; staring at the jagged end of the peculiar object in her hand, she envisioned stabbing the Madman in the throat.

She actually saw it happen in her mind's eye; him falling backwards into the padded wall clutching at the severed arm sticking from his torn throat. Blood bubbled and sprayed in high arcs from punctured arteries as he choked and drowned on his own blood and bile.

Melina felt energized by the fantasy in her head. Visualizing the Madman struggling to breath gave her focus and strength. She stood up with the combo Todd-chair arm still in her hand and took a step towards the Madman.

However, the next words that came out of his mouth took all of the fight out of her.

"I just wanted you to see what I have planned for your brother if he doesn't fulfill his end of our arrangement."

Melina stopped and let go of Todd's hand. The thought of Roberto strapped to a chair, beaten to a pulp and waiting to be blown apart, was too much for her to handle. In her blind desire for revenge, Melina lost sight of the most important reason she had to persevere.

Roberto was her only family and she had deeply regretted those two and half years they were apart. The entire time she was at UCLA she counted the days until she could be reunited with her older brother. It was that intense desire that drove her to excel in school. She needed to graduate at the top of her class so she could have her pick of graduate schools. When she had received the honor of being accepted into the New York University School of Law J.D. Program, she was more thankful for the opportunity to be back with Roberto above anything else that came with that honor.

They were the last of the Sanchez line from La Joya. The deep connection they shared while growing up remained even with the almost three thousand miles that divided them these past several years. When Roberto's heart hurt, she felt it; when she passed an exam, he knew it. All they had to do was think of the other and within minutes the phone would ring.

All those years while their parents had worked their fingers to the bone so that they could enjoy even the most meager of life's pleasures, Roberto and Melina had each other; and as dire as the past two weeks seemed, deep down Melina's will to endure had come from one main source. She had to survive to get back to her brother.

As Melina stood deflated before the Madman she realized that attacking him with Todd's severed arm was not a well thought out approach. Melina clutched her fists, felt her knuckles pop and her nails dig deep into the meat of her palm.

Her chance would come.

The Madman seemed to be aware that he had just won a small victory from Melina. Maybe it was her demeanor or maybe, like before, they had some degree of psychic connection. Melina couldn't quite explain it as much as she felt it. But, somehow she sensed the Madman in her mind and it made her feel violated; almost like being mind raped.

The smile on his face was nauseating to Melina; and when he spoke again, she wanted to scream and claw out his eyes, but she simply complied with his next request.

"So far your brother has been doing a wonderful job. I stopped by just the other day to say hello to him, but he was too busy. So I merely took the liberty of leaving him a few presents at the office and around his apartment."

The Madman reached into his long-tail suit jacket and produced a deck of cards. At first it appeared as if he was a magician about to perform a trick; then Melina recognized the shape as the same as what was taped to Todd's chest. She knew right away she was looking at another bomb.

Pleased with the look he saw on her face, he knew the redesigned pack of Bicycle playing cards required no further explanation, so he simply continued as he slid the deck back into his jacket pocket.

"Sorry to say, you won't be around to clean up his mess; but at least you can pretend while you clean up this one. You will find that the panel under the chair there lifts up like a trap door. I wouldn't go down there if I was you, unless you like to bathe in lye. That is where you will dispose of all of these nasty pieces of my former employee; he always was a useless fucking moron."

The Madman paused briefly as he shook his head thinking of something more that went unspoken. Walking over to the near corner behind the door he tucked his fingers into one of the seams set into the padding on the walls and swung forward a hidden door exposing a large closet. In addition to an industrial sink basin, the closet was stocked with mops and brooms and cleaning products that would be the envy of any hospital janitorial crew.

Turning back to Melina with a hideously smug grin; very proud of himself at once again at having astonished his guest, he told her that he expected the room to be spotless when he returned in the morning for her. The exact phrasing he used was; "In the same condition as when you found it, minus the roommate of course."

Pausing briefly before he closed and locked the door, the Madman stopped and pointed at Todd's severed arm on the floor; "Please, go ahead, finish your dinner. I'm sorry I interrupted."

(Unedited excerpt from the manuscript)

The view of the St. Regis was spectacular from The Tap. There was about a 2 minute delay between keying in the last number and the explosions.

I know this is an odd place to discuss the Theory of Relativity, especially since it isn't relevant, but it still may make sense even to those of you not really capable of grasping an understanding of matters beyond your meager existence.

I can see the confused expression on your face, so I'll try to simplify what I mean...

Time is relevant based on your point of reference at a specific moment as it relates to your level of anticipation pertaining to a specific event. If you remove or reduce the level of anticipation, then you no longer have a pivotal point of reference and therefore no true concept of time moving at a rate that is pertinent; hence, you are left with the feeling that time moved quickly. However, in contrast, when you accentuate the level of anticipation, you focus on an acute awareness pertaining to the rate that time appears to be moving; hence, you are left with the feeling that time has slowed down or completely stopped.

Okay, now that I've cleared that up...

The point I'm making is that while I was waiting for the wireless connection to be made, those 2 minutes seemed like a half hour to me.

I was starting to feel very uncomfortable.

Very exposed.

Everything that possibly could go wrong came flooding in at me all at once. Schematics of soldered wires on computer chip boards, untested nickel cadmium batteries, wireless 'dead-zones' and prematurely discovered gym bags danced through my mind; each image posing as a potential reason for why the signal was not being received.

I remember a cold sweat beading up on my forehead as I began thinking about what would happen if the gym bags were discovered. At the time I was stuffing them full of C4, I wasn't really concerned about leaving my fingerprints in the clay. I was so focused on the end result of the explosions that I forgot to concentrate on the bigger picture.

This was a great lesson.

I'm a firm believer in that everything happens for a reason. The level of panic I experienced in those 2 minutes was meant to remind me how important it is to not only have a plan, but to make sure all your ducks are in a row.

It is so much easier to kill all the ducks when they are standing perfectly still and all in a row.

💣

Still to this day, I remember that feeling deep in the pit of my stomach; a mixture of frustration and fear.

It was terrible.

Meanwhile, I had Beach-Bimbo Barbie trying to whore a drink from me every 15 seconds and it was getting very annoying.

As much as I had appreciated her being a receptacle for my sperm donation earlier, I was seriously contemplating grabbing her by her blond hair and repeatedly smashing her head into the concrete right there at poolside.

I was right there on the edge of losing my composure. No telling what would have happened next if the top of the St. Regis didn't finally erupt in a cacophony of color and sound.

It was beautiful.

It was soothing.

It was just what the doctor ordered.

As the tempo of the day shifted into panic, I finally felt at ease.

The second explosion in the Health Spa occurred about 10 seconds after the first and occurred in such a manner that the entire hotel collapsed upon itself.

I wished I had a better view.

From where I sat a few blocks up the street at The Tap it appeared that the towering inferno that had engulfed the rooftop of the St. Regis got sucked straight down as if the earth had opened up below the building.

Almost instantly a plume of smoke and debris shot straight up into the air, rising high above where the building had originally peaked. The heat contained within of the rising column of soot glowed as fire trails swirled around within the mounting cloud of wreckage.

It was a great day for math and physics.

I've called that imagery to mind on several occasions since I left Florida. Something about it stirs an emotion deep inside me. Maybe it was because the erupting column of debris and flame was like a mental orgasm. It was a visual release that soothed the anxiety that I had been feeling only moments before.

I'm not ashamed or embarrassed to admit that I've used that image and those feelings during those few times when I've had trouble climaxing with a date or some club-slut. I had become so used to associating violence and torture with climaxing, that my body had difficulty pollinating the flowers I had been picking.

Don't misunderstand what I'm saying, I've never had any trouble getting it up and keeping it up; the problem was making Mr. Happy Stick throw up.

On a few occasions after I moved back to New York and took a position with Citibank (that reminds me... the men won the game at the St. Regis) I had almost resorted back to my old ways.

I was very much like an addict trying to exist without his fix. I thought about raping and torturing and bludgeoning. I missed the screams and the begging and the blood. I craved to have my dick thrust inside a warm hole I had just created.

I remember that first night in New York, I was longing for the taste of blood on my lips; the mayhem of the Lauderdale strip had faded quickly as the miles between my old home and new home increased.

With the need for murder pulsing in my veins, I left my Soho loft on the prowl; like a werewolf under the glow of a full moon.

I walked aimlessly for a couple hours trying to get a grip on the voices screaming in my head. Their cries for cold blooded murder providing background music as I moved through the streets of the East Village; eventually, I found myself at the doorstep of the historic Webster Hall on E. 11th.

Nostalgia brought me back to a degree of sanity. I used to get my stick wet at Webster Hall back in the day. If I was in the city and I wasn't at the Limelight I was at Webster Hall.

I went in with the intention of just checking the old place out but I ended up bringing home some skanky Puerto Rican club-slut.

I knew at some point I needed to test myself and I figured that there is never a better time than the right here and the right now. So I locked myself in my apartment with a needle, a spoon and a couple grams of heroin named Daisy.

💣

Daisy was a lot of fun.

We fucked hard for a couple of hours; actually christened every room in my new Soho loft, some twice.

But I didn't cum.

I couldn't cum.

My cock was throbbing and hard and in desperate need for release; but I couldn't cum.

I needed the heroin.

Daisy was trying so hard to milk the prize out of me when I caught a glimpse of the vegetable peeler I had left on the kitchen counter earlier in the day.

Envisioning the club-slut tied to my custom made wrought iron poster bed, dragging the peeler across her face as layers of skin curled off her. Imagining the tip of her nipples slicing off as the open groove of the peeler took hold and tore away the tender tips. I pictured myself ramming the peeler deep into her belly button and using it like a handle to pull her down over my cock.

The mind is a powerful tool.

Finally it was my turn to explode.

💣

Chapter 71

Becca couldn't believe her luck as she turned off of First Avenue onto 69th Street. A black car was pulling out of a parking spot directly in front of her apartment building. The odds of that ever happening again were slim to none. The simple fact that Becca didn't need to spend the next hour looking for a parking space brought such an overwhelming sense of relief that and she actually shed a tear of joy.

Becca was emotionally exhausted. It had been a rollercoaster of a weekend; and she had been firing on all cylinders since she meet Roberto at his office Friday afternoon.

During the remainder of her ride home from Long Island, Becca kept her focus on the road by blasting the radio. Q104.3, New York's classic rock station, played the extended version of *Ina-Gada-Da-Vida* by Iron Butterfly. Other than a few flashbacks to her high school days and of her father, who had always been a card-carrying, head-banging, Heavy Metal enthusiast, she managed to stay focused on her driving

Becca's lung-searing chants of 'Da-da Da-da-da Da, Da-da-da' kept her hands drumming the wheel at ten and two across the Triborough Bridge and down the FDR to her apartment on 69th.

Turning off the engine, Becca checked the side mirror of her Nissan to insure that no cars were speeding up the narrow cross-street. She had come too close too many times to losing the driver's side door and possibly her legs.

Becca swiveled out and waved hello to Rudy, one of the building's doormen.

Becca hated doormen. Not that she had anything specific against Rudy, it was doormen in general; she just felt uncomfortable with them. Becca was the type of person who preferred to help herself. She didn't need them opening the door for her. She didn't need them running out in the rain to assist her with packages as she stepped out of a taxi. She didn't need them asking her how she was; and she definitely didn't need to feel required to make small talk with them about the weather.

Rudy was the worst of them all. Again, nothing against Rudy, he was a nice enough kid; but, he was Hispanic and seemed to feel it was his duty, his obligation to communicate with Becca in his native tongue. Not once did Becca ever respond in Spanish and yet Rudy was relentless about communicating with her that way. It was as if somehow, the fact that they were both of Latino heritages they belonged to the same club.

Becca was always especially sensitive to that type of behavior because she felt it just further accentuated the rift between cultures. How were people supposed to come together as equals if everyone constantly perpetuated their differences?

With one other exception, the doormen of the 333 building on East 69th were Italian; not a Mafioso type of situation, but close. Becca was also one of the few tenants of the building that had a strong Latino presence and with that came another whole slew of issues from the doormen. It had nothing to do with the 'door' part; it had everything to do with the 'men' part. Becca was used to the comments and the looks she got from the overly aggressive, uncouth male breed of the species out in the streets. But, when it came to her home, Becca expected a degree of sanctuary from the verbal and visual abuse.

Improper looks and comments were just the beginning. Becca found the doormen on the inside of her gated, street-level patio on more than one occasion. Supposedly 'cleaning and tidying up' the outside of the building took a lot more effort and time around Becca's windows than it did for the other tenant's apartments.

Becca had filed an official complaint to the building's Condo Association but had received back a less than favorable response regarding their willingness to support her allegations of improper etiquette.

The Condo Association, which had barely approved her purchase in the first place, was comprised of predominately older, Jewish couples that were desperately trying to hold onto a segregated neighborhood. A concept and a battle that was lost fifty years earlier. However, they took the opportunity to respond to Becca's grievance with a venomous aspiration that maybe she should consider moving to a part of the city where she wouldn't feel so much as an outsider. The Association also suggested that possibly a good, hard look in the mirror might lend some explanation as to why people might get the wrong impression. It was in their opinion that Becca's choice of clothing was nothing more than a blatant cry for sexual attention. In closing, the Association explained that the over-worked, under-appreciated doormen should not have to worry about being subjected to potential frivolous sexual harassment suits from any of the foreign, single women tenants.

From that day forward, Becca made it a point to predominately use her street-level entrance. In addition, she ignored the doormen as if they didn't exist, with the exception of Rudy, who truly meant no harm and who was also treated poorly by the tenants and other doormen. But, the thing that changed most of all was that Becca made it a point to say hello and act mildly inappropriate with all the husbands of the Coots and Biddies from the Association.

Dropping her notebook and emptying her pockets onto the glass coffee table, Becca flopped down hard onto her living room sofa with a heavy exhale.

Leaning back and rubbing her eyes, Becca slipped off her shoes and let them fall to the wood paneled floor. In desperate need of a hot shower, a soothing cup of Chamomile tea and good night's sleep; Becca began undressing on the couch. Lifting her bottom up off the sofa cushion, Becca shimmied out of her skirt until it landed on the floor next to her shoes. Next she removed her shirt and unfastened the front clasp on her bra. After rubbing at the indentations the restrictive article of clothing had left on her upper body, her shirt and bra joined the pile on the floor.

Traditionally, Becca was a very neat and orderly person. Removed clothes were usually separated into two hampers; one for normal washing and one ready to go to the dry-cleaners. Tonight though, exhaustion had given way to a breach in the routine. Becca was a firm believer in the concept of handling a piece of paper just once. Something she had learned from her fiancé, once high school guidance counselor, Mr. 'call me Jeremy' Young.

Jeremy always said, "If it is in your hand, why not put it where it belongs right then. Maximize your efforts, why handle the same piece of paper more than once?"

Becca recalled one of the first times they were together sexually after years of friendship; she held his erect shaft in her hand and commented on how since it was in her hand, she was going to put it where it belonged; she then proceeded to file the stiff member in her mouth.

Sitting almost completely naked on the couch, wearing only her black lace panties, Becca arched her body and stretched as far as she could against the back of the sofa. With arms extended back beyond her head, Becca realized that her blinds were still open and any passerby would have gotten one heck of a striptease. But, the sidewalk was empty and Becca felt somewhat disappointed.

No wonder the doormen spend extra time tending to her garden patio. Standing and moving slowly to the window, Becca twisted the tilt-wand and rotated the slats on the Venetian blinds until they provided a degree of privacy that was commonly acceptable.

No longer under the prying eyes of the city, Becca gave her body another sky reaching stretch while taking in a deep breath through her mouth; and then in slow graceful move, she bent down to touch her toes while exhaling slowly from her nose. With her palms flat on the floor next to her feet, Becca held that pose feeling the pull in her lower back.

Thoughts of a hot shower with the pulsating jets of her Shower Massage pounding against her body got her moving towards the bathroom.

Passing by the couch and the clutter she had made on and around the coffee table, Becca paused to gather up her discarded clothes and distribute them in the proper wash hampers before they mocked her laziness any more.

Becca's attention was drawn to the irregular folded piece of newsprint lying next to her notebook on the coffee table. Becca was unable to readily place what the object represented and sat down briefly on the couch to unfold the mystery.

Unveiling the torn off portion of the Newsday puzzle section she had obtained at Kyra's house earlier, Becca realized that she was more exhausted than she was giving herself credit for. Typically, Becca was able to recall things that happened within the past few hours.

Glancing over at the clock above the kitchen doorway Becca had to rub her eyes to make sure she was seeing the display properly. Shaking her head in disbelief because it seemed much later, the big hand showed that it was barely on the left side of 5:30.

Looking back down at the unfolded piece of paper in her hands; Becca's eyes danced down the word jumble and across her own handwriting. The Norwegian toy company, WINSTON HORGHBRALL, would have to wait until later or maybe tomorrow for further research; meanwhile, SKAM, DYNAC, GRANDO and FLINTIO were about to get her immediate attention.

The jumbled words were entered into her mind and would be joining her as she headed towards the bathroom in pursuit of a hot, pulsating shower.

(Unedited excerpt from the manuscript)

Daisy left my Soho loft intact. She truly had no idea how close she had come to dying that evening.

We never fucked again, although we did run into each other at Webster's every now and then. It seemed that Daisy and I were similar in at least one aspect; we were both sexual predators who enjoyed capturing prey and fucking them to death for the evening.

I can't speak for Daisy, but I quickly started getting bored with just the simple club pick up. There were just too many times that I grabbed the girl who was a great dancer, the one who was writhing and gyrating her hips around in the club like she was double jointed, only to find out that she was like a dead fish in bed.

Sometimes it was really hard not to kill.

After a while I needed something more to keep me from going back to the needle.

New York City is just like a live version of the internet. Meaning that if you type in the right words, the search engine will provide you with more than you've bargained for; and, the best part is, that it is all right there at your fingertips, just on the other side of your door.

I graduated from picking up club-sluts to being a regular at some Gothic venues and S & M member clubs.

I could go into a lot of twisted, bizarre, sordid details about fucking in coffins and fantasy vampirism ritualistic orgies. Plus, I could write pages upon pages about sexual gratification through the means of inflicting physical and mental pain on others...

Wait a minute... I already have.

The only difference is, and trust me when I tell you it is a huge difference; was that nobody died.

Not nearly as much fun; but it did keep me off the needle.

If I hadn't been working diligently on my plans to blow most of you faceless fucks up; I probably would have gone crazy.

We're basically done here.

All that's left to do is sit back and make phone calls.

I can't wait to get started.

Every 7 calendar days for a year.

I do plan on taking Christmas and New Years off, so you can enjoy time with your families.

I mean, come on, I'm not a monster.

Alright, it's time to wrap this puppy up; I will however just quickly share with you how easy it was to fulfill my dream thanks to Citibank Bank. They were after all, instrumental in laying down the foundation for that which is to come.

I couldn't believe how lax the inner controls were for the bank. Once I discovered how easy it was to open accounts for businesses that didn't even exist; and, to be able to have loans funded to them without any collateral, I was like a kid in candy shop getting fat.

Company A would lend money to Company B; Company C would use its money to pay back the original loans from Company A, meanwhile Company B would make a few bad investments involving Company D who lent money back to Company C at high interest rates forcing Company B out of business... and so on.

Multiply that and similar concepts of money manipulation by hundreds of companies where Citibank ended up on the short end of the stick every time; someone like myself could end up very rich, even after they purchased a private island and resort.

We all should have retirement plans; don't you agree?

That wasn't the only scam I was able to run from being on the inside of one of the worlds largest financial institutions. Utilizing the multitude of names and social security numbers I had stock piled from Florida, I was able to create an overlapping network of personal accounts; and, once I integrated them with an equally staggering amount of legitimate, dormant account holders, the money just kept flooding in.

I'll slow down that explanation for you stupid fucks that can't grasp the simplicity of what I did.

An account goes dormant after 2 years of inactivity. No money in and no money out. I figured the likelihood of those dormant account holders even opening up their statements was slim to none. These are typically accounts of individuals that have no particular use for the money other than to have it sit there until they die.

The beauty of everything I did was complimented by the luxury of time. There was no need to rush anything I was doing.

Haste makes mistakes.

First, I added joint account holders to the dormant accounts and made a nominal withdrawal into separate accounts held in sole ownership by the fictitious owner. Once two full monthly statement cycles went by without any problems, I would liquidate the dormant account with a cashier's check made payable to a third party who would then wire transfer the funds into an off shore account. From there the money could reenter the United States as investments into any number of legitimate businesses.

And that's all I'm going to tell you.

💣

This seems like a good time for my acceptance speech...

"I'd like to thank the Academy and its members; I've worked hard my whole career and feel blessed to be recognized for this special honor. I need to thank Amanda Farber and the entire Hollingsworth Family for giving me the opportunity and means to develop my skills at such an early age. There have been so many of you around the world that have contributed to my growth and progress, that I couldn't possibly take the time to thank you all; but, please know that each and every one of you holds a special place in my heart. Lastly, I'd be negligent if I didn't thank The Creator, with whom none of this would be possible." (Cue music and cut to commercial).

🌑

Chapter 72

Becca admired her almost thirty year old body in the full length mirror on the back of the bathroom door. Time had been generous to her. Although she didn't regularly work out or religiously watch her weight; Becca still sported a body that would be the envy of most females at any age.

As the water in the shower heated up, steam fogged the mirror and Becca's body slowly faded from view.

Taking in a deep breath, enjoying the warm wet air as it entered her body, Becca scribed into the wet dew that laced the mirror before her. Becca's hand flowed through the moist film as she transformed the jumbled letters from the Newsday Word Jumble into coherent everyday words.

As Becca took SKAM and created MASK, and DYNAC became CANDY; another part of Becca's mind brought up the image of the Norwegian toy company's logo. The metallic gold lettering framed on either side by a toy jack sparkled in her mind's eye; WINSTON HORGHBRALL, *Importer of Norwegian Novelties Since 1980.*

Once again, Becca thought to herself how sad it was that the family reached at anything that suggested the existence of a renegade brother as her hand wrote HOLLINGSWORTH BARN into the mirror.

Becca stared at the lettering she had just written; the full impact not quite hitting home until she wrote DRAGON out of the jumbled GRANDO below it, and then her knees buckled.

Shutting off the shower and wrapping herself in the red Teri-cloth robe that hung on a hook to the right of the bathroom door; Becca basically ran to the kitchen and picked up the phone. Her hands were shaking so fiercely that she needed to redial Roberto's home number three times before she got it right.

Pacing back and forth as the connection simply rang and rang, Becca's mind reeled with mixed emotions. The reality that Jack Thomas and the Norwegian toy company were connected had her absolutely blown away.

After what must have been the thirtieth ring, Becca slammed the phone back into its cradle and headed into the living room to retrieve her cell phone from her purse. Although she knew Roberto's home number, Becca needed the help of her cell phone for his office and cell numbers.

She had been able to dial Roberto's home number from her memory. It was just one of those things that stuck from their years of dating; that, and it was a simple pattern on the phone's keypad. Becca always said his number went around and around, very much like their relationship. Roberto never saw the humor in that concept the same way Becca did; but that was just par for the course.

A different taste in comedy was another facet that became a wedge between them as their relationship struggled. It's funny, so to speak, that when a relationship starts to go sour, how all the little things start to become big things. It becomes easy to nitpick at that very same person you, until recently, thought was flawless. It becomes easy to find fault and be annoyed with the same attributes of a person that you originally found so endearing.

When you really look at how fickle we are as a species, it is amazing that any of us are with another person for any given length of time. We can barely stand being with ourselves for extended periods, let alone sharing time and space with another.

As Becca fished out her cell phone from her purse, she looked at the torn piece from the Long Island Newsday puzzle section sitting on the glass coffee table. Taking the pen from its sleeve in her notebook, Becca wrote HOLLINGSWORTH BARN under her earlier handwriting of WINSTON HORGHBRALL and although the exercise was unnecessary, Becca cross-referenced the letters.

A perfect match.

Becca questioned what else she may have missed now that this new element of the Madman's game was unveiled. The last thing she wanted to do was read through the psychopath's manuscript again.

With a heavy sigh, Becca let her mind contemplate that very undesirable undertaking; while her hand officially filled in the words on the daily jumble. Because everyone knows, that fog on a bathroom mirror is not considered as an official entry of word jumble answers.

MASK, CANDY, DRAGON... FLINTIO?

FLINTIO?

Becca closed her eyes and let the lettered flashcards go through their rearrangement dance in her mind as she heard her mother's voice; "Let go and let God."

Chapter 73

Roberto made it to his office just as the phone had stopped ringing.

He wanted to scream.

Looking at the display screen, Roberto was able to tell that the call had been re-routed from his apartment on 17th Street. He had programmed his home phone to ring into his cell phone on Saturday night. The idea to have all calls coming into a centralized location had just been one of his revelations as he emerged from the cold water with a fire in his heart and a focus in his mind.

Roberto wondered who the call had come from, and kicked himself for not keeping the phone closer within reach.

The call could have come from anybody, but the caller ID simply identified the call as coming from his own apartment.

A shiver ran down his spine as he contemplated the idea that maybe it wasn't a re-routed call, but rather a call that originated from his apartment. If that was the case, that meant that someone was in his apartment.

Roberto had a flashback of a scene from that old horror movie where the babysitter is getting prank phone calls and gets the police involved monitoring the phone lines. When the call comes again the police call back and tell her that the call came from inside the house. The call came from inside the house… The caller is inside the house... GET OUT!!!!

Feeling jumpy and exhausted from a long day, Roberto figured he was reading too much into the missed call. Checking for the time on his wrist once more, Roberto found himself needing to adjust the distance his arm was from his face. They say the eyes are the first to go as you get older and Roberto was guessing they were right.

As the hands on the watch became clearer, Roberto was able to decipher the time to be ten after six and realized that the re-routed call could simply be from a telemarketer. Roberto hated telemarketers even though he understood the need for that form of a sales approach. He also realized that although he would never buy anything that way, quite a large number of people must, or else companies wouldn't spend billions of dollars marketing through the phone.

Roberto was just guessing at the figure of 'billions of dollars'. It just seemed like the right number though. Another flash and his mind brought up an image of Carl Sagan, the famous astronomer, who was renowned for using the term 'billions and billions'; enunciated slowly through a constricted throat so as every word appeared to be a struggle to say and therefore must be very important if Carl Sagan was willing to risk his life to utter the sentence.

Realizing the insanity of his thought patterns; Roberto still found himself unable to control them and therefore had to let Carl Sagan finish what he was trying to say. "Every year, billions and billions of dollars are spent on the telemarketing industry and despite recent reforms, these billions and billions of pesky phone calls find their way into our homes at an alarming rate, invading our meal times and providing a source of constant irritation."

Thank you Carl; now back to our previously scheduled nightmare…

There was really no way for him to know for sure; but, Roberto's gut feeling told him that it had been Becca who had called him. His gut also told him that she had good news to share.

Becca.

Roberto found himself thinking about Becca quite a bit since she had come to the office Friday afternoon. It was hard to believe that that was only two days ago. It felt like weeks had gone by since he received the manuscript.

Throughout the underlying horror that the past several days had brought into his life; Becca was there once again as a beacon of hope. Roberto caught himself having thoughts of reuniting their relationship once all of this Rush Hour Madman stuff was behind them. But for now, Roberto remained focused on Melina's safe return; anything else that may or may not come, was for later consideration.

Roberto picked up his cell phone and began to scroll through the directory for Becca's number. With the phone flipped open in the palm of his hand, Roberto just stared at the display. It was as if he was gathering his nerves for some reason; just like he had done when they had first met. He couldn't decide if it was caused by a nervous anticipation of the impending news she may have had or if he was experiencing the nerves of a high school boy about to call the girl he liked.

Chapter 74

Standing on her tiptoes, Becca reached deep into the cabinet above the stove. She knew there was another box of Chamomile tea in there somewhere. Becca kept her variety of teas better stocked than most stores.

Moving aside spare boxes of Saran Wrap cellophane and Reynolds Wrap aluminum foil, Becca stopped in mid-motion.

Earlier, she couldn't concentrate and decipher the meaning of the remaining jumbled word, FLINTIO. With everything else going on in her head, Becca decided that a cup of Chamomile tea with a hint of lavender extract would go a long way in relaxing her mind, body and soul.

If she could be seen from the outside, Becca looked like a statue, frozen in a pose for all eternity. Stretched out to the full extent that her robust five foot five body would allow; calve muscles taught with feet extended to their toes like a ballerina, one arm bracing on fingertips spread out on top of the stove while the other arm held the blue metallic box of Reynolds Wrap.

Momentarily abandoning her Chamomile quest, Becca broke her statuesque pose and moved quickly and gracefully back into the living room. The open Teri-cloth robe fluttered behind her naked body like a super hero's cape blowing in the wind.

Checking off one more item from her mental list, Becca completed the Word Jumble by writing TINFOIL next to FLINTIO. Snapping the pen down with a triumphant *thwap* on the paper, Becca leaned back into the white scalloped couch allowing the cool breeze from the air conditioning vents to bring fresh goose-bumps to her skin.

Having checked off the Word Jumble, Becca's thoughts returned to the pulsating jets of her shower massage and her intention of thoroughly 'washing' herself.

Becca couldn't believe how horny she still felt.

Thoughts of the shower brought her mind back to the mirror and her discovery of the Hollingsworth Barn anagram.

Becca needed to call Roberto.

Fishing through her satchel for the tiny cell phone hidden amongst the random chaos that seemed to always find its way into her handbags; Becca tried to organize her thoughts to share her day with Roberto. She didn't want to get caught up in a lengthy conversation, but she wanted to let him know that he had been correct in his assumption about what she would uncover.

The brothers did know more than they knew they knew, and the Jack Thomas connection to the mystery birthday gifts, Becca hoped would prove to be his downfall. The excitement and subsequent surge of adrenaline that thought brought to Becca made her realize that no matter how tired her body felt, sleep wasn't going to come easy that evening.

Armed with her cell phone in hand, Becca flipped open the devise and scrolled through the directory to 'RJ aka SAD SACK'. Pushing the left soft key instead of the send button, Becca navigated the menu-bar to the edit selection and modified the description to simply read 'RJ'.

Becca sat with the open phone in her hand and reflected on the change she had witnessed in Roberto since this whole fiasco had begun. The confidence that emanated from him was comforting and somewhat sexy. Becca always liked a take-charge kind of man. The determination and clarity of thought Roberto had displayed at breakfast that morning had Becca's mind wandering places she swore it would never go again.

The phone in Becca's hand rang just as she was just about to press the send button causing her to utter a small scream and drop the phone onto the hard wood floor.

Fortunately the phone was fine and kept playing the assigned ring tone she had allocated to all of Roberto's possible numbers. As *Round and Round* by Aerosmith entered into the second verse, Becca listened to the lyrics before she answered the call. Although the display just said 'RJ' now; the lyrics still meant the same old thing. Everything changes.

Chapter 75

Becca woke up disoriented. She was lying on the outside edge of a couch and there was a human arm draped across her chest. She could feel this person's warm rhythmic breathing on the back of her neck.

There was a clock sitting at a slight angle, centered on a short table inches from her face. Liquid blue numbers glowed in its display telling Becca that it was 1:49am.

Slowly, the gravity of the colossal mistake she had made crept back into reality.

Becca eased herself from beneath Roberto's arm and slinked off the couch taking extreme care so as not to awaken him.

Replaying the evening's events in her mind, Becca gathered up her clothes that were scattered around the office and began to dress herself. Ashamed, angry and embarrassed, she shook her head as she watched Roberto sleeping soundly on the couch before her. He was such a sweet man and Becca hated that this situation was going to end up hurting him.

Becca knew better and should have maintained a degree of self control. If Becca was a man, someone would have told her that she had been thinking with her dick. However, in her own defense, she did tell him that there were no strings attached.

Earlier when she had answered Roberto's call at her apartment there had been such pride in his voice as he shared his accomplishments of the day. Becca had relayed that she also had exciting news and before she knew what was happening, she was asking Roberto if he would mind if she came over to tell him face to face.

At the office they chatted and laughed at the crazy day Becca had with Jack's brothers and their wives. Becca left out all of the sexual fantasies she had been having through out the day; but there was no stopping them from resurfacing in mind as she was retelling Roberto her saga and that got her juices flowing once again.

Together, Becca and Roberto moved all of the printed manuscripts down to the shipping platform and cleaned up the presses for the staff's arrival the following morning. Once the production floor appeared that nothing out of the ordinary had happened over the weekend, Becca and Roberto retired into his office to take a well deserved break before they headed to their respective homes.

Without a doubt, Becca was to blame for what transpired next. Leaning back against the front edge of his desk, Roberto simply stretched and moaned. As he complained about how he hadn't had a work out like that in a long time, Becca's eyes were drawn to the well defined abdomen that appeared when his shirt lifted above his waistline.

Roberto stated how was going to feel the ache in the morning and Becca seized the opportunity to satisfy the itch that had plagued her all day. Standing up from the couch where she had been admiring his physique, Becca approached Roberto and guided him into one of the short-backed leather chairs in front of his desk.

A shoulder massage, turned into a frenzied, throw the items off the desk, all out fuck fest. Becca clawed off Roberto's jeans and sucked at his cock until she felt him almost ready to explode. She then forced him out of the chair and onto his desk and climbed aboard. With her feet planted firmly on the desk straddling his erection; Becca rocked herself back and forth, and up and down on Roberto. Driving him deeper and deeper into her wetness, Becca thrust her body until she felt him climax inside of her.

Shifting her legs down next to his, Becca laid her sweat covered body down gently atop of Roberto. Keeping his still swollen member tucked safely inside of her warmth, Becca nestled her face into his neck and began nibbling at his earlobe. When she felt him stiffen back to full attention, Becca slid off and guided him over to the couch where she positioned and presented herself to him for more.

On her knees with legs spread, using the back of the couch for support, Becca reached between her legs and pulled Roberto back inside of her from behind. Roberto reached around and under; cupping both of her large breasts in his rough hands, he forced himself further and further into Becca. Matching his forward motion with timed, rhythmic, downward thrusts, Becca climaxed with explosive shudders.

Disengaging from each other's mess, the former lovers repositioned themselves on the couch. Lying together like perfectly matched puzzle pieces, Becca and Roberto slipped off into an exhausted slumber.

Becca looked around the office once more and took a mental inventory of everything she had brought with her; comfortable she was leaving nothing behind, Becca knelt down beside Roberto.

Earlier they had decided that they would try to meet for lunch on Monday. The beginning of the workweek was typically a fast paced whirlwind in the news industry. Not only were you faced with the normal zigs and zags of everyday news and events; but, special features and exposes were discussed and assigned in chop-shop type meetings.

Becca had promised Roberto that she would find time to SNIPH around on the background and affiliations of the Winston Horghbrall Novelty Toy Company as soon as possible. Becca was going to talk to her editor about maybe getting some official time off to continue following the Jack Thomas leads. Regardless, Becca let Roberto know that she had every intention of pursuing the Madman with or without official time off.

Becca realized that Jack Thomas and his psychotic manuscript were her meal ticket out of freelance writing for the Post. Even if nothing else transpired, the information she had on the Madman was front page exclusive news once the manuscript hit the bookshelves. Becca envisioned herself being interviewed on *Dateline* and *60 minutes*. She would then catapult into stardom as the most widely sought out female news anchor in history.

As Becca sat there watching Roberto's eyes move back and forth under his lids, she thought that finally something worthwhile had come out of their relationship. She hoped that he would understand when nothing developed from the evenings escapades. She would like to remain friends but couldn't envision going through another round of an intimate relationship with him. Despite all the changes she had witnessed in him over the past few days, she had to imagine that beneath it all was still the same jealous, needy RJ that sucked all the life out of her too many times before.

Deciding not to wake him, Becca bent forward and gave Roberto a soft kiss on his forehead. Knees popping as she stood up, Becca headed for the office door hoping that she would quickly find a cab on Third Ave at two o'clock in the morning. With her hand on the doorknob and trying to be as quiet as possible, Becca almost screamed when a voice spoke out from behind her.

(Unedited excerpt from the manuscript)

The time has come for me to bid you faceless fucks a sweet adieu...

In closing, I want to remind you that although I sincerely despise the so called moral majority, the explosive revelations (pun intended) that are soon to wreak havoc amid your favorite cities are not statements of a political or religious nature.

I do what I do, as I have done and will continue to do, simply for the thrill; for the pure beauty of chaos and disorder.

I am guessing that some of you have put together enough clues from this manuscript to accurately predict the first attack. I'm also guessing that if you have, it still doesn't matter.

Even if I spelled it out for you phonetically, you'd still find a way to mispronounce your own fate. The point is that thousands of you will die that day at that time.

Do you know why?

I do.

You're fucking complacent.

It would take a stick of J-J Walker brand dynamite shoved directly up your ass for you to even realize you've got a potential problem.

With that being said...

Your final clue isn't a clue; it's a hint.

Do you understand the difference?

There are 50 cities in my crosshairs; all of the fundamental nouns have been locked and loaded. I'm positive there isn't a damn thing you can do to prevent the first one. The next 3 will produce a pattern for you to follow throughout the rest of the year.

Not that it will matter, because even if you do catch on, you won't be able to stop it; and that's the whole point of this little game.

There really isn't much left to tell you; other than, goodbye and thanks for listening.

As if you had a choice.

You faceless fuck.

As you go scurrying beneath the refrigerator and diving into the cracks in your walls, don't forget what this manuscript was intended to do.

Let the mayhem begin...

Thump-thump.

💣 💣 💣

Chapter 76

"I see how you are... Leave me here for dead. Steal all my bodily fluids and just go. You're a regular modern day sex vampire."

Roberto could tell he had spooked her and actually enjoyed doing so. Becca turned from the door and pretended that she hadn't been startled.

"I just didn't want to wake you. I need to get home. I have an early staff meeting."

"Some things never change." Roberto said and Becca thought that she had just been thinking the very same thing.

Roberto continued, "You'll see, one of these days soon, you will break out of that rat race. Karma will reward you for everything you've done for me these past few days."

Becca was actually at a loss of words, she wasn't prepared for Roberto to say such an unselfish thing. In the past, her comment would have been followed up with something more along the lines of; 'you think you're the only one who has to get up early.' Becca just smiled and walked back across the office floor to the couch where Roberto had himself propped up on his side. Lying naked, resting on an elbow with one leg bent up at the knee, Roberto looked like he was the centerfold picture for *Playgirl* magazine.

Becca's eyebrows rose involuntarily as she scanned Roberto's well toned body. She had noticed earlier that he must have been working out. He was definitely in much better shape now than when they were dating. Becca also found herself admiring his penis as it rested soft but thick across his thigh. That too seemed to be in much better shape than she had remembered.

Becca's mind swayed as if on a pendulum and she found herself momentarily entertaining the possibility of another ride on the RJ Express. Not just wrapping her hands around his exposed member; but, actually entertaining a renewed undertaking of their relationship.

Catching herself before she could say, or do, something she would terribly regret later. Even more so than she had already accomplished in the past several hours; Becca just gave Roberto another peck on the forehead and told him she would call him later.

In his new persona and very uncharacteristic of the old RJ she had broken up with; Roberto simply thanked her for coming over and told her to get home safe.

It was odd; but when Roberto said, "Call whenever you can." Becca found herself wanting to call as soon as possible.

Chapter 77

Despite the overpowering stench of cleaning products, a mixture of pine and lye, plus the incessant glow of the overhead lights, Melina had slept relatively well.

It had been quite a while since she felt the comfort of a mattress beneath her body; and when she first awoke, she thought she was in the living room of her brother's apartment on the pullout Futon.

The dismal reality of her surroundings quickly replaced the slight confusion that accompanied her waking state of mind. Melina looked around the white padded room and recalled the tedious and revolting task she had endured well into the early hours of the morning.

All of her anger and frustration came flooding back through her veins in raging rivers of purpose. Last night, every scrub and scour fueled her fire like coal feeds a steam engine. As she gathered up Todd's tattered body parts and dropped them down into the lye well beneath the trap door in the center of the room; Melina thought of Roberto and the threat the Madman had made. He had said, "Sorry to say, you won't be around to clean up his mess; but at least you can pretend while you clean up this one."

Melina didn't know what to think anymore, and maybe that was part of his twisted game. One moment the Madman would make a comment that made her think she was going to survive, and all she had to do was hang on, just endure one more torture, and then she'd be free.

However last night's comment had Melina convinced that not only was she going to die, but that Roberto was going to die as well; that he was going to be blown up and scattered around like Todd. That he'd be turned into torn, broken, bloody body parts no longer resembling a human being; and that Melina would have to identify his body and then clean it up.

Melina's head swam. She was light headed from the cleaning fumes and weak from lack of food.

The door swung open and she instinctively curled into a ball on the clean side of the soiled mattress.

With fresh make-up on his face, painted all white with black spikes dripping out of the corner of his eyes and from his lips; the Madman walked towards Melina while surveying the room. Wearing a long black wig that made him look like Alice Cooper, the Madman wore his black long-tail coat and sported a top hat that he tipped to Melina as he bid her a good morning welcome.

"Top of the morning to ya, my fine lass. It's going to be a lovely day."

Shirtless and barefoot, the Madman only wore a pair of faded blue jeans to compliment his jacket and hat. Bidding her to reciprocate, the deranged Ring Master extended a hand towards Melina. Slow with stiffness and shaky with weakness, Melina complied and reached up into the psychopath's proffered hand.

With his hand placed on her back, the Madman guided Melina in front of him and told her what a wonderful job she had done cleaning the room. As they moved slowly towards the open door, the Madman explained that she deserved a present; that he was going to make her feel like a woman again. His hand moved slightly up and down her back as he ran his fingers through her hair. He told her how proud he was of her and how he had never allowed someone to share so much with him. He told her how she should feel honored and special to be a part of what's to come.

Pausing briefly at the open doorway, gently rubbing the small of her back, Melina could feel the heat building up in his hand and began to fear what was about to transpire. The Madman's hand slid down over the rise of her butt and came to rest firmly on her right cheek. He then pivoting around in front of her and backed Melina up into the doorjamb and pressed himself against the full length of her body.

Trapped between the edge of the doorframe jutting into her back and the pressure of the Madman's swollen erection pressing into her crotch, Melina turned her head up and away from the vile odor that wafted out of his mouth as he spoke to her.

"You're going to help me make America hold her breath and her heart skip a beat."

Melina had two thoughts run through her head at the same time. *With breath like yours; you're not going to need my help...*and...*If you don't back the fuck up off me; I'm gonna stab your eyes out with my thumbs.*

Melina's fear of clowns was replaced by utter revulsion; an emotion she could deal with and react to. Fear left her quivering. Revulsion left her angry. The Madman's advances upon her body overrode any common sense warnings that her brain was putting out. So, when his hand slid up her belly and cupped her breast, she saw nothing but red and reacted without a second thought.

Melina regained consciousness.

Slowly she opened her eyes but still could not see. The darkness around her was so complete that she could have been blind in both eyes.

This time, she was.

Chapter 78

For everyone else, by comparison, Monday morning was primarily uneventful.

Becca made it to her staff meeting on time but couldn't concentrate. Her mind kept bouncing from one thought to another before any one concept was even remotely satisfied.

She had the attention span of a gnat.

Her overlapping thoughts featured three main topics. First, was her upcoming date with Christopher John and the realization that she needed to become more knowledgeable on the subject of Long Island's founding families to uphold her cover story. Next, there was her desire to dig deeper into Jack Thomas's involvement with the Winston Horghbrall Company and provide Roberto with something concrete to pursue. Lastly, Becca kept thinking about what she had done to Roberto. She felt like the world's biggest ass and was physically nauseated by the prospect that she may have hurt Roberto at a terribly inappropriate time in his life.

Becca completely missed her weekly assignment because she was too distracted by the three ring circus that was performing in her head.

Michael Matelski, Becca's new special features editor, asked to her to see him in his office before she went out into the field for the day.

Becca hated Michael.

Michael was a young kid who took over the position when the prior special features editor retired. It just so happened, that Michael was the previous editor's nephew; and in Becca's opinion, he didn't have the experience to warrant the position.

Becca couldn't decide what her number one reason was for despising Michael. It was a toss up between the fact that she had also applied for the editor's position and wasn't even granted an interview and the fact that Michael openly talked down to her and treated her breasts as if they were her face. Either way, it was all Becca could do, not to quit right there on the spot when Michael called her into his office.

"Are you alright today, Ms. Willis? You seemed a little out of it at the meeting... rough weekend?"

Becca took a deep breath before answering and watched as Michael's eyes gleamed at the expansion of her shirt. She couldn't afford to tell the little shit what she really thought about him, his lack of talent and his more than likely under developed set of balls would have to wait for the time being.

Becca needed to ride out at least the next couple of days before she could tell young Michael Matelski where he could put the Post's laptop when she returned it. Becca figured she'd be utilizing the SNIPH program to dig deeper into Jack's Norwegian toy company as well as to uncover more information on Long Island's early settlers.

Becca had resolved to finally stop talking about all the great changes she was going to make in her life and just make them. The feeling that accompanied that resolution was one she hadn't felt in a long time. The excitement that stirred deep in her bones was reminiscent of when she had first gotten accepted to Columbia. It was like her life would be staring all over again and achieving her dreams was a real possibility.

By using the manuscript and her search for Jack Thomas, Becca was sure that she could take that leap into the spotlight and springboard her career in front of the cameras as a leading news anchor.

But first things first; Becca needed to deal with Michael Matelski. Standing before him in his office as he lecherously stared at her breasts awaiting a response to his question, Becca exhaled, and despite how ever much it repulsed her, she asked; "I was hoping you could help me." Two quick bats of the eyes, a demure look down, eye contact with raised eyebrows and then wait.

Michael was more than happy to help Becca. Little, wimpy men like Michael, feel big when they feel like they are in control; especially in regards to women. Michael wasn't too far removed from his years in high school and the two year community college he supposedly went to, and Becca assumed that he still carried some of that hostility he had acquired. It was a type of hostility that someone like Michael develops from years of being rejected by the opposite sex and by not fitting in with his own. Michael was a geek, a nerd, a dweeb. Becca could call him whatever she liked; but, the bottom line was that he was still her boss and she needed to play the game.

Becca had received her assignment from Michael, another follow-up piece on the rise of paparazzi related brawls that started out in Los Angeles; a popular trend that was making its way to the East Coast. Personally, Becca was all for the paps getting their ass's kicked; they constantly overstepped their bounds and created unsafe situations for the general public. In addition, the pap's unethical behavior trickled down into her own profession and made it impossible for sincere journalists to get close enough to the celebs for any honest news; on the rare occasion that it did happen.

Although it would be fun to attack the paparazzi, Becca had a feeling that she wouldn't be turning in this week's assignment. If all went well, she had plans of turning in her resignation instead.

Chapter 79

Melina felt the weight of the shackle around her ankle and knew right away she was back in familiar territory. Melina's body had been violated in more ways than one; and, the entire time that the Madman was torturing her, he kept reminding her how lucky she was to still be alive.

Melina wasn't so sure.

Struggling against the aches and pains that racked her naked body, Melina fought her way into a sitting position and backed herself up against the wooden wall. Bringing her hands up to her face to try to steady the throbbing agony that resounded in her head, Melina's fingers grazed the crusting remnants of her ruined eyes. The pain was beyond intense and brought with it bright flashes of white light in her mind's eye.

The heart wrenching anguish that accompanied the reality that her face was horribly scarred and that she was forever blinded brought a wave of nausea that produced painful expulsions of bile and blood from her empty stomach. Tears that no longer had ducts in which to travel ran freely out of Melina's nose in a mixture of mucus, pus and blood.

The searing pain that crisscrossed over her chest and abdomen brought with it vivid mental images of the torture she had endured. The Madman had easily fought off her ridiculous attempt at aggression in the padded room. Melina was able to superficially scratch his face on both cheeks before he grabbed her wrists and head butted her on the bridge of her nose. Weak from lack of food and high on fumes, Melina's knees crumbled beneath her.

The Madman then picked her up off the floor by grabbing her ears in clenched fists and held her up high so her feet dangled limply above the floor. His scolding's fell upon deaf ears and an unconscious mind as he knocked her senseless by repeatedly smashing her head into the metal doorframe.

When Melina initially opened her eyes, she knew she hadn't endured the worst of what was to come. Readying her mind and body for the sting of the whip's crack across her exposed skin, she quickly realized that that would have been a blessing.

Secured to the wall by leather straps, her arms were stretched out to the sides and pulled up over her head while her body was being lifted off the floor by her knees. Although her head throbbed from the bludgeoning, she could distinctly hear the Madman talking to her as her body rose higher and higher.

Keeping his voice calm and under control; he spoke to her as a father would speak to his child. Extreme disappointment bled through every sentence as he explained how he had given her the benefit of the doubt. How he thought she understood what an honor he had bestowed upon her by making her part of his grandiose plan. How she was blessed with the honor of being his first to live and confirm his existence to the world.

Melina began to mutter a sincere and pathetic apology but the Madman assured her there was no need to apologize; she hadn't changed a thing. Well, maybe just a little; but not to worry because it wasn't going to be any skin off his face.

Naked and suspended in the air, Melina was repeatedly and violently raped and sodomized. The Madman was able to insure Melina's enthusiastic participation by utilizing an old trick of the trade. Controlled sprays of lighter fluid followed by the touch of a match. This technique not only guaranteed the hardcore ride that the Madman needed on his engorged member; but, also left the first targeted city's initials scorched across Melina's chest and abdomen.

Determined to get off twice, the Madman was relentless in his drive and determination. Once finished, the Madman walked behind Melina still hanging in the air and grabbed her face. Bending her head backwards and stretching her neck as if preparing to slit her throat, the Madman asked that she remain very still while he gently slid his thumbs behind her eyeballs and popped them out of their sockets.

Even though he was sure she couldn't hear him over her own screaming; the Madman rhetorically said to Melina, "See what you made me do?"

Chapter 80

Becca snapped her laptop into the docking station on her desk. She had decided to utilize her office versus heading back uptown to her apartment. It was still early Monday morning and the hustle and bustle of the millions of commuters clogging the streets, subways, buses, bridges and tunnels would steal away precious time from an already 'not enough time in the day' kind of day.

The thought of all those people crowded together, bottle-necked with nowhere to go, brought a case of *The Jack Thomas Chills* scurrying down her spine. She could imagine what it would be like if a coordinated bombing went off during the city's rush-hours. Bridges collapsing and depositing thousands of cars into the East River; tunnels imploding, allowing millions of gallons of salt water to come rushing in from the Hudson. Underground subway cars exploding and splintering like grenades. The streets above them, crumbling and raining down into the void they created. The compromised foundation would then topple the massive structures they supported. Collapsing buildings would then fill the chasm, burying the already dead and sealing in the fate of the wounded.

Becca could hear the screams of the hundreds of thousands of New Yorkers caught up in such an attack and realized that it could be a catastrophe on the same scale as nine-eleven, if not worse.

Becca was feeling dizzy and needing to step away from her office. Sliding back her plastic chair out of the sterile cubicle, Becca went to the break room for a cup of tea.   Becca used to have a regular office with a nice view of Rockefeller Center. But all that changed when Mr. Vertically-Challenged, Michael Matelski, decided that the freelance writers on staff would be moved to what he called the work-pool; a series of free-standing slat walls that were merely dividers and not truly walls at all. Cheap plywood desks and plastic chairs replaced the solid wood and leather chairs of management past; and sloppy wiring provided electrical outlets for the desk's laptop docking stations. If a writer needed to make phone calls; "that's why God created cell phones" was the response they received. Michael Matelski was a firm believer in cutting costs at any and anyone's expense as long as it produced the desired results; and unfortunately it did, and upper management loved him for it.

Normally Becca avoided the work-pool area like the plague and had found herself working from home on most occasions. However, today the other seven stations were unoccupied and Becca felt like she at least had the illusion of privacy. The other five freelance writers on staff seemed to feel the same way about the work-pool as she did.

Settling back down in front of her laptop with a hot cup of tea, her own soothing blend of chamomile, rosemary, lavender and spearmint; Becca brought up the SNIPH program and began researching the Norwegian toy company, Winston Horghbrall; the clever anagram for Hollingsworth Barn.

Speaking aloud, Becca said, "Alright Jack... It's Showtime."

Chapter 81

Roberto was feeling great. He was able to contact all of the distributors for Barnes and Noble, as well as Waldenbooks by eleven o'clock. All but one appreciatively accepted the opportunity and Roberto received the approvals and corresponding purchase order numbers he required to have the books shipped and displayed. Despite the 'no-brainer' offer, Roberto actually had to do a hard sell to the Mid-West Regional distributor for the Waldenbooks Mall Division. Tom Lance was a giant of a man in physical appearance, but he was somewhat of a dip-shit when it came to negotiating.

Tom was always after the 'what's in it for me' angle; the total off the top profit margin he was making for the company didn't seem to be enough. Roberto had to promise him and his wife a special invitation to the Wiley Publishing Christmas Gala that was predominately held for the industry's bigwigs.

Tom's underlying issue was that he was a frustrated, unrecognized, no-talent, self-proclaimed author; who by career choice was constantly faced with the successful established writers, in addition to being on the bus that drove the upcoming authors to stardom.

By inviting Tom and his wife to an annual event that didn't exist, comfortable in the fact that he wasn't going to be around to hear the ramifications anyway; Roberto secured the buy-ins to release *The Rush Hour Madman* across the country. According to his own calculations, the book should be on store's shelves by the weekend; almost a full week ahead of the Madman's demand.

Roberto still possessed a reasonable expectation that Melina would be returned back home safely once the psychopath's conditions had been satisfied; there was however, a slight shadow of a doubt that had crept in over the past few days and it could be seen in the corner of his eyes.

Marissa Colmenares was respectful of her boss's obvious desire to not be questioned about the mystery production of 16,500 books and the 1,375 corresponding shipping orders. Marissa had been hired at the same time Roberto was brought on board by the Wiley family to assist spearheading the Hispanic division of the organization.   Roberto   and   Marissa   formed   an   instant camaraderie on their first day in the office. Marissa was also instrumental in bringing Roberto and Becca Willis together; if it hadn't been for her speed-dating suggestion, the two of them never would have met. Although Marissa was ten years his junior, she often took on a maternal role in regard to Roberto and his well-being.

Sensing that something enormous was going on; but, also sensing the extreme sensitivity of the situation, Marissa kept their conversations light and focused primarily on general work related topics. Marissa just assumed that the project had something to do with Wiley Publishing, and that for some reason it was being kept 'hush-hush'; more than likely it had something to do with the recent acquisition of Hungry Minds Incorporated. With all the Wileys out of town last week, Roberto was probably enlisted as the inside man on some secretive publicity campaign.

Even though her boss was obviously keeping something from her, she just couldn't resist asking Roberto about Becca. Marissa was busting at the seams wanting to know what had transpired between them. When she left on Friday, both Becca and Roberto were in his office talking; which, to Marissa was a great sign that hopefully the two of them were going to get back together. Throughout their whole 'on-again-off-again' relationship, Marissa knew it was just a matter of time before the flower had only one more petal and it was the 'he/she loves me' petal.

Roberto's face threatened to be split in half by his smile at the mention of Becca's name. Marissa knew right away what that smile meant and didn't pry for details other than expressing how happy she was for the both of them. Roberto accepted the uncontrollable embrace his admin threw around his body and headed down to the shipping floor to insure that the freshly printed orders were given top priority.

Alone in the stairwell, Roberto stopped and let out a heavy gust of air from his lungs as he brought up his hands and gave his forehead a hearty rub. It was overwhelming trying to digest all that had transpired since Thursday when the manuscript had arrived. The incredible mosaic of emotions, the myriad of highs and lows, the astounding depth of personal revelations and life changing insights were unparalleled to any other moment in his lifetime. Even the death of his parents at the hands of those cracked-out teenagers on the outskirts of Dodger's Stadium all those years ago, didn't leave him as altered as the events of the last few days had.

Roberto was no longer the same man who had gotten out of bed on Thursday morning last week; and he never would be again, not ever.

Regardless of the circumstances, or maybe because of the circumstances, Roberto found himself thinking about Becca almost constantly. He knew he cared, but he didn't realize how much he cared until Marissa mentioned her name.

Thinking about Becca was an easy diversion from the painful thoughts he regularly found himself obsessing on regarding his sister's dilemma. But, for the most part, it was because he never stopped loving Becca and always hoped that they would have a chance again.

Roberto realized that the forceful, passionate sex they had shared the night before was more of a physical escapade than it was an emotionally involved moment for Becca. He could tell the difference, and he knew that just because they had shared spit and sweat the night before, that it didn't mean that they were now back together.

Being completely honest with himself, Roberto didn't know if he could've been able to tell the difference even just a week ago; and he definitely knew he wouldn't have been able to handle it, at least not the way he found himself doing so now.

Thoughts of Becca had been keeping him somewhat sane these past few days. She was providing a support network that would otherwise have seen him alone trying to cope with the misfortune, heartbreak and calamity that had entered his life two weeks ago when Melina didn't return home for dinner.

Roberto also discovered that Becca was the best medicine for counterbalancing the overwhelming stream of thought waves coming to him from his sister. A constant torrent of confusion, fears, and hunger; overlaid with panic, pain and anger. Roberto was inundated with emotions from Melina; and, although it troubled him, at the same time it was very comforting knowing that she was still alive.

The connection they shared had never wavered over the years, no matter how much time had passed them by and no matter how many miles separated the two siblings. Even if they had been twins, the last of the Sanchez clan from La Joya, Mexico could not have been any more connected.

Standing there in the stairwell on his way down to the shipping platform, Roberto was suddenly blindsided by a commanding force. Stabbing pain in his eyes, followed by a relentless headache brought Roberto to his knees and he knew Melina's predicament had just escalated.

Chapter 82

The SNIPH archives were able to pull up some interesting facts on the Norwegian toy company, Winston Horghbrall. Although the company was founded in 1980, the same year that Jack Thomas supposedly died at Old Man's Cave; Becca deemed that to be nothing more than a coincidence. In 1980, the company's name was Star Bright; a world renowned manufacturer of classic wooden toys produced under the brand name of Uncle Goose. It wasn't until 1997, when the company changed ownership that Becca realized that she had stumbled onto something big.

Pulling out her copy of the manuscript, Becca confirmed what she already knew; Jack Thomas wasn't as good at covering his trail as he thought he was. The Star Bright Company was acquired by a Hong Kong based company called The Paper Airplane.

Using the SNIPH program and infiltrating the Asian database which contained details of Hong Kong's registered companies, Becca discovered that The Paper Airplane Company was merged into an operation called Synergistic Research as part of a court ordered takeover in December of '91.

Becca wasn't about to be misled by the company's assimilation into Synergistic Research. Becca knew a smokescreen when she saw one. By cross-referencing data found in an article from a Hong Kong newspaper, Becca hit the trifecta.

Four names kept appearing on the screen that gave Becca rock solid answers and new directions on which to focus. Becca had Jack Thomas in her sights and was setting the targeting sequence.

The first name was Andrew Palmer. Becca came across Andrew Palmer when she unearthed the original founding owner of The Paper Airplane Company.

Andrew Palmer was an eighteen year old from North Kensington, a suburb just outside of London. Becca found a story that had appeared in the London Daily newspaper simply as a human interest story; but to her it meant so much more.

The article stated that Andrew had left his foster home in 1980 to study at Ohio University by utilizing a trust fund that was established for him by his parents before they were killed in the 1975 IRA car bombing at the Hilton Hotel.

Another article in The Standard, Hong Kong's newspaper, offered additional information about Andrew in a 1992 article which stated that after losing his company in a hostile, court approved takeover, Andrew Palmer took his own life by jumping off the balcony of his thirty-seventh floor apartment in Tai Tam.

It appeared that Jack finalized things in Hong Kong a little more so than he had indicated in his manuscript, and Becca could certainly understand why. Becca was positive that the suicide was in fact, just another cover-up murder that Jack had used to protect himself from obvious repercussions created when he accidently butchered the daughter of his associate's client.

Having outlived its usefulness, the prolonged existence of Andrew Palmer, Jack's college roommate, ended. The corpse in the corner grave of the Rockville Cemetery finally had a name.

Becca had to admit, Jack was clever as well as dangerous. She was impressed with his ingenuity, what better way to stay alive than to already be thought of as dead. But he was also proving to be careless. The more she looked the more she was finding. The Winston Horghbrall lead was like finding that perfect loose thread; the more she pulled on it, the more the warm sweater Jack thought he was hiding in became unraveled.

The other three names Becca made note of were, Mei Ling Huang and two Europeans, Jonas and Martha McTik. The three of them were listed as the owners of Synergistic Research and by extension, the new owners of The Paper Airplane.

There was no doubt in Becca's mind that she would now be able to follow a trail that was going to lead her to Jack's present day whereabouts. Not only did Becca discover that Jack had, and may still have, continued dealings with Mei Ling, his former `associate's wife; but, Becca figured out something else. Something that she was sure Jack Thomas never thought would have been discovered by anyone.

Ever since Becca found the anagram hidden within the Norwegian toy company's name, she was looking for more; and as soon as Becca saw the names Jonas and Martha McTik, her mind reformed the letters.

She had him.

Jonas and Martha McTik was an anagram for Jack Martin Thomas.

Becca glanced over at the clock in the lower right hand corner of her laptop and had to confirm what she saw by looking at her watch. It was 11:30; three hours had gone by in what appeared to be twenty minutes. As if disbelieving the two clocks, Becca lifted up her still full cup of tea and found it to be ice cold.

Reaching into her satchel, Becca recovered her cell phone and saw that she had missed a call from Roberto. She had forgotten to switch the ringer back on after her staff meeting with Mr. Vertically Challenged, who insisted that phone settings be kept on vibrate or off during *his* time.

There was a very disturbing voice message from Roberto, something about time running out for Melina and wondering if Becca had found out anything that might be useful.

Initially Becca was expecting the message to be more related to their encounter last night and a request to have lunch; when it wasn't, Becca found herself to be a little disappointed.

She had been so determined in her resolve to not ever consider rekindling her relationship with Roberto that somehow the idea had slipped through the cracks. As if justifying her one-eighty turnaround, Becca ran down a mental list of all the things that had changed in Roberto and reasons why she would revise her decision and entertain the possibility of giving their past a chance in the present. Who knows, Becca told herself, maybe this time there would be a future.

The call had come in almost two hours before Becca had noticed the message on her phone and when she had finally gotten a hold of Roberto, his voice was much calmer than it had been in the original message.

After a quick explanation about the somewhat psychic connection he shared with his sister their whole life, Roberto shared with Becca what had happened in the stairwell. Becca wasn't sure what to make of the allegation that Melina was now in more trouble than she was three hours ago; and honestly, she thought that maybe Roberto just didn't get enough sleep the night before.

Regardless of the reasoning and regardless of weather or not Roberto and Melina shared some form of psychic connection; in Becca's mind it really didn't change anything as long as Roberto was still determined to not go the police.

Since their offices were only a few blocks from each other, Becca suggested that they meet in the middle for a quick lunch. They both decided on an old meeting place they frequented back when they were dating, the front steps of the New York Public Library on Fifth Ave.

Often they would sit while consuming New York's finest cuisine, a street-vendor hotdog and soda, on the front steps of the library while making comments about the tourists passing by. When time allowed they would walk hand in hand through the short pathways that wound around through Bryant Park located right behind the library.

How does it make you feel when you see someone cry?

Becca decided that that question was a defining proposition regarding your undefined feelings towards another person.

When she saw Roberto hang his head and sob as he retold his story about his connection with Melina, what had happened in the stairwell and what he feared it meant; she felt Roberto's pain deep in the fiber of her own existence. At that moment Becca knew, without a doubt, that she did care very much for Roberto. The prospect of them reuniting their relationship was something that Becca not only foresaw as a probability, but it was something she wanted to happen.

Being with Roberto seemed to be falling into its proper place right along with her resolve to finally take control of her life and obtain all the things she ever wanted. Fate or destiny, whatever you want to call it, has a strange way of finding you even when you do your best to hide from it.

Becca brought Roberto up to speed on what she had uncovered about the Norwegian company and the connections she had made with the Madman's own admissions in the manuscript. Becca explained how *finally*, it felt like she had found the trail of breadcrumbs.

Although he would have to take a rain check on a reminiscent walk through Bryant Park with her, Roberto made clear that he wanted Becca to get back to her research as soon as possible.

Becca couldn't agree more and told Roberto that she looked forward to that moment when all of this was behind them and they could move forward once again.

Chapter 83

Becca stopped by the office just long enough to pack up her laptop and clear out her personal selection of teas from the break room. Becca had an unshakable feeling that she was leaving the building for the last time. Mixed emotions ran through her head, she was sad, excited and nervous all at the same time. The feelings reminded Becca of the time when she had graduated from Samuel

J Tilden High School; looking out amongst the crowd of parents as she accepted her diploma, realizing that an age of innocence was ending and life was about to happen. It was a feeling of fear, the fear of walking away from what you knew; the fear of stepping into the unknown without MapQuest.

Riding the 6 train beneath Lexington Avenue from Grand Central Station to the Hunter College stop at Sixty-Eighth Street, Becca sorted through the slight dilemma she had created by putting in motion the rebirth of a relationship with Roberto hours before her date with Christopher John. Not exactly the way she wanted to start over. She tried to convince herself that they hadn't officially started anything yet; but, she wasn't buying her own line of bullshit and took that as a good sign.

Needing to make a quick and honest decision about Christopher John, Becca's father's words came to mind once again; '*It's always best to hide behind the truth*', and she knew right then what she had to do.

It's amazing how much someone's attitude can change in such a short period of time and Becca thought of something else her father used to say to her; 'Life can change in a split second'. He was predominately referring to being careful and mindful about life's frailties. It was a saying that began around the time Becca began to drive, but it did apply to everything. Words, actions, even thoughts sometimes, can completely alter everything around you in a split second.

Everything changes.

Becca had thought that exact phrase yesterday when she was reminiscing about her on again, off again, relationship with Roberto. Kyra had mentioned it when talking about how fast children grow up; and Becca had heard it coming from her phone as Aerosmith announced Roberto's call.

The one and only constant variable that you could take to the bank; one of life's few guarantees. Given time, everything changes.

Becca always was on the negative side of that concept; and for the first time, she felt like she was on the positive side. Everything seemed to be changing for the better; Roberto, her career, and even her initial dead-end search for the Madman, seemed to focus on the silver linings instead of the normal grey clouds.

Becca spent the rest of the afternoon multitasking in her apartment. She was running side-by-side SNIPH programs on her laptop; and although the dual process slowed down the response time greatly, Becca made good use of the rotating hourglasses.

While one program continued to follow leads branching off from The Paper Airplane's network of companies and the other brought up information on the Hollingsworth family and Long Island's history; Becca moved around her small apartment cleaning and dusting, getting ready for her 'meeting' with Christopher John.

Becca tried to convince herself that she was no longer getting ready for a date, but rather a get together with someone who offered to help her with information she was seeking. She knew better than to think that Christopher John's offer to help her with research on a book was nothing more than that; he was still a man, and therefore had one thing on the brain. He wanted to get her naked as much as the next guy. It didn't matter that he was wealthy and well groomed. It probably actually made it worse. In his mind he more than likely thought women were falling all over themselves just to put his dick in their mouth.

Becca had to admit to herself that she was one of them up until earlier that afternoon; but now things were different.

Everything changes.

First of all, she wasn't feeling as far removed from the 'God, it's been so long since I've been fucked' stage anymore; her romp with Roberto the night before took care of that. Secondly, she was feeling like she was back in a relationship; and that meant something, she was not, and never would be, a cheater. If Becca was involved with someone, it was a total, one-hundred percent commitment, of mind, body and soul.

Becca decided that she would immediately tackle any potential misunderstandings with Christopher John as soon as he arrived. She would thank him for taking time out of his busy schedule to meet with her to talk about her book; and, she would insist that dinner was 'on' her, and not up for discussion.

Pleased with her plan, Becca dressed in an outfit that was conservative and business like, rather than her original idea of wearing a tight fitted, knit button down dress that would be primarily unbuttoned to reveal ample doses of both cleavage and thigh.

The SNIPH searches were providing streams of useful information and Becca continued adding to two legal pads that sat on either side of the computer. Both lists looked like family trees, and in essence that's exactly what they were. But, instead of searching through family names, her genealogical research was stemming from a Hong Kong based company called The Paper Airplane and an area of land originally owned by the Rockaway Indians.

The one list was providing Becca with a complex network of companies located around the world, and while the names of Jonas and Martha McTik never resurfaced beyond the original Asian company, Synergistic Research, which acquired the Hong Kong company, The Paper Airplane; Becca was still confident of Jack Thomas's involvement in the elaborate web.

Becca had developed a keen awareness of when a story was reaching a climatic conclusion. Her years of schooling and her not quite ten years with the Post, had honed that awareness to an almost psychic level. Becca could feel it, she knew she was getting close; it was just a matter of time before she gathered that next set of parameters, the precise information needed for the SNIPH search engine to produce a company right here in New York.   A name and location that Becca knew would take her to the Madman's front door and Melina.

The other list was slowly assembling information it was gathering from County Auditor's websites and financial archives of banks long since closed and or merged with other institutions. Becca was following the ownership of the land that provided the setting for the Hollingsworth family's farm and the infamous barn. Previously, Becca had followed the trail through the history of the Rockaway Indian's sacred burial grounds to the failed businesses of the founding Hollingsworth clan.

Becca was now SNIPHing around for information about the property post 1970, the year that Sarah Hollingsworth murdered her husband and four children. According to the manuscript, the farm remained around for at least the next ten years, so it stood to reason that somebody owned it; and Becca was determined to find out who, if for no other reason than to be able to come off believable with Christopher John when he arrived. She did after all tell him she was writing a book about the area, and it only made sense that she would be aware of how his company had come to take possession of the land.

Oddly enough, Becca discovered that the deed to the Hollingsworth property remained in the family's name right up until the summer of 1980 when it was acquired by Freedman, Wexelblatt and Marcus, a law firm located on Hempstead Avenue in Lynbrook. Becca needed to SNIPH a little deeper before she discovered that the law firm of Freedman, Wexelblatt and Marcus was not exactly the owners of the property, but rather the managing firm of a Limited Liability Company called The Swing Set Emporium. Becca was having trouble locating the name or names of the owner or owners of The Swing Set Emporium due to the protections provided to the LLC; however, *The Jack Thomas Chills* that caressed her spine, told her all she needed to know. That, and the fact that Freedman, Wexelblatt and Marcus were revealed to be the lawyers that drafted young Jack's Last Will and Testament some twenty-eight years ago. Not picture perfect yet; but, it was enough for Becca to put them in the same room and prompt further SNIPHing.

Time slipped away from her once again as she was lost in the depths of the SNIPH process. Becca loved this type of discovery; one hidden gem producing the top of a buried pyramid filled with lost chambers of untold wonders.

Christopher John would be ringing her doorbell in less than a half hour and Becca needed at least an hour in the bathroom. Plus, she still hadn't found the Pharaoh's sarcophagus.

It was also time for her to pick up the phone and make the call to Roberto she promised herself she would make. He deserved to know where she was in her search, and he deserved to know about her upcoming meeting with; as Becca planned on calling him, 'a historian who could provide some insight we may have missed regarding the Hollingsworth connection to Jack Thomas'.

It's always best to hide behind the truth.
Roberto took the news better than Becca had ever expected that she was about to meet a man for dinner. He actually didn't even flinch and Becca found herself once again feeling a little cheated out of his old, jealousy laden responses. She realized that was insane; but, at the same time gained an appreciation of the concealed message that was typically obscured in the negative comments that Roberto used to make. As self-destructive as they were, they arose from feelings of love and fear of loss.

The heart felt appreciation that Roberto exhibited for all her time and effort in the day's search touched Becca in a way she didn't expect; and, for the second time that day, she was overwhelmed by her feelings towards a man she thought she could never love again.

Becca ended her call to Roberto by telling him that the 'historian' was arriving shortly and that she would talk to him later.

Chapter 84

Arriving promptly at seven, Becca opened her street level patio door to the debonair Mr. Christopher John. Bathed in the orange glow of the setting sun, Christopher John offered Becca an expensive bouquet of rare orchids. Standing there with his chiseled features and penetrating grey-blue eyes; Christopher John was dressed in a stylish Joseph Abboud khaki seersucker sportcoat with matched linen pants. Looking like he had just stepped out of a Fifth Avenue catalogue, Becca realized that she was going to have a hard time keeping her hands off this man as she accepted the bouquet and welcomed him into her apartment.

Hard, but not impossible; Becca was determined to keep the evening's events on a completely professional level. His charm and good looks were somewhat distracting; and therefore, it wasn't until later, that Becca realized she had missed a key warning sign that she was in trouble.

Returning into the living room with a glass vase tall enough to accommodate the orchids, Becca found Christopher turning the pages of one of the legal pads that sat by her laptop. With his eyebrows raised and his head nodding up and down in approval, the evening began with the professional turn that Becca had been hoping would happen.

"Rebecca, you've quite outdone yourself here; you seemed to have gathered more information on the old Hollingsworth property than is commonly known, or for that matter, available to the public."

When Christopher first addressed Becca as Rebecca, she was a little thrown off and then remembered that was how she had introduced herself. Feeling a bit silly about having done so, she offered that he call her Becca, emphasizing that there was no need for them to be so formal. Christopher John appeared quite pleased and reciprocated by telling her to call him CJ.

Setting down the legal pad, Christopher approached Becca and offered his right hand in what appeared to be an extension of a greeting. Placing her hand in his, he brought it up to his mouth where he gently placed a kiss atop her fingers as he stared into her eyes and stated; "Well then, Miss Becca Willis, it is once again an honor to be in your company." Becca fought back a natural impulse to blush and coyly look away. Continuing on, Christopher said, "As your research shows, you are, to a certain extent, head and shoulders above your fellow cockroach scurrying around in today's bourgeois rat-race."

Becca was confused by the comment he had just made. She was picking up on conflicting signals. His words seemed insulting although his expression and tone seemed complimentary; however, an underlying air of contempt and disdain sent an unexplainable parade of *The Jack Thomas Chills* running through her veins.

Saved by the beeping from her laptop, signaling that another phase of a SNIPH search was completed, Becca withdrew her hand from his. Needing to turn her body and sidestep around her house guest, thus being forced to press her chest against his as she slid past. Becca was confused by the abrupt change in Christopher John, who seemed to arrogantly hold his ground and force Becca to navigate by him.

Becca began to feel uncomfortable with the obvious stranger she had let into her apartment. It was as if by calling himself CJ, it brought a totally different persona to the surface. Truth be told, Becca realized that she actually didn't know who Christopher John was either. Just because he was a well mannered hunk of a male specimen, that didn't mean that he came with the Good Housekeeping Seal of Approval.

Stepping up directly behind her, Christopher peered over her shoulder as Becca piloted the arrow cursor to the flashing SNIPH program parked in the task bar along the bottom edge of the computer screen.

Expanding up and out, the familiar message encompassed the entire monitor of the laptop:

SNIPH SEARCH SUCESSFULLY COMPLETED
COMPILING DATA PLEASE BE PATIENT

Chapter 85

Framed by the SNIPH program's proprietary insignia, the Panda Bear Farm logo appeared on the screen of Becca's laptop. Below the logo was the corporately registered name, Anda Bear Farm; the official name had no cute depiction of an actual Panda Bear sitting in profile next to the 'A' to complete the word. The screen also provided the owner's information, a Mr. Christopher John, as well as the text of the original corporate resolution.

Already knowing that the SNIPH search she was performing in regards to the ownership of the land that dated back to the Rockaway Indians would end with the company she had seen standing there on the old Hollingsworth property with her own eyes; Becca had a feeling that Christopher John's company, Panda Bear Farm, was chronologically next after the LLC that the lawyers had managed.

However, when Becca realized that the SNIPH program that had called her attention was in fact the one doing research on the extended network of The Paper Airplane's companies, and *not* the one doing property research around the Hollingsworths, her heart began beating so hard that she thought there were tribal drums playing in her apartment.

So many things happened simultaneously that it was hard to tell how much time had transpired from the moment she heard the computer beeping to the moment she finally lost consciousness.

Starring in disbelief at the computer screen, trying to somehow invalidate the idea that Jack Thomas and Christopher John were one in the same person, Becca's vision began to blur and she was afraid she was going to faint.

This couldn't possibly be happening.

She had to be wrong. As if in response to her request for validation, the blurry letters of the Panda Bear Farm logo transformed before her eyes to spell Amanda Farber with a cute picture of a bear left over.

Becca's perspective shifted and images flashed through her mind's eye reflected in the light of a brand new day. But it was a dark and dreary day. A day of nightmares. A day of impending doom. A day that showed you your own death.

Becca recalled her first encounter with Christopher John on the grounds of the old Hollingsworth Farm; him peering into her car after her visit with Bud Farber, the copy of the 1980 Lynbrook High School yearbook sitting out in the open on the passenger seat. He knew from the start that she was on his trail. The Asian woman who arrived at the facility; it had to be Mei Ling.

All those feelings of being watched over the past two days were probably well founded. He had been playing with her. Becca remembered the black car that had pulled away from in front of her apartment the other night when she had come home from Long Island.

The door! How could she have been so blind? She opened her patio door to let him in! There are no numbers on the outside doors!

"It's the little things that make it all worthwhile."

When Christopher John spoke, Becca lost the ability to breath; it seemed like her pounding heart had exploded and clogged her esophagus cutting off the passageway to her lungs.

In slow motion, Becca turned to face the Madman as the heavy glass vase that was still in her hand slipped away from her grip and shattered on the hard wood floor.

A noticeable twinkle sparkled in the corner of his piercing grey-blue eyes as his lips curled into a sinister smile as he spoke the words that made Becca's knees weaken beneath her.

"*Thump-thump.*"

The final confirmation of her dire mistake came as his arms rocketed up from his sides. In an instant, his left hand reached around the back of her head where he secured a handful of black hair. Forcing her forward into his other hand, he covered her mouth and nose with a moist rag.

Becca knew immediately that she was breathing in fumes from a chloroform laden rag and tried her best not to breathe. Twisting and turning, trying to break free from the vice grip he had on her head; Becca's arms flailed and knocked her laptop to the ground. The electric cord had been snaked around a floor lamp which fell off its axis and also shattered on the hard wood floor next to the vase.

Instinct took control and years of self-defense classes rose to the surface seconds before Becca would have been forced to suck in a deep breath of the debilitating substance.

In a swift and powerful motion, Becca brought her right knee up and into the groin of the Madman.

"Mother-fucker!" burst out of his mouth in a spray of venomous spit and hatred as he released his death grip on Becca's head; though, not without consequence.

Although the one hand securing the doused rag was removed from her face allowing her to take in a much needed waft of air, his other hand came away from the back of her head still clenching the wad of hair it held. Becca could feel the mass being torn from her scalp at the roots and the subsequent sting that accompanied the exposed flesh.

Stumbling backwards away from the lunatic, Becca knocked into the glass coffee table with such force that the thick top slid off its base and hit the floor with enough power to send shockwaves through the apartment and create a gash in the hard wood floor. The ensuing clatter of the teacup, saucer and spoon that followed the tabletop to floor, coupled with the noise created by the breaking vase and the falling lamp, was enough noise to finally stir the attention of the doorman on duty.

Rudy slowly rose from his chair in the mailroom where he was taking an undeserved break and meandered down the hall to inspect the disturbance.

Spinning away from the cacophony crashing to the floor, Becca half-sat-half-rolled off the corner of the white scalloped couch and fell to her knees. Feeling the flesh peel away from her kneecaps as she skidded along the polished wood flooring; Becca continued moving forward and scurried in crablike fashion towards the apartment's main door.

Hearing his mutter curses and feeling his impending presence, Becca calculated the distance to the door and realized that she wasn't going to make it before the Madman would be upon her. Quickly adjusting her course of action, Becca turned, rose to her feet, and headed back across the apartment to the patio door placing the couch between her and her assailant as a barrier.

Altering his path in perfectly synced symmetry to hers' as if it had been choreographed and rehearsed a thousand times before; Christopher John leapt up and over the toppled coffee table and then catapulted himself up and over the back of the couch. As he called out, "This is a fun first date Miss Rebecca!" the Madman collided with his escaping prey.

Landing firmly beside Becca on the run, Christopher John shoved her towards the floor-to-ceiling mirrored wall that ran the full length of the short wall of the apartment. Originally intended to give the illusion of depth and a bigger place, the mirror now acted as a window into her up coming pain and misfortune. Becca watched herself as she awkwardly stumbled and staggered in an uncontrollable dance and face-planted into the silvered glass.

The mirror splintered and imploded beneath Becca's forehead. Tendrils of hairline fractures raced up and out from the epicenter of the impact creating a spider's wed design that would be the envy of any arachnid. Random triangular shaped shards of lethal glass showered down around Becca. While smaller ones nicked and sliced at her arms and legs; a larger section barely avoided being impaled into her skull, but succeeding in severing off a piece of her ear.

Picking her up by another handful of tangled hair, the Madman brought her face inches from his own as he spoke through clenched teeth.

"You of all people should know that I hate having my plans ruined."

Becca found herself being tossed like a ragdoll towards the back end of her couch. Falling forward, Becca ended up bent over the seatback; face down with her rear in the air. Christopher John was quickly up behind her with his hands firmly on her hips grinding his crotch into her ass with hard upward thrusts.

"We were going to have a nice dinner first and then I was going to let you suck my cock. But no; you had to go and spoil the evening."

Lifting her up by the inner thighs, Christopher John flipped Becca the rest of the way forward off the couch where she landed with a crash onto the gnarled wood base of the coffee table.

Slowly walking around the couch to where Becca lay in a crumpled mess of torn clothes and blood, the Madman could see her eyes flutter and begin to roll backwards into her head.

"Don't you dare pass out on me; the fun is just about to begin."

Terror struck Becca so deep that she no longer felt the throbbing of the rising welt on her forehead, or the sting of her right ear where the backend was sliced off, or the deep splinter that had penetrated her back when she had landed on the coffee table's base.   Becca now was snapped back into full consciousness by the horrifying awareness that if she didn't do something she was going to end up in Jack Thomas's next book.

Turning her head, looking for anything to use as a weapon, Becca saw her cell phone under the white couch now streaked with red stripes from her blood.

Not a weapon, but Becca reached for it anyway.

Snaking her fingers around the small object, Becca brought it forth like it was The Shield of Hercules and flipped open the top while staring up at Christopher John as he made the final turn around the couch's end. In an absurd act of defiance, Becca held her pointed finger inches from the phone's number pad as if to threaten the Madman with her intent of making a call.

Quickening his step and swinging his leg, Becca's head was snapped back on her neck as the Madman connected under her jaw with his shoe. The phone sailed out of her hand and Becca lost consciousness; but, not before she was able to stab at her phone and hit the redial key.

Chapter 86

As Becca lay limp at the foot of the couch like a discarded pillow; Rudy's knock resounded through the apartment.

"Now what?" Christopher John muttered to himself as he strode over to answer the questions coming though the door.

"Ms. Willis... It's Rudy... The doorman... Is everything all right in there? I thought I heard some noise... Did you break something? Do you need me to help you clean it up? ...Ms. Willis?"

Swinging the door open with a fierce inward jerk, Christopher John reached out and grabbed Rudy by the lapel and pulled the doorman into the apartment.

Quickly closing the door behind them, Christopher John began talking frantically and thereby kept the doorman off guard and confused about what was truly happening.

"Thank goodness you came when you did. Ms. Willis is having some kind of fit. You've got to help us. Do you know CPR?"

With the doorman's lapel still in his grasp, Christopher John led the doorman over the shards of broken mirror around the couch to where Becca lay unconscious.

"I'm going to call for help; you see what you can do for her, you better take her blouse off and remove her bra."

Manipulating Rudy like a puppet without the strings, Christopher John had the situation completely under his control. As soon as Rudy slid aside the gnarled wood base of the coffee table and bent over the motionless body of his favorite tenant, hands wrapped around his chin and forehead and snapped his neck in a quick fluid motion.

Wrenching the head of the already dead doorman, listening to the severed bones grinding and chipping against one another, Christopher John stretched and twisted Rudy's head around until it was facing completely backwards and then dragged the lifeless body across the room. Using his foot for leverage, Christopher John fractured Rudy's spine as he forced him into a reverse seated position on the loveseat next to the apartment's main door.

After admiring his creative, spur-of-the-moment display of art, Christopher John surveyed the chaos that had erupted in the apartment around him and realized that the mess was beyond cleaning up. Luckily he had a few special decks of playing cards in the car and would therefore be able to clean up with just one simple phone call as soon as he was on his way back to Long Island.

Rummaging around in the kitchen, Christopher John found a roll of duct tape and was able to secure Becca's wrists and ankles before he headed out to move his car. He would need to double park on 69th Street by the patio door. He had faith that an opportunity would present itself to facilitate the covert transport of the body into his Mercedes.

He was pleased that despite the vast change in his original plans for the evening, everything was still falling into place. He was remaining level headed and was able to keep a focus on the big picture. He was feeling very confident that he had the situation under control and was not missing anything that could put him in harm's way. Even when he was duct taping the dropped chloroform rag back over Becca's mouth, the open cell phone lying against the wall didn't concern him.

Chapter 87

Roberto knew Becca was in ominous trouble even before the phone began ringing. He felt its impending approach earlier when she mentioned her plans for the evening with 'the historian'.

That special place in his gut told him that something was wrong.

Roberto could only describe what he was feeling by comparing it to the imagery of Becca chasing a tiger around a circle; and that, although she was getting closer and closer to grabbing the tiger by the tail. The circle was also getting smaller and smaller with each turn; and therefore, the tiger was getting just as close to being right behind Becca as she was to it.

Unable to sit still since he had received her phone call, Roberto paced around in his apartment on 17th Street watching the snail's pace of the clock which sat above the black screen of the television. He contemplated picking up the phone several times to warn Becca of his premonition of danger. Afraid that she would misinterpret the motivation for his warning as jealousy; Roberto chose not to call.

Instead shoved the .38 caliber Magnum into a backpack and ran down to the street and hailed a taxi heading uptown on Third Avenue.

Sitting in the rear of the checkered cab, Roberto felt the heft of the gun in his backpack; he still couldn't believe how easy it was to acquire. All it took was a little courage to walk into Tompkins Square Park after their breakfast on Sunday morning while Becca was on her way out to Long Island.

Tompkins Square Park is considered a dead zone. Located where the famous East Village street, St. Marks Place, either ends or begins, depending on your point of view, at Avenue A; an area of Manhattan that holds so much bloodshed and history best forgotten, that most ignore its very existence.

As soon as the phone rang, Roberto broke out in a cold sweat and his heart began pounding in his chest when he looked at the caller ID. Even before he answered the call, he knew that Becca was in desperate need of assistance and he was still twenty blocks away and stuck in traffic that was only moving the taxi's meter.

Listening to the calamity that ensued on the other end of the phone, Roberto was frozen under the weight of his fear that he was too late. Everything that his ears witnessed happened so fast that his mind struggled to comprehend the reality of what had just occurred.

Needing to reaffirm that the call had come from Becca's cell phone, Roberto rechecked the caller ID. Not once did he hear Becca's voice. Initially just silence; and then a lot of banging, followed by the muffled sounds of two men talking hurriedly, and then more silence. The clips and clops of footfalls on a wood floor, followed by a heavy object being dragged; and then the grunts and deep breaths of labored movement.

Although Roberto couldn't put distinct visuals to the sounds he was hearing, the message was clear in his heart and soul; some crazy shit was going down and he needed to bust a move and get his ass up there quickly if he wanted to save Becca's life.

Tossing a twenty dollar bill up into the driver's section of the cab to cover the thirteen-fifty that read on the meter; Roberto jumped out of the backseat and began running the remaining mile to Becca's on East 69th Street and First Avenue

Chapter 88

Over the next few minutes, several things happened within mere seconds of one another and even someone with a bird's-eye view couldn't tell that the events were related to each other. Had these events occurred any closer in time and space, the outcome for so many people would have been so very different.

But, that is the way life works.

Timing is everything.

A well groomed gentleman got in and closed the door of a black Mercedes double parked by the 333 building on East 69th Street as Roberto was flying around the corner off Second Avenue, almost completing a six minute mile and barely out of breath.

Roberto did see the car, but from that distance, he couldn't be sure of its exact location and he certainly couldn't see the small spatters of blood on the man's clothing; and only Superman would have noticed the bound passenger in the trunk.

However, Roberto did take notice that, as the black Mercedes drove up East 69th Street, the driver was nice enough to give him a friendly wave and a smile as he passed by. Roberto chuckled to himself and thought that at least someone is having a nice evening.

Finally reaching the main entrance to Becca's building, Roberto stiff-armed his way through the double doors and was thankful that he didn't have to deal with a 'holier-than-thou' doorman just as the first police car was speeding around the corner off First Avenue and onto East 69th Street.

With only its red and blue strobe-lights flashing, the police car stealthily came to a halt just inside the 'No Parking Zone' in front of the building's double glass doors Roberto had just entered.

The Sergeant, along with the rookie officer he was training, stepped out of the patrol car and onto the curb as Roberto was sliding his key into the hallway door of Becca's apartment. First hoping that she hadn't changed the locks and secondly, Roberto was hoping that he wasn't too late.

The key slid into the lock like an old friend just as a second police car arrived with two more officers and the Sergeant in charge gave the orders to move in.

Roberto pulled the Magnum from his backpack and held it up next to his face as he had seen all good heroes do in the movies and turned the doorknob to Becca's home. Just as Roberto was taking a deep breath, trying to calm his nerves and prepare himself to storm the apartment; the Sergeant and his rookie partner entered the building through the building's glass double doors.

Outside, at the very same moment, after circling the block, the black Mercedes was pulling into a new parking space on First Avenue. It had a perfect cattycorner view of the developing drama, the Madman watched as a pair of officers readied themselves to provide backup through the patio entrance to Becca's empty apartment.

Just as Roberto was about to swing open the door, the Sergeant stepped into the hallway and dropped into another popular movie stance and yelled. "Freeze! Drop the gun scumbag and get your hands in the air!"

Despite looking up and seeing the officer's firearms drawn and pointed in his direction, Roberto didn't comprehend that he was being considered as 'the bad guy' and immediately took a step towards the police to enlist their help in saving Becca.

The shot that rang out from the Sergeant's 9mm Beretta not only knocked the Magnum from Roberto's grasp, but also threw him back six feet down the hallway.

Hearing the shot and therefore no longer waiting to hear the 'On-3' call from the Sergeant, the outside team engaged the lock-pick gun and kicked open the patio door. Twenty feet away, on the other side of the apartment's hallway door, the Sergeant bent over and picked up Roberto's dropped Thirty-Eight.

All of this happened at the exact moment that a final number was keyed into a cell phone held by a well dressed gentleman in the black Mercedes.

The first officer to enter in from the patio door was blown backwards like a cannonball into the second officer. Lifting them both up and across the street over a parked car and through the windshield of a dark green 2008 Cadillac CTS parked on the opposite side.

A concurrent blast inside the apartment shot flames and glass shrapnel out from under the hallway door slicing into the extended wrist and Achilles tendon of the bent over, soon to be retired, Sergeant.

Chapter 89

Becca slowly regained consciousness. The amplified effects of the prolonged exposure to the Chloroform left her vision blurry and her mind groggy.

At first, as her eyes adjusted and she became aware of her location, Becca was convinced that she was still unconscious. Her mind just couldn't accept the reality of what her eyes were taking in, and she decided that she must be in the midst of a very vivid nightmare.

Hanging naked from the ceiling like a chandelier, Becca was bound at the wrists and attached to a chain that hung down from a pulley system in the rafters. She felt like she had been in a car accident and was lucky to be alive. Her entire body ached and every beat of her heart reminded her of the beating she had taken in the apartment.

Becca's pain rapidly increased in intensity as the anesthetic effects of the Chloroform dissipated from her body. Simultaneously, her mind began to clear and she slowly became hauntingly aware that her surroundings were not a dream.

Looking around the inside of the Hollingsworth Barn from her suspended vantage point, Becca recalled all the past atrocities that had happened within the wooden slat walls. Whether it was the remaining toxins of the Chloroform still poisoning her thoughts, or whether she actually conjured up the ghosts of the

Madman's victims, Becca could see them all parading around the barn in their final fits of agony and despair.

There was Amanda Farber walking shakily and disoriented from out of the corner. Her right arm extended, using the horse stall wall for support while her left hand tried in vain to hold in the sloppy entrails of her own intestines. With every step, steamy, bloody loops of her innards slipped and slid over her arm as they oozed out from the torn, jagged hole in her abdomen.

The red-headed prostitute named Roxie crawled around on the floor, unable to stand on legs that were sizzling and popping, discarding hunks of dissolved flesh in her wake. Roxie's petite frame was being rapidly eaten away by the caustic lye that had been dumped on her still breathing body. Ribbons of shredded skin and severed veins hung in tatters from the self inflicted holes in Roxie's wrists. Trails of fresh blood painted the ground behind her as she pulled her dying body through the dirt.

Angela Henry stumbled about trying to replace the bloody mask of fleshy tissue that used to be her face; while, Andrea Blackman rolled around on the ground screaming silently as her head smoldered and charred chunks of flesh slid off her face like meat from the bone.

Countless others, equally maimed and horrifically brutalized, all wandered around the hallowed halls of the Hollingsworth barn. Silent pleas for help and release were directed upward towards Becca as the flock gathered beneath her dangling presence with outstretched hands.

Begging and pleading for extrication of their trapped souls, Becca could feel their desperate cries as they looked to her as their savior. Suddenly, all heads turned as one to the far corner of the barn where a door slowly opened inward. Becca watched as the Madman entered his lair and all spirits disappeared in a collective wisp of invisible smoke.

Barefoot and shirtless, Christopher John wore only a pair of designer faded blue jeans. His well defined muscles rippled as he swaggered into his sanctuary.

Looking up and seeing that Becca was awake, the Madman sincerely beamed as he spoke to her. "I am so glad you finally decided to join us. I was getting worried that we might have exceeded the recommended dosage of Chloroform."

Following close behind, moving on her hands and knees, naked and dirty, was Roberto's sister, Melina. Her matted hair, bruised features and the black, clotted scabs that filled the sockets where her eyes used to be, made her almost unrecognizable as a person and Becca thought that the Madman had entered the barn with some type of dog on a leash before she realized that it was a human being.

Walking over to a small card table that had previously gone unnoticed by Becca, the Madman produced a clicking sound out of the corner of his mouth and told his pet human to sit. Melina complied without hesitation and curled up into a fetal position at the foot of the table.

Kneeling down, the Madman patting the matted hair on her head and told Melina that she was a good girl. Then, as he stared up at Becca, he slid his hand over the contours of Melina's side, and Becca watched in dismay as Roberto's sister pivoted her body in the dirt and spread her legs open and appeared to whimper in longing as she offered herself to the psychopath.

Having read the manuscript several times, Becca thought she knew what Jack Thomas was capable of doing. But now, having witnessed what he had done to Melina, how he had turned a well educated human being into an animal willing to derogate herself; Becca was quickly becoming acutely aware that she had no idea what she was up against. She was in way over her head and when Jack stood up and said, "Let's play a game." Becca felt a fear so intense and so profound that her bladder lost all control. Ignoring the yellow fluid that ran down between her legs, the Madman walked over to the wall, armed himself with a bullwhip, turned a lever, and watched as Becca began to drop.

Timing the slow descent, waiting for the perfect moment when she almost came into full contact with the ground, when she was just barely touching down on the balls of her feet; the Madman flipped the switch back to its resting position and the chain ceased its movement.

Pausing briefly to enjoy Becca's toe-tapping dance as she tried in vain to find stability in the dirt, the Madman continued to speak as he set up the table in front of his guest of honor, the Madman produced a familiar satchel and emptied out its contents. Becca watched as her notebooks and laptop were removed and displayed on the tabletop.

"The game we are going to play is very simple; I will ask you questions and you will give me answers that prevent me from slicing your body to ribbons. Before we get started, do you have any questions?"

With a voice that trembled and cracked, Becca asked the first question that had popped into her head when she had regained consciousness and found herself hanging in a room that she had been convinced no longer existed.

"W-Where are we?"

Smiling from ear to ear, Jack Thomas raised his arms and extended his hands as he twirled around and presented the room for one and all's viewing pleasure.

Laughing sardonically, the Madman lifted the notebook from the table and waved it at her face as if the gesture would jog her memory. "You know exactly where we are; you were writing a book on it. Don't you remember? It's right here in your notes. You were going to call it *The Hollingsworth Triangle*."

Jack thoroughly enjoyed the momentary expression of anger that brushed across Becca's face almost as much as he enjoyed watching it dissipate back into an expression of helplessness. He nearly felt admiration for Becca Willis; she *had* done an outstanding job researching his background, and then on top of that, she followed a thin trail of breadcrumbs that almost led her ahead of all his hard work over the past decade. Regrettably for her, the powers of the Universe were on his side; why else would he have been led to her apartment at the exact moment that she was getting too close?

It was unfortunate that he had to kill her; but at least he could grant her a decent answer to her question.

"As you can see, the barn never did burn down. You made the common mistake of taking things for granted and accepting what you read. You actually were standing only about three hundred yards from the barn the other day. You see Ms. Willis, very much like Jack, the barn needed to disappear; and what better way to get a fresh start, than to get a makeover?"

The look on Becca's face told the Madman that she didn't understand what he was telling her. Fighting back the urge to pick up the bullwhip from the table and crack some sense into her, Jack took a deep breath and clarified, this time being a little more blunt; after all, he would have the opportunity to beat her to death soon enough.

"After I inherited Scott Lee's drug money, I purchased the Hollingsworth's farm from the bank; and, given its bloody past, they basically gave it to me. I built the warehouse you saw the other day around the barn protecting her from the weather and prying eyes. After all, she was mine; I found her abandoned by the Hollingsworth's. I alone kept her spirit alive. I fed her earth the blood she craved. I was the one who answered the calls of the Rockaway and in turn was guided by the Creator. I was shown the path of righteousness and given the strength and foresight to punish you faceless fucks polluting the planet."

Veins protruded from the Madman's neck and also pulsed in his forehead as his dissertation grew in intensity and volume. His simple explanation of the barn's existence turned into an explosive expose revealing his core delusions of grandeur.

Becca got her wish; she had received an impromptu interview with the psychopath named Jack Thomas. The further research necessary to confirm the roots of Jack's debauchery would never come. Answers to questions the likes of which would define what came first, the chicken or the egg, would go unasked and therefore unanswered. Truths and lies about ancient burial grounds, hinted to, but left unconfirmed, would remain a mystery for nobody to even wonder about.

The sharp turn of events left Jack in a quiet rage that needed release. Walking briskly back over to the table, ignoring his concubine pet, Jack traded the notebook for the bullwhip and told Becca it was time to play his game.

"First question..."

Chapter 90

Roberto awoke in the same hospital that they were treating Sergeant Justin Bell's lacerations. Although his chest ached and it felt like a hot spike was being driven into his lungs every time he tried to take a breath; Roberto called out to one of the attending nurses.

Several officers lingered in the hallways and cafeteria of the New York Weill Cornell Medical Center on East 68th and York Ave awaiting news on the patients in ER106 and ICU29. The awakening of Roberto Sanchez, who they no longer deemed as the perpetrator of the events that unfolded at 333 East 69th, gave them something to focus on while they awaited the final disposition on the severity of the injuries Sergeant Bell had suffered.

Initial reports indicated that although massive damage was sustained to the ligaments and tendons of the Sergeant's wrist, he would regain full use of his hand after several months of physical therapy. However, despite the best efforts to reattach his severed Achilles tendon, the Sergeant would be left with less than ten percent mobility for the remainder of his life.

Roberto on the other hand had been fortunate enough to only endure a fractured rib thanks to a new 'safe bullet' the NYPD were piloting for the country. Similar to the technology used in an automobile's safety airbag; a human rights activist invented a 9mm slug that projects an expanding dense foam sandbag-type bullet. Able to be chambered and shot from any standard 9mm police issued Glock-19 or Beretta-M9; the 'safe bullet' was designed to incapacitate a potential threat while reducing the loss of life typically associated in those situations.

Circumstances left Roberto with no options other than to involve the police. He was no longer concerned about the Madman's original threat. Roberto figured that bridge had been crossed when the Madman had tried to blow them all up. Besides that, if his sister had any chance of making it out of this nightmare alive; it was no longer based on the delivery of the manuscript to bookstores. At this point, all bets were off.

Roberto was released and transported from the hospital to the 19th Precinct on 67th Street. Propped up in the world's most uncomfortable chair and surrounded by both plain clothes and uniformed officers in the crowded interrogation room, Roberto tried to maintain his composure as he told his story to the police.

Starting from the beginning with the disappearance of his sister two weeks earlier and ending with the call he had received from Becca's cell phone just three short hours ago; Roberto left nothing out, not a conversation, not a thought and not a bead of sweat.

Even before his tale was done, phone calls were made and officers were deployed to both Roberto's office and to his apartment on 17th Street. The original manuscript was taken into police custody for forensic processing and psychiatric profiling, and statewide APB's were issued for both Melina Sanchez and Rebecca Willis.

Chapter 91

Carrying the bullwhip coiled around his hand with its twelve inch wooden handle sticking out like a club; Jack repeatedly asked Becca the same two questions over and over again while he circled around her hanging body.

"Who else knew I was coming over tonight?"
"Who else knew about your research?"
"Who else knew I was coming over tonight?"
"Who else knew about your research?"
"Who else knew I was coming over tonight?"
"Who else knew about your research?"

Mixing up the rhythm of the same questions trying to break her, Jack whispered into her ears, all the while touching her body, moving his hand over the full, firm mounds of her chest on one pass, and then sliding his hand down over her toned abdomen and around her waist. Then on the next pass, he took his hand across the small of her back and eased it lower and lower; caressing the smooth skin of her butt cheeks, gently digging in his nails across her hips and then pausing as he pressed the palm of his hand over the soft, protruding tuft of hair between her legs.

Each and every time Becca answered, she assured him that no else knew anything. But the Madman was unable or unwilling to accept her answers, and he continued circling and touching and whispering his questions until Becca screamed; "I didn't tell anyone! Why can't you believe me?"

Grabbing the short hair on the back of Becca's neck and yanking it backwards, the Madman pulled Becca forward. Running his tongue up her throat, under her chin and around to the base of her ear, licking at the salty mixture of sweat and tears, the Madman bit down hard onto Becca's earlobe and felt her body stiffen. Thrusting his hand holding the bullwhip up between her legs, the Madman shoved the twelve inch wooden handle inside Becca at the same time he wrenched her head back even further, cutting off any chance of sound escaping her collapsing windpipe.

Forcing the jagged wooden handle deeper into her with a violent upwards thrust, feeling the gnarled wood tear through a momentary blockage, the Madman spoke almost musically through clenched teeth into Becca's ear.

"I can't believe you because I don't think you are aware of my motivation. Let me explain; I am angry. You appear to have stepped a little to close to something I have spent a decade preparing. I want information, and you are going to give it to me, or I will make this not only the last day of your life, but also the worst."

A rush of warm blood flowed down over his hand and wrist as he ripped the bullwhip's handle out from between Becca's legs and released the hold he had on her neck. Listening to her cough and moan, Jack walked back over to the table and dropped the wet bullwhip on top of Becca's notebooks.

Propped up against the edge of the table, the Madman leaned back and unbuttoned his jeans and zipped open his fly. At the sound of the zipper, Melina was immediately up on her knees and shuffling through the dirt, hands outstretched, blindly groping for her master's cock. Smiling at the spectacle that inched forward towards him, Jack spoke to Becca; "Let's take a commercial break. That was the end of Round One and as you can see, I've got a hard on that needs milking."

Once Melina had swallowed the last of the Madman's seed, he dismissed her by pushing her to the ground and kicking her in the ribs while he told her to go lay down. Slinking away, Melina moved off into the shadows of the barn while the Madman picked up the bullwhip, still sticky with Becca's blood, and announced the beginning of Round Two.

"In Round Two, I'll be asking the same questions you had a chance to familiarize yourself with in Round One. Hopefully your answers will be a little more truthful or at least a little more convincing. Are you ready?"

Not waiting for a verbal response from Becca, assuming that her whimpering and labored breathing were indications that she was ready, the Madman asked his questions.   "Who else knew I was coming over tonight?"

"Who else knew about your research?"

"Who else knew I was coming over tonight?"

"Who else knew about your research?"

"Who else knew I was coming over tonight?"

"Who else knew about your research?"

"Oh God, oh God, please no!" were definitely not the right answers; because in one smooth fluid motion, the Madman's arm raised and his wrist snapped back as the bullwhip unfurled in a graceful backwards wave and then cracked forward with lightning speed. Strands of nylon fishing line attached to the tapered end of the whip sliced through the air. Razor thin openings cut deep into the soft, tender flesh of Becca's left nipple as the Madman wildly called out; "Bull's-eye!"

The sting that followed the whip's cruel attack was nothing like Becca had ever experienced. The pain traveled deep inside igniting nerve endings all the way up into her armpit; and when the second assault over her right nipple sliced the areola in half, Becca screamed in agony.

Dancing a jig and raising his arms up high in triumph, the Madman exclaimed; "Another direct hit!"

Dropping the whip and rapidly approaching his screaming prey, the Madman cold cocked Becca in the face with a closed fist. Surprised and terrified she stopped screaming even when the Madman followed up his battering by viciously seizing hold of her torn breasts forcing a warm flow of blood from the open wounds.

Feeling the freshly open wounds tear further apart beneath his vice grip, the Madman screamed into Becca's face; tepid spittle landing in her eyes and open mouth as the questions were asked one final time.

"Who else knew I was coming over tonight?"

"Who else knew about your research?"

Unable to speak, teetering on the verge of unconsciousness from the sadistic torture she was experiencing; Becca's eyes rolled up to their whites and her face fell forward on neck tendons too weak to support her head.

Apparently upset with the lack of response he was receiving; the Madman smashed his fists against the sides of her head. Grabbing fistfuls of hair, clamping his bloody hands firmly over her ears, he pulled Becca forward.

The concussion of pain and sound caused by the Madman's hands clapping down over her ears brought Becca back from the edge of unconsciousness. Her eyes tried to regain their focus as her brain attempted to formulate some semblance of understanding.

Bringing her face inches from his own, looking deep into her faraway eyes, the Madman calmly asked in a raspy voice; "Are you giving up? I'm not done playing our game."

With a violent sideways toss the Madman threw Becca into a spin that lifted her feet up off the ground and arched her body in such a way that she could have been auditioning for Cirque du Soleil.

The strain on her shoulders was unbearable. Becca felt and heard the tendons rip in her shoulders and the bones pop out of their sockets. Becca imagined that soon her body would fall to the ground and she'd be starring up at her arms dangling by the wrists, still attached to the chain hanging down from the rafters, as she bled to death from the holes torn in her torso.

Becca finally stopped spinning and hung motionless for what seemed like an eternity. Suspended center stage in the Hollingsworth's notorious barn, Becca was like a fly caught in a spider's web; trapped, helpless, waiting to die.

Chapter 92

Shortly before Jack had arrived back at the barn with his new guest, Melina's pounding headache finally become manageable. Not that it had gone away, but rather that, Melina was able to adjust to the crippling pain that it had been plaguing her with.

It is amazing how the human body adapts to pain and discomfort. We truly are a very resilient species when it comes to survival. We are able to adjust to a loss of a limb, we are able to adjust to the loss of one of our senses, and we are able to adjust to sudden and extreme changes in our surroundings. We make these adjustments without thinking and without skipping a beat. We prove our desire to survive everyday. We demonstrate our flexibility year after year. Floods, hurricanes, earthquakes, shootings and bombings; we adjust, we adapt, we survive.

After the vicious assault and blinding she had succumbed to at the hands of the Madman, Melina's bat-like radar sense had been replaced with a dark abyss of throbbing pain.

Even though being able to 'see' without her eyes had only developed since her weeks of captivity in the dark, Melina felt as if it had been a part of her since birth; and when it was gone for those few hours, Melina mourned its loss like it was her child.

Slowly, as Melina took control over the dull pain that had her head in a vice-grip, the familiar blue hues and textures of her radar vision reappeared, and she could 'see' again.

From her vantage point in the dirt, chained to the barn's south wall, Melina watched as the Madman towed the naked woman's body into the center of the barn. Melina knew right away who the woman was; Roberto had mailed her plenty of pictures out in California when the two of them were dating.

Melina witnessed as Becca was being attached to the chain and lifted up off the ground; and, her first reaction was that she was being replaced. Melina was terrified that Becca was going to be the Madman's newly selected spokesperson.

Melina was mindful that whatever her purpose had been, and whatever the hold was that she had provided to her captor in regards to her brother; Becca could very easily bestow that same benefit.

Fearful that her life was now being measured by hours, maybe minutes, maybe even seconds; Melina's heart pounded in terror thinking that Becca was now blessed with the honor of being the Madman's first to live and confirm his existence to the world.

For most of the movie, she had enjoyed the leading role; now Melina felt that she was just another extra waiting to die in the final scene of the horror show.

Melina's mind scrambled for a way to survive. Fearful that she was running out of time, utilizing her radar-sense of sight, Melina followed Jack Thomas's movements as he left the barn by its only door in the north wall and focused her attention on Becca.

Becca was barely breathing and Melina wondered if she was even alive. Despite how nauseated the thought made her, Melina found a dark place inside herself wishing that Becca wasn't alive, not that she wanted to be responsible for any harm that would befall Becca; but, Becca's death *would* eliminate any risk of Melina loosing her position with the Madman.

If Becca was dead, Melina would maintain the honor of being the Madman's first to live and confirm his existence to the world.

It was a simple matter of survival, nothing more.

But, with Jack's brisk return into the barn carrying a card table and a satchel filled with what appeared to be books; Melina knew with a depressing sense of extreme anxiety, that Becca was in fact still alive. In the blue hues of her radar vision, Melina watched as the Madman set up the table directly to the east of his new guest hanging high from the center beam.

Without the need of make up to hide his identity in the presence of blindness, Jack stretched his body until an audible pop from his back was heard. Melina witnessed as the Madman groped himself; sliding his hand inside his waistband, grabbing hold of his thickening member, squeezing it as he starred up at his new prize; it was at that moment, that Melina knew what she needed to do.

Writhing and moaning in the dirt while vigorously pleasuring herself, Melina caught the attention of the Madman and he shifted his focus and marched towards the south wall.

Hiding her ability of heightened awareness, Melina tuned up onto her knees and reached out as any blind person would do; absently groping at the air until she came in contact with the approaching Madman's thighs.

Once having found purchase, Melina's hands eagerly and hungrily moved up Jack's legs, pulled down his fly, and slid off his jeans.

Using one hand to cradle and massage his balls while the other stroked him to full attention, Melina skillfully used her lips to suck at the tip of his cock. Flicking and rolling her tongue around the ridge, tantalizing and teasing the underside of the massive helmet on his throbbing member, Melina finally engulfed his full presence into her open mouth. Wrapping her hands around the Madman's ass, slightly digging her nails into the meaty flesh, Melina pulled his stiff length deep down her throat.

To her own dismay, Melina found herself getting aroused as she worked the Madman to a fulfilling climax. Turning around and bracing herself on all fours, Melina raised her ass into the air and presented herself for penetration. However, the Madman told her that she would have to wait her turn as he had more pressing business to attend to; but he would be happy to bring her along for the ride.

Pushing Melina down into the dirt, Jack told her to lie down and be a good girl. Complying immediately, curling into her familiar fetal position, Melina watched the Madman with her radar sense as he walked over to the north wall and returned with a key, a collar, and a leash.

Freeing Melina's ankle from her shackle, Jack secured the thick leather collar around her neck and attached the leash. Considering that the collar was nothing like the sharpened choke collar used on her previously, Melina took it as a positive sign that she was back in the good graces of her captor; and she willingly followed him around like a good girl.

Melina's consciousness was stepping dangerously close to the edge of loosing herself in the game she decided to play in hopes of surviving.

You often reach a point of no return when making a life altering decision and Melina was dancing dangerously close to that mark. The future of her sanity was at risk. Sometimes you can play a game too well.

Chapter 93

Becca's eyes stopped swimming and she looked up to find Jack at the table rifling through the pages of her notebook.

Sensing that he was being watched, the Madman slowly looked up with an evil crooked grin and winked at Becca. Walking around the table, never taking his eyes away from hers, the Madman spoke. His sentences first came out in slow, methodical fragments and then rushed together in a disharmony of insane rhetoric.

"While you were just hanging around... I reread your notes... and I've come to the conclusion... that fate... once again... has illustrated an overwhelming consent in support of my intentions. It seems that the forces of the Universe and the Great Creator have delivered me to your apartment at the exact moment of your discovery, and thereby have bestowed upon me the blessings of preventing you from interfering with our cleansing process."

Pausing in his dissertation, not so much as to allow for some form of a response from Becca; but, more to allow the chaotic symphony within his own head to slow down and present him with his next course of action.

Appearing to be satisfied with what the voices in his head told him to do; the Madman walked forward, slowly and silently, until he was only inches from Becca's face. Staring into her bloodshot eyes, he whispered into her mouth; "I'm finished playing with you; the Rebecca Willis show has been canceled... it's time to die."

Stepping back a few feet, cracking his knuckles and stretching out his neck like a boxer does before a fight, the Madman began dancing around Becca. Throwing punches and jabs into the air while intoning the *Rocky* theme music, the Madman kept circling around Becca.

Finally coming to a halt directly in front of her, the Madman explained that it had been quite a while since he had beat someone to death and he hoped that she would enjoy herself.

The first few blows to Becca's midsection fractured a couple of ribs as Jack chucked and jived as if he were dodging another boxer's returned attacks.

Taking a half step back and leaning into it, the right cross that connected with Becca's jaw sent her up and snapping back down on the chain she was suspended from. Although Becca tried, she couldn't mask the excruciating pain that was created from the vicious assault on her already destroyed shoulders. The obvious agony and the animalistic sound it brought up from Becca's insides, thrilled the Madman to such an extent, that he threw his arms up in the air and began a joyous reprise of the *Rocky* theme music.

Becca hated herself for giving the Madman any sense of satisfaction. She honestly didn't know how much more she would be able to take; and then out of the corner of her eye, swelling shut from the beating, Becca noticed what Melina was doing and realized there might be a chance of survival.

Chapter 94

Melina became aware of a window of opportunity and without hesitation put a plan in motion that one way or another was going to be her last heroic act.

Cowering in the shadows, watching the Madman whip and beat Becca, Melina realized that she was momentarily forgotten. Even while Becca spun around and around, and the Madman was focused on the books at the table, Melina was conscious to the fact that she was almost invisible.

Whether her captor felt that his blind pet was of no concern and posed no threat, or whether he felt that she was now trained and obedient, or whether he truly forgot about her, was completely irrelevant; Melina was presented with a chance to go on the offensive.

Seeing Becca being helplessly beaten, Melina moved over to an area in the dirt floor where, several days earlier in her captivity, she had buried a long thick shard of wood she had freed from the wall. Silently approaching the Madman as he rained down blow upon blow on the vulnerable Becca, Melina held the weapon firmly in her grasp as she crawled forward.

The closer Melina crept, the more fearful Becca became of the Madman turning around and catching her before she was close enough to strike. The thought of how the blind girl was stalking her attacker never occurred to Becca, and she reached down deep inside herself and found the energy to speak.

"I told your brothers."

The words were barely audible as Becca tried to use her broken jaw and split lips; blood and saliva ran freely out of her mouth and formed a bubble that glistened in the barn's light.

The words that came out of her mouth stopped Jack Thomas in his tracks. His right arm cocked back to deliver what could have been the final blow dropped back to his side as he asked Becca to repeat herself.

"I said... I told your brothers... you pathetic psychopath."

Becca was no longer feeling any pain; she didn't know if it was because her spinal cord had been severed in one of his flurried bombardments to her body, or if her adrenaline had kicked in as she and Melina were orchestrating the final chapter of *The Rush Hour Madman*.

Blinking his eyes and openly flabbergasted at Becca's blatant verbal disrespect, the Madman asked; "I'm sorry, are you fucking mad? Do you have any idea what I can do to you? We can carry on and do this for days?"

Ignoring his questions, simply trying to maintain his undivided attention while Melina continued to close the gap between them; Becca spat out a wad of blood laden flem only to have it barely cross over her torn lips and fall in the short gap between them.

The wild, wide-eyed look on Jack's face was priceless as Becca began her final piece; "I told... I told your brothers... all about you..."

Having finally taken the bait, Jack Thomas allowed himself to be drawn into a conversation that Becca hoped was going to be his last.

Laughing, although with a hint of uncertainty, the Madman replied; "What could you have possibly told them? You didn't know anything. Your futile attempts at survival are only going to make this worse."

Becca cut him off as Melina slowly rose up from the ground behind the Madman; "I told them... how you killed... your parents..."

Enraged the Madman turned to retrieve the notebooks as Melina shot up from her crouched position; and, with a firm grip on the thick wooden shard, Melina angled it out before her and thrust it up into the soft tissue under the Madman's jaw line. The wooden blade slid in smoothly until Melina felt it come into contact with something hard inside his head.

Not knowing what hit him, the Madman fell forward before he could even cry out and Melina quickly sidestepped out of the way and allowed the Madman to fall straight down. Jack's arms never moved from his sides to cushion the fall; and the Madman landed firmly on his face, forcing in the remaining few inches of the wooden spike into his head with an audible crunch.

Chapter 95

From Melina's perspective the entire event happened in slow motion with an intense audio soundtrack.

Staring at the motionless body of her tormentor for what seemed like an eternity; half expecting him to rise up at any second, laughing as he pulled the bloody spike from his head, lick the gummy substance from its shaft and grab her by the throat.

When that didn't happen, Melina finally turned to share the joyous moment with Becca; however, she found herself alone.

Becca's body sagged motionless from her distended arms. Her head hung down and blood flowed freely from her ears and nose. Rapid, raspy breaths struggled to escape over her shredded lips and Melina knew she was watching the final moments of a dying woman if she didn't get medical attention very soon.

Without any further hesitation, Melina hobbled on her own aching frame to the north wall and opened the barn's only functioning door.

The heavy wooden door opened up into the brightly lit hallway of the warehouse Jack had built around the barn after he had acquired the Hollingsworth's land from the bank. Melina realized immediately that she had been in these halls before. This is where the Madman had taken her when she thought she must have blacked out and awoken somewhere else.

This is where the War Room was.

This is where she had watched Todd Hem-something blown apart.

This is where she had lost her innocence.

This is where she had attempted her futile attack.

Wandering through the somewhat familiar hallways, Melina wound herself around the corridors until her intuition and radar sensory perception led her to the warehouse's front doors.

Naked and in need of her own medical attention, Melina stepped out into the cool August night air. Goosebumps covered her sweaty skin as she walked across the parking lot to the chain-link fence that surrounded the perimeter of the property. The warehouse, located behind the Panda Bear Farm's distribution facility, faced the southern stretch of Central Avenue.

Guided by pure instinct, Melina painfully climbed over the eight foot high fence. Staggering across to the other side of Central Avenue, Melina angled to the right and headed down Hillside Avenue like a moth in the dark. A solitary light illuminating someone's front porch halfway down the street marked Melina's destination.

The row of dense trees that guarded the suburban sidewalks kept Melina predominately in heavy shadows at the center of the road as she approached the tiny house at 14 Hillside Avenue. Not only was the porch light on, but every light in the house was ablaze.

As Melina neared the front steps, the soft, scratchy voice of an elderly woman emanated from the open window next to the solid wood door.

"Todd? Is that you? Todd? Are you home?"

Chills ran down over Melina's already chilled skin, for she knew that Todd would never be answering his mother's call ever again.

Suffering from the late stages of dementia, Sue Hemsoth had been sitting vigil for three days awaiting the arrival of her son; who, in her mind, was just running a little late getting home from work.

Stepping out from the shadows and up into the porch light, Melina replied; "No ma'am, it's not Todd... My name is Melina Sanchez and I need your help."

Chapter 96

Roberto watched in awe as his sister navigated around their new two bedroom apartment on Manhattan's Upper East Side. He would never fully understand the amazing gift of blind perception Melina possessed. Although several doctors did comment about being familiar with similar cases of what they called 'blind-sight'; none could recall anything even remotely as developed, or as accurate, as what Melina's condition illustrated.

It had been exactly one year since the *The Rush Hour Manuscript* had arrived on his desk at Wiley Publishing; and exactly fifty, long and painful weeks since he began his mourning of Becca Willis. Her death left a hole in his heart that could never be filled.

The Madman's warehouse had exploded with such a force, that neighborhoods, ten miles away, in Uniondale, Syosset and Port Washington, were awakened by the blast in the early morning hours of that fateful Tuesday.

Initial efforts of the local police and fire departments produced no evidence to support the allegations of multiple bodies on the scene. However, in all fairness, their investigation was cut short. As soon as the identity of the brutalized blind girl reached the airwaves in response to the APB; the Lynbrook Police Department's jurisdiction was revoked.

After Roberto had been released and transported from the hospital to the 19th Precinct, where he openly shared his story with the authorities, he was charged with withholding information as it pertains to national security and detained for further questioning by the Department of Homeland Security.

The DHS was in the midst of questioning Roberto for what seemed like the hundredth time in his holding cell on 67th Street when the call about locating Melina Sanchez had arrived and a second team from the DHS was deployed out to Long Island.

Both Melina and Roberto spent the next several weeks under the care and supervision of our government's finest medical and psychological research teams who took control of the "situation" as they called it, at an undisclosed location. It was a full two weeks before the siblings were allowed any contact with one another and receive the much needed, in the flesh confirmation of the other's survival.

Fortunate enough to have each other for comfort, Roberto and Melina learned of Becca's unfortunate fate; and, they were questioned enough to have surmised that the remains of Jack Thomas were never located. Despite the concern and alarm this caused them; they were assured that there were "top people" working on the "situation".

The Department of Homeland Security blocked the release of the Madman's manuscript under the widely accepted mandate of never giving in to a terrorist's demands.

For whatever reason, the attacks as threatened in the manuscript never happened that fall; but the Madman had proven his ability to hibernate and be patient in the past and there was no reason to believe anything different now.

On the anniversary of the arrival of the manuscript, there was still no word regarding the whereabouts of Jack Thomas. Despite the fact that it was no longer headline news, or even sideline news for that matter, most authorities assumed him still to be at large but had stopped looking.

Roberto and Melina shared a common belief that this was exactly what the Madman had been waiting for; because we *are* complacent, we *are* forgetful, we *are* vulnerable. Just as Jack said we were.

The Madman had a plan; and that plan was methodically put to paper, it is just a matter of time.

Thump-thump...Thump-thump...Thump-thump...

&END&

Pat Addams is divorced with two grown children and travels the countryside from coast to coast, gaining inspiration from this wonderful country's natural cast of characters and locales. Pat has resided around the world, experiencing diverse cultures and has worn several hats throughout a short but fulfilling lifetime.

Pat Addams has written several short stories, catering predominately to private audiences, and hopes you have enjoyed the first of many full-length novels to be publically displayed. Pat is currently working on a horror fiction novel titled *Shadows and Reflections, Tangents of the Mind*.

Pat Addams welcomes your questions and comments via info@pataddams.com

2336259

Made in the USA